HOME ON THE RANCH:
STANDOFF

New York Times Bestselling Author
B.J. DANIELS

USA TODAY Bestselling Author
DELORES FOSSEN

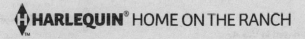

H HARLEQUIN® HOME ON THE RANCH
™

ISBN-13: 978-1-335-02046-8

First published as Big Sky Standoff by Harlequin Books in 2007 and Branded by the Sheriff by Harlequin Books in 2009.

Home on the Ranch: Standoff
Copyright © 2018 by Harlequin Books S.A.

The publisher acknowledges the copyright holders of the individual works as follows:

Big Sky Standoff
Copyright © 2007 by Barbara Heinlein

Branded by the Sheriff
Copyright © 2009 by Delores Fossen

Recycling programs for this product may not exist in your area.

Printed in U.S.A.

www.Harlequin.com

Praise for *New York Times* bestselling author B.J. Daniels

"Crossing multiple genres, Daniels successfully combines Western romance, suspense and political intrigue with ease."
—*RT Book Reviews* on *Hard Rain*

"Forget slow-simmering romance: the multiple story lines weaving in and out of Big Timber, Montana, mean the second Montana Hamiltons contemporary...is always at a rolling boil."
—*Publishers Weekly* on *Lone Rider*

"Daniels is truly an expert at Western romantic suspense."
—*RT Book Reviews* on *Atonement*

"Will keep readers on the edge of their chairs from beginning to end."
—*Booklist* on *Forsaken*

Praise for *USA TODAY* bestselling author Delores Fossen

"The perfect blend of sexy cowboys, humor and romance will rein you in from the first line."
—*New York Times* bestselling author B.J. Daniels

"From the shocking opening paragraph on, Fossen's tale just keeps getting better."
—*RT Book Reviews* on *Sawyer*, 4½ stars, Top Pick

"*Rustling Up Trouble* is action packed, but it's the relationship and emotional drama (and the sexy hero) that will reel readers in."
—*RT Book Reviews*, 4½ stars

CONTENTS

B.J. Daniels is a *New York Times* and *USA TODAY* bestselling author. She wrote her first book after a career as an award-winning newspaper journalist and author of thirty-seven published short stories. She lives in Montana with her husband, Parker, and three springer spaniels. When not writing, she quilts, boats and plays tennis. Contact her at bjdaniels.com, on Facebook or on Twitter, @bjdanielsauthor.

Books by B.J. Daniels

Harlequin Intrigue

The Montana Cahills

Cowboy's Redemption

Whitehorse, Montana: The McGraw Kidnapping

Dark Horse
Dead Ringer
Rough Rider

HQN Books

A Cahill Ranch Novel

Renegade's Pride
Outlaw's Honor
Hero's Return

Visit the Author Profile page
at Harlequin.com.

BIG SKY STANDOFF

B.J. DANIELS

This one is for Harry Burton Johnson Jr.
Who knows how different our lives would
have been had you lived.

Chapter 1

Dillon Savage shoved back his black Stetson and looked up at all that blue sky as he breathed in the morning. Behind him the razor wire of the prison gleamed in the blinding sunlight.

He didn't look back as he started up the dirt road. It felt damn good to be out. Like most ex-cons, he told himself he was never going back.

He had put the past behind him. No more axes to grind. No debts to settle. He felt only a glimmer of that old gnawing ache for vengeance that had eaten away at him for years. An ache that told him he could never forget the past.

From down the road past the guardhouse, he saw the green Montana state pickup kicking up dust as it high-tailed toward him.

He shoved away any concerns and grinned to himself. He'd been anticipating this for weeks and still couldn't believe he'd gotten an early release. He watched the pickup slow so the driver could talk to the guard.

Wouldn't be long now. He turned his face up to the sun, soaking in its warmth as he enjoyed his first few minutes of freedom in years. Freedom. Damn, but he'd missed it.

It was all he could do not to drop to his knees and kiss the ground. But the last thing he wanted was to have anyone know how hard it had been doing his time. Or just how grateful he was to be out.

The pickup engine revved. Dillon leaned back, watching the truck rumble down the road and come to a stop just feet from him. The sun glinted off the windshield in a blinding array of fractured light, making it impossible to see the driver, but he could feel the calculating, cold gaze on him.

He waited, not wanting to appear overly anxious. Not wanting to get out of the sun just yet. Or to let go of his last few seconds of being alone and free.

The driver's side door of the pickup swung open. Dillon glanced at the ground next to the truck, staring at the sturdy boots that stepped out, and working his way up the long legs wrapped in denim, to the firearm strapped at the hip, the belt cinched around the slim waist. Then, slowing his eyes, he took in the tucked-in tan shirt and full rounded breasts bowing the fabric, before eyeing the pale throat. Her long dark hair was pulled into a braid. Finally he looked into that way-too-familiar face under the straw hat—a face he'd dreamed about for four long years.

Damn, this woman seemed to only get sexier. But it was her eyes that held his attention, just as they had years before. Shimmering gray pools that reminded him of a high mountain lake early in the year, the surface frosted over with ice. Deeper, the water was colder than a scorned woman's heart.

Yep, one glance from those eyes could freeze a man in his tracks. Kind of like the look she was giving him right now.

"Hi, Jack," he said with a grin as he tipped his battered black Stetson to her. "Nice of you to pick me up."

Stock detective Jacklyn Wilde knew the minute she saw him waiting for her beside the road that this had been a mistake.

Clearly, he'd charmed the guards into letting him out so he could walk up the road to meet her, rather than wait for her to pick him up at the release office. He was already showing her that he wasn't going to let her call the shots.

She shook her head. She'd known getting him out was a gamble. She'd foolishly convinced herself that she could handle him.

How could she have forgotten how dangerous Dillon Savage really was? Hadn't her superiors tried to warn her? She reminded herself that this wasn't just a career breaker for her. This could get her killed.

"Get in, Mr. Savage."

He grinned. Prison clearly hadn't made him any less cocky. If she didn't know better, she'd think this had been his idea instead of hers. She felt that fissure of worry work its way under her skin, and was unable to shake the feeling that Dillon Savage had her right where he wanted her.

More than any other woman he'd crossed paths with, she knew what the man was capable of. His charm was deadly and he used it to his advantage at every opportunity. But knowing it was one thing. Keeping Dillon

Savage from beguiling her into believing he wasn't dangerous was another.

The thought did little to relieve her worry.

As she slid behind the wheel, he sauntered around to the passenger side, opened the door and tossed his duffel bag behind the seat.

"Is that all your belongings?" she asked.

"I prefer to travel light." He slid his long, lanky frame into the cab, slammed the door and stretched out, practically purring as he made himself comfortable.

She was aware of how he seemed to fill the entire cab of the truck, taking all the oxygen, pervading the space with his male scent.

As she started the truck, she saw him glance out the windshield as if taking one last look. The prison was small by most standards—a few large, plain buildings with snow-capped mountains behind them. Wouldn't even have looked like a prison if it wasn't for the guard towers and razor-wire fences.

"Going to miss it?" she asked sarcastically as she turned the truck around and headed back toward the gate.

"Prison?" He sounded amused.

"I would imagine you made some good friends there." She doubted prison had taught him anything but more ways to break the law. As if he needed that.

He chuckled. "I make good friends wherever I go. It's my good-natured personality." He reached back to rub his neck.

"Was it painful having the monitoring device implanted?" A part of her hoped it had given him as much pain as he'd caused her.

He shook his head and ran his finger along the tiny white scar behind his left ear. "Better anyday than an ankle bracelet. Anyway, you wanted me to be able to ride a horse. Can't wear a boot with one of those damn ankle monitors. Can't ride where we're going in tennis shoes."

She was willing to bet Dillon Savage could ride bare-ass naked.

His words registered slowly, and she gave a start. *"Where we're going?"* she asked, repeating his words and trying to keep her voice even.

He grinned. "We're chasing cattle rustlers, right? Not the kind who drive up with semitrucks and load in a couple hundred head."

"How do you know *that?*"

He cocked his head at her, amusement in his deep blue eyes. "Because you would have caught them by now if that was the case. No, I'd wager these rustlers are too smart for that. That means they're stealing the cattle that are the least accessible, the farthest from the ranch house."

"It sounds as if you know these guys," she commented as the guard waved them past the gate.

Dillon was looking toward the mountains. He chuckled softly. "I'm familiar with the type."

As she drove down the hill to the town of Deer Lodge, Montana, she had the bad feeling that her boss had been right.

"What makes you think a man like Dillon Savage is going to help you?" Chief Brand Inspector Allan Stratton had demanded when she told him her idea. "He's a *criminal.*"

"He's been in prison for four years. A man like him, locked up…" She'd looked away. Prison would be hell for a man like him. Dillon was like a wild horse. He needed to run free. If she understood anything about him, it was that.

"He's dangerous," Stratton had said. "I shouldn't have to tell you that. And if you really believe that he's been masterminding this band of rustlers from his prison cell… Then getting him out would accomplish what, exactly?"

"He'll slip up. He'll have to help me catch them or he goes back to prison." She was counting on this taste of freedom working in her favor.

"You really think he'll give up his own men?" Stratton scoffed.

"I think the rustling ring has double-crossed him." It was just a feeling she had, and she could also be dead wrong. But she didn't tell her boss that.

"Wouldn't he be afraid of them implicating him?"

"Who would believe them? After all, Dillon Savage has been behind bars for the past four years. How could he mastermind a rustling ring from Montana State Prison? Certainly he would be too smart to let any evidence of such a crime exist."

"I hope you know what you're doing," Stratton said. "For the record, I'm against it." No big surprise there. He wasn't going down if this was the mistake he thought it was. "And the ranchers sure as hell aren't going to like it. You have no idea what you're getting yourself into."

Stratton had been wrong about that, she thought, as she glanced at Dillon Savage. She'd made a deal with the devil and now he was sitting next to her, looking as if he already had her soul locked up.

She watched him rub the tiny scar behind his left ear again. It still surprised her that he'd agreed to the implanted monitoring device. Via satellite, she would know where he was at any second of the day. That alone would go against the grain of a man like Dillon Savage. Maybe she was right about how badly he'd wanted out of prison.

But then again, she knew he could very well have a more personal motive for going along with the deal.

"So the device isn't giving you any discomfort?" she asked.

He grinned. "For a man who can't remember the last time he was in a vehicle without shackles, it's all good."

As she drove through the small prison town of Deer Lodge, past the original jail, which was now an Old West museum, she wondered what his life had been like behind bars.

Dillon Savage had spent his early life on his family's cattle ranch, leaving to attend university out East. Later, when his father sold the ranch, Dillon had returned, only to start stealing other people's cattle. Living in the wilds, with no home, no roots, he'd kept on the move, always one step ahead of her. Being locked up really must have been his own private hell.

Unless he had something to occupy his mind. Like rustling cattle vicariously from his prison cell.

"I'm surprised you didn't work the prison ranch," she said as she drove onto Interstate 90 and headed east.

"They worried that their cattle would start disappearing."

She smiled not only at his attempt at humor, but also at the truth of the matter. It had taken her over two years to catch Dillon Savage. And even now she wasn't sure how that had happened. The one thing she could be certain of was that catching him had little to do with her—and a whole lot to do with Dillon. He'd messed up and it had gotten him sent to prison. She'd just given him a ride.

* * *

Reda Harper stood at the window of her ranch house, tapping the toe of her boot impatiently as she cursed the mailman. She was a tall, wiry woman with short-cropped gray hair and what some called an unpleasant disposition.

The truth? Reda Harper was a bitch, and not only did she take pride in it, she also felt justified.

She shoved aside the curtain, squinting against the glare to study her mailbox up on the county road. The red flag was still up. The mailman hadn't come yet. In fact, Gus was late. As usual. And she knew why.

Angeline Franklin.

The last few weeks Angeline had been going up the road to meet mailman Gus Turner, presumably to get her mail. By the time Angeline and Gus got through gabbin' and flirtin' with each other, Reda Harper's mail was late, and she was getting damn tired of it.

She had a notion to send Angeline one of her letters. The thought buoyed her spirits. It was disgraceful the way Angeline hung on that mailbox, looking all doe-eyed, while Gus stuttered and stammered and didn't have the sense to just drive off.

The phone rang, making Reda jump. With a curse, she stepped away from the window to answer it.

"Listen, you old hateful crone. If you don't stop—"

She slammed down the receiver as hard as she could, her thin lips turning up in a whisper of a smile as she went back to the window.

The red flag was down on her mailbox, the dust on the road settling around the fence posts.

Reda took a deep breath. Her letters were on their way. She smiled, finally free to get to work.

Taking her shotgun down from the rack by the door,

she reached into the drawer and shook out a half-dozen shells, stuffing them into her jacket pocket as she headed to the barn to saddle her horse.

A woman rancher living alone had to take care of herself. Reda Harper had had sixty-one years of practice.

"I want to make sure we understand each other," Jacklyn Wilde said, concentrating on her driving as an eighteen-wheeler blew past.

"Oh, I think we understand each other perfectly," Dillon commented. He was looking out at the landscape as if he couldn't get enough of it.

A late storm had lightly dusted the tops of the Boulder Mountains along the Continental Divide to the east. Running across the valley, as far as the eye could see, spring grasses, brilliantly green, rippled in the breeze, broken only by an occasional creek of crystal clear water.

"I got you an early release contingent on your help. Any misstep on your part and you go back immediately, your stay extended." When he said nothing she looked over at him.

He grinned again, turning those blue eyes on her. "We went over this when you came to the prison the first time. I got it. But like I told you then, I have no idea who these rustlers are. How could I, given that I've been locked up for four years? But as promised, I'll teach you everything I know about rustling."

Which they both knew was no small thing. Jacklyn returned her gaze to her driving, hating how smug and self-satisfied he looked slouched in her pickup seat. "If at any time I suspect that you're deterring my investigation—"

"It's back to the slammer," he said. "See, we understand each other perfectly." He tipped his Stetson down, his head cradled by the seat, and closed his eyes. A few moments later he appeared to be sound asleep.

She swore softly. While she hadn't created the monster, she'd definitely let him out of his cage.

Dillon woke with a start, bolting upright, confused for an instant as to where he was.

Jacklyn Wilde had stopped the truck in a lot next to a café. As she cut the engine, her gaze was almost pitying.

"Prison makes you a light sleeper." He shrugged, damn sorry she'd seen that moment of panic. Prison had definitely changed his sleep patterns. Changed a lot of things, he thought. He knew the only way he could keep from going back to jail was to keep the upper hand with Ms. Wilde. And that was going to be a full-time job as it was, without her seeing any weakness in him.

"Hungry?" she asked.

He glanced toward the café. "Always." It felt strange opening the pickup door, climbing out sans shackles and walking across the open parking lot without a guard or two at his side. Strange how odd freedom felt. Even freedom with strings attached.

He quickened his step so he could open the restaurant door for her.

Jacklyn shot him a look that said it wasn't going to be *that* kind of relationship. He knew she wanted him to see her as anything but a woman. Good luck with that.

He grinned as she graciously entered, and he followed her to a booth by the window as he tried to remember the last meal he'd had on the outside. Antelope steak over a campfire deep in the mountains, and a can of cold beans. He closed his eyes for a moment and could almost smell the aroma rising from the flames.

"Coffee?"

He opened his eyes to find a young, cute waitress standing next to their table. She'd put down menus and two glasses of water. He nodded to the coffee and made a point of not letting Jacklyn see him noticing how tight the waitress's uniform skirt was as he took a long drink of his water and opened his menu.

"I'll have the chef salad," Jacklyn said when the waitress returned with their coffees.

Dillon was still looking at his menu. It had been four years on the inside. Four years with no options. And now he felt overwhelmed by all the items listed.

"Sir?"

He looked up at the waitress and said the first thing that came to mind. "I'll have a burger. A cheeseburger with bacon."

"Fries?"

"Sure." It had been even longer since he'd sat in a booth across from a woman. He watched Jack take off her hat and put it on the seat next to her. Her hair was just as she'd worn it when she was chasing him years ago—a single, coal-black braid that fell most of the way down her slim back.

He smiled, feeling as if he needed to pinch himself. Never in his wildest dreams did he ever think he'd be having lunch with Jacklyn Wilde in Butte, Montana. It felt surreal. Just like it felt being out of prison.

"Something amusing?" she asked.

"Just thinking about what the guys back at the prison would say if they could see me now, having lunch with Jack Wilde. Hell, you're infamous back there."

She narrowed her gaze at him, her eyes like slits of ice beneath the dark lashes.

"Seriously," he said. "Mention the name Jacklyn Wilde and you can set off a whole cell block. It's said that you always get your man, just like the Mounties. Hell, you got me." He'd always wondered how she'd managed it. "How exactly *did* you do that?"

He instantly regretted asking, knowing it was better if he never found out, because he'd had four long years to think about it. And he knew in his heart that someone had set him up. He just didn't know who.

"I'll never forget that day, the first time I came face-to-face with you," he said, smiling to hide his true feelings. "One look into those gray eyes of yours and I knew I was a goner. You do have incredible eyes."

"One more rule, Mr. Savage. You and I will be working together, so save your charm for a woman who might appreciate it. If there is such a woman."

He laughed. "That's cold, Jack, but like I said, I understand our relationship perfectly. You have nothing to worry about when it comes to me." He winked at her.

Jack's look practically gave him frostbite.

Fortunately, the waitress brought their lunches just then, and the burger and fries warmed him up, filling his belly, settling him down a little. He liked listening to the normal sounds of the café, watching people come and go. It had been so long. He also liked watching Jacklyn Wilde.

She ate with the same efficiency with which she drove and did her job. No wasted energy. A single-minded focus. He hadn't entirely been kidding about her being a legend in the prison. It was one reason Dillon was so damn glad to be sitting across the table from her.

He'd been amazed when she'd come to him with her proposition. She'd get him out of prison, but for his part, he had to teach her the tricks of his trade so she could catch a band of rustlers who'd been making some pretty big scores across Montana. At least that was her story.

He'd seen in the papers that the cattlemen's association was up in arms, demanding something be done. It had been all the talk in the prison, the rustlers becoming heroes among the cellies.

What got to him was that Jack had no idea what she was offering him. He hadn't agreed at first, because he hadn't wanted to seem too eager. And didn't want to make her suspicious.

But what prisoner wouldn't jump at the chance to get out and spend time in the most isolated parts of Montana with the woman who'd put him behind bars?

"Where, exactly, are we headed?" he asked after he'd finished his burger. He dragged his last fry through a lake of ketchup, his gaze on her. It still felt so weird being out, eating like a normal person in a restaurant, sitting here with a woman he'd thought about every day for four years.

Her gray eyes bored into him. "I'd prefer not to discuss business in a public place."

He smiled. "Well, maybe there's something else you'd like to discuss."

"Other than business, you and I have nothing to say to each other," she said, her tone as steely as her spine.

"All right, Jack. I just thought we could get to know each other a little better, since we're going to be working together."

"I know you well enough, thank you."

He chuckled and leaned back in the booth, making himself comfortable as he watched her finish her salad. He could tell she hated having his gaze on her. It made her uneasy, but she did a damn good job of pretending it didn't.

He'd let her talk him into the prerelease deal, amused by how badly she'd wanted him out of prison. She needed to stop the rustlers, to calm the cattlemen, to prove she could do her job in a macho man's West.

Did she suspect Dillon's motives for going along with the deal? He could only speculate on what went through that mind of hers.

She looked up from her plate, those gray eyes cold and calculating. As he met her gaze, he realized that if she could read his mind, it would be a short ride back to prison.

She said nothing, just resumed eating. She was wary, though. But then, she had every reason to be mistrustful of him, didn't she.

Chapter 2

Rancher Shade Waters looked across the table at his son, his temper ready to boil over—lunch guest or not.

In fact, he suspected Nate had invited her thinking it would keep Shade from saying anything. He hadn't seen his son in several days, and then Nate had shown up with this *woman*.

"I suppose you heard," Shade said, unable to sit here holding his tongue any longer. "Another ranch was hit last night by that band of rustlers. If they don't catch those sons of—"

"Do we always have to talk ranch business at meals?" Nate snapped. "You're ruining everyone's appetite."

Nate's appetite seemed to be fine, and Shade couldn't have cared less about Morgan Landers's. From what he could tell, she ate like a bird. Their guest was like most of the women his son dated: skinny, snobby and greedy. He'd seen the way she'd looked around the ranch house. As if taking inventory of the antiques, estimating their worth at an auction.

Shade had no doubt what Morgan Landers would do with the ranch and the house if she got the chance.

But then, he wasn't about to let her get her hands on either one.

"Please don't mind me," Morgan said. "This rustling thing is definitely upsetting."

"No one can stop them. They've fooled everyone and proved they're smarter than the ranchers and especially that hotshot stock inspector, Wilde," Nate said, clearly amused by all of it.

"I beg your pardon?" Shade snapped, no longer even trying to keep his temper under control. How could his son be so stupid? "You sound like you admire these thieves."

"Well, they haven't hit our ranch, so what do you care?"

Shade was speechless. He'd never understood his son, but it had never crossed his mind that Nate was just plain stupid.

He heard his voice rising as he said, "As long as those men are out there stealing cattle, this ranch is at risk. I won't rest until they are all behind bars. And as for the man who's leading this ring, I'd like to see him hanged from that big tree down by the creek, like he would have been if your grandfather was still alive."

Nate chuckled and looked at Morgan, the two sharing a private joke. "As if he can be caught."

"Do you know something I don't?" the rancher asked between gritted teeth.

"The leader of the rustlers is already behind bars," Morgan said. "Everyone knows it's Dillon Savage. Who else could it be?"

"Really?" Shade looked at his son.

"Who else *could* it be?" Nate said. He had the irritating habit of parroting everything Morgan said.

"Well, for your edification, Dillon Savage is not behind bars anymore. Jacklyn Wilde got him out of prison."

Nate had the sense to look surprised—and worried. "Why would she do that?"

"Supposedly to help her catch the rustlers. Isn't that rich?" Waters said, and swore under his breath.

Nate looked upset, but Shade doubted his concern was for their cattle. No, he thought, looking over at the woman beside his son, Nate had other worries when it came to Dillon Savage.

"The whole damn thing was kept quiet," Shade said, fighting his anger. "For obvious reasons." He would have fought it tooth and nail had he known.

"Like I said, do we have to talk about this now?" Nate asked pointedly.

"Your *guest* might have more of an interest in the topic than you think," he replied. "After all, she was Dillon Savage's…" he looked at Morgan as if he wasn't sure what to call their relationship "…girlfriend."

Nate shot him a warning look as the cook came in with another basket of warm rolls. Morgan was picking at her salad. It galled Waters that while he and Nate were having beefsteaks, Morgan had opted for rabbit food. The woman was dating a cattle rancher, for hell's sake.

The rancher cursed under his breath, angry at his son on so many levels he didn't even know where to begin. Nate not only looked like his mother—blond with hazel eyes, and an aristocratic air about him—he'd also gotten her softness, something Shade had tried to "cowboy" out of him, although, regretfully, he hadn't succeeded.

He wished he hadn't let Nate's mother spoil the boy

so. Now in his early thirties, Nate stood to inherit everything Shade had spent his life building. Nate had no idea the sacrifices his father had made, the obstacles he'd had to overcome, the things he'd had to do. Still had to do. Nate, like his mother, would have been shocked and repulsed if he'd known.

Fortunately, Elizabeth had always turned a blind eye to anything her husband did, although Shade wondered if it wasn't what had put her in an early grave. That and the loss of her firstborn son, Halsey.

While Halsey had loved everything about ranching, Nate never took to it. And just the thought of ever turning the W Bar over to him was killing Shade.

Nate leaned toward Morgan now, whispering something in her ear that made her chuckle coyly—and turned Shade's stomach.

"I'm sorry, Morgan, is talk of Dillon Savage making you uncomfortable?" he asked innocently.

Nate shot him a warning look.

"It's all right, Nate," she said, smiling at the older Waters. "Yes, I knew Dillon…well." Her smile broadened. "Do I care that he's out of prison? Not in the least. Dillon and I were over a long time ago."

Shade looked at his son to see if he believed any of that bull. Nate had never had any sense when it came to women. Apparently, he was buying everything Morgan told him, probably because he had a good view of the woman's breasts in that low-cut top.

"Then you didn't write him while he was in prison or go see him?" Shade asked, ignoring the look his son gave him.

"No," Morgan said, her smile slipping a little. "We'd

gone our separate ways long before Dillon went to prison."

She was lying through her teeth. He suspected that she'd been keeping Dillon up on everything going on in the county, especially at the W Bar.

"Well," Shade said, with exaggerated relief, "I guess the only thing Nate and I have to worry about with Savage out is losing our cattle." He dug into his steak as he noted with some satisfaction that his son had lost *his* appetite.

As Jacklyn Wilde drove east past one small Montana town after another, Dillon realized he didn't have any idea where they were headed or what she had planned for him.

But that was the idea, wasn't it? She wanted to keep him off balance. She didn't want him to know too much—that had been clear from that first day she'd come to see him in prison.

He glanced over at her now. Back when she'd been trying to catch him rustling, he'd known only what he'd heard about her. It wasn't until he'd come face-to-face with her and the gun she had leveled at him that he'd looked into her steel-gray eyes and realized everything he'd heard about her just might be true.

She was relentless, clever and cunning, cold and calculating. Ice water ran through her veins. In prison, anyone who'd crossed her path swore she was tougher than any man, but with a woman's sense of justice, and therefore more dangerous.

He couldn't argue the point, given that she was the one who'd put him behind bars.

"So when are you going to tell me the real reason you got me out?" he asked now.

Outside the pickup, the landscape had changed from mountains and towering, dark green pines to rolling hills studded with sagebrush. Tall golden grasses undulated like waves in the breeze and the sky opened up, wide and blue from horizon to horizon. It truly was Big Sky Country.

"I thought I made myself clear on that point," she said, keeping her eyes on the road. "You're going to help me catch rustlers."

He chuckled and she finally looked over at him. "Something funny about that?"

"You didn't get me out of prison to catch rustlers. You are perfectly capable of catching any rustler out there and we both know it." He met her gray eyes. In this light, they were a light silver, and fathomless. The kind of eyes that you could get lost in. But then the light changed. Her gaze was again just a sheet of ice, flat and freezing.

"I need your expertise," she said simply.

Right. "Well, I'll be of little help to you if you keep me in the dark," he said, smiling wryly as he changed tactics. "Unless you have something besides rustling on your mind. I mean, after what happened the first time we met…"

Her eyes narrowed in warning. "The only reason you aren't still behind bars is because you were good at rustling. That's the only talent of yours I'm interested in."

He lifted a brow, still smiling. "That's too bad. Some of my other talents are even more impressive. Like my dancing," he added quickly. He could see she hadn't expected that was where he was headed.

"I'm surprised you had the time, given how busy you were stealing other people's cattle."

He shrugged. "All work and no play... What about you, Jack? What do you do for fun?"

"Mr. Savage, I told you, our discussions will be restricted to business only."

"If that makes you more comfortable... How about you tell me where we're headed then, Jack."

"You'll be updated on a need to know basis, Mr. Savage, and at this point, the only thing you need to know is that I'm Investigator Wilde or Ms. Wilde. Not Jack."

"Still Ms., huh? I guess it's hard to find a cowboy who's man enough to handle a woman like you."

Her jaw tightened, but she didn't take the bait.

He gazed out the windshield, enjoying himself. There were all kinds of ways to get even, he realized. Some of them wouldn't even get him sent back to prison.

Too bad he'd so often in the past four years revisited the day she'd caught him. It was like worrying a sore tooth with his tongue. He'd lost more than his freedom that day.

There'd been only one bright spot in his capture. After she'd cuffed him, he'd stumbled forward to steal one last thing: a kiss.

He'd taken her by surprise, just as she had him with the capture. He'd thought about that kiss a lot over the years. Now, as he glanced over at her, he wondered if he'd be disappointed if he kissed her again. *When* he kissed her again, he thought with a grin. And he *would* kiss her again. If only goodbye.

"Is there a problem, Mr. Savage?" she asked.

"Naw, just remembering the day you caught me," he said, and chuckled.

"Lewistown," she said irritably, making him laugh. "We're headed for Lewistown."

"Now that wasn't so hard, was it?" The center of the state. A hub of cattle ranches. How appropriate, given that rustlers had run rampant there back in the 1800s. It had gotten so bad that some ranchers took matters into their own hands. On July 4, 1884, a couple of suspected rustling ringleaders, "Longhair" Owen and "Rattlesnake Jake" Fallon, were busy shooting up the town when a band of vigilantes gunned them down in the street. Longhair Owen took nine bullets and Rattlesnake Jake eleven.

Dillon wondered how long it would be before a band of vigilantes started shooting first and asking questions later, given how upset the ranchers were now over this latest ring of rustlers. Was that why Jack had gotten him out? Was she hoping some ranchers would string him up?

Staring out at the landscape, he knew that the only reason she'd told him where they were headed was because he wouldn't be getting an opportunity between here and there to call anyone and reveal their destination.

"Your lack of trust cuts me to the core," he said as he ran his finger along the tiny scar behind his left ear, where the chip was embedded under his skin.

Much like Jacklyn Wilde had gotten under his skin and been grating on him ever since. He told himself he'd be free of both before long. In the meantime, he tried not to think about the fact that Jack as well as her superiors would know where he was at any given moment.

"You sure that monitoring chip isn't bothering you?" she asked, frowning at him.

He hadn't realized she'd been watching him. Apparently she planned to keep a close eye on him—as well as monitor his every move.

"Naw," he said, running his finger over the scar. "I'm good."

Her look said he was anything but, and they both knew it.

Shade Waters always made a point of walking up the road to the mailbox after lunch, even in the dead of winter.

While it was a good half mile to the county road and he liked the exercise, his real motive was to get to the mail before anyone else did.

The letters had been coming for years now. He just never knew which day of the week, so he always felt a little sick as he made the hike up the road.

Even after all this time, his fingers shook a little as he pulled down the lid and peered inside. The envelope and single sheet of stationery within were always a paler lavender, as if the paper kept fading with the years.

Today he was halfway up the ranch lane when he saw Gus come flying down the county road, skidding to a stop and almost taking out the mailbox.

"What the hell?" Waters said under his breath as he watched the carrier hurriedly sort through the mail, open the box and stuff it inside. He had been running later and later recently.

Gus saw him, gave a quick wave and sped off almost guiltily.

Waters shook his head, already irritated knowing that his son and Morgan Landers were back at the house together. He had to put an end to that little romance. Maybe Dillon Savage being out of prison would do the trick.

At least something good would come of Savage being on the loose again.

When Shade finally reached the mailbox, he stopped to catch his breath, half dreading what he might find inside. Fingers trembling, he pulled down the lid, his gaze searching for the pale lavender envelope as he reached for the mail.

Even before he'd gone through the stack, he knew the letter hadn't come. A mixture of disappointment and worry washed over him as he slammed the box shut. He hadn't realized how much he anticipated the letters. What if they stopped coming?

He shook his head at his own foolishness, wondering if he wasn't losing his mind. What man looked forward to a blackmail letter? he asked himself as he tucked the post under his arm and headed back up the lane.

Jacklyn had just left the town of Judith Gap when her cell phone rang and she saw with annoyance that it was her boss. She glanced over at Dillon, wishing she didn't have to take the call in front of him, because more than likely it would be bad news.

"Wilde."

"So how did it go?" Stratton asked, an edge to his voice. He was just waiting for things to go badly so he could say I told you so.

"Fine," she said, and glanced again at Dillon. He was chewing on a toothpick, stretched out in the seat as if he was ready for another nap.

"I hope you aren't making the biggest mistake of your career. Not to mention your life," Stratton said.

So did Jacklyn. But they'd been over this already. She waited, fearing he was calling to tell her the rustlers had hit again. She knew he hadn't phoned just to see how she was doing. Stratton, too, had a receiver terminal that told him exactly where Dillon Savage was at all times. Which in turn would tell her boss exactly where she was, as well.

"Shade Waters wants to see you," Stratton said finally.

She should have known. Waters owned the W Bar, the largest ranch in the area, and had a habit of throwing his weight around. "I've already told him I'm doing everything possible to—"

"He's starting what he calls a neighborhood watch group to catch the rustlers," Stratton said.

"Vigilante group, you mean." She swore under her breath and felt Dillon Savage's gaze on her.

"Waters has all the ranchers fired up about Savage being released. He's got Sheriff McCray heading up a meeting tomorrow night at the community center. I want you there. You need to put a lid on this pronto. We can't have those ranchers taking things into their own hands. Hell, they'll end up shooting each other."

She groaned inwardly. There would be no stopping Waters. She'd already had several run-ins with him, and now that he knew about her getting Dillon Savage out of prison, he would be out for blood. Hers.

"I'll do what I can at the meeting." What choice did she have? "Will you be there as well?"

"I'm not sure I can make it." The chicken. "You do realize by now that you've opened up a hornets' nest with this Savage thing, don't you?" He hung up, but not before she'd heard the self-satisfied "I told you so" in his voice.

Dillon watched Jack from under the brim of his Stetson, curious as to what was going on. Unless he missed his guess, she was getting her butt chewed by one of her bosses. He could just imagine the bureaucratic bull she had to put up with from men who sat in their cozy offices while she was out risking her life to protect a bunch of cows.

And from the sounds of it, the ranchers were doing exactly what he'd expected they would—forming a vigilante group and taking the law into their own hands. This situation was a geyser ready to go off. And Dillon had put himself right in the middle of it.

He watched her snap shut the phone. She squared her shoulders, took a deep breath and stared straight ahead, hands gripping the wheel as she drove. He knew she was desperate. Hell, she wouldn't have gotten him out of prison if she hadn't been. She'd stuck her neck out and she would have to be a fool not to realize she was going to get it chopped off.

For a split second, he felt sorry for her. Then he reminded himself that Jacklyn Wilde was the enemy. And no matter how intriguing he found her, he would do well to remember that.

"Everything all right?" he asked innocently.

She shot him a look that said if he wanted to keep his head he wouldn't get smart with her right now.

Unfortunately, he'd never done the smart thing. "Why do you do it?"

"What?" she snapped.

"This job."

She seemed surprised by the question. "I *like* my job."

He scoffed at that. "Putting up with rich ranchers, not to mention your arrogant bosses and all that bureaucrat crap?"

"I'm good at what I do," she said defensively.

"You'd be good at anything you set your mind to," he said, meaning it. She was smart, savvy, dedicated.

Plus her looks wouldn't hurt. "You could have any job you wanted."

"I like putting felons behind bars."

"You put *cattle rustlers* behind bars," he corrected. "Come on, Jack, most people see rustling as an Old West institution, not a felony. Hell, it was how a lot of ranchers in the old days built their huge spreads, with a running branding iron, and a little larceny in their blood. Rustling wasn't even a crime until those same ranchers started losing cattle themselves."

"Apparently that's an attitude that hasn't changed for two hundred years," she snapped. "Rustling, with all its legends and lore." She shook her head angrily, her face flushed. "It's why rustlers are seldom treated as seriously as burglars or car thieves."

He shrugged. "It comes down to simple math. If you can make ten grand in a matter of minutes easier and with less risk and more reward than holding up a convenience store, you're gonna do it." He could see that he had her dander up, and he smiled to himself, egging her on. "I see it as a form of living off the land."

"It's a *crime*."

He laughed. "Come on, everyone steals."

"They most certainly do not." Her hands gripped the wheel tightly, and she pressed her foot on the gas pedal as her irritation rose. He saw that she was going over the speed limit, and grinned to himself.

"So you're telling me that you've never listened to bootleg music?" he asked. "Tried a grape at the supermarket before buying the bunch? Taken a marginal deduction on your taxes?"

"No," she said emphatically.

"You're *that* squeaky clean?" He shook his head,

studying her. "So you've never done *anything* wrong? Nothing you've regretted? Nothing you're ashamed of?" He saw the flicker in her expression. Her eyes darted away as heat rose up the soft flesh of her throat.

He'd hit a nerve. Jack had something to hide. Dillon itched to know what. What in her past had her racing down the highway, way over the speed limit?

"You might want to slow down," he said quietly. "I'd hate to see you get a ticket for breaking the law."

Her gaze flew to the speedometer. A curse escaped her lips as she instantly let up on the gas and glared at him. "You did that on purpose."

He grinned to himself yet again as he leaned back in the seat and watched her from under the brim of his hat, speculating on what secret she might be hiding. Had to have something to do with a man, he thought. Didn't it always?

Everyone at prison swore she was an ice princess, cold-blooded as a snake. A woman above reproach. But what if under that rigid, authoritarian-cop persona was a hot-blooded, passionate woman who was fallible like the rest of them?

That might explain why she was so driven. Maybe, like him, she was running from something. Just the thought hooked him. Because before he and Jacklyn Wilde parted ways, he was determined to find her weakness.

And use it to his advantage.

Rancher Tom Robinson had been riding his fence line, the sun low and hot on the horizon, when he saw the cut barbed wire and the fresh horse tracks in the dirt.

Tom was in his fifties, tall, slim and weathered. He'd

taken over the ranch from his father, who'd worked it with *his* father.

A confirmed bachelor not so much by choice as circumstances, Tom liked being alone with his thoughts, liked being able to hear the crickets chirping in the sagebrush, the meadowlarks singing as he passed.

Not that he hadn't dated some in his younger days. He liked women well enough. But he'd quickly found he didn't like the sound of a woman's voice, especially when it required him to answer with more than one word.

He'd been riding since early morning and had seen no sign of trouble. He knew he'd been pushing his luck, since he hadn't yet lost any stock. A lot of ranchers in this county and the next had already been hit by the band of rustlers. Some of the ranchers, the smaller ones, had been forced to sell out.

Shade Waters had been buying up ranch land for years now and had the biggest spread in two counties. He had tried to buy Robinson's ranch, but Tom had held pat. He planned to die on this ranch, even if it meant dying destitute. He was down to one full-time hired man and some seasonal, which meant the place was getting run-down. Too much work. Not enough time.

On top of that, now he had rustlers to worry about. And as he rode the miles of his fence, through prairie and badlands, he couldn't shake the feeling that his luck was about to run out. This latest gang of rustlers were a brazen bunch. Why, just last month two cowboys had driven up to the Crowley Ranch to the north and loaded up forty head in broad daylight.

Margaret Crowley had been in the house cooking lunch at the time. She'd looked out, seen the truck and had just assumed her husband had hired someone to move some cattle for him.

She hadn't gotten a good look at the men or the truck. But then, most cowboys looked alike, as did muddy stock trucks.

Tom could imagine what old man Crowley had said when he found out his wife had just let the rustlers steal their cattle.

Tom was shaking his head in amusement when he spotted the cut barbed wire. Seeing the set of horseshoe prints in the dirt, he brought his horse up short. He was thinking of the tracks when he heard the whinny of a horse and looked up in time to see a horse and rider disappear into a stand of pines a couple hundred yards to the east.

Tom was pretty sure the rider had seen him and had headed for the trees just past the creek. From the creek bottom, the land rose abruptly in rocky outcroppings and thick stands of Ponderosa pines, providing cover.

"What the hell?" Tom said to himself. He looked around for other riders, but saw only the one set of tracks in the soft earth. He felt his pulse begin to pound as he stared at his cut barbed wire fence lying on the ground at his horse's feet.

Tom swore, something he seldom did. He squinted toward the spot where he'd last seen the rider. This part of his ranch was the most isolated—and rugged. It bordered the Bureau of Land Management on one corner and Shade Waters's land on the other.

The man had to be one of the rustlers. Who else would cut the fence and take to the trees when seen?

Still keeping an eye on the spot where the horse and rider had disappeared, Tom urged his mount forward, riding slowly, his hand on the butt of his sidearm.

Chapter 3

Jacklyn silently cursed Dillon Savage as she drove, glad she hadn't gotten a speeding ticket. Wouldn't he have loved that? It was bad enough she'd proved his point that everyone broke the law.

She couldn't believe she'd let him get to her. Like right now. She knew damned well he wasn't really sleeping. She'd bet every penny she had in the bank that he was over there smugly grinning to himself, pleased that he'd stirred her up. The man was impossible.

She tried to relax, but she couldn't have been more tense if she'd had a convicted murderer sitting next to her instead of a cattle rustler. But then, she'd always figured Dillon Savage was only a trigger pull away from being a killer, anyway.

She could hear him breathing softly, and every once in a while caught a whiff of his all-male scent. With his eyes closed, she could almost convince herself this had been a good idea.

Desperate times required desperate measures. She had

her bosses and a whole lot of angry cattlemen demanding that the rustlers be stopped. Because of her high success rate in the past—and the fact that she'd brought in the now legendary Dillon Savage—everyone expected her to catch this latest rustling ring.

She'd done everything she could think to do, from encouraging local law enforcement to check anyone moving herds late at night, to having workers at feedlots and sale barns watch for anyone suspicious selling cattle.

Not surprisingly, she'd met resistance when she'd tried to get the ranchers themselves to take measures to ward off the rustlers, such as locking gates, checking the backgrounds of seasonal employees and keeping a better eye on their stock.

But many of the ranches were huge, the cattle miles from the house. A lot of ranches were now run by absentee owners. Animals often weren't checked for weeks, even months on end. By the time a rancher realized some of his herd was missing, the rustlers were long gone.

Everyone was angry and demanding something be done. But at this point, she wasn't sure anyone could stop this band of rustlers. These guys were too good. Almost as good as Dillon Savage had been in his heyday.

And that was why she'd gotten him out of prison, she reminded herself as she turned on the radio, keeping the volume down just in case he really was sleeping. She liked him better asleep.

Lost in her own private thoughts, she drove toward Lewistown, Montana, to the sounds of country music on the radio and the hum of tires on the pavement. Ahead was nothing but trouble.

But the real trouble, she knew, was sitting right beside her.

* * *

Dillon stirred as she pulled up in front of the Yogo Inn in downtown Lewistown and parked the pickup.

He blinked at the motel sign, forgetting for a moment where he was. His body ached from the hours in the pickup, but he'd never felt better in his life.

Opening his door, he breathed in the evening air. A slight breeze rustled the leaves on the trees nearby. He stretched, watching Jack as she reached behind the seat for her small suitcase.

"I can get that," he said.

"Just take care of your own," she replied, without looking at him.

Inside the motel, Dillon felt like a kept man. He stood back as Jack registered and paid for their two adjoining reserved rooms, then asked about places in town that delivered food.

"What sounds good to you?" she asked him after she'd been given the keys, both of which she kept, and was rolling her small suitcase down the hallway.

She traveled light, too, it appeared. But then, he expected nothing less than efficiency from Jack.

"What sounds good to me?" He cocked a brow at her, thinking how long it had been.

"For *dinner*," she snapped.

"Chinese."

She seemed surprised. "I thought you'd want steak."

"We had steak in prison. What we didn't have was Chinese food. Unless you'd prefer something else."

"No, Chinese will be fine," she said as she opened the door to his room.

He looked in and couldn't help but feel a small thrill. It had been years since he'd slept in a real bed. Past it, the bathroom door was open and he could see a bathtub. Amazing how he used to take something like a bathtub for granted.

"Is everything all right?" Jack asked.

He nodded, smiling. "Everything's great." He took a deep breath, surprised how little it took to make him feel overjoyed. "Would you mind if I have a bath before dinner? In fact, just order for me. Anything spicy."

Her look said she should have known he'd want something spicy. "I'll be right next door," she said, as if she had to warn him.

The last thing on his mind was taking off. All he could think about was that bathtub—and the queen-size bed. Well, almost. He looked at Jack. Past her, down the hall, he spotted a vending machine.

"Is there something else?" she asked.

He grinned. "Do you have some change? I'd really like to get something out of the vending machine."

She glanced behind her, then reached into her shoulder bag and handed him a couple of dollars.

"Thanks." He looked down at the money in his hand. He hadn't seen money for a while, either. He tossed his duffel bag into the room and strode down the hallway, knowing she was watching him. From the machine, he bought a soda and, just for the hell of it, a container of sea scent bubble bath.

She was still standing in the hallway, not even pretending she wasn't keeping an eye on him.

"You'll ruin my reputation if you tell anyone about this," he said, only half joking as he lifted the package of bubble bath. "But when I saw that bathtub... We only had showers in prison," he added when he saw her confusion.

"I hadn't realized..."

"It's scary enough in the showers," he said with a shake of his head. "Can't imagine being caught in a bath-tub there."

She ducked her head and put her key into the lock on her room door, as if not wanting to think about what went on in prison. "I'll let you know when our dinner arrives." She opened her door, but didn't look at him. "Enjoy your bath."

He chuckled. "Oh, I intend to."

Jacklyn swore as she closed her room door. The last thing she wanted to do was imagine Dillon Savage loung-ing in a tubful of bubbles.

Bubble bath? Clearly, he didn't worry about his mas-culinity. Not when he had it in spades. But she knew that hadn't been his reason for buying the bubble bath. He'd wanted her imagining him in that tub.

She opened her suitcase and took out the small re-ceiver terminal with the built-in global positioning sys-tem, turning it on just in case the bath had been a ruse. The steady beep confirmed that he was just next door. In fact, she could hear the water running on the other side of the adjoining door.

In the desk drawer, she found a menu for the local Chinese restaurant, and ordered a variety of items to be delivered, all but one spicy. It seemed easier than going out, since after they ate, she wanted to get right down to business.

With luck, she'd be ready when the rustlers struck again.

Her cell phone rang. She checked the number, not sur-prised that it was her boss again. "Wilde."

"Is he there?"

"No. He's in the adjoining room."

"He's probably using the motel room phone to call his friends and let them know where he is and what your plans are," Stratton said, sounding irritated.

"The phone in his room is tapped," she said. "If he makes a call, he'll be back in prison tomorrow. But he isn't going to call anyone and warn them. I haven't told him anything."

"Good. I didn't want him to hear this," Stratton said. "The rustlers hit another ranch. Bud Drummond's."

The Drummond ranch was to the north, almost to the Missouri River. Jacklyn swore under her breath. "When?"

"He's not sure. He'd been out of town for a few days. When he got back, he rode fence and found where the rustlers had cut the barbed wire and gotten what he estimates was about twenty head."

Less than usual. "Why didn't they get more? Is it possible someone saw them?"

"Doubtful. It's at the north end of his ranch, a stretch along the river," Stratton said. "I told him you were going to be up that way tomorrow, anyway, so you'd stop by."

It had rained the day before. Any tracks would be gone. She doubted there would be anything to find—just like usual.

"Savage giving you any trouble?" Stratton asked.

"No." No trouble, unless you counted the psychological games he played. She had a mental flash of him in the tub, sea scent bubbles up to his neck. Exactly the image she knew Dillon had hoped she'd have when he'd bought the bubble bath.

"I shouldn't have to remind you how clever he is or how long it took you to catch him the last time. Don't underestimate him."

She heard the water finally shut off next door. She checked the monitor. Dillon was exactly where he'd said he would be.

"Trust me," she said, "I know only too well what Dillon Savage is capable of."

Tom Robinson dismounted in the dry creek bottom and pulled out his handgun. He hadn't realized how late it was. He was losing light. A horse whinnied somewhere above him on the hillside. He moved behind one of the large pines and listened, trying to determine if the horseback rider was moving.

He knew the man was still up there. This was the only cover for miles. At the very least he was trespassing. But Tom knew that, more than likely, the rider was one of the rustlers. Since the man was alone, maybe he was just checking out the ranch layout, finding the best access to the cattle in this section of pasture.

Tom had gotten only a glimpse of him, but that glimpse was more than anyone else had gotten of the rustlers. His heart began to pound at the thought of catching the man, being the one who brought down the rustling gang.

He had two options. He could wait for the intruder to break cover and try to make a run for it.

Or he could flush him out.

Leaving his horse, Tom worked his way up the steep incline, taking a more direct route on foot than the horseback rider had. Pebble-size stones rolled under his boots and cascaded down with every step he took.

Halfway up, he stopped, leaning against one of the large rocks to thumb off the safety on his weapon. His hands were shaking. It had crossed his mind belatedly that there might be more than one rider now on his spread. Maybe they'd planned to meet here in the trees. There could be others waiting in ambush at the top of the hill.

He considered turning back, but this was his land and he was determined to defend it and his livestock. He knew he had at least one man cornered. Once he broke from the shelter of trees, Tom would see him. With luck, he would be able to get off a shot. Unless the intruder was waiting for the cover of darkness.

This, Tom knew, was the point where the cops on television called for backup. But even if he'd had a cell phone, he wouldn't have been able to get service out here. Nor could he wait for someone to arrive and help him even if he could call for assistance.

No, he was going to have to do this alone.

Would the man be armed? Tom could only assume so.

He was breathing hard, but his hands had steadied. He had no choice. He had to do this.

Climbing quickly upward, staying behind the cover of rocks and trees as best he could, Tom topped the hill, keeping low, the gun gripped in both hands.

He knew he couldn't hesitate. Not even an instant. The moment he saw the rustler he would have to shoot. Shoot to kill if the individual was armed. He'd never killed a man. Today could change that.

As Tom Robinson moved through the trees at the edge of a small clearing, he heard a horse whinny off to his left, and spun in that direction, his finger on the trigger.

The moment he saw the animal, and the empty saddle, he realized the mistake he'd made. He spun back around and came face-to-face with the trespasser. Shocked both by who it was and by the tree limb in the man's hands,

Tom hesitated an instant too long before pulling the trigger.

The shot boomed among the trees, echoing over the rocks, the misguided bullet burying itself in the bark of a pine off to the trespasser's left.

It happened so fast, Tom didn't even realize he'd fired. He barely felt the blow to his head as the man swung the thick limb like a baseball bat. Instead, Tom just heard a sickening thud as the limb struck his temple, felt his knees give out under him and watched in an odd fascination as the dried needles on the ground came up to meet his face, just before everything went black.

Jacklyn Wilde started at the sound of a knock on the hall door to her motel room. "Delivery."

She sat up in confusion, horrified to realize that she'd dozed off. After the phone call from Stratton, she'd lain down for only a minute, but must have fallen asleep.

She rushed to the receiver terminal, half expecting to see that Dillon was no longer in his room.

But the steady beep assured her he was right next door. Or at least his tracking device was.

She thought about knocking on his door to check, using the food as an excuse. But instead she went to tip the deliveryman, closing her door behind him.

As she placed the Chinese food sacks on the table in the corner of her room, she heard a soft tap on the door between their rooms.

"Dinner's here," she called in response. Unconsciously, she braced herself as he stepped into her room.

His hair was wet and curled at his neck, his face flushed from his bath, and he smelled better than sweet and sour shrimp any day of the week. On top of that, he looked so happy and excited that anyone with a heart would have felt something as he made a beeline for the food.

She knew she was considered cold and heartless with no feelings, especially the female kind. It made it easier in her line of work to let everyone think that.

But how could she not be moved to see Dillon like a kid in a candy store as he opened each of the little white boxes, making delighted sounds and breathing in the scent of each, all the time flashing that grin of his?

"I can't believe this. I think you got all my favorites," he said, turning that grin on her. "You must have read my mind." The look in his eyes softened, taking all the air from the room.

She turned away and pretended to look in her suitcase for something.

"Come on," he said. "Let's eat while it's hot. Work can wait. Can't it?"

She pulled out the map she'd planned to show him later, and glanced toward the small table in the corner and Dillon. "Go ahead and start."

He shook his head. "My mother taught me better than that."

Reluctantly, she joined him as he began to dish up the rice. "I just want a little sweet and sour shrimp."

He looked up. "You can't be serious. Who's going to eat all this?"

She couldn't help her smile. "I figured you would. You did say you've been starved for Chinese food."

His grateful expression was almost her undoing—and his subsequent vulnerability as well. He ducked his head as if overcome with emotions he didn't want her to see, and spooned sweet and sour shrimp onto a plate for her.

She made a job of putting the map on the chair beside her, giving him a moment. Maybe she'd underestimated what four years in prison had done to him. Or what it must be like for him to be out.

When she looked up, however, there was no sign of anything on his face except a brilliant smile as he dished up his own plate. She warned herself not to be taken in by any of his antics as she took a bite of her meal and watched him do the same.

He closed his eyes and moaned softly. She tried to ignore him as she pretended to study the map on the chair next to her while she nibbled her food.

"You have to try this."

Before she could react, he reached across the table and shoved a forkful of something at her. Instinctively, she opened her mouth.

"Isn't that amazing?" he asked as he intently watched her chew.

It *was* amazing. Spicy, but not too hot. "Which one is that?" she asked, just to break the tense quiet in the room as he stared at her.

"Orange-peel beef." He was already putting some on her plate. "And wait until you try this." He started toward her with another forkful.

She held up her hand, more than aware of how intimate it was to be fed by a man. She was sure Dillon Savage was aware of it, too. "Really, I—" But the fork had touched her lips and her mouth opened again.

As he dragged the fork away slowly, she felt a rush of heat that had nothing to do with the spicy food.

She met his gaze and felt a chill run the length of her

spine. The smile on his lips, the teasing tilt of his head, couldn't hide what was deep in those pale blue eyes.

She had forgotten that she'd been the one to put him behind bars, but clearly, Dillon Savage had not.

Chapter 4

Dillon stared into Jack's gray eyes. For a moment there he'd been enjoying himself, so much that he'd forgotten who she was: the woman who'd sent him to prison. His mood turned sour in an instant.

He dragged his gaze away, but not before she'd seen the change in him. Seen his true feelings.

She shoved her plate aside, her appetite apparently gone, and spread the map out on the table like a barrier between them. "We need to get to work, so as soon as you've finished eating…"

He ate quickly, but his enjoyment of foods he'd missed so much was gone. He told himself it was better this way. Jack had to be aware of how he felt about her. She would have been a fool not to, and this woman was no fool.

But he doubted she knew the extent of his feelings. Or how he'd amused himself those many hours alone in his bunk. He'd plotted his revenge. Not that he planned to act on it, he'd told himself. It had just been something to do. Because he would need to do *something* about the person who'd betrayed him. And while he was at it, why not do something about Jack?

Only he would have to be careful around her. More careful than he'd been so far.

Food forgotten, he shoved the containers aside and stood to lean over the map. But his attention was on Jack. He could tell she was still a little shaken, and wanted to reassure her that he was no longer a man driven by vengeance. No easy task, given that he didn't believe it himself.

But that wasn't what bothered him as he pretended to study the map. As a student of human nature, he couldn't help but wonder why, when he'd been so careful to mask his feelings for years, he had let that mask slip— even for an instant—around the one woman who controlled his freedom.

Jacklyn watched his eyes. They were a pale blue, with tiny specks of gold. Eyes that gave away too much, including the fact that behind all that blue was a brain as sharp as any she'd run across. And that made him dangerous, even beyond whatever grudges he still carried.

On the map, she'd marked with a small red *x* each ranch that had lost cattle. Next to it, she'd put down the number of livestock stolen and the estimated value.

Some of the cattle had been taken in broad daylight, others under the cover of night. The randomness of the hits had made it impossible to catch the rustlers—that and the fact that they worked a two-hundred-mile area, moved fast and left no evidence behind.

Dillon had been leaning over the table, but now sat back and raked a hand through his still-wet hair.

"Something wrong?" she asked. Clearly, there was. She could see that he was upset. If he was the leader of the rustlers, as she suspected, none of this would come as a surprise to him. Unless, of course, his partners in crime had hit more ranches than he was aware of. Had they been cheating him? What if they'd been double-crossing him? She could only hope.

She reminded herself that there was the remote chance Dillon Savage wasn't involved, which meant whoever was leading this band of rustlers was as clever as he had been. Another reason Dillon might have looked upset?

"Just an interesting pattern," he said.

She nodded. She'd been afraid he was going to start lying to her right off the bat. "Interesting how?"

He gave her a look that said she knew as well as he did. "By omission."

"Yes," she agreed, relieved he hadn't tried to con her. "It appears they are saving the biggest ranch for last."

He smiled at that. "You really think they're ever going to stop, when things are going so well for them?"

No. That was her fear. Some of the smaller ranchers were close to going broke. The rustlers had taken a lot of unbranded calves this spring. Based on market value, the animals had been worth about a thousand dollars a head, a loss that was crippling the smaller ranches, some of which had been hit more than once.

Worse, the rustlers were showing no sign of letting up. She'd hoped they would get cocky, mess up, but they were apparently too good for that.

"What do you think?" she asked, motioning to the map.

He leaned back in his chair. "I'm more interested in what you think."

She scowled at him.

"I'm not trying to be difficult," he contended. "I'm just

curious as to your take on this. After all, if we're going to be working together…"

She fought the urge to dig in her heels. But he was right. She'd gotten him out of prison to help her catch the rustlers. It was going to require some give and take. But at the same time, if he was the leader…

"I think they're going to make a big hit on Shade Waters's W Bar Ranch. It's the largest spread in the area and the rustlers have already hit ranches around him for miles, but not touched his."

Dillon lifted a brow.

"What?"

"I suspect that's exactly what they want you to think," he said.

She had to bite her tongue. Damn him and his arrogance. "You have a better suggestion as to where they'll go next?"

He leaned forward to study the map again. After a long moment, he said, "Not a clue."

She swore under her breath and glared at him.

"If you're asking me what the rustlers will do next, I have no idea," he said, raising both hands in surrender.

"What would *you* do?" she snapped.

Dillon shrugged, pretty sure now he knew why Jack had gotten him out of prison. "Like I told you back at the prison weeks ago, I'm not sure how I can help you find these guys."

He saw that she didn't believe that. "Look, it's clear that they are very organized. No fly-by-night bunch. They move fast and efficiently. They know what they're doing, where they're going to go next."

"So?" she asked.

"If you think I can predict their movements, then you

wasted your time and your money getting me an early release. You might as well drive me back to prison right now."

"Don't tempt me. You said you think they want me to assume they're going to hit Waters's ranch. What does that mean?"

"They wouldn't be that obvious. Sorry, but isn't the reason this bunch has been so hard to catch the fact that they don't do what you expect them to? That gives them the upper hand."

"Tell me something I don't know, Mr. Savage."

He sighed and looked at the map again. "Are these the number of cattle stolen per ranch?" he asked, pointing to the notations she'd made beside the red *x*'s.

She gave him an exasperated look, her jaw still tight.

He could see why she thought the ring would be looking for a big score. The rustlers were being cautious, taking only about fifty head at a time, mostly not-yet-branded calves that would be hard to trace. Smart, but not where the big money was.

Jacklyn got up from the table as if too nervous to sit still, and started clearing up their dinner.

"It's not about the money," he said to her back.

She turned as she tossed an empty Chinese food box into the trash. "Stop trying to con me."

"I'm not. You're looking at this rationally. Rustling isn't always rational—at least the motive behind it isn't. Hell, there are a lot of better ways to make a living."

"I thought you said it was simple math, quick bucks, little risk," she said, an edge to her voice.

So she had been listening. "Yeah, but it's too hit-or-miss. With a real job you get to wear a better wardrobe, have nicer living conditions. Not to mention a 401 K salary, vacation and sick pay, plus hardly anyone ever shoots at you."

"Your point?" she said, obviously not appreciating his sense of humor.

She started to scoop up the map, but he grabbed her hand, more to get her attention than to stop her. He could feel her pulse hammering against the pad of his thumb, which he moved slowly in a circle across the warm flesh. His heart kicked up a beat as her eyes met his.

What the hell was he doing? He let go and she pulled back, her gaze locked with his, a clear warning in all that gunmetal gray.

"All I'm saying is that you have to think like they think," he said.

She shook her head. "That's *your* job."

"The only way I can do that is if I know what they really want," he said.

"They want *cattle*."

He laughed. "No. Trust me, it's not about cattle. It's always about the end result. The cattle are just a means to an end. What we need to know is what they're getting out of this. It isn't the money. They aren't making enough for it to be about money. So what do they really want?"

"The money will come from a big score. Waters's W Bar Ranch."

"After they've telegraphed what they are going to do so clearly that it's what you're expecting?" He snorted. "No, they have something else in mind."

She shook her head as if he was talking in riddles. "I won't know what they want until I catch them."

He grinned. "Catching them is one thing. Finding out who they are is another."

She was glaring at him again.

"You've been trying to catch an unnamed ring of cattle rustlers," he said patiently. "What do these men do when they aren't rustling cattle? You can bet they work on these ranches," he said, pointing at the map.

She sat back down very slowly. He could tell she was trying to control her temper. She thought he was messing with her.

"Look," he said softly. "You already know a lot about these guys." He ticked items off on his fingers. "One, someone smart is running this operation. That's why these characters seem to know what they're doing and why they haven't made any mistakes. Two, they know the country." He nodded. "We're talking some inside jobs here. They know not only where to find the cattle, but which ones to take and when. They either work on the ranches or have a connection of some kind."

She crossed her arms, scowling but listening.

"Three, they're cowboys. They're too good at working with cattle not to be, and they've used horses for most of their raids. I'll bet you these guys can ride better at midnight on a moonless night in rough terrain than most men can ride in a corral in broad daylight."

She actually smiled at that.

He smiled back, then asked, "What's so humorous?"

"You. You just described yourself," she said, her gaze locking with his. "We're looking for someone just like you. How about that."

When the call came hours later, Jacklyn was in the middle of a nightmare. She jerked awake, dragging the bad dream into the room with her as she fumbled for her cell phone beside the bed.

"Tom Robinson's in the hospital," Stratton said without preamble. "He's unconscious. The doctors aren't sure he's going to make it."

Jacklyn fought to wake up, to make sense of what he was saying and what this had to do with her. Although she couldn't remember any specifics of the nightmare, she knew it had been about the leader of the rustling ring. He'd been trying to kill her, stalking her among some trees. She could still feel him out there, feel the danger, the fear, sense him so close that if she looked over her shoulder... It had been Dillon, hadn't it?

"It seems like he might have stumbled across the rustlers," Stratton said. "His hired hand found him near a spot where someone had cut the fence."

She glanced at the clock next to the bed. It was just after midnight.

"Are you there?" Stratton asked irritably. Like her, he'd obviously been awakened by the call about Tom. "When Tom didn't return home for dinner, his hired hand tracked him down, and got him to the hospital. You know what this means, don't you?"

Jacklyn threw off the covers and sat up, trying to throw off the remnants of the dream and the chilling terror that still had her in its grip, too. Snapping on the light beside the bed, she asked, "Did they get any cattle?"

"No. He must have scared the rustlers away."

More awake, she said, "You told everyone to stay out of the area, right? To wait until I got there before they fix the fence?"

"Sheriff McCray already went out to the scene tonight."

She swore under her breath.

"I told Robinson's hired man that you'd be there first thing in the morning. The rustlers have moved up a level on the criminal ladder. If Tom dies, they've gone from rustling to murder." With that he hung up.

She closed her cell phone and, bleary-eyed, glanced again at the clock, then at the monitor. She'd turned it down so there was no steady beep indicating where Dillon Savage was at the moment.

But she could see that he was in the room next door. Probably sleeping like a baby, without a care in the world.

With both a real nightmare and a bad dream hanging over her, she fought the urge to wake him up and ruin his sleep, just as hers had been. She wondered what Dillon Savage's reaction would be to the news.

She turned out the light and crawled back under the covers, even though she doubted she'd get back to sleep. Silently, she prayed that Tom Robinson would regain consciousness and be able to identify his assailants.

The rustlers had messed up this time. They'd been seen. It was their first mistake.

Chapter 5

The drive north the next morning was like going home again for Dillon Savage. Except for the fact that he had no home. Which made seeing the land he knew so well all that much harder to take.

Not to mention that Jack wasn't talking to him. She'd broken the news at breakfast.

"You all right?" he'd finally asked, over pancakes and bacon. She'd seemed angry with him all morning. He couldn't think of anything he'd done recently that would have set her off, but then, given their past...

She'd looked up from her veggie omelet and leveled those icy gray eyes on him. "Tom Robinson was found near death yesterday evening on his ranch. Apparently, he stumbled across the rustlers. He's in the hospital. His ranch hand found him—along with a spot in the fence where the barbed wire had been cut." She'd stared at Dillon, waiting.

"I'm sorry to hear about Tom. I always liked him," he

had said, meaning it. But his words only seemed to make Jack's mood more sour, if that was possible.

Tom Robinson was one of the few neighbors who still had his place. Dillon had often wondered how he'd managed to keep his spread when almost all the other ranchers around the W Bar had sold out to Shade Waters.

"If Tom was attacked by the rustlers, then they just went from felony theft to attempted murder," Jack had pointed out. "But the good news is that when Tom regains consciousness, he'll be able to identify them."

"Good," Dillon had said, seeing that she was bluffing. She had no way of knowing if Tom Robinson had gotten a good look at whoever had attacked him, let alone if it was the rustlers. "Sounds like you got a break." She was staring at him, so he frowned at her. *"What?"*

"Come on, Dillon," she'd said, dropping her voice. It was the first time she'd called him by his first name. "You and I both know you're the leader of this rustling ring. Once Tom identifies who attacked him, your little house of cards is going to come tumbling down. Tell me the truth now and I will try to get you the best deal I can."

He had laughed, shaking his head. "Jack, you're barking up the wrong tree. I'm not your man." He'd grinned and added, "At least not for that role, anyway. I told you. I've gone straight. No more iron bars for me."

She hadn't believed him.

He should have saved his breath, but he'd tried to assure her she was wrong. "There's a lot of injustice in the world. I'm sorry Tom got hurt. But Jack, if you think I have anything to do with this—"

"Don't even bother," she'd snapped, throwing down her napkin. Breakfast was over.

Since then, she hadn't said two words to him.

He stared out his window. The golden prairie was dotted with antelope, geese and cranes, and of course, cows. This was cattle country and had been for two hundred years. Ranch houses were miles apart and towns few and far between.

It amazed Dillon how little things had changed over the years. He kept up on the news and knew that places like Bozeman had been growing like crazy.

But this part of Montana had looked like this for decades, the landscape changing little as the population diminished. Kids left the farms and ranches for greener pastures in real towns or out of state.

But as isolated and unpopulated as this country was, there was a feeling of community. While there had been little traffic this morning, everyone they passed had waved, usually lifting just a couple of fingers from the steering wheel or giving a nod.

There was so much that he'd missed. Some people didn't appreciate this land. It was fairly flat, with only the smudged, purple outline of mountains far in the distance. There was little but prairie, and a pencil-straight, two-lane road running for miles.

But to him it was beautiful. The grasses, a deep green, undulated like waves in the wind. The sky was bluer than any he'd ever seen. Willows had turned a bright gold, dogwood a brilliant red. Everywhere he looked there were birds.

God, how he'd missed this.

He'd known it would be hell coming back here. Especially after his four-year stint in prison. He'd never dreamed he'd return so soon—or with Jack—let alone have a microchip embedded behind his left ear. Life was just full of surprises.

The farther north Jacklyn drove, the more restless Dillon became. He'd hoped the years in prison had changed him, had at least taught him something about himself. But this place brought it all back. The betrayal. The anger. The aching need for vengeance.

"I'm sorry, where did you say we were going?" he asked. Jack, of course, hadn't said.

"Your old stompin' grounds," she said.

That's what he was afraid of. They'd gone from the motel to pick up a horse trailer, two horses and tack. He couldn't wait to get back in the saddle. He was just worried where that horse was going to take him. Maybe more to the point, what he would do once he and Jack were deep in this isolated country, just the two of them.

Jacklyn had her own reasons for not wanting to go north that morning. The big one was that Sheriff Claude McCray had sent word he had to see her.

Claude was the last man she wanted to see. And with good reason. The last time she'd been with him they'd gotten into an argument after making love. She'd broken off their affair, knowing she'd been an idiot to get involved with him in the first place. She was embarrassed and ashamed.

When Dillon had asked her if she didn't regret something she'd done, she'd thought of Sheriff McCray. Since the breakup, she'd made a point of staying out of his part of Montana.

But today she had no choice. And maybe, just maybe, the reason McCray wanted to see her had something to do with Tom Robinson and the men who had attacked him, given the fact that the sheriff had gone to her crime scene last night.

The day was beautiful as she drove out of Lewistown pulling the horse trailer. Behind her, in her rearview mirror, she could see the Big Snowy Mountains and the Little Belts. Once she made it over the Moccasins and the Judiths, the land stretched to the horizon, rolling fields broken only occasionally by rock outcroppings or a lone tree or two.

Jack stared at the straight stick of a road that ran north, away from the mountains, away from any town of any size, and dreaded seeing Sheriff Claude McCray again—especially with Dillon Savage along.

She'd never forgive herself for foolishly becoming involved with someone she occasionally worked with. Not a good idea. On top of that, she'd gotten involved with Claude for all the wrong reasons.

Jacklyn turned off the two-lane highway onto a narrow, rutted dirt road. As far as the eye could see there wasn't a house or barn. Usually this open land comforted her, but not this morning, with everything she had on her mind. She felt antsy, as if she were waiting for the other shoe to drop.

She'd called the hospital before she'd left the motel. Tom Robinson was in critical condition. It was doubtful he would regain consciousness. She was angry and sickened. She liked Tom.

Selfishly, she'd wanted him to come to in the hopes that he could ID at least one of the rustlers. With just one name, she knew she could put pressure on that individual to identify the person running the ring. Dillon Savage.

She glanced over at him. She'd give him credit; he'd seemed genuinely upset over hearing about Tom. But was that because he'd known and liked the man, as he'd said? Or because his little gang of rustlers had gone too far this time and now might be found out?

He didn't look too worried that he was going to be caught, she thought. He was slouched in the seat, gazing out the window, watching the world go by as if he didn't have a care. Could she be wrong about him? Maybe. But there *was* something going on with him. She could feel it.

"So we're heading to the Robinson place," Dillon said, guessing that would be at least one of their stops today.

"After that we're going to the W Bar."

He could feel her probing gaze on him again, as if she was waiting for a reaction.

But he wasn't about to give her one. He just nodded, determined not to let her see how he felt about even the thought of crossing Shade Waters's path. He hadn't seen Waters since the day Jack had arrested him.

The truth was she'd probably saved his life, given that Shade had had a shotgun—and every intention of killing Dillon on the spot that day.

"Waters know you got me out of prison?" he asked.

"Probably the reason he wants to see me."

Dillon chuckled. "This should be interesting then."

"You'll be staying in the pickup—and out of trouble. Your work with me has nothing to do with Shade Waters," she said in that crisp, no-nonsense tone.

He smiled. "Just so I'm there to witness his reaction when you tell him that. Unless you want to leave me at the bar in Hilger and pick me up on your way back."

She shot him a look. "Until this rustling ring is caught, you and I are attached at the hip."

"I do like that image," he said, and grinned over at her.

She scowled and went back to her driving. "Any animosity you have for Waters or any other ranchers, you're to keep to yourself."

"What animosity?" he asked with a straight face. "I'm a changed man. Any hard feelings I had about Shade Waters I left behind that razor wire fence you broke me out of."

She gave him a look that said she'd believe that when hell froze over. "Just remember what I said. I don't need any trouble out of you. I have enough with Waters."

"Don't worry, Jack, I'll be good," Dillon said, and pulled down the brim on his hat as he slid down in the seat again. He tried not to think about Tom Robinson or Shade Waters or even Jack.

Instead, he thought about lying in the bathtub last night at the motel, bubbles up to his neck. And later, sprawled on the big bed, staring up at the ceiling, trying to convince himself he wasn't going to blow his freedom. Not for anything. Even justice.

The bath had been pure heaven. The bed was huge and softer than anything he'd slept on in years. In prison, he'd had a pad spread on a concrete slab. A real bed had felt strange, and had made him wonder how long it would take to get used to being out.

How long did it take not to be angry that normal no longer felt normal? Maybe as long as getting over the fact that someone owed him for the past four years of his life.

Sheriff Claude McCray wasn't in, but the dispatcher said she was expecting him, and to wait in his office.

Ten minutes later, Claude walked in. He was a big man, powerfully built, with a chiseled face and deep-set brown eyes. He gave Jacklyn a look that could have wilted lettuce. His gaze turned even more hostile when he glanced at Dillon.

McCray chuckled to himself as he moved behind his desk, shaking his head as he glared at Jacklyn again. "Dillon Savage. You got the bastard out. What a surprise."

She met his eyes for only an instant before she looked away, not wanting to get into this with him. Especially in front of Dillon, given what Claude had accused her of nearly four years ago.

"You're obsessed with Dillon Savage," McCray had said.

"Excuse me? It's my job to find him and stop him," she'd snapped back.

"Oh, Jacklyn, it's way beyond that. You admire him, admit it."

"Wh-what?" she'd stammered, sliding out of bed, wanting to distance herself from this ridiculous talk.

"He's the only one who's ever eluded you this long," Claude had called after her. "You're making a damn hero out of him."

She had been barely able to speak, she was so shocked. "That's so ridiculous, I don't even— You're jealous of a cattle rustler?"

He'd narrowed his eyes at her angrily. "I'm jealous of a man you can't go five minutes without talking about."

"I'm sorry I bothered you with talk about my job," she'd snapped as she jerked on her jeans and boots and looked around for her bra and sweater.

Claude was sitting up in the bed, watching her, frowning. "I'd bet you spend more time thinking about Dillon Savage than you do me."

She'd heard the jealousy and bitterness in his voice

and had been sickened by it. He'd called her after that,
telling her he'd had too much to drink and didn't know
what he was saying.

For all his apologies, that had been the end of their affair. She'd caught Dillon a few days later and had made
a point of staying as far from Sheriff Claude McCray as
possible, even though he'd tried to contact her repeatedly
over the past four years.

Now, as Claude settled into his chair behind the large
metal desk, she noticed that he looked shorter than she
remembered, his shoulders less broad. Or maybe she
couldn't help comparing him to Dillon Savage. They
were both close to the same age, but that was where the
similarities ended.

"What's the world coming to when we have to get
criminals out of prison to help solve crimes?" McCray
said as if to himself, looking from Dillon to Jack.

"Is there anything new on the Robinson case?" she
asked, determined to keep the conversation on track.

"Why don't you ask your boyfriend here," McCray
quipped.

Dillon was watching this interplay with interest. She
swore under her breath, wishing that she'd come alone.
But she didn't like letting Dillon out of her sight. Especially now that the stakes were higher, with Tom Robinson critical.

"Sheriff, I just need to know if you have any leads. I
understand you went out to the crime scene last night."
She had to bite her tongue to keep from saying how stupid it was to go out there in the dark and possibly destroy
evidence. "I'm headed out there now."

"Don't waste your time. There's nothing to find."

She would be the judge of that. "What about the Drummond place?"

Claude was shaking his head. "Wasn't worth riding back in there for so few head of cattle."

Bud Drummond might argue that, she thought.

She rose from her chair, anxious to get out of Claude's office. She'd thought about not even bothering to come here, but he'd sent word that he wanted to see her. She should have known it wasn't about the Robinson case.

Her real reason for coming, she knew, was so he wouldn't think she was afraid to face him. Perish the thought.

"If Tom Robinson dies, it will be murder," McCray said, glaring at Dillon. "This time you'll stay in prison."

Dillon, to his credit, didn't react. But she could see that this situation could escalate easily if they didn't leave. Claude seemed to be working himself up for a fight.

"We're going," Jacklyn said, moving toward the door.

The sheriff rose, coming around the desk to grab her arm. "I need to speak with you alone."

Jacklyn looked down at his fingers digging into her flesh. He let go of her, but she saw Dillon leap to his feet, about to come to her defense.

That was the last thing she needed. "Mr. Savage, if you wouldn't mind waiting by the pickup…" She had no desire to be alone with Claude McCray, but if she was anything, she was no coward. And he just might have something to tell her about the investigation that Dillon shouldn't hear.

Dillon frowned, as if he didn't like leaving her alone with McCray. Obviously, she wasn't the only one who thought the man could be dangerous.

She indicated the door and gave Dillon an imploring look.

"I'll be right outside if you need me," he said as he opened the door and stepped out, closing it quietly behind him.

"That son of a bitch." The sheriff swore and swung on her. "He acts like he owns you. Are you already sleeping with him?"

"Don't be ridiculous. What was it you had to say to me?"

He glared at her, anger blazing in his eyes. "If you're not, it's just a matter of time before you are. You've had something for him for years."

"If that's all you wanted to say…" She started for the door.

He reached to grab her again, but this time she avoided his grasp. "Don't," she said, her voice low and full of warning. "Don't touch me."

He drew back in surprise. "Jackie—"

"And don't call me that."

He stiffened and busied himself straightening his hat, as if trying to get his temper under control.

What had she ever seen in him? She didn't want to think about why she'd ended up with McCray. And it wasn't because she hadn't known what kind of man he was. She'd been looking for an outlaw during the day and had wanted one at night, as well.

Too late she'd realized Claude McCray was a mean bastard with even less ethics than Dillon Savage.

"Was there something about the case?" she asked as she reached for the doorknob.

He glared at her for a long moment, then grudgingly said, "My men found something up by where the rustlers cut the barbed wire of Robinson's fence last night," he said finally. "I'm sure it's probably been in the dirt for years and has nothing do with the rustlers, but I was told to give it to you." He reached toward his desk, then turned and dropped a gold good-luck piece into her palm.

"You have any idea who this might belong to?" she asked.

"Someone whose luck is about to turn for the worst," McCray said cryptically. "At least if I have anything to do with it."

Chapter 6

"You all right?" Dillon asked as Jack came out of the sheriff's office.

"Fine," she said, whipping past him and heading for the truck.

He followed, thinking about what he'd seen in there. Definitely tension between the lawman and Jack. Dillon had never liked that redneck son of a bitch, McCray. He'd seen plenty of guys like him at prison. What he'd witnessed in the office hadn't made Dillon dislike him any less.

In fact, it had been all he could do not to punch the man. But if Dillon had learned anything it was that you didn't punch out a sheriff. Especially when you had just gotten a prerelease from prison and were treading on thin ice as it was.

Jack started the pickup as Dillon slid in and slammed the door. She seemed anxious to get out of town. He knew that feeling.

"So what did the bastard do to you?"

She jerked her head around to look at him and almost ran into the car in front of them.

He saw the answer in her expression and swore. "McCray. Oh man." Dillon had hoped the animosity between them just had to do with work, but he'd known better. He just hadn't wanted to believe she'd get involved with Claude McCray, and said as much.

"Don't," she warned as she gripped the wheel. The light changed and she got the pickup going again. "You and I aren't getting into this discussion."

He shook his head. "I've made some big mistakes in my life, but Claude McCray?"

She slammed on the brakes so hard the seat belt cut into him. "I will not have this discussion with you," she said, biting off each word. The driver behind them laid on his horn. Jack didn't seem to notice. She was clasping the wheel so tightly her knuckles were white, her eyes straight ahead, as if she couldn't look at him.

"Okay, okay," Dillon said, realizing this had to be that big regret he'd sensed in her. Jack's big mistake.

It was so unlike her. She had more sense than to get involved with McCray. Something must have caused it. "When was it?"

"I just said—"

He swore as he remembered something he'd overheard while in the county jail. "You were seeing him when you were chasing me."

She groaned and got the pickup going again. "Could we please drop this? Can't you just sit over there and laugh smugly under your breath so I don't have to hear it?"

She still hadn't looked at him.

He reached over and touched her arm. Her gaze shifted

to him slowly, reluctantly. He looked into her eyes and saw a pain he couldn't comprehend. No way had McCray broken it off between them. No, from the way the sheriff had been acting, Jack had dumped *him*.

So what was with this heartache Dillon saw in her eyes?

Tom Robinson's ranch house was at the end of a narrow, deeply rutted road. The ranch was small, a wedge of land caught between Waters's huge spread and Reda Harper's much less extensive one.

The ride north had been pure hell. Though Dillon finally shut up about her and Sheriff McCray, Jack knew he was sitting over there making sport of her entire affair. She hated to think what was going through his mind.

After a few miles, she stole a glance at him. He had his hat down over his eyes, his long legs sprawled out, his hands resting in his lap. To all appearances, he seemed to be sleeping.

Right. He was over there chortling to himself, pleased that he'd stirred her up again. Worse, that he now had something on her. The man was impossible.

She would never figure him out. Earlier, when he'd forced her to look at him, she'd thought she'd seen compassion in his eyes, maybe even understanding.

But how could he understand? She didn't herself.

Dillon Savage was like no man she'd ever known. When she'd been chasing him before, she'd been shocked to learn that he didn't fit any profile, let alone that of a cattle rustler. For starters, he was university educated, with degrees in engineering, business and psychology, and he'd graduated at the top of his class.

If that wasn't enough, he'd inherited a bundle right before he started rustling cattle. He had no reason to commit the crime. Except, she suspected, to flout the law.

Dillon stirred as she pulled into Tom Robinson's yard. She felt the gold good-luck coin in her pocket. She'd almost forgotten that she'd stuck it there, she'd been so upset about McCray—and Dillon.

She knew it might not be a clue. Anyone could have dropped it there at any time. While the coin did look old, that didn't mean it was. Nor would she put it past Claude McCray to lie about where he'd found it, just to throw her off track. Worse, she suspected it might be fairly common, even something given out by casinos, since Montana had legalized gambling.

If it had belonged to one of the rustlers, any fingerprints on it had been destroyed with McCray handling it.

She sighed and reached into her pocket for the coin, thinking about what McCray had said about luck changing for the person who'd been carrying it.

"I need to ask you something," she said, turning to Dillon. "I need you to tell me the truth."

He nodded and grinned. "Did I tell you I never lie?"

"Right."

Dillon looked at the hand she held toward him, her fingers clasped around something he couldn't see, her eyes intent on his face.

He felt his stomach clench as she slowly uncurled her fingers. He had no idea what she was going to show him. And even though he suspected it wasn't going to be good, he wasn't prepared for what he saw nestled in her palm.

"You recognize it!" she accused, wrapping her fingers back around it as if she wanted to hit him with her fist. "So help me, if you deny it—"

"Yeah, I've seen it before. Or at least one like it."

She was staring at him as if she was surprised he'd actually admitted it. "Who does it belong to?"

"I said I'd seen one like it, I didn't say—"

"Don't," she snapped, scowling at him.

"Easy," he said, holding up his hands. "A friend of mine used to have one like it, okay? He carried it around for luck. But he's dead."

"And you don't know what happened to his?"

Dillon couldn't very well miss her sarcasm. "May I look at it?"

She reluctantly opened her hand, as if she thought he might grab it and run.

He plucked the good-luck coin from her warm palm, accidentally brushing his fingertips across her skin, and saw her shudder. But his attention was on the coin as he turned it in his fingers. The small marks were right where he knew they would be, leaving no doubt. His heart began to pound.

"Where did you say you got this?" he asked as he handed it back.

Her gaze burned into him. "I didn't."

Dillon could only assume that, since she'd gone to the sheriff about Tom Robinson, McCray had given it to her. Which had to mean that she suspected one of the rustlers who'd attacked Tom had dropped it.

"So who was the deceased friend of yours who had one like it?" she asked, clearly not believing him.

"Halsey Waters. And as for what happened to his coin," Dillon said, "I personally put it in his suit pocket at his funeral."

"Halsey *Waters?* Shade's oldest son?"

"That's the one." Out of the corner of his eye, Dillon

saw the ranch house door open and a stocky cowboy step out. Arlen Dubois.

It was turning out to be like old home week, Dillon thought. All the old gang was back in central Montana. Just as they had been for Halsey Waters's funeral.

Arlen Dubois was all cowboy, long and lanky, legs bowed, boots run-down, jeans worn and dirty. He invited them into the house, explaining that he was looking after everything with Tom in the hospital.

Jacklyn watched Arlen take off his hat and nervously rake a hand through short blond curls. His skin was white and lightly freckled where the hat had protected it from the sun. The rest of his face was sunburned red.

He looked from Jacklyn to Dillon and quickly back again. "I'd offer you something to drink…"

"We're fine," Jacklyn said, noticing how uncomfortable the cowboy was in the presence of his old friend. Arlen had a slight lisp, buckteeth and a broad open face. "I just want to ask you a few questions."

He shifted on his feet. "Okay."

"Do you mind if we sit down?" she asked.

Arlen got all flustered, but waved them toward chairs in the small living room. Jacklyn noticed that the fabric was threadbare, and doubted the furnishings had been replaced in Tom's lifetime.

Arlen turned his hat in his hands as he sat on the edge of one of the chairs.

"You work for Tom Robinson?" she asked.

"Yep, but you already know that. If you think I had anything to do with what happened to Tom—"

"How long have you worked for Mr. Robinson?"

Arlen gave that some thought, scraping at a dirty spot

on his hat as he did. "About four years," he said, without looking up. The same amount of time Dillon Savage had been behind bars.

"You and Mr. Savage here have been friends for a long time, right?"

Arlen started. "What does that have to do with this? If you think I ever stole cattle with him—"

"I was just asking if you were friends."

Arlen shrugged, avoiding Dillon's gaze. "We knew each other."

Yeah, she would just bet. She'd long suspected Dillon hadn't done the rustling alone. He would have needed help. But would he have involved a man like Arlen Dubois? Word at the bar was that Dubois tended to brag when he had a few drinks in him, although few people believed even half of what he said.

"Have you seen anyone suspicious around the ranch? Before Tom was attacked?" she asked, knowing that most of her questions were a waste of time. She had just wanted to see Arlen and Dillon together.

Dillon seemed cool as a cucumber, like a man who had nothing to hide.

"Nothin' suspicious," Arlen said, with a shake of his head.

"You know of anyone who had a grudge against Tom?"

The cowboy shook his head again. "Tom was likable enough."

Dillon was studying Arlen, and making him even more nervous. Maybe she should have left him in the truck.

"If you think of anything…"

Arlen looked relieved. "Sure," he said, and rose from his chair. "You ready to ride out to where I found Tom?"

Jacklyn nodded. "One more thing," she said as she stood and reached into her pocket. "Ever seen this before?"

Arlen reacted as if she'd held out a rattlesnake. His gaze shot to Dillon's, then back to the coin. "I might have seen one like it once."

"Where was that?" she asked.

"I can't really recall."

Both of Arlen's responses were lies.

"Mr. Savage, would you mind waiting for me in the pickup?" she asked.

"Not at all, Ms. Wilde."

She ground her teeth as she waited for him to close the front door behind him. "Anything you want to tell me, Arlen?"

"About what?" he asked, looking scared.

"Did you happen to be at Halsey Waters's funeral?"

All the color left his face. "What does that have to do with—"

"Yes or no? Or can't you remember that, either?"

He had the good grace to flush. "I was there, just like all his other friends."

She detected something odd in his tone. Today was the first time she'd heard anything about Halsey Waters. But then, she wasn't from this part of Montana. "How did Halsey die?"

Arlen looked down at his boots. "He was bucked off a wild horse. Broke his neck."

All the old demons that had haunted him came back with a vengeance as Dillon rode out with Arlen and Jacklyn, across rolling hills dotted with cattle and sagebrush. He breathed in the familiar scents as if to punish himself. Or remind himself that even four years in prison couldn't change a man enough to forget his first love. Or his worst enemy.

The air smelled so good it made him ache. This had once been his country. He knew it even better than the man who owned it.

They followed the fence line as it twisted alongside the creek, the bottomlands thick with chokecherry, willow and dogwood. Jacklyn slowed her horse, waiting for him.

The memories were so sharp and painful he had to look away for fear she would see that this was killing him.

Or worse, that she might glimpse the desire for vengeance burning in his eyes.

"I've always wanted to ask you," she said conversationally. Arlen was riding ahead of them, out of earshot. "Why three university degrees?"

Dillon pretended to give her question some thought, although he doubted that's what she'd been thinking about. She'd made it clear back at the ranch house that she thought he and Arlen used to rustle cattle together. It hadn't helped that Arlen had lied through his teeth about the good-luck coin.

Shoving back his hat, Dillon shrugged and said, "I was a rancher's son. You know how, at that age, you're so full of yourself. I thought the last thing I wanted to do was ranch. I wanted a job where I got to wear something other than jeans and boots, have an office with a window, make lots of money."

She glanced over at him, as if wondering if he was serious. "You know, I suspect you often tell people what you think they want to hear."

He laughed and shook his head. "Nope, that's the real reason I got three degrees. I was covering my bets."

She cut her eyes to him as she rode alongside him, their legs almost touching. "Okay, I get the engineering and business degrees. But psychology?"

He wondered what she was really asking. "I'm fascinated by people and what makes them tick. Like you," he said, smiling at her. "You're a mystery to me."

"Let's not go there."

"What if I can't help myself?"

"Mr. Savage—"

He laughed. "Maybe before this is over I'll get a glimpse of the real Jack Wilde," he said, her gaze heating him more than the sun beating down from overhead.

He could see that she wished she hadn't started this conversation when she urged her horse forward, trotting off after Arlen Dubois.

As Dillon stared after her retreating backside, he suspected he and the real Jacklyn Wilde were more alike than she ever wanted to admit—and he said as much when he caught up to her.

Jacklyn pretended not to hear him. His voice had dropped to a low murmur that felt like a whisper across her skin. It vibrated in her chest, making her nipples tighten and warmth rush through her, straight to her center.

Dillon chuckled, as if suspecting only too well what his words did to her.

She cursed her foolishness. She should have known better than to try to egg Dillon Savage on. He was much better at playing head games than she was.

In front of her, Arlen brought his horse up short. She did the same when she noticed the cut barbed wire fence. Dismounting, she handed the cowboy her reins and walked across the soft earth toward the gap.

There was one set of horseshoe tracks in the dirt on the other side of the cut fence, a half-dozen on this side, obliterating Tom's horse's prints. Sheriff McCray and his men. She could see where they had ridden all over, trampling any evidence.

But she no longer thought McCray had planted the lucky gold coin. Not after both Dillon's and Arlen's reactions. She just didn't know what a coin belonging to the deceased Halsey Waters had to do with this ring of rustlers. But she suspected Dillon and Arlen did.

Bending down, she noted that there was nothing unique about the trespasser's horse's prints. She could see where Tom had followed the man toward the creek bottom.

Arlen Dubois had tracked Tom and found him. At least that was the cowboy's story. Unfortunately, McCray and his men had destroyed any evidence to prove it.

She swung back into her saddle. "Show me where you found Tom," she said to Arlen. Turning, she looked back at Dillon. He seemed lost in thought, frowning down at the cut barbed wire.

"Something troubling you?" she asked him.

He seemed to come out of his daze, putting a smile on his face to cover whatever had been bothering him. If he was the leader of the rustlers, then wouldn't he feel something for a man who might die because of him and his partners in crime?

She followed the trampled tracks in the dust, feeling the hot sun overhead. It wasn't until she reached the trees and started up the hillside that she turned, and wasn't surprised to see Arlen and Dillon sitting astride their horses, engaged in what appeared to be a very serious conversation below her.

At the top of the ridge, she found bloodstained earth and scuffed tracks—dozens of boot prints. There was no way to distinguish the trespasser's. Had that been Sheriff McCray's intent? To destroy the evidence? Her one chance to maybe find out who the rustlers were? McCray would do it out of spite.

But there was another explanation, she realized. McCray might be covering for someone. Or even involved...

She couldn't imagine any reason Claude McCray would get involved in rustling. But then, she wasn't the best judge of character when it came to men, she admitted as she looked down the slope to where Dillon and Arlen were waiting.

By circling the area, she found the trespasser's tracks, and followed them to where he'd made a second cut in the barbed wire to let himself and his horse onto state grazing land.

Then she headed back to where she'd left the two men. As she approached, she noticed that Dillon had ridden over to a lone tree and was lounging under it, chewing on a piece of dried grass, his long legs stretched out and crossed at the ankles, his hat tilted down, but his eyes on her. He couldn't have looked more relaxed. Or more sexy. She couldn't help but wonder what he'd been talking about with Arlen.

Back at the ranch, she let Dillon unsaddle their horses while she went out to the barn, where Arlen was putting his own horse and tack away. He seemed surprised to see her, obviously hoping that she'd already left.

"Thanks for your help today," she said, wondering

what he would do for a job if Tom Robinson didn't make it. "Looks like you could use a new pair of boots."

Arlen looked down in surprise. "These are my lucky boots," he said bashfully. He lifted one leg to touch the worn leather, and Jack saw how the sole was worn evenly across the bottom.

Lucky boots. Good-luck coin. Cowboys were a superstitious bunch. "You'll be walking on your socks pretty soon," she said. "I saw you talking to Dillon. Mind telling me what you two were chatting about?"

Arlen gave a lazy shrug. "Nothin' in particular. Just talking about prison and Tom and—" he dropped his gaze "—you. Don't mean to tell you your business, but if I were you, I'd be real careful around him. When he's smiling is when he's the most dangerous."

Dillon watched Jack come out of the barn, and knew Arlen had said something to upset her.

Dillon had loaded the horses into the trailer and was leaning against the side, waiting for her in the shade. He hadn't been able to get Halsey's good-luck coin off his mind.

"Get what you needed?" he asked as Jack walked past him to climb behind the wheel.

He opened his door and slid in.

"I saw you and Arlen talking. Looked pretty serious," she said, without reaching to start the truck.

"Think we were plotting something?" He laughed.

"You said yourself that the rustlers might work for the ranchers they were stealing cattle from."

Dillon let out a snort. "Arlen? That cowboy can't keep his mouth shut. If he was riding with the gang, you'd have already caught them. The guy is a dim bulb."

Maybe. Or maybe that's what Dillon wanted her to believe. She looked back at Arlen. He was standing in the shade of the barn, watching them.

Dillon sighed. "I was asking him what he was going to do now. He said even if Tom regains consciousness, his injuries are such that he won't be running the ranch anymore. Waters has offered Arlen a job."

"What's wrong with that?" Jacklyn asked, as she heard Dillon curse under his breath.

"Arlen? He's worthless. Tom just kept him on because no one else would hire him. The only reason Waters would make the offer is so Arlen keeps him informed on everything that's going on with Tom and the ranch." At her confused look, Dillon added, "Waters has been trying to buy the Robinson ranch for years."

"Tom is in no condition to sell his ranch—"

"Tom has a niece back East, his only living relative. In his will, apparently he set it up so if anything happened to him and he couldn't run the place or he died...."

"You think she'll sell to Shade Waters."

"Waters will make sure she does."

Jacklyn could understand how Shade might want Tom Robinson's ranch. With it, he would own all the way to the Missouri on this side of the Judith River. The Robinson spread had been the only thing standing in his way.

Chapter 7

Jacklyn followed the county road as it wound around one section of land after another, until she saw the sign that marked the various directions to ranches in the area.

At one time there'd been a dozen signs tacked on the wooden post. But over the years, most ranches had been bought out, all of them by Shade Waters.

Now there were only three signs on the post, pointing to Shade Waters's W Bar Ranch, Tom Robinson's ranch and Reda Harper's RH Circle Cross.

Jacklyn saw Dillon glance at the signs, his gaze hardening before it veered away. Not far up the road, she turned to drive under an arched entry with W Bar Ranch carved into the graying wood.

"I'll stay in the pickup," he said as she pulled up in the ranch yard.

She looked at him, then at the sprawling ranch house. Shade Walters had come out onto the porch. Always a big man, he wasn't quite as handsome as he'd been in his younger days, but he was still striking. He stood in the shadow of the porch roof, an imposing figure that demanded attention.

The front door opened again and his son Nate came out, letting the door slam behind him. She saw Shade's irritated expression and the way he scowled in Nate's direction.

Nate was in his early thirties, big boned and blond. Unlike his father, his western clothing was new and obviously expensive. Shade Waters looked like every working rancher she'd known, from his worn western shirt to his faded jeans and weathered boots.

She couldn't help but think that whoever had attacked Tom Robinson had come by way of the W Bar, Shade Waters's land.

Nate was staring toward her passenger, and it dawned on her that Dillon and he were close in age and must have gone to school together. The old Savage place had been up the road. Had they once been friends, as had Dillon and Nate's brother, Halsey?

Nate's frown and the intense silence coming from the man next to her made it clear that the two were no longer friends, whatever their relationship had been in the past.

"You won't get out of the pickup no matter what happens?" she asked quietly, without looking at Dillon.

"Nope."

As Jacklyn started to open her door, a pretty, dark-haired woman joined the two men on the porch. Jacklyn felt Dillon tense beside her. The woman looped her arm through Nate's and gazed out at the pickup, as if daring anyone to try to stop her—including Shade Waters. Judging from his expression, he wasn't happy to see the woman join him, any more than he had been his son.

But it was Dillon's reaction that made Jacklyn hesitate before she climbed out of the truck.

Dillon knew the woman. Not just knew her. His left hand was clenched in a fist and his jaw was tight with anger.

She knew he blamed Shade Waters for what had happened not just to his family ranch but to his father. But was there more to the story? Was there a woman involved?

This dark-haired beauty?

"Holler if you need me," Dillon said as she started to climb out of the truck.

She shot him a look as he drew the brim of his hat down over his eyes and leaned back as if planning to sleep until she returned.

Right. As if he wouldn't be watching and listening to everything that was said. She noticed that he'd managed to power down his window before she turned off the pickup engine.

"Enjoy your nap," she said, knowing he wouldn't.

His lips tipped up in a smile. He wasn't fooling her and he knew it.

As Jacklyn closed the truck door, she noticed that the woman had her own gaze fixed on the passenger side of the pickup. On Dillon.

Jacklyn knew there'd been women in Dillon's life. Probably a lot of them. Had he turned to crime because of one of them? Maybe this one?

Jacklyn approached the porch slowly, afraid all hell was about to break loose. She just hoped Dillon Savage wasn't going to be in the middle of it.

Morgan Landers. Dillon couldn't believe his eyes. He'd

heard she'd gone to California. Or Florida. That she'd snagged some old guy with lots of bucks.

But as he watched her lean intimately into Nate Waters, Dillon knew he shouldn't have been surprised that Morgan had come back—or why.

What did surprise him was his reaction to seeing her. He hadn't expected ever to lay eyes on her again. Especially not here. It felt like another betrayal, but then he suspected it wasn't her first. Or her last.

What bothered him was that he knew Jack had seen his reaction. She missed little. Now she would think he still felt something for Morgan.

From under his hat, he watched Jack walk to the bottom step of the porch. Clearly, Shade Waters wasn't going to invite her inside the house. Manners had never been the man's strong suit. No, Waters wanted to intimidate her. How better than to stand on the porch, literally looking down on her?

Dillon smiled to himself. He'd put his money on Jack anyday, though. Not even Shade Waters could intimidate a woman like Jacklyn Wilde.

The rancher glanced at the pickup, no doubt seeing that Dillon had has side window down. Another reason Waters wouldn't invite Jack inside. He'd want Dillon to hear whatever he had to say. And Dillon was sure Waters had a lot to say, given that he'd demanded Jack stop by to see him.

Also, Dillon thought with a grin, Waters wouldn't want to go in the house knowing that a Savage was on his property, alone. Waters would be afraid of what Dillon might do.

As Dillon shifted his gaze from Morgan Landers to

the elderly man he'd spent years hating, he thought Waters was wise to worry.

Jacklyn looked up at the three standing on the porch. They made no move to step aside so she could enter the house—or even join them in the shade.

"I can handle this," Shade said, scowling over at his son. But Nate didn't move. Nor did the woman beside him.

Jacklyn couldn't help being curious about the woman, given that Dillon obviously had some connection to her. "I don't believe we've met," she said. "I'm Jacklyn Wilde."

The brunette had the kind of face and body that could stop traffic, but that had nothing to do with the dislike Jacklyn had felt for her instantly.

"Morgan Landers." She flicked her gaze over Jacklyn dismissively, her brown eyes lighting again on the pickup and no doubt the passenger sitting in it.

"If we're through with introductions…" Shade Waters snapped.

Jacklyn waited. She could see how agitated the rancher was, but wasn't entirely certain it had anything to do with her.

"Do you people have any idea what you're doing?" he finally demanded, tilting his head toward the pickup and Dillon.

"You want the rustlers caught?" she asked, resenting him trying to tell her how to do her job.

Waters smirked. "The rustler was *already* behind bars. That is, until you got him out. What the hell were you thinking?"

"Dillon Savage is my problem."

"You're right about that," the big man said angrily. "You going to try to tell me he doesn't know anything about what's been going on?"

She wasn't. Nor was she about to admit that she suspected the same thing he did when it came to Dillon Savage.

"It's his boys who are stealing all the cattle," Waters said with a curse. "That bunch he used to run around with. He's been orchestrating the whole thing from prison, and now you go and get him out so he can lead you in circles. You don't really think he's going to help you catch them, do you?"

"What bunch are we talking about?" she asked, ignoring the rest of what he'd said.

"Buford Cole, Pete Barclay, Arlen Dubois—that bunch," Waters snapped.

"What makes you think it's them? Or are you just making unfounded accusations? Because if you have some evidence—"

Waters let out another curse. "Hell, if I had evidence I'd take it to Sheriff McCray and the rustlers would be behind bars. Everyone in the county knows that Buford Cole and Arlen Dubois were riding with Savage before he went to prison."

"There was never any evidence—"

"Don't give me that evidence bull," Waters snapped. "Just because you couldn't prove it."

"I'm confused. Arlen Dubois just told me you offered him a job. If you really believe he's one of the rustlers…"

Waters's smile never reached his eyes. "Sometimes it's better to have the fox living in the henhouse so you can keep an eye on him. That's one reason I hired Pete Barclay. He also used to run with Savage."

That was also never proved, but she decided not to argue the point. "What about Buford Cole?"

"He's working at the stockyard," Waters stated, and raised a brow as if that said everything.

She looked at Nate. "Didn't you used to run with those same cowboys?"

Nate appeared surprised that she'd said anything to him. "What?"

"I heard you were all friends, including Dillon and your brother, Halsey."

The older Waters's face blanched and he looked as if he might suddenly grab his chest and keel over.

"Now just a minute," Nate said.

"What the hell are you trying to do?" Waters interrupted, taking a step toward her. "Don't you ever bring up Halsey's name in the same breath as those others!"

She noticed he was fine with Nate's name being mentioned with the others. Nate had noticed it, too, and was scowling in his father's direction.

"I'm just saying that because this group used to be friends, there is no evidence they are now involved in rustling cattle together." Her gaze went to Morgan Landers. She was smiling as if enjoying this.

"The damn rustlers are closing in on my ranch. Even you should be able to see that." Waters's face was now flushed, his voice breaking with emotion. "I can't protect my land or my livestock, not even if I hire a hundred men. Not when half of the range is badlands and only accessible by horseback."

She wanted to point out that the rustlers would have the same problem. But Waters was right. Huge sections of his land were inaccessible except by horseback, and given the size of the place, it would take several days to ride across the length of the W Bar. No amount of men could protect it completely.

"Your ranch hasn't been hit by the rustlers," she pointed out. "Do you have some reason to believe it will be?"

Waters looked flustered, something she didn't think happened often. "They must know I'll shoot to kill if they try to take my cattle."

"I wouldn't advise that," Jacklyn said.

"Then what are you going to do to stop them?" he demanded.

"I'm going to catch them, but I'll need your help. Tell me where your cattle are, what precautions you've taken and what men you have available to guard the key borders."

Waters looked at her, then glanced toward the pickup and laughed. "You don't really think I'm going to give you that information, do you? Why don't I just run it in the newspaper so the rustlers know exactly when and where to steal my cattle?"

"If this is about Mr. Savage—"

"You can try to explain until you're blue in the face why you got Dillon Savage out of prison, young woman, but I'm not giving you a damn thing. I'll take care of my stock as best I can. Just know I'll do whatever I have to, and that includes killing the sons of bitches." He was looking toward the truck again. "I have the right to protect my property."

"Mr. Waters—"

"I don't have time for this," he said, and thumped down the steps and past her, headed toward the barn.

"Like we're going to hold our breaths and wait for you to catch the rustlers," his son muttered.

"Shut up, Nate," Waters snapped over his shoulder.

"Mr. Waters," Jacklyn said, trailing after him. "I want your permission to put some video devices on your ranch. If you're right, the rustlers have probably been watching your operation already."

"No," he said, without stopping or looking back. "I told you I was going to take care of things my own way."

"If your own way is illegal—"

He swung around so fast she almost ran into him. "Listen, maybe you will catch the rustlers. But it won't be on my ranch. I won't be spied on."

"Spied on?"

"Videos and all that paraphernalia. No. Maybe that's the way it's done nowadays, but I don't want a bunch of your people on my land, and I know for a fact you can't force them on me."

Jacklyn glanced back at the truck. She couldn't see Dillon's face through the sunlight glinting off the windshield, but she knew he hadn't missed a thing.

Then she followed Shade Waters into the barn, determined to do her job despite him.

Dillon watched Morgan give him a backward glance before she followed Nate Waters into the house. She'd stared in his direction, as if she'd been expecting to see him.

Unlike him, who hadn't been prepared to see her again ever. As the front door closed, he sat without moving, bombarded by memories of the two of them.

Morgan. There'd been a time when she'd made him think about buying another ranch and settling down. But even Morgan couldn't still the quiet rage inside him. Not that Morgan had wanted him to be anything but a rustler. She liked the drama. She'd never wanted him to quit rustling.

She was hooked on the danger, never knowing when he would sneak into town and into her bed, never knowing if her house would be raided by the sheriff's men.

And since Morgan had no way of knowing about Dillon's inheritance, she'd just assumed he would never have enough money to keep her in the way she wanted to live, so she'd never even mentioned marriage. And he'd never told her different.

He wondered idly if she was serious about Nate Waters. Or if she was only serious about his money. Morgan would like the power that came with the Waters name, as well.

As Jacklyn disappeared into the barn with the rancher, Dillon fought the turmoil he felt inside. Seeing Morgan had brought back the past in a blinding flash. All his good intentions not to let what had happened drag him back into trouble again seemed to fly out the window. He felt the full power of the old bitterness, the resentment, the injustice that burned like hot oil inside him.

Worse, while he'd always suspected that he'd been set up four years ago, that someone close to him had betrayed him, he hadn't wanted to believe it.

In prison, he'd told himself it didn't matter. That all of that was behind him.

But as he thought about the look Morgan had given him before going back into the house, the image now branded on his mind, he knew it *did* matter—would always matter. He'd been kidding himself if he thought he could forgive and forget—at least not until he found out who had betrayed him.

And Morgan was as good as any place to start.

* * *

Jacklyn should have saved her breath. Shade Waters was impossible. She'd tried to talk to him, but he seemed distracted as he looked in on one of the horses. She saw him frown and touch the horse's side, apparently surprised to find that it was damp, as if recently ridden.

"Is something wrong?" she asked, noting that he seemed upset.

He shook his head irritably. "I told you. I don't have time for this. Shouldn't you be out looking for the rustlers instead of driving me crazy?" he snapped, then sighed, looking his age for a moment. "I just got a call a few minutes before you got here. Tom Robinson's condition is worse."

Her heart dropped, and instantly she felt guilty, because she'd been praying he would regain consciousness. She'd been counting on Tom being able to identify at least one of the rustlers.

"I'm sorry to hear that," she said, a little surprised how hard Waters was taking the news, given that he would now probably get the Robinson ranch, just as Dillon had said. Was Tom's worsened condition really what had Waters upset?

The rancher didn't seem to hear her as he began to wipe down the horse. Jacklyn wondered where Pete Barclay was.

She let herself out of the barn, knowing she wasn't going to get anywhere with him. But she couldn't shake the feeling that Dillon Savage might be right. Maybe there was more going on than she'd thought.

As she started toward her pickup, what she saw stopped her dead. The truck was empty. Dillon Savage was gone.

Chapter 8

Jacklyn couldn't believe her eyes. No. For just an instant there, she'd believed Dillon, believed she'd been wrong about him, believed he really was trying to help her catch the rustlers.

What a fool she was!

"Excuse me," she said as she spotted a man trimming a hedge that ran along one side of the ranch house. "Did you happen to notice the man who was waiting in the pickup?" She pointed to her truck.

He nodded, shoving back his hat to wipe the sweat from his forehead. "He said to tell you he'd meet you in town if he missed you."

She raised a brow. Town was twenty miles away. Trying not to show her panic or her fury, she asked, "And how, exactly, was he planning to get back to town? Did he say?"

The man shrugged. "He said he needed to take a walk."

Take a walk? Oh, he'd taken a walk all right. She

would kill him when she found him. And she *would* find him.

She thanked the gardener and, hoping Shade Waters wasn't watching, tried not to storm to the pickup. There were going to be enough people saying I told you so, starting with Waters.

As she climbed in and started the engine, she looked down the long dirt road. Empty. Just like the truck.

Still fighting panic and fury, she drove until she topped a hill and couldn't see the ranch house anymore. Pulling over, she opened the tracking receiver terminal and started to push the on button, afraid of what she would find.

She knew Dillon Savage. Better than she wanted to. He was too smart. Too charming. Too arrogant for words. But there was something about him, something wounded that had softened her heart to him four years ago, when she'd captured him.

How could he do this? Didn't he realize it was going to get him sent back to prison? Unless he thought he could evade her as he had for so long before.

But the only way he could do that was to disable the monitoring device or cut the thing out. If he had, she'd be lucky if she ever saw him again.

She wasn't even thinking about her career or her anger as she turned on the receiver terminal, her heart in her throat. In those few seconds, she felt such a sense of dread and disappointment that she only got more angry—angry at feeling anything at all for this man.

Until that moment, she hadn't realized how badly she wanted to believe in his innocence.

The steady beep from the terminal startled her. "I'll

be…" According to this, he was still on the ranch—and moving in her direction.

Or at least his monitoring device was.

If she drove on up the road, she should connect with him about a half mile from here.

Why would he head for the road, when he could have gotten lost in the mountains and led her on a wild-goose chase? One that she wouldn't have been able to hide from her boss?

As she topped the next rise, she spotted a figure walking nonchalantly across open pasture, headed for the road. He had to have heard the pickup approaching, and yet he didn't look up. Nor did he make any attempt to run away.

He vaulted over the barbed wire fence as she brought the truck to a dust-boiling stop next to him.

She was out of the vehicle, her hand on the butt of her pistol, before he reached the road.

"Don't you ever do that again," she shouted at him.

He held up both hands in surrender.

Had he grinned, she feared she would have pulled the pistol and shot him.

"I'm sorry. I couldn't very well tell you where I was going under the circumstances," he said contritely.

"Circumstances?"

"You were with Shade Waters, and I didn't want him to know I was following one of his stock trucks."

She stared at Dillon. "Why would you follow one of the Waters's stock trucks?" she demanded suspiciously.

"To see what was going on." He glanced up as if he heard someone coming. "Could we talk about this somewhere besides the middle of a county road?"

She sighed, torn between anger and overwhelming relief. She removed her hand from her gun butt and turned back toward the pickup. She'd left the driver's door open. As she slid behind the wheel, he climbed in the passenger side and saw the monitoring device on the seat between them.

"Thought I'd skipped out on you, did you?" He chuckled. "So much for trust. You want me to help you catch these guys? Then you have to give me a little leeway. Keep me on too short a leash and I'm useless to you."

She wasn't so sure he wasn't useless to her, anyway. "So why did you follow the stock truck?"

"I went for a little walk. Took your binoculars," he said, handing them back to her. "Hope you don't mind. I just happened to see a couple of ranch hands loading something into the back of a stock truck. They acted suspicious, you know? Looking around a lot. I made sure they didn't see me, and when the truck stopped so one could open the gate, I hopped in the back."

As she got the pickup moving, she looked over at Dillon, convinced he was either lying or crazy or both. Then she caught a whiff of his clothing and wrinkled her nose. "Let me guess what was in the back. Something dead."

"Half-a-dozen dead calves."

She shot him a look, the truck swerving on the gravel road. "They were probably just taking them to the dump."

He shook his head. "They were headed north. Waters's dump is to the south."

"He probably has a new dump since you've been here," she said irritably. "Why would you get in the truck with the dead calves?"

He lifted a brow. "*Six* dead calves. Doesn't that make even *you* suspicious?"

Everything made her suspicious. Especially him. "Every rancher loses a few calves—"

"Six all dead at the same time? Not unless they're sick with something."

She glanced over at him. "What do you think killed them?"

"Lead poisoning." He grinned at her obvious surprise. "That's right, Jack, they each had a bullet hole right between their eyes. But that's not the best part. They were missing a patch of hide—right where their brands should have been—and notches had been cut in their ears. You guessed it, no ear tags."

She slammed on the brakes, bringing the truck to another jarring stop. "What are you talking about?"

He nodded, still grinning. "I knew Shade Waters was still up to no good."

Jacklyn was shaking her head. "You went looking for trouble, didn't you? This walk you took, you just happened along on a stock truck with six possibly rustled dead calves? Where was this?"

"A mile or so from the ranch house."

Her brows shot up.

"I walk fast. I figured I'd be back before you finished with Waters. I told the gardener so you wouldn't worry. I'm telling you the truth, Jack. I swear."

She glared at him and turned back to her driving, not believing anything he said. "So who were these ranch hands?"

"I didn't get a good look at them. When the truck started moving, I took off running, so I could jump in the back."

"Right. But you're sure they work for Waters?" she asked, trying to rein in her temper.

"They were on his land, driving one of his stock trucks," Dillon said.

She could hear the steel in his voice. She shot him a suspicious look. He had to realize that all she had was his word for this, and right now her trust in him was more than a little shaky.

"And you have no idea where they were taking the calves," she said.

"No," he replied through gritted teeth. "North. I would assume to bury them. Look, under other circumstances, I would have stayed with that truck till the end. But I knew you'd flip if you came out and found me gone." His gaze narrowed. "And you did."

"I could have tracked you and the truck," she pointed out.

"I thought of that. But I also really didn't want every lawman in the county coming after me, ready to shoot to kill, before I got to explain that I hadn't just taken off. Even you believed that's what I'd done, didn't you?"

He was right. Even if she'd had faith that he wouldn't run off, Stratton would have had a warrant out on Dillon Savage before the ink dried.

"Plus I had no weapon and was a little concerned about when the truck got to its destination," Dillon said. "I didn't want to end up buried with those calves. For all I knew they might have been meeting more ranch hands up the road."

If he was telling the truth, he'd done the only thing he could do. And if so, he'd certainly made more progress than she had in the case.

"I'm sorry," she said. "You did the right thing." She could feel his gaze on her.

"You believe me then?"

She glanced back at him. "Let's say I'm considering the possibility that you're telling the truth."

To her surprise, he laughed. "Jack, you're killing me. But at least that's progress." He turned toward her. "Don't you see, this proves what I've been saying. Waters is your man. He's behind this rustling ring."

She met his gaze, knowing he was capable of making up this whole thing to even the score with his archenemy. "You can't be objective when it comes to Waters."

"There's a reason his ranch hasn't been hit by the rustlers and you know it," Dillon said.

She shook her head. All she knew was that if Dillon was behind the rustling, then by not stealing from Waters, he would make him look guilty. Just as coming up with a story about a stock truck filled with bullet-ridden calves missing their brands would do.

"You're trying to tell me that Waters is rustling cattle from his neighbors, then killing them, cutting off the brands and ear tags and burying them? Why? He's not even making any money, that I can see, on the deal."

Dillon rolled his eyes. "Waters doesn't need the money. I told you there was another motive. He's getting something out of this, trust me."

She shook her head. "I know you believe he was the cause of your father losing his ranch, but you have to realize there were other factors." She saw his jaw tighten.

"I do. Dad made some business mistakes after my mother died. But ultimately, Waters wanted our ranch and he got it."

"Exactly. He's bought up almost all of the ranches around him, so what—"

"There are still two he wants. And with Tom Robinson gone, he's got that one. That leaves the Harper place."

"Reda will never sell," Jacklyn said, remembering her visit to the Harper ranch when she was talking to local folks about the rustlers. "She hates Waters. Maybe worse than you do."

Dillon lifted a brow. "We'll see. Tom said he'd never sell, either. Jack, we have to get on Waters's ranch and find out where they're taking those calves. You want evidence? It's on the W Bar."

"And what do you suggest I do? Trespass? Waters has already said he won't have us on his ranch."

Dillon grinned. "We need to make Waters think we aren't anywhere near his ranch."

"If you're suggesting—"

"You have to make sure everyone believes you've gotten a new lead and will be to the south, nowhere near the W Bar."

She shook her head. "Stratton would never let me do that."

"That's why you have to tell him you got a tip that the Murray ranch is going to be hit."

"Lie?" Jacklyn fought the sick feeling in the pit of her stomach. "Are you trying to set me up?" she asked, her voice little more than a whisper.

Dillon didn't answer. She looked over at him and saw anger as hard as granite in his blue eyes. "Waters is your man. You want to catch the rustlers?"

She couldn't even acknowledge that with a response.

"When are you going to trust me? I'll tell you what. Let's put something on it. A small wager."

"I don't want your money."

"Don't worry, you won't get it. No, I was thinking of something more fun."

She shot him a warning look.

"A dance. If I'm right, you'll owe me a dance."

"And if you're wrong and it turns out you're involved with this rustling ring?" she asked, studying him as she headed for Lewistown.

He grinned. "Then I'll be back in prison. What do you have to lose? One dance. Deal?"

Was he that sure she'd never prove he was involved? Or was he really innocent—this time? "Deal," she said, ninety-nine percent certain she would never be dancing with Dillon Savage, and a little sad about it.

"So are you going to take my advice?" he said as they shook on their bet.

Not a chance. Waters didn't want her on his ranch. She'd have to get a warrant to go there and she had no evidence to get Stratton to go along with it, not to mention a judge.

"There's a meeting of the ranchers this evening in town," she said noncommittally. "Let's see how that goes."

Reda Harper checked the time on the dash of her pickup as she cut across her pasture, opened a gate posted with No Trespassing signs and, thumbing her nose at Waters and his W Bar Ranch, drove along what once had been a section road between his spread and the Savage Ranch.

The road had long since grown over with weeds, but Reda was in one of her moods, and when she got like this, she just flat-out refused to drive past the W Bar ranch house. She not only didn't want to see Shade Waters, she also didn't want him seeing her.

As she drove, darkness settled in, forcing her to turn on her headlights. The last thing she wanted was to be caught trespassing on Shade's land. Her own fault. As it would be if she was late for the meeting Shade Waters had called about the rustling problem.

"If you're late, it's your own blamed fault for being so stubborn," she told herself as her pickup jostled along. "You should have taken the main road. Shade is probably already in town, anyway. Damn foolish woman."

On the other hand, it aggravated her that she had to take the back roads to town to avoid seeing Shade Waters. Just the thought of him angered her. She would blame him if she got caught trespassing on his land. But then, she blamed him for most everything that had happened to her in the last forty years.

She blamed herself for being a fool in the first place. What had she ever seen in Shade? Sure, he'd been handsome back then. Hell, downright charming when he'd wanted to be.

She swore at even the thought of him. It still made her sick to think about it. She hated to admit she could have been so stupid. Shade Waters had played her. Tempting her with sweet words and deeds, then reeling her in. His professed love for her nothing more than an attempt to take her ranch.

But in the end, she'd outfoxed him, she reminded herself.

As she came over a rise in the road, she saw a light flicker ahead, off to her left. She frowned as the light flashed off, pitching the terrain back into darkness—but not before her headlights had caught a stock truck pulling behind a rock bluff a good twenty yards inside the fence line.

There was nothing on this road for miles. Nothing but sagebrush and rock. Shade didn't run cattle up here.

Never had. Too close to the badlands. Too hard to round 'em all up. Not to mention he had so much land he didn't need to pasture his cattle in the vicinity.

So what would a stock truck be doing up here? As far as she knew, no one used this road. Hadn't since Waters bought the Savage Ranch.

She slowed. In her headlights, she could see where the truck had trampled the grass as it drove back between the bluffs. How odd.

Reda powered down her window, pulling the pickup to a stop to stare out. The night was black. No moon. The stars muted by wisps of clouds. She couldn't see a damn thing. If she hadn't seen the light, she would never have known there was a truck out there among the rocks.

What had her curiosity going was the way the truck had disappeared, as if the driver didn't want to be seen.

The air that wafted in the window was warm and scented with dust and sage. She listened. Not a sound. And yet she'd seen the light. Knew there was a truck in there somewhere.

She felt a cold chill and shuddered as a thought struck her. Whoever was there hadn't expected anyone on this road tonight. The driver had turned out the lights when he'd seen her come flying over the rise. For some reason he hadn't heard her approaching.

Whatever he was doing, he didn't want a witness.

Reda knew, probably better than anyone in four counties, what Waters was capable of. But she had a feeling this wasn't his doing.

On a sudden impulse, she reached for the gearshift and the button to power up her window, telling herself she wanted no part of whatever was going on.

But as the window started to glide upward, she heard

a sound behind her pickup, like the scuff of a boot sole on a rock.

Her foot tromped down on the gas pedal. The tires spat dirt and chunks of grass as she took off, her blood pounding in her ears, her hands shaking.

When she glanced into her rearview mirror, she saw the black outline of a man standing in the middle of the road.

He'd been right behind her truck.

She was shaking so hard she had trouble digging her cell phone from her purse while keeping the pickup on the road between the fence posts.

Was it possible he was one of the rustlers?

Her cell phone display read No Service. She swore and tossed the phone back into her purse. Worthless thing. She only used the damn gadget to call from town to the ranch. Only place she could get any reception.

She glanced behind her again, afraid she'd see lights. Or worse, the dark silhouette of a stock truck chasing her without its headlights on.

But the road behind her was empty.

She drove as fast as she dared, telling herself she had to notify someone. Not Shade Waters, even though it was his property. It would be a cold day in hell if she ever spoke to him again.

No, she'd drive straight to the meeting. Sheriff McCray would be there. She'd tell him what she'd seen.

Her pulse began to slow as she checked her mirror again and saw no one following her. Even in the dark, she would have been able to see the huge shape of a stock truck on the road. She was pretty darn sure she could outrun a cattle truck.

As she swung into the packed lot at the community center, she felt a little calmer. More rational.

Maybe it had been rustlers. Maybe not. Shade Waters was the only rancher who hadn't lost cattle to that band of thieves she'd been hearing about. It made sense that the rustlers had finally gotten around to stealing some of his livestock.

Except that Waters wasn't running any cattle in that area.

Reda parked and headed for the meeting. As she pushed open the door to the community center, the first man she saw was Sheriff Claude McCray. She started to rush to him, her mouth already open as she prepared to tell him about what she'd seen on the road.

But then she saw the man he was deep in conversation with: Shade Waters. Their heads were together as if they were cooking up something.

Her mouth snapped shut, the words gone like dead leaves blowing away in the wind. She walked past both men, her head held high. The sheriff didn't seem to notice her, but Shade Waters did.

She could feel his gaze on her, as intense and burning as a laser beam. She waltzed right on past without even a twinge of guilt. She hoped the rustlers cleaned Shade Waters out. Hell, she wished she had stopped and helped them.

On the drive back to Lewistown, Jack had seemed lost in thought, which was just fine with Dillon. He tried not to think about Waters or the fact that Jack didn't believe him. Those problems aside, he couldn't get Morgan Landers off his mind—or the fact that she was apparently now with Nate Waters.

Jack stopped by the hospital to see how Tom Robinson was doing, and Dillon went in with her even though he hated to. The last time he'd been in a hospital was after his father's heart attack.

The moment he walked in, he was hit by the smell. It took him back instantly, filling him with grief and guilt. His father would have been only fifty-eight now, young by today's standards, if he had lived. If Shade Waters hadn't killed him as surely as if he'd held a gun to his head.

Tom was still unconscious. His recovery didn't look good, which meant that the chances of him identifying the rustlers wasn't good, either.

Dillon could see the effect that had on Jack. She'd been counting on a break in the rustling case. As they left the hospital, he could feel her anger and frustration.

"Would you please stop looking at me as if I was the one who put Tom in that hospital bed?" Dillon said as she drove back toward the motel.

"Aren't you?"

He groaned. "Jack, I'm telling you I have nothing to do with this bunch of rustlers. You've got to believe that." But of course, she didn't have to.

She shot him a quizzical look. Clearly, she didn't believe anything he said.

"How can I convince you?" he asked. "We already know who the rustler is, but you don't believe that, either. I told you what we have to do to catch him, except you aren't willing to do that. So what else can I say?" He shook his head.

"Don't you find it interesting that some of your old friends are working ranches around here?" she asked.

So she'd been thinking about some of the cowboys

he'd run around with: Pete Barclay, Buford Cole, Arlen Dubois.

"*Former* friends," he said. "We haven't been close for years. A lifetime ago."

"I know for a fact that Buford Cole came to visit you in prison."

It shouldn't have taken him by surprise, but it did. Of course she would have checked to see who his visitors had been during his four years at Montana State Prison.

"Buford and I used to be close," he admitted. "He only came that one time. I haven't heard from him since."

"What about Pete Barclay?"

Dillon chuckled. "Yeah, he came to visit me in prison several times."

"He works for Waters."

"I'm aware of that. You want to know why he came to see me?" Dillon asked. "To deliver threats from his boss about when I got out."

She swung her gaze to him. "Is that true?"

"I told you I don't lie."

"Right. How could I forget?" She pulled into the motel parking lot and glanced at her watch. "We have to get to the ranchers' meeting. I just need to change." She settled her gaze on him. "Maybe you shouldn't go. You could stay in the motel room. You'd be monitored the whole time, of course."

"Of course," he said disagreeably. He hated to be reminded of how little freedom he had. Or how little trust she had in him. Not that he could blame her. He hated being constantly watched. But that was the deal, wasn't it?

"I'm going with you," he said, meeting her gaze head-on.

"I'm not sure that's a good idea."

"I'm not afraid of any of them, and I have nothing to hide."

She gave him one of her rock-hard looks, as if nothing could move her.

"Jack, come on. You think I have that much control over everything that is happening now?" He couldn't help but smile and shake his head. "You give me too much credit."

"On the contrary. I think you are capable of just about anything you set your mind to."

He made a face, recognizing his own words to her earlier. "That almost sounded like a compliment," he joked. "So you got me out of prison thinking you'd give me enough rope that I'd hang myself? That's it, isn't it?" He saw that he'd hit too close to home, and chuckled at her expression.

"If not you, then who?" she demanded. "And don't tell me Shade Waters." She cocked an eyebrow at him, her eyes the color of gunmetal. There was a pleading in her expression. "Whoever is leading this band of rustlers is too good at this. Is it possible there is someone who's even better than the great Dillon Savage?"

He shrugged, but admitted to himself that she had a point. Waters was a lot of things, but what did he know about rustling? Whoever was leading the ring knew what he was doing. But if it wasn't Shade Waters, was it someone who worked for him?

Chapter 9

The lot was full of pickups as Jacklyn tried to find a place to park at the community center. Clearly, many ranchers had arrived early, not about to miss this.

She couldn't help but think it was the last place Dillon wanted to be. She looked around for a large tree, figuring one of the ranchers might have a rope and this could end in a hangin' before the night was over. And it would be Dillon Savage's neck in the noose.

"I'd prefer if you don't say anything during the meeting," she said as she cut the engine and looked over at him.

"No problem." He glanced toward the building. All the lights were on and a muted roar came from inside. A few ranchers were out on the steps, smoking and talking in the darkness. They'd all glanced toward the state pickup as she'd parked.

"You sure about this?" she asked.

"If I don't go in," Dillon said, "they'll assume you're trying to protect me."

That was exactly what she hoped to do. "Maybe I'm trying to protect us both."

He smiled at that. "We're both more than capable of taking care of ourselves."

She wasn't so sure. The ranchers were furious. Shade Waters had them all stirred up about Dillon being out of prison. And unfortunately, Dillon had enemies in there waiting for him—and so did she.

Jacklyn stepped from the pickup, her hand going to the gun at her hip as she started toward the community center and the angry-looking men now blocking the doorway. Dillon walked next to her. She dreaded the moment he would come face-to-face with Shade Waters, not sure what either of them would do.

The men on the steps finally parted so she and Dillon could enter. The room was already buzzing as she pushed open the door. She wasn't surprised to find the center packed, a sea of Stetsons.

As she started down the aisle between the chairs, she could feel Dillon right behind her. A wave of stunned silence seemed to fill the place, followed at once by a louder buzzing of voices as heads turned. They hadn't expected her to bring Dillon. He'd been right about coming.

She didn't look at any of them as she made her way toward the front of the room. But Shade Waters stopped her before she could reach it. "No one invited you. Or your *friend*."

Dillon Savage was far from her friend, but she wasn't here to debate that with Waters.

"I'm here to clear up a few things," she said over the drone of voices.

"Things are damn clear," Waters said angrily. "The state isn't doing a thing to protect us ranchers."

"What's this *us?*" called a female voice from near the front. "Your cattle haven't been stolen. So what are you all worked up about?"

Jacklyn recognized the strident voice as Reda Harper's.

"You think my ranch isn't next?" Waters demanded to the crowd, apparently ignoring Reda. "Only it won't be fifty head of cattle. The bastards will hit me harder than any of you, and we all know it."

"That's why I'm here," Jacklyn said. "So that doesn't happen. But just this afternoon you denied me access to your land."

There were murmurs from the crowd.

"And you know damn well why," Waters snapped, glaring at Dillon.

Was Dillon the reason? Or was he telling the truth and there was a lot more going on here than missing cattle.

"You didn't protect *my* ranch," said an angry male voice.

"You're finally going to do something because it's the W Bar?" called another. "What about the rest of us?"

"Let her talk," cried one of the ranchers.

"Yeah, I'd like to hear what she has to say," Reda declared.

Waters scowled at Jacklyn, visibly upset that she'd come, and maybe even more upset that Reda Harper had been heckling him. He turned his scowl on Dillon and cursed. "I'd like to hear what Dillon Savage has to say for himself," Waters bellowed.

A few in the crowd were agreeing with him as Jacklyn stepped up on the stage. She glanced around the room, recognizing most of the faces. Waters's son, Nate, was slumped in the first row, looking bored.

As she stepped behind the podium, Dillon joined her, standing back but facing the angry crowd.

"Yeah, what the hell is the story?" called out one of the ranchers. "You get a rustler out to catch rustlers? What kind of sense is that?"

She raised a hand. When the room finally quieted, she waited for Shade Waters to sit down, glancing at him pointedly until he took his seat.

"Most of you know me. I'm Stock Detective Jacklyn Wilde," she began. "And I know most of you. Because of that you know I'm doing everything I can to catch the rustlers." She hurried on as the room threatened to erupt again.

"Dillon Savage is helping with the investigation of the rustling ring operating in this area." As expected, a wave of protests rang out. Again she raised a hand and waited patiently for the room to go quiet.

"I will not debate my decision to have Mr. Savage released early to help in that investigation. You want the rustlers caught?" she demanded, above the shouts and angry accusations. "Then listen to me."

"We've listened to you long enough," Shade Waters said, getting to his feet again. "It's time we took matters into our own hands."

"That's right!" A dozen ranchers were on their feet.

She saw her boss and several others come in through the back door. Chief Brand Inspector Allan Stratton walked up the aisle to the stage and stepped to the podium, practically shoving her aside.

Jacklyn edged back, hating the son of a bitch for upstaging her in front of the ranchers.

"Finally we're going to get some answers," Waters

called. "You sent us a damn woman, when we need a man for *this* job."

Others began to applaud Stratton, echoing Waters's sentiments.

Jacklyn felt her face flame. It was all she could do not to walk off the stage. She felt Dillon move to her side, as if in a show of support for her. The move would only antagonize the ranchers, and worse, Sheriff McCray, whom she spotted standing on the sidelines, glaring at her.

Stratton raised his arms and waited for the room to quiet down before he spoke. "I don't have to tell any of you how hard it is to stop rustlers. Livestock are a very lucrative source of income."

There were nods across the room, some murmurs.

"A thief who breaks into a house and steals a television or CD player can try to sell the equipment either at a pawnshop or on the black market, but will likely only get about ten percent of the actual value of the property," Stratton continued. "Someone who steals a cow, on the other hand, can sell the animal at a packing plant or an auction market and receive one hundred percent of the value."

There were more murmurs of agreement, but some restless movement as the smarter ranchers began to realize Stratton wasn't telling them anything they didn't already know.

"Improvements in transportation, the interstate, bigger cattle trailers, all make it easier for criminals to load up cattle and haul them across state lines before you even realize the animals are missing," he continued. "I don't have to tell you that thieves can steal more and move farther and faster than in the old days. A rustler can steal cattle here today, and this afternoon or early tomorrow morning be in Tennessee or California."

"Don't you think we know all that?" one of the ranchers demanded.

"What I can tell you is that we need to work together to stop these rustlers," Stratton said.

"You know a lot of us can't afford to hire more hands or buy special equipment," a man said from the front row.

"The state can't afford to hire staff to watch your cattle, either," Stratton said, as if it hurt him personally to say that. "That's why we need each of you to help us. Experienced cattle thieves will watch a ranch for a while, get to know the schedule of the owner and hired hands, and the times of day when no one will be around. You can keep an eye out for strangers hanging around or hired help that's too curious."

Jacklyn couldn't believe Stratton thought the rustling gang was that stupid. They weren't like some bumbling amateurs who left a gas receipt or wallet at the scene of the crime. These guys always got away clean. Except possibly for a good-luck coin. And even that could have been dropped by anyone at any time.

But for sure, the rustlers wouldn't be asking stupid questions of ranchers.

"You can also run checks on the men you hire," Stratton was saying, over an uproar from the floor. "I know society is so mobile that you're lucky to get a ranch hand to stay a season, let alone longer, and most ranches don't keep good records when it comes to seasonal help."

The crowd was getting restless.

Stratton had to raise his voice as he explained how every rancher should brand even dairy cows. "One white or black cow looks exactly like another. We have no way of telling them apart."

"I thought some states were using DNA?" a rancher asked over the growing murmuring.

"It's expensive, and we have to have some idea where the cow was stolen so we can try to match the DNA," he replied. "The best place to stop rustlers is at livestock sales. We need those people to be attentive. There are also radio-frequency chips that we're looking into. It's an expense for all of you, I know, but—"

"It sounds like you're expecting everyone else to do your job," a rancher called.

"Yeah," Waters agreed. "What's the bottom line here? You're telling us you aren't going to do a damn thing?"

"The only way we can beat the rustlers is to work together." Stratton was forced to yell to be heard over the uproar. "You have to trust—"

Jacklyn walked over to the podium and kicked it over. Stratton jumped back as if he'd been shot. The boom as the podium hit the floor sent a shock wave through the room, instantly quieting everyone. All attention was fixed on her.

She barely had to raise her voice. "You want to know how easy is it to steal your cattle? Simple as hell. If there is nobody watching them tonight, the rustlers are out there taking a dozen, two dozen, three dozen right now. You probably won't even know for weeks, maybe months, that they're gone. As for the rustlers, they made a quick getaway. Your cattle *could* be in another state. Or already butchered. Doesn't matter, because they aren't going to turn up. You just lost ten, twenty thousand dollars."

She looked out at the stunned audience of ranchers. "*That's* the reality. I plan to catch these rustlers. But even if I do, there will be others. Unless you help, we'll never be able to protect your property. That, Mr. Waters, is the bottom line."

With that she turned and walked off the stage as the room went from stunned silence to a clamor of voices. She saw a group of ranchers corner Stratton, blocking his exit, as she and Dillon slipped out the side into the cool darkness.

Dillon let out a low whistle as he joined her outside. "You all right?"

She'd stopped at the street, as if she'd forgotten where she'd parked the truck. When he touched her shoulder, he could feel her shaking.

"I'm fine." She took a step forward to break the contact, but made no move toward the pickup.

"That was great back there. You got the respect of every man in that room."

A small sound like a chuckle came out of her. "*That* just cost me my job."

"No way. The bastard tried to make you look bad, and only succeeded in ticking off everyone in the center. He won't come at you like that again. And once you catch the rustlers…"

She spun on him, her face contorting in anger. "You know damn well I'm not going to catch the rustlers. It's the only reason you agreed to pretend to help me."

"You're wrong."

"Damn it, Dillon, I know you're the one who's leading them. It's how they keep one step ahead of me. Just like you used to."

He shook his head. "You're wrong about that, too."

The anger was gone as quickly as it had appeared. "It doesn't matter now, anyway."

"The hell you say. Come on, Jack. We can do this. I'll help you. Really help you. After all, it's the only way I can prove to you how wrong you are about me."

She seemed to study him in the lamplight. Behind him, the community center was in an uproar. "How can I trust you?"

He smiled. "You can buy me a steak. Come on," he said again, as some of the ranchers began to leave the meeting. "There's a steak house just a short walk from here. I don't know about you, but I could use some fresh air." He took her arm before she could object, and they started down the street. It was a good walk, but he figured they both could use it.

Also, he didn't want a run-in with the ranchers. Not for himself, but for Jacklyn. She'd been through enough tonight. He saw her look over at him as if trying to make up her mind about him.

Funny, but at that moment he wanted to be the man his father always told him he could be. The last thing Dillon wanted to do was disappoint Jacklyn Wilde.

Unfortunately, there was little chance of him doing anything *but* disappointing her.

Jacklyn couldn't believe she'd let Dillon talk her into this.

"After everything you've been through tonight, I say we celebrate," he'd said as they walked into the steak house.

"Celebrate?" Had he lost his mind?

"You still have a job. I'm not on my way to prison.

Yet," he added with a grin. "Tell me that isn't cause for celebration."

She might have argued that keeping her job was nothing to celebrate. Maybe Dillon was right. Maybe she was a fool for thinking that her job mattered. Right now not even the ranchers thought so.

The steak house was crowded, especially at the bar. They were shown to a booth in the rear. She noticed that Dillon made a point of sitting with his back to the wall rather than the room. Something he'd picked up in prison?

To her surprise, the waitress put a bottle of her favorite wine on the table and a cold beer in front of Dillon, no glass.

She looked up at him in surprise.

He grinned. "I grabbed a waitress on the way in and told her it was urgent."

"How did you—"

"Know your favorite wine?" His grin broadened. "It's not my psychic ability. I asked. It's what you ordered the last time you were in here. Apparently, you made an impression."

She groaned inwardly. The last time was right before she'd gotten Dillon out of prison. She'd been feeling anything but confident about her decision, and had definitely imbibed more than she should have. No wonder the waitress remembered what wine she'd ordered.

Dillon poured her a glass of wine, then lifted his bottle of beer in a toast, his gaze locked with hers. "To a successful collaboration."

She slowly picked up the glass, clinked it softly against his beer bottle and took a sip, not any more sure of the appropriateness of the toast than she was about drinking even one glass of wine with Dillon Savage.

He took a long swallow of his beer, then stared at the bottle, his thumb making patterns on the sweating glass. "I can't remember the last beer I had." He looked up, scanning the noisy steak house and bar. "It still all feels surreal."

Just then a man who'd had too much to drink stumbled into their table, startling them both and jostling her glass and spilling some of the wine. But it was Dillon's instant reaction that startled her the most.

In a flash, he'd grabbed the beer bottle by its neck, brandishing it like a weapon as he shot to his feet, ready to defend himself and her.

The drunken man raised both hands. "Sorry. My apologies," he said, backing away. "Just clumsy. No harm done, right?"

Dillon sat back down, turning the bottle as he did and gently setting it on the table as beer spilled down the sides. He'd gone pale, his eyes wide. She thought she saw his hand shaking as he rubbed it over his face. "Old habits die hard," he said quietly. "Sorry."

She stared at him, shocked by how quickly he'd changed when he'd felt threatened. "Was it that dangerous in there?" she asked, before she could stop herself.

He looked up at her, his grimace slow and almost painful. "Prison? Dangerous? With people who are crazy, mean, strung out?" He shook his head. "What makes it dangerous is a lack of hope. A lot of those people will never see the outside again and they know it. Because of that, they have nothing to lose."

He smiled as if to lighten his words. "If you're smart, you do your time, stay out of trouble, make the right friends." He grinned. "Like I said, I make friends easily, and you know what they say. What doesn't kill you makes you stronger."

She heard something in his tone that tore at her heart.

The waitress hurried over to mop up the mess, then returned with another beer for Dillon. "That gentleman over there sends his apologies," she said.

Dillon looked in the drunken man's direction and gave a nod.

Jacklyn took a drink of her wine to try to wash down the lump in her throat, and busied herself with her menu. What was wrong with her, having sympathy for a criminal? A criminal *she'd* put behind bars? Dillon had the same options as everyone else. He didn't have to rustle cattle. He'd chosen the route that had led him straight to prison. He had only himself to blame.

So how could she feel sorry for him?

Because, she thought, lowering her menu to peer across the table at him, Dillon Savage wasn't the criminal stereotype. Instead he was educated, smart, from a good family. And, she suspected, a man with his own code of ethics. So what had made him turn to crime?

She tried to concentrate on her menu, but when she looked up again, she saw that Dillon was no longer gazing at his. Instead, he was staring toward the bar, a strange expression on his face.

She turned to follow his gaze. A few cowboys were standing together, the back door closing as someone left. All she caught sight of was one denim-clad shoulder and a glimpse of a western hat.

She searched the group at the bar and recognized only Arlen Dubois, from earlier today on Tom Robinson's ranch.

Was that who Dillon had noticed? Or had it been whoever had just left? In any case, Dillon looked upset.

"Who was that?" she asked, turning back to him.

His expression instantly changed, to an innocent look.
"I beg your pardon?"

"You saw someone, someone you recognized?" He'd
spotted someone he hadn't wanted to see. She was sure
of it. She tried to read his expression, but his eyes showed
only the vast blue of an endless sky. She would have
thought she was wrong about him seeing someone he
knew if it hadn't been for the twitch of a muscle along
his jaw.

He was looking at her now, studying her the way she'd
been studying him. He always seemed slightly amused—
and wary.

The woman was perceptive. Much more than Dillon had realized. He smiled at her, meeting her gaze,
cranking up the charm as he tried to mask whatever had
alerted her.

"What makes you think I wasn't just staring off into
space, thinking about the meeting tonight and Shade Waters?"

She cocked her head, her look one of disappointment.
"How about the truth? Try it, you might like it."

He rubbed the back of his neck and smiled faintly at
her.

"The person who just left. You knew him."

He frowned. "What would make you think that?"

"Don't play games with me," she snapped. "And stop
answering my questions with one of your own."

"Okay," he said. "What say we flip for it?" He pulled

a quarter from his pocket and spun it between his fingers. "A little wager of sorts. Truth for truth."

"You like to gamble, don't you?"

He grinned. "I like to take my chances sometimes, yes. And I never lie, remember?"

She drew a breath, her gaze on the silver flicker of the quarter in the dim light of the restaurant. "Is it that hard for you to tell the truth that you have to flip for it?"

He did his best to look offended. "Don't assume just because I have a proclivity for cattle rustling that I'm a liar—and a gambler."

"Of course not."

He turned serious for a moment. "Have I ever lied to you?"

She met his gaze. "How would I know?"

"You could look into my eyes." His gaze locked with hers. "So what do you say? A flip of the coin. Heads, I tell you whatever you want to know. Tails, you tell me something I'd like to know."

She watched the quarter for a moment, then held out her hand. "I'll flip the coin if you don't mind."

He pretended to be hurt by her lack of trust.

"You'll answer truthfully?"

He nodded. "And you?"

"I'm always honest."

He smiled at that. "I guess we'll see about that."

Jacklyn didn't like the gleam in his eyes, but anything was better than talking about his prison stay. She'd seen a side of him with the drunken man that had scared her, and at the same time made her want to comfort him.

Fear of Dillon Savage was good—and appropriate. Sympathy on any level was dangerous.

Probably as dangerous as this game he had her play-

ing. But against her better judgment, she believed him
when he said he'd tell her the truth if she won the coin
toss. And since she was no doubt going to get fired before the night was over, and Dillon would be going back
to prison, what did it hurt?

He was watching her, humor dancing in his eyes, as
she inspected the coin. "You're the least trusting woman
I've ever known."

"Then the women you've known didn't know you very
well."

He laughed. It was a nice sound. He took a long drink
of his beer and seemed to relax. She hadn't noticed, but
apparently he'd refilled her wineglass.

It crossed her mind that he might be trying to get her
drunk. She met his gaze, then tossed the coin up, catching it and bringing it down flat on the tabletop.

He took on an excited, eager look as he stared down
at her hand and waited for her to lift it from the coin.

Drawing a breath, she did so, instantly relieved to see
it was heads.

She smiled at him and took a drink of her wine.

He leaned back, raising his hands in defeat and grinning. "You win, and I'm a man of honor whether you
believe it or not. So what do you want to know? The
truth, I swear."

"Who did you see earlier going out the back door?"

He glanced toward the bar, clearly hesitating, then
slowly said, "Truthfully? I'm not even sure. I just caught
a glimpse of the man. Actually, it was the way he moved.
It reminded me of someone I used to know. But it couldn't
have been him, because he's dead."

She eyed Dillon suspiciously. "What was his name?"

"Halsey Waters." Dillon met her gaze, and she saw

pain and anger. "I guess it's because I've been thinking about him."

"He was a good friend?"

Dillon nodded. "We were best friends. He was like a brother to me. I've never been that close to anyone since." He smiled ruefully. "Just one of those regrets in life, you know what I mean?"

"Yes," she said, and looked toward the bar, wondering who Dillon had seen that might remind him of Halsey Waters. Or if he'd made up the whole thing.

"Trust," he said, with his usual amusement.

Then Morgan Landers walked in the door with Nate Waters.

Chapter 10

Jacklyn couldn't very well miss the instant that Dillon saw Morgan. His entire demeanor changed. Like him, she watched the two come in on a cool gust of night air, Morgan laughing, Nate totally absorbed in her.

When Jacklyn turned back to Dillon, he was on his feet, excusing himself to go to the restroom. He walked away, not looking back. Jacklyn turned, pretty sure she'd find Morgan watching Dillon go, but her view was blocked by a man standing next to her table.

"Jacklyn Wilde?" he asked, but before she could answer he slid into the seat Dillon had just vacated. "I'm Buford Cole. A friend of Dillon's."

She studied the man across from her. He looked like most of the other cowboys, wearing jeans, boots, a western shirt and hat. His face was weathered from a life outdoors, and crow's-feet bracketed his brown eyes.

"How much do you know about Dillon Savage?" Buford asked before she could comment.

His question took her by surprise. "Not much," she said, telling herself how true that was.

"He ever tell you how he got into rustling cattle?" Buford didn't wait for an answer. "Dillon believes that his family's ranch was stolen."

"Stolen?" she asked, even though she knew that's how Dillon felt.

Buford nodded. "Cattle disappeared, others got accidentally closed off from water and died. There were a lot of strange accidents around the ranch, including his father's near-death accident that left him dependent on a cane. After that his dad just gave up. His spread was bought by Shade Waters. Dillon's always believed his father died of a broken heart. That ranch was his life."

She'd suspected as much.

"But even if Dillon believed that Shade Waters stole his family ranch, why not alert the authorities or just steal cattle from the W Bar if he wanted revenge?" she asked. "Why steal from all his neighbors?"

"Dillon's father tried to get the neighboring ranchers to join forces and fight Waters. They all turned a blind eye to what was happening on the Savage Ranch. By the time it started happening to them, Dillon's old man was dead, the ranch lost. Then Waters bought up one ranch after another, usually after each had had its share of bad luck."

"Are you trying to tell me that Waters—"

"I'm trying to tell you what Dillon believes," Buford interrupted, glancing toward the hallway to the restrooms where Dillon had disappeared. "In the end, all but two of the ranchers sold out to Waters."

"Why, if what Dillon believes is true, weren't those two forced to sell as well then?"

"You ever meet Reda Harper? As for Tom Robinson,

he was barely hanging on by a thread. Now after what happened…" The cowboy shook his head. "Word is that Waters has already bought it from Tom Robinson's niece. As for Reda… She's old. Waters can wait her out."

"You sound as if you don't like Shade Waters any more than Dillon does."

"I don't like fighting battles I know I can't win. Dillon's an idealist. He still believes in justice. And vengeance."

"You think Dillon is out for revenge?" she asked, thinking about the ranchers that Dillon had rustled cattle from. They'd all later sold out to Waters. When she'd finally caught him, he'd been on the W Bar, Shade's own ranch. She'd thought Dillon had gotten greedy and that had been his downfall. Now she wondered.

She'd seen how much Waters and Dillon hated each other, but the big rancher's hatred of Dillon seemed out of proportion to the amount of cattle he'd lost over the years.

"Why does Shade hate Dillon so much?" she asked, feeling the effects of the wine.

"Did you ask Dillon?"

She shook her head.

"Shade Waters blames him for his son's death."

"Halsey," she murmured, frowning to herself. "But he was Dillon's best friend."

Buford smiled at that. "We were all friends. Did you ever wonder what happened to the cattle Dillon rustled?" he asked. "Dillon put them in with Waters's herd."

She stared at him. Wouldn't she have heard this from Waters if that were true?

The cowboy chuckled. "The cattle just seemed to disappear. Who knows what Waters did with them."

Jacklyn thought about the dead calves in the stock

truck that Dillon swore had been shot. Is that what Shade Waters had done with the rustled cattle he'd found among his herd?

And then what? Just taken them out and buried them? What a waste. And for what?

She couldn't believe the lengths Dillon had gone to. But was any of this true? Or was it just the way he rationalized his thieving ways to his friends?

"You seem to know a lot about Dillon's rustling activities," she said.

Buford smiled. "You aren't going to ask me if I was in on it with him, are you?"

"You were one of his closest friends, right? This gang of rustlers—you think he has anything to do with them?"

Buford looked wary. "I wouldn't know."

"But you think it's possible."

He sighed, still not looking at her. "I just know Dillon isn't finished with Waters." He shook his head as he rose from the booth. "He won't be, either, until Waters is either behind bars or dead. Unfortunately, Dillon Savage is the kind of man who takes a grudge to the grave. I would just hate to see him in an early grave."

Why was Buford telling her all this? Buford appeared to be genuinely worried about his old friend. But didn't he realize this only made Dillon look guilty of being the leader of this latest band of cattle rustlers?

As Buford walked away, Jacklyn saw that Nate Waters was sitting alone. Where was Morgan? And why hadn't Dillon returned?

Morgan gasped as Dillon stepped directly into her path. Her hand went to her throat, her eyes looking around wildly as if searching for a way to escape the dim restaurant hallway.

"Dillon."

He smiled as he moved so close he could see the fear in her eyes. "Morgan."

She licked her lips and smiled back nervously. "What are you doing here?" Without Nate Waters beside her, she'd lost a lot of her haughtiness.

"I wanted to see you, Morgan. Don't tell me you didn't expect to meet up with me again."

"I didn't think you could...that is, I thought you weren't allowed to go anywhere alone."

He smiled at that. "Is that what you thought?"

She swallowed, looking again for a way to escape, but he was blocking the hallway. She'd have to go over him to get back to Nate.

"We should get together sometime," she said, shifting nervously. "To talk. A lot has happened since you've been gone."

"So I gather. You and Waters." Dillon shook his head. She would turn Nate any way but loose before she was through.

"Nate and I are getting married."

"You're perfect for each other."

She frowned, thinking he was being facetious.

"Seriously, I wish you all the best."

"You're not upset?" She was eyeing him now, obviously not wanting to believe that he'd gotten over her.

"I had a lot of time to think in prison," he said, his gaze locking with hers. "It cleared up a lot for me. Like, for instance, how I just happened to get caught."

She shifted again, pulling her shoulder bag around to the front, her hand going to it.

He put his hand over hers and smiled. "Carrying a gun now? You have something to fear, Morgan?"

Her gaze hardened as she jerked her hand away from his.

"You set me up that day, didn't you?"

She was shaking her head. "You're wrong. I swear to you."

"Come on, Morgan, you were the only person who knew where I would be."

"No, the others knew. It had to be one of them. Or maybe your luck just ran out."

"Yeah, maybe that was it." He reached into her purse and pulled out the gun, swinging the barrel around until the end was pointed at her forehead. Her eyes widened as she heard him snap off the safety.

"Here's the one-time deal," he told her. "The truth for your life. Because, Morgan, I'm going to find out who set me up. Tell me the truth now and I walk away. No foul, no harm. For old time's sake, I'll give you this chance. But," he added quickly, "if I find out you lied, I'll come back and all bets are off. So what's it going to be?"

"I'm telling you the truth. I didn't say a word to anyone. I swear. It wasn't me, Dillon. I couldn't do that to you."

He would have argued the latter, but his time was up. Jacklyn would have realized by now that he was missing. He couldn't chance her finding him holding a gun on Morgan.

He emptied the gun, snapped the safety back on and dropped the weapon into her purse, pocketing the bullets. "Wouldn't want you to accidentally shoot anyone," he said with a grin.

It would have been like Morgan to shoot him in the

back and say it was self-defense. And with the Waters family behind her, she would have probably gotten away with it.

"I'm sure we'll be seeing each other again," he said.

"Not if I see you first," Morgan snapped back.

He chuckled to himself as he turned and walked away. Behind him, Morgan let out a string of curse words. That's what he'd loved about her: she was no lady.

Back at the table, Jack seemed relieved to see him. As Morgan returned to her own table, Jack shot Dillon a suspicious look.

He picked up his menu and studied it. But he could feel both Jack and Morgan looking in his direction. He'd known what kind of woman Morgan was. The kind who would lie through her teeth. The fact that she was carrying a gun didn't bode well in the truth department. She was afraid of someone. Him, no doubt. Which led him to believe she had something to hide.

She'd said the others knew where he'd be that day.

Yes, the others. His friends, his partners, the men he'd trusted with his life. He'd have to have a little talk with each of them. If he helped Jack bust up this rustling ring, he'd get the opportunity, he was sure.

"Have you made up your mind?" Jack asked.

He couldn't help but wonder if Morgan might not be involved. She was carrying a gun and had hooked up with the son of one of the richest and most influential ranchers in the state of Montana.

He looked up from his menu. "Definitely," he said, smiling at her.

"About what you're going to order," she said, but not with her usual irritation at his foolishness.

The wine had mellowed her some. Her cheeks were

a little flushed. She looked damn good in candlelight. Dillon had the wildest urge to reach across the table and free her hair from that braid.

The waitress appeared at that moment, saving him. After they'd ordered, he stole a glance in the direction of Morgan's table.

Morgan and Nate were gone.

Jacklyn couldn't help thinking about everything Buford Cole had told her as she ate her dinner. The wine had left her feeling too warm, too relaxed, too intent on the man across the table from her.

Dillon was his usual charming self. And she found herself enjoying not only the meal, but also the company.

But what difference did it make? She was sure she'd lost her job tonight. In fact, she was surprised that Stratton hadn't already called to fire her.

After dinner they walked back toward the community center, both falling into silence as if a spell had been broken. The night was dark and cold. Lewistown was close to the mountains, so that often made nights here chilly, especially in spring.

Without a word, Dillon took off his jacket and put it around her shoulders. She thought about protesting, but was still in that what-the-heck mood.

Tonight he'd sweet-talked her, stood up for her, wined and dined her, and she'd liked it. In the morning, she'd be her old self again. Not that it mattered. She was sure Stratton would be picking up Dillon to take him back to prison, and would fire her.

What would *she* do? She didn't have a clue. But for some reason not even that bothered her right now.

"Pretty night," Dillon said, as he stopped to look up at the stars.

She stopped, too, taking a deep breath of the clean air, feeling strangely happy and content. A dangerous way to be feeling this close to Dillon Savage.

His hand brushed her sleeve, and she turned toward him like a flower to the sun. They were so close she couldn't be sure who made the first move. All she knew was that when his lips brushed hers, she felt sparks.

She leaned into him, wanting more even as the sensible Jacklyn Wilde tried to warn her that she'd regret it in the morning. Heck, she'd probably regret it before the night was over.

Dillon pulled back. "Jack, you sure you know what you're doing?"

"This isn't the first time I've kissed someone," she said.

He laughed. "No, I didn't think it was. It's just that—" He looked past her and let out a curse.

She turned and saw her pickup sitting alone in the community center parking lot. Sitting at an odd angle.

"Someone slashed your tires," Dillon said, sounding miserable.

To her surprise, she found she was fighting tears. The slashed tires were the last straw. She marched toward her pickup, angry at the world.

"I'm sure you had nothing to do with this, either," she snapped over her shoulder.

He caught up to her as she reached the truck. She started to open the driver's door to get out her insurance card and call for towing, but he slammed it shut, flattening her back to the side of the vehicle.

"How can you say that?" he demanded, his voice hoarse with emotion. "I was with you all night."

"Right, you have the perfect alibi. You were getting me drunk."

He raised a brow. "Is that what that kiss was about? You just had too much to drink?"

She didn't answer, couldn't. She wanted to push him away, to distance herself from him. Every instinct told her that Dillon Savage was nothing but trouble. And these feelings she had for him, had had for him years ago when she'd spent days learning everything she could about him, chasing him across Montana and finally coming face-to-face with him, well, they were feelings she was damn determined not to have. Especially now.

"Jack?"

She pushed on his chest with both hands, but he was bigger and stronger than she was, and he had her pinned against the truck with his body.

"Trust me, Jack," he said, his eyes dark with emotion. "I know you want to. Let me prove to you that I'm through with that life."

Her eyes filled with tears. She wanted to believe him. But she'd seen the other look in his eyes, the hatred, the need for vengeance. He would never forget that she'd put him in prison. No matter if she believed anything Buford had told her, she believed Dillon Savage was a man who held a grudge.

"Damn it, Jack," he said with a groan. He dragged her to him, his mouth on hers, his arms surrounding her and pulling her in.

He caught her off guard. Just like the first time he'd kissed her, the day she'd captured him. Her lips parted now of their own accord. Just as they had the first time.

And just like the first time, she felt the stars and planets fall into line.

Noise erupted from a bar down the street. Dillon stepped back as abruptly as he'd kissed her. She followed his gaze, surprised and disappointed that he'd ended the kiss.

That is, until she saw the lone man standing outside the bar, watching them. As he scratched a match across his boot and lifted the flame to the cigarette dangling from his mouth, his face was caught in the light.

Sheriff Claude McCray.

Dillon felt shaken. He'd seen the look on the sheriff's face. All Dillon had done was bring Jack more trouble—as if she needed it.

Worse, she'd given him nothing but silence and distance ever since. But at that moment he would have done anything to convince Jack she was wrong about him. As if a kiss would do that! And yet, it had been one hell of a kiss. He'd felt a connection between them. Just as he had the first time. It had haunted him for the past four years, locked up in prison.

Just as this kiss would haunt him.

He mentally kicked himself on the way back to the motel. She was skittish again when it came to him. Distrustful.

He almost laughed at the thought. Hell, as it was, she didn't trust him as far as she could throw him. How could it be any worse?

But he knew the answer to that.

She could send him back to prison.

He was probably headed back there for another year, anyway. If she lost her job, which appeared likely, then this deal was over. He knew Stratton hadn't wanted him out to begin with, and with pressure from Shade Waters...

But that wasn't what worried him. It was Sheriff Claude McCray. McCray had seen the two of them together by the truck. He would make trouble for Jack. Dillon didn't doubt that for a second.

The tow truck driver finally arrived. Jack had been leaning against the side of the disabled pickup, arms crossed, a scowl on her face.

Dillon had had the good sense to leave her alone. Now he listened to Jack give the tow truck operator instructions to take the pickup to a tire shop, have the slashed tires replaced, the state billed, and the truck delivered to the motel in the morning.

The driver, a big burly guy with grease-stained fingers, grunted in answer before driving off with the pickup in tow.

"Pleasant fellow," Dillon commented as he and Jack were left alone in the dark parking lot.

She grunted in answer and started walking toward the motel. He guessed she needed the fresh air so he accompanied her and kept his mouth shut.

They hadn't gone a block, though, when her cell phone rang. She shot him a look. He felt his gut clench. It was the call they'd both been expecting all night. Once Stratton fired her, Dillon would be on his way back to Montana State Prison.

Well, at least he'd gotten a kiss, he told himself. And Chinese food. Sometimes that was as good as it got.

He could tell that Jack didn't want to talk to anyone, after everything that had happened tonight. As she checked her caller ID, he figured that, like him, she was worried it would be the sheriff.

"It's Stratton," she said, and gazed at Dillon. They'd both been expecting this. He sure was calling late, though.

Was there some reason it had taken him so long? Maybe like he was giving it some consideration—until he got a call from the sheriff?

She snapped open the phone. "Wilde."

Dillon watched her face. A breeze stirred the hair around her face, and her eyes went wild, like those of a deer caught in headlights.

"I see." She listened for a while, then stated, "Fine. No, I understand. If that's what you want." She snapped the phone shut.

Dillon stared at her, trying to gauge the impact of the call. She looked strange, as if all evening she'd been preparing herself for the worst. Earlier, he'd had the feeling that she'd already given up the job. There'd been a freedom in her that had drawn him like a moth to a flame. "Well?"

"The rustlers hit again. Leroy Edmonds's ranch, to the east. Stratton thinks it was the same bunch. One of the ranch hands just found where the barbed wire fence was cut. Not sure when or how many head were stolen."

"Did Stratton…?"

"Fire me? No." She shook her head, as if this had been the last thing she'd expected. Maybe still couldn't believe it. "Waters apparently talked him out of it. Seems Waters has had a change of heart."

"Not likely," Dillon said with a curse, wondering what the bastard was up to.

Just as she had earlier, Jack looked to be close to tears.

Tears of relief? Or just exhaustion? This day had to have played hell on her. He wished there was something he could do to make things easier for her. But he wasn't going to make the mistake of trying to kiss her again.

That woman at the steak house, the one who'd laughed and drank wine and seemed free, was gone. This one was all-business again.

"So you're telling me Waters has agreed to let us on his ranch?" Dillon asked, more than a little surprised.

"Sounds that way."

"Why the change of heart?" he had to ask.

"Shade says one of his ranch hands saw someone watching a grazing area with binoculars He's agreed to let us talk to the hired hand and even have access to that section," she said. "That's a start."

She seemed relieved that she hadn't been fired. But there was also a sadness about her. Dillon felt a stab of guilt for denigrating her job earlier.

"The sneaky son of a bitch," he said with a laugh. "He's that sure we won't catch him at whatever he's up to. Tell me this doesn't feel like a setup."

"I have to treat it like a legitimate lead," she said, sounding as if she wasn't any more happy about this than he was.

"I know. It's your job. But just do me one favor. No matter how sure you are that Waters is innocent, don't ever underestimate the bastard."

Jacklyn smiled. "Funny, that's what everyone keeps telling me about you."

Chapter 11

The next morning, with new tires on the truck, Jacklyn filled up the gas tank, then picked up the horse trailer and enough supplies to last a good three days.

"So we're headed for Leroy Edmonds's place?" Dillon asked, as Jack pointed the rig north again. "I thought you said his ranch was to the east?"

"First stop is Waters's spread. I need to talk to the hand who says he saw someone up in the hills scoping out the herd," she said.

He nodded, but sensed there was more going on with her this morning. Unless he was mistaken, there'd been a change in Jack. Not quite a twinkle in her eye, but close. He'd bet money she was up to something.

It was one of those blue-sky days that was so bright it was blinding. There wasn't a cloud in the sky and the weather was supposed to be good for nearly a week.

Dillon still couldn't believe he wasn't headed back to prison. It made him a little uneasy. "So who's the ranch hand?"

"Pete Barclay. He's worked for Waters ever since you went to prison," she said, glancing over at him.

She wasn't fooling him. All his old cowboy buddies were back in central Montana. Neither of them thought that was a coincidence.

He sighed deeply. "Pete Barclay."

"What? I thought Pete was your friend? Or are you going to tell me that he's now in cahoots with Waters?"

Dillon shook his head. There was no telling her anything. "Pete actually saw one of the rustlers?"

"The person was up in the hills. He saw a flash of light up in the rocks that he believes came from binocular lenses. When he went up to investigate, he found tracks. Look, I'm not sure what I believe at this point. That's why I want to talk to Pete."

"Right." There was more to it, sure as hell.

"If it makes you feel any better, I don't trust Waters," she admitted, as if the words were hard to say.

Dillon looked at her in surprise. That was the most honest she'd been with him. Not to mention that she'd just taken him into her confidence. Maybe he was finally making inroads with her. Or maybe she was just telling him what she thought he wanted to hear.

Reda Harper had never been good at letting sleeping dogs lie. She hadn't slept well last night, tossing and turning, her mind running over the meeting at the community center and, even more, what she'd seen on the W Bar.

She'd made a few calls first thing this morning to find out if the rustlers had struck again.

She'd been shocked to hear that, sure enough, they had hit another ranch. One to the east, though, not Waters's. How was that possible, when she'd have sworn she saw them on the W Bar last night? Unless she'd seen them *after* they'd hit Edmonds's ranch.

But what had she really seen?

"Isn't any of my business," she said to herself, even as she sat down at her desk and pulled out the pale lavender stationery. Caressingly, she ran her fingertips over the paper. Nicer than any paper she would have bought for herself. The stationery had been a gift from her lover.

"The no-good son of a bitch," she said under her breath. Her lips puckered, the taste in her mouth more sour than lemons as she picked up her pen and, with a careful hand, began to compose one of her infamous letters.

The mistake she'd made wasn't in mailing the letter, she realized later. It was in not leaving well enough alone and *only* sending the letter.

Even as she was pocketing shells and picking up her shotgun, she knew better. Not that she'd ever drawn the line at butting into other people's business. In fact, it was the only thing that gave her any satisfaction in her old age.

No, it was not leaving well enough alone when it came to Shade Waters. Her mother, bless her soul, had always said that Reda's anger would be the death of her.

Of course, her mother had never known about Reda's affair with Shade, so she'd never witnessed the true extent of her daughter's fury.

Had there been someone around to give Reda good advice, he or she would have told her not to get into her pickup armed with her shotgun. And maybe the best advice of all, not to go down that back road to where she'd seen that stock truck last night.

* * *

Jacklyn turned at the gate into the W Bar Ranch, taking a breath and letting it out slowly.

Last night she hadn't been able to sleep—not after the ranchers' meeting, everything she'd learned at the steak house with Dillon, and finally Stratton's call.

At least that's what she told herself. That it had been Dillon who gave her a sleepless night—and not just the kiss.

The night before had left her off balance. Even a little afraid. That wasn't like her, and she knew part of it was due to Dillon Savage. She'd known he was dangerous, but she'd underestimated his personality. Even his charm, she thought with a hidden smile.

But last night, unable to sleep, she'd realized what she had to do. As she drove into the W Bar, she knew the chance she was taking. She was no fool. She'd gotten Dillon out of prison for the reason he suspected: to give him enough rope that he would hang himself. She'd been that sure he was the leader of the rustling ring.

Now she suspected that Stratton was doing the same thing with her.

This morning before they left, she'd called Shade Waters. He'd been almost apologetic. She'd questioned him why this was the first time she'd heard about one of his men seeing someone on the ranch. Why hadn't he mentioned it yesterday at his place? Or last night at the meeting?

"I just heard about it. I guess he told Nate and—" Waters let out a low curse "—Nate had other things on his mind and forgot to mention it until late last night."

"I want to talk to the ranch hand."

"I'll make sure he's here in the morning."

She'd wondered even then if Waters was making things too easy for her, setting her up, just as Dillon suspected. Or was she just letting Dillon sway her, the same way she'd let him kiss her last night?

As she parked in front of the ranch house, she was glad to see there wasn't a welcoming reception on the porch this time. "I need to talk to Pete alone."

"I'll be right here," Dillon said, lying back and pulling his hat down over his eyes. He gave her a lazy grin.

"Make sure you stay here," she said.

He cut his eyes to her. They seemed bluer today than she'd ever seen them. Just a trick of the light. "At some point, you might want to give me more to do than sleep."

Soon, she thought. Very soon.

Dillon's intention had been to stay in the pickup. The last thing he wanted to do was make Jack mad again, he thought, as he watched her walk toward the barn. She did fill out her jeans nicely, he decided. He groaned, remembering the hard time he'd had getting to sleep last night, just thinking about their kiss.

He'd figured this early release would be a cakewalk. Just hang back, let things happen, do as little as he could. Jack was good at her job. She didn't need him.

But that had been before last night. Now he felt frustrated, on too many levels. He couldn't sit back and let Jack make the biggest mistake of her life.

The thought made him laugh. The biggest mistake of her life would be falling for him.

Yeah, like that was ever going to happen.

No, Jack was going at this all wrong. She was never going to catch the rustlers at this rate. She needed to investigate the W Bar and Waters.

Was she dragging her feet because of Dillon's own past with the rancher? He swore under his breath and sat up. The place was quiet. Maybe too quiet?

He told himself he had to think of what was best for him as well as Jack. She needed his help. He wondered how long it would be before he was headed back to prison, if she didn't get a break in this case.

Something shiny caught his eye. Grillwork on an old stock truck parked in tall weeds, behind what was left of a ramshackle older barn.

He thought of Jack for a moment. She'd disappeared into the new barn, closer to the house. He knew why she had balked at investigating Waters on the q.t. behind her supervisor's back. Because she didn't have a criminal mind.

But he did, he admitted with a grin, as he popped open his door and slipped out of the pickup. He wouldn't go far, but he definitely wanted to have a look at that truck. He was betting it was the same one he'd hitched a ride in just the day before.

Sneaking along the side of the building, Dillon kept an eye out for Jack. He hated to think what she would do if she caught him.

The W Bar definitely seemed too quiet as he neared the front of the truck. He hesitated at the edge of the building, flattening himself against the rough wood wall to listen. He could hear crickets chirping in the tall weeds nearby, smell dust on the breeze, mixed with the scents of hay and cattle, familiar smells that threatened to draw him back into that dark hole of his past.

After a moment, he inched around the corner of the barn and along the shady side of the stock truck. It was cool here, wedged between the truck and the barn. He stayed low, just in case he wasn't alone. Strange that no one was around, other than the hired hand Jack was meeting with in the other barn. Pete Barclay, she'd said. He and Pete had never been close. Pete was a hothead.

That fact made Dillon nervous about Jack being in the barn alone with him. He reminded himself that she was wearing a gun, this was what she did for a living, and he had to trust her judgment.

Still, he was worried as he moved past the driver's door and along the wooden bed of the truck. He grabbed hold of one of the boards and climbed up the side, hesitating before he stuck his head over the top. He still hadn't heard any vehicles. No tractors. No ranch equipment. Not even the sound of a voice or the thunder of horses' hooves. Where was everyone?

As he finally peered over the top of the stock rack, Dillon wasn't all that surprised by what he found. The back of the truck had been washed out. There was only a hint of odor from the dead calves that had been in it yesterday.

Climbing down, he noticed that the truck was older than he'd realized yesterday. Probably why it was parked back here. Because it was seldom used.

He started around the corner of the barn, sensing too late that he was no longer alone.

Jacklyn found Pete Barclay where Waters had told her he would be. In the barn. On her walk there, she saw no one else. She hadn't seen Waters's car, nor Nate's, for that matter, and suspected they might have gone into town to avoid her.

Which was fine with her.

Pete Barclay was a long, tall drink of water. He had a narrow face that she'd once heard called horsey, and

he wore a ten-gallon Stetson that he was never going to
grow into. His long legs were bowed, his clothing soiled,
she noted, when she found him shoveling horse manure
from the stalls.

"Mornin'," he said when he saw her, and kept on working.

"Shade told you I was coming out?"

Pete nodded.

"I just wanted to ask you a few questions."

"Sure." He shoveled the manure into a wheelbarrow,
not looking at her.

"Shade said you saw someone watching the ranch?"

Pete dumped another shovelful into the wheelbarrow,
the odor filling the air. Had Waters purposely told him
to do this job this morning, because she would be talking to him?

"Can't say I saw anyone, just kind of a reflection. You
know—like you get from binoculars."

"So you investigated?"

He nodded as he scooped up more manure. "Just found
some boot and horseshoe prints. The ground was kind of
trampled. Looked like someone had been hanging around
behind a rock up there."

"And where was this, exactly?"

He told her. He still hadn't looked at her.

"Shade said you told Nate?"

He gave another nod.

"How many cattle would you say Mr. Waters has in
that area?" she asked. She couldn't see Pete's face, but
his neck flushed bright red.

"Mr. Waters said I wasn't to be giving out any numbers. Truth is he's talking about moving the cattle closer
to the ranch house until the rustlers are caught."

"That's a good idea," she agreed, wondering if Shade had any idea what a terrible liar Pete was.

"He said to tell you to take the Old Mill Road. The country back in there is pretty rough. It's a good day's ride on horseback."

"Then I'd better get started," Jacklyn said.

Shade Waters stepped out in front of Dillon, blocking his way, as he came around the corner of the barn.

Dillon had often thought about what he would do if he ever caught the rancher in a dark alley, just the two of them alone, face-to-face.

"You and I need to talk," Waters said.

Dillon cocked his head, studying the man. Did the rancher have any idea how much danger he was in right now? Up close, Waters looked much older than he remembered him. He had aged, his skin sallow and flecked with sun spots. But there was still power in his broad frame. Shade Waters was still a man to be reckoned with.

"What could you and I possibly have to talk about?"

"Your father."

Dillon couldn't hide his surprise. He glanced toward the pickup, but didn't see Jack. "I don't think you want to go down that road."

"You're wrong about what happened," Waters said, sounding anxious. "I liked your father—"

"Don't," Dillon said, and pushed past the older man, striding toward the pickup, telling himself not to look back. His hands were shaking. It was all he could do not to turn around and go back and—

"I have a proposition for you," Waters said from behind him.

Dillon stopped walking. He took a deep breath and slowly turned.

"You want your father's ranch back? It's yours."

Dillon could only stare.

"I'll throw in the old Hanson place, as well."

Dillon took a step toward him, his fists clenched at his sides, anger making his head throb. "You think this will make up for the past?"

"I don't give a rat's behind about the past," Waters snapped. "This isn't a guilty gesture, for hell's sake. This is a business deal."

Dillon stopped a few yards from Waters. "Business?"

He couldn't believe this old fool. Waters had no idea the chance he was taking. In just two steps Dillon could finally get vengeance, if not justice.

"I give you the ranch, you take Morgan Landers off my hands," Waters said.

Dillon couldn't have been more astonished. "I beg your pardon? Off *your* hands?"

"Don't play dumb with me, Savage. What I always admired about you was your intelligence. You know damn well what I'm asking. I want her away from my son. Name your price."

Dillon shook his head, disbelieving. "My price?" he asked, closing the distance between them. This was the man who had destroyed his family, stolen his ranch and now thought he could buy him as well.

Dillon reached out and grabbed the man's throat so quickly Waters didn't have a chance to react. He shoved the rancher against the side of the barn. "My price?"

"Dillon," Jacklyn said calmly, from behind him.

Waters's face had turned beet-red and he was making a choking sound.

"Dillon," Jacklyn repeated, still sounding calm and not overly concerned.

Dillon shot a look over his shoulder at her, saw her expression and let go of the rancher's throat.

Waters slumped against the side of the barn, gasping for air. "I'll have you back in prison for assault," he managed to wheeze as he clutched his throat.

"No, you won't," Dillon said to him quietly. "Or I'll tell your son what you just tried to do. Better yet, I'll tell Morgan."

Waters glared at him. "Get him the hell off my property," he growled to Jacklyn.

"We were just leaving," she said.

Next to her, Dillon walked toward the pickup, neither looking back.

"What was that about?" she asked under her breath, sounding furious.

"The bastard offered to give me back my ranch."

She shot him a look.

"And the old Hanson place thrown in."

"He admitted he'd stolen your ranch?" she said, once they were at the pickup and out of earshot.

"Yeah, right." Dillon glanced back. Waters was still standing beside the barn, glaring in their direction. "It was a business deal. He wanted me to take Morgan Landers off his hands."

As Jack opened her door, she glanced toward him in surprise. "You aren't serious."

"Dead-on," Dillon said as he joined her in the cab. He was still shaking, his heart pounding, at how close he'd come to going back to prison for good.

"He wants her out of his son's life that badly?"

Dillon laughed and leaned back in his seat as she

started the engine and got rolling. "Waters is one manipulative son of a bitch. But I'd say he's met his match with Morgan Landers."

Jacklyn watched Dillon's face as he glanced out in the direction of what had once been his family's ranch. "Tempted?" she asked.

He smiled but didn't look at her. "That train has already left the station."

She thought about the lovely Morgan Landers, heard the bitterness in his voice. Jacklyn had little doubt that Dillon could get the woman back if he wanted. Nate was no match for Dillon Savage.

"The sooner we catch these guys, the sooner you can get your life back," she said.

"What life?" He looked over at her and sighed. "I guess I do need to start thinking about the future."

She nodded. "Have you thought about what you want to do?"

"Sure." He looked out at the rolling grasslands they were passing. "I thought about leaving Montana, starting over."

"Using one of your degrees?"

He nodded, his expression solemn.

"But you can't leave here, can you?"

He turned to her again, then smiled slowly. "I don't think so."

But he couldn't stay here unless he let go of the past, and they both knew it.

Ahead, Jacklyn spotted the turnoff to the Old Mill Road. She slowed the truck. "You wouldn't have killed him."

Dillon laughed. "Don't bet the farm on it."

She shook her head. "You're not a killer, Dillon Savage."

He looked over at her and felt a rush of warmth that surprised him. Whether true or not, he liked that she seemed to believe it. He reminded himself that while she might not consider him capable of murder, she *did* believe he was behind the rustling ring. Or did she really?

Jacklyn turned down the road, amazed by the lengths Shade Waters would go to get what he wanted. Was it possible Dillon had been right about him all along?

The road was rutted and rough, and obviously didn't get much use. But clearly, a vehicle had been down here recently. There were fresh tire tread patterns visible in the dust.

As she topped a small rise, the huge old windmill, with only a few of the blades still intact, stood stark against the horizon. Near it, she spotted two vehicles parked in the shade of a grove of trees.

She swore under her breath as she recognized both of the people standing beside the vehicles, having what appeared to be an intimate conversation.

"And what do we have here?" Dillon said, as Sheriff McCray turned at the sound of the truck coming over the hill.

Jacklyn saw the sheriff's angry expression. He left Morgan and walked over to stand in the middle of the road, blocking it.

"Tempted?" Dillon said with amusement when Jacklyn brought the pickup to a stop just inches from McCray's chest.

With a groan, she powered down her window as the sheriff walked around to her side of the vehicle. He didn't look happy to see her. Or was it that he wasn't happy to be caught out here with Morgan?

"What are you doing here?" McCray demanded, glancing from her to Dillon. "You spying on me?" Clearly, he was upset at being caught. But caught doing what?

She glanced toward Morgan, who had gotten into her SUV and was now leaving. "Shade said one of his men noticed someone watching this end of the ranch. I told him I'd check it out."

McCray frowned. "Why would he tell you that? There's no cattle in here." His eyes narrowed. "You're going to have to come up with a better story than that."

No she wasn't. "My mistake." She shifted the pickup into Reverse and, backing up the horse trailer into a low spot, turned around.

But McCray wasn't done with her. He stepped up to her window. "Or maybe you had another reason for coming out here," he said, scowling at Dillon.

"I could ask what *you* are doing out here," Jacklyn snapped, before she could stop herself.

"I'm doing my job," he retorted defensively. "Shade asked me to keep an eye on his place."

"Really?" She glanced toward the retreating Morgan Landers. "Or did he make you an offer you couldn't refuse?" Claude ignored that.

"I see you got yourself some new tires," he said with snide satisfaction, no doubt to let her know he'd seen Dillon kissing her last night in the community center parking lot.

"Don't let me keep you from your...*work*," she said as she let the clutch out a little quicker than she'd planned. The pickup lurched forward, the tire almost running over the sheriff's foot.

He jumped back with a curse. As she turned the wheel and left, she saw him in her rearview mirror, mouthing something at her. She gave the pickup more gas and heard Dillon chuckle.

"I wonder what Waters offered *him?*" Dillon said. "That looked like a lovers' tryst to me. I just hope I'm around when Morgan finds out that Shade Waters is trying to sell her to anyone who'll take her."

As Jacklyn drove back the way they'd come, she only momentarily wondered just how far Shade would go to protect his son from Morgan Landers—and what Nate would do if he found out.

But her mind was on what McCray had said about Waters not running any cattle in that section of the ranch. She'd known Pete Barclay was lying, but now she knew that Waters was, as well.

Chapter 12

As Jacklyn reached the county road, a truck whizzed past, headed in the direction of the W Bar Ranch.

"That's odd," she said, as she caught a glimpse of the man behind the wheel. Buford Cole had to have seen them, but appeared to turn away, as if not wanting to be recognized.

"Looks like he's headed for Waters's ranch," Dillon said, lifting a brow.

She was reminded of what Buford had told her at the steak house. "He's a friend of yours." She hadn't meant to make it sound so much like an accusation.

Dillon looked away. "I lost some friends when I went to prison. Buford was one of them."

That surprised her. "Why was that?"

He turned to smile at her. "You tell me. Was he the one who helped you capture me? I've always wondered who betrayed me."

She heard the pain in his voice. But it was the underlying anger that worried her. "No one helped me."

He gave her a look that said he didn't believe that for a minute.

"Buford used to rustle cattle with you, didn't he?"

Dillon didn't reply. But then, she thought she knew the answer. Buford had known too much about Dillon's motives not to have helped him.

And what about Dillon's other buddies, Pete Barclay and Arlen Dubois? Dillon hadn't seemed happy to see any of them. And now that she thought about it, they were giving him distance, as well. Because they didn't want her to know that they were still involved in rustling together?

"If I were you, I wouldn't trust anything Buford told you," Dillon said finally.

"Why?"

He looked at her as if she wasn't as smart as he'd thought. "Because he can't be trusted."

"Unlike you. Is Buford smart enough to be running this latest rustling gang?"

Dillon shook his head without hesitation. "He's smart enough, but he has no imagination."

"Rustling requires imagination?" she asked, half-mockingly.

He grinned. "As a matter of fact, it does. Whoever is running this gang has imagination. Look what they pulled off at the Crowleys'. Stealing the cattle in broad daylight right in front of the house. That took imagination. And bravado."

She heard admiration in his voice.

"Don't be giving me that look," he said. "If I was the one behind this gang, do you think I'd be bragging on myself?"

"As a matter of fact...."

* * *

Dillon glanced up as she pulled off the road. Out the windshield, all he could see was pasture beyond the barbed wire fence gate. He shot Jack a questioning look. She appeared to be waiting for him to get out and open a gate that hadn't been opened for some time. The fence posts on both sides were clearly marked with orange paint.

In Montana any fool knew that a fence post painted orange meant no trespassing. It meant prosecution under the law if caught on that land. And up here, especially with a band of rustlers on the loose, the rancher would be prone to shoot first and ask questions later.

Especially this rancher, because the land on the other side of that gate was W Bar property, belonging to Shade Waters.

"What the hell?" Dillon asked quietly as he met her gaze.

"I called Stratton this morning and told him we would be going north up by the Milk River for a few days, to follow a lead," she said.

Dillon felt an odd ache in his chest. She'd lied to her boss, just as he'd suggested she should do. "Are you sure about this?"

"No," she said without hesitation. "If you want to know the truth, I suspect you're setting me up. But Waters lied about having cattle down by the old windmill and Pete lied about seeing someone in that area. I can only assume Shade was just trying to keep me busy. And that makes me wonder if he isn't trying to keep me away from another part of his ranch. You said that stock truck was headed north, right?"

Dillon nodded slowly.

"Toward your old ranch."

"Looked that way."

"Any thoughts on why he would get rid of the rustled calves on your family's old place?"

Dillon smiled at that. "For the same reason you're thinking. To make it look like I had something to do with it."

She nodded.

"So when I told you about the calves in the back of the stock truck, you *believed* me?" he asked.

"I wouldn't go that far. I wanted to do a little investigating on my own first." She reached into the glove box, pulled out a map and spread it on the seat between them. "Okay, Waters's ranch house is here. Most of his cattle are in this area." She looked up at Dillon. "I had a friend who owns a plane fly over it early this morning."

He met her gaze. "You are just full of surprises."

"The problem is there's no way to get to your old ranch anymore without driving right past Waters's house." She pointed to the map. "Reda Harper's place is past his. According to the map, there used to be a section road that connected with another county road to the east, but that's now part of the W Bar."

"Waters closed the road after he bought our ranch," Dillon said, trying to keep the emotion out of his voice. Waters had had his family's ranch house razed.

"Can I ask you something?"

Her tone as much as her words surprised him. And he knew before she asked that her question wasn't about cattle rustling business.

"This bad blood between you and Shade Waters, am I wrong in suspecting it goes deeper than his ending up with your ranch?" she asked.

Dillon chuckled and looked toward the mountains in the distance. "I told you Nate had an older brother. He was killed trying to ride a wild horse." His voice sounded flat over the painful beating of his heart. "Halsey was my best friend." He looked at her. "It happened on our ranch."

She let out a breath as if she'd been holding it, compassion and understanding in her eyes. "Shade blamed you."

He nodded. "And my family. Halsey was…" He chewed at his cheek for a moment. "Well, there just wasn't anyone like him. A day hasn't gone by that I haven't missed him."

"It must be worse for Shade," she said.

"Halsey was definitely his favorite of the two boys." Dillon looked down at the map. "So what we need is a way to get to my old ranch without Waters or his men seeing us, right?" he asked, hoping she'd let him change the subject.

"Right," she said, to his relief. "I thought you might have some ideas."

He managed a grin. "You know me. I'm just full of good ideas."

"Let's see if we can find those calves," Jack said. "Open the gate, Mr. Savage. You're about to get us both arrested for trespassing."

Jacklyn wound her way among rocks and sage, across open grasslands. As soon as she reached a low spot where she was sure the truck and horse trailer couldn't be seen from the county road, she cut the engine.

The former Savage Ranch land was miles away, but the only way to get there without being seen was by horseback. Water and wind had eroded the earth to the north, carving canyons and deep ravines that eventually spilled into the Missouri River. It was badlands, inaccessible by anything but horseback, and isolated. They would have a long ride. That's why she'd brought provisions in case they had to camp tonight.

Jacklyn didn't doubt for an instant that Waters would have them arrested for trespassing if he caught them before they could find the evidence they needed to open up an investigation.

"You suspected the calves are buried on my family's former ranch the minute I told you about the dead calves, didn't you?" Dillon said with a grin as they saddled up their horses and loaded supplies into the saddlebags.

She just smiled at him. The truth was she'd had a hard time believing his story. Why kill the calves? What was the point of rustling them in the first place?

But the more she'd pondered the topic, the more she couldn't help thinking about what Dillon had said regarding motive. Was there a chance it had nothing to do with money? That the rustlers didn't want the calves—they just wanted them stolen?

It made no sense to her, but it seemed to make sense to Dillon. If what Buford had told her was true, Dillon had rustled cattle as retribution against his neighboring ranchers and Waters. He hadn't wanted the cattle, either.

Which made her suspicious, given that the current rustlers appeared to have a similar, nonmonetary motive.

"Don't you wonder why the rustled calves are being dumped on my former land?" Dillon asked.

"Like you said, it makes you look guilty."

"But you know I'm too smart for that," he said, grinning at her.

Again Jack smiled back. "Right. You're so smart you would have the rustled cattle put on your land to frame

Waters, by making it look like he was trying to frame you."

Dillon laughed, shaking his head.

But the truth was he looked worried. And maybe with good reason. If DNA tests were run on the dead calves he'd seen, she'd bet it would match cattle stolen from the same ranches that he had stolen from in the past.

"What if you never get justice?" she asked seriously.

Dillon seemed surprised by her question. "Isn't that the reason you do the job you do? To make sure justice is served?" He winked at her. "See, you and I aren't that different after all, Jack. We just have our own way of getting the job done."

She watched Dillon ride on ahead of her. He looked at home in the saddle. She'd come to realize there was little Dillon Savage wasn't capable of doing. Or willing to do for justice. Was that why he was helping her now?

As if he felt her eyes on him, he slowed his horse, turning to look back at her. Their gazes locked for a moment. He smiled as if he knew that she'd been studying him.

She looked away, hating that he made her heart beat a little faster. Worse, that he knew it. Dillon Savage was arrogant enough without seeing any kind of interest in her eyes.

"Everything all right?" he asked, reining in his horse to ride next to her again.

"Fine."

His grin broadened. "You don't have to always play the tough guy."

"Who's playing?"

He laughed. "You know, Jack, I like you. I don't care what other people say about you."

It was an old joke, but it still made her smile. Maybe

because she knew at least the part about other people was true.

"Some men may hold a grudge toward you," he said as he rode alongside her. "But you and I understand each other."

She glanced at him, wondering if that was true.

Shade Waters stood at the front window, watching his son's SUV barrel up the road. Nate hadn't come home last night. Where had he been? Shade could only guess. He'd been with Morgan Landers.

Waters waited anxiously, having made a decision. He had to tell Nate exactly what would happen if he persisted in dating this woman.

As the car came to a stop, Shade saw that Nate wasn't alone, and swore. Morgan. Well, he'd have one of the ranch hands take her back to town, because he couldn't put off this talk with his son. He wouldn't.

Waters didn't turn at the sound of footfalls on the porch or the opening and closing of the door. He realized he was shaking, his entire body trembling.

"Nate." He cleared his voice, raising it. "Nate. I need to talk to you. Alone."

He finally turned as Nate entered the room. His son looked like hell. Obviously hungover, as if he'd pulled an all-nighter. Waters felt disgust as he stared at his youngest offspring. If only his elder son, Halsey, had lived.

"Dad…" Nate said, and Morgan appeared at his side, looping her arm through his, a big, victorious smile on her face.

Shade felt his heart drop. "I want to speak to my son alone." He saw Morgan give a little tug on Nate's arm.

"Dad," Nate began again. "There's something I need

to tell you." He didn't sound happy about it. Or was he just afraid of Shade's reaction? "Morgan and I got married last night."

Shade felt the floor beneath him threaten to crumble to dust. He watched his every dream fly out the window. He'd always hoped that Nate would change, that he'd grow up and want to take the ranch to the next level. He'd hoped Nate would make the Waters name known not only all across Montana, but also the Northwest. Maybe even farther. Anything would have been possible.

But as he looked at his son's hangdog face, Shade knew that Nate would only run the ranch into the ground. And Morgan... He looked at her self-satisfied expression and knew she would bleed the place dry, then dump Nate for someone with more to offer.

He saw every dream he'd ever had for the W Bar disappear before his eyes.

"Congratulations," he said, hoping the break in his voice didn't give him away. He stepped to his son and shook his hand, squeezing a little too hard.

Then he kissed Morgan on the cheek, embracing her, even smiling. Both newlyweds were surprised and taken aback. They'd run off to get married, afraid he'd try to stop them. Now they expected him to be upset, even to rant and rave and threaten them.

Clearly, neither knew him very well.

"I wish you both the best," he said, almost meaning it. "This calls for champagne. You will join me for dinner tonight, won't you?"

They both readily agreed, and Waters smiled to himself.

He'd break the news at dinner.

* * *

Jacklyn rode the horse across sun-drenched, rolling hills miles from the nearest road, the grasses vibrant green, the air sharp with the scents of spring. Dillon rode next to her, his gaze more often than not on the horizon ahead—on land that had once been in his family for five generations.

For a long time, neither spoke. She could see how much Dillon was enjoying this. There was a freedom about him even though she had the tracking monitor in her saddlebag.

They stopped for lunch in a stand of trees, letting their horses graze while they ate their sandwiches. Out here, Jacklyn felt as if she was a million miles from civilization.

After lunch, they rode on again, across land starting to change from prairie to badlands.

"So tell me about your childhood," Dillon said out of the blue once they were back in the saddle. "Come on, Jack, we've got a long ride today. If you don't want me to sing—and believe me, you don't—then talk to me. You a Montana girl or a transplant?" When she didn't answer, he said, "Okay, if you want me to guess—"

"Montana. I grew up around West Yellowstone. I was an only child. My mother taught school. My father was a game warden."

Dillon let out a low whistle. "That explains a lot. Now I see where you get it."

"The game warden father," she said sarcastically.

"No, the schoolteacher mother," he joked, and she had to smile. "See? That wasn't so hard."

"So tell me about you," she said.

"Come on, Jack, you know my whole life story. What

you didn't already know I'm sure Buford Cole filled you in on the other night at the steak house."

She couldn't hide her surprise.

He grinned. "Yeah, I saw him talking to you. I can just imagine what he had to say."

"Can you? He said you're a man who holds a grudge."

His grin broadened. "Buford should know. We're cut from the same cloth."

"He also said he wouldn't be surprised if you were leading this gang of rustlers."

Dillon laughed. "You don't believe that anymore," he said as he rode on ahead.

When she caught up to him, Dillon could tell she had something on her mind. "Come on, let's have it," he said.

"I was just thinking how different you are from your cousin Hud."

Oh boy, here it comes. As if he hadn't heard that his whole life. "How is Hud?" he asked, although he knew.

"He married his childhood sweetheart, Dana Cardwell. She owns a ranch in the Gallatin Canyon."

Dillon nodded. He liked her voice, her facial expressions when she spoke. "I heard something about a lost will," he said, encouraging her.

"Dana's mother had told her she made up a new will leaving the ranch to her, with some of the income divided among the siblings, along with some other assets. For a while Dana couldn't find the document leaving her the ranch, and it looked like she would have to sell to settle with her sister and brothers."

"But the ranch was saved," Dillon said, hating the bitterness he heard in his voice.

Unfortunately, Jack heard it, too. "Weren't you away when your father sold the family ranch?"

He gave her a self-deprecating grin. "You know I was. But then, like I said, you know everything about me. You probably know when I had my first kiss, my first—"

"I know it is hard to lose something you love," she said quickly, to cut him off, no doubt afraid of where he was headed.

"Have you ever lost something you loved?" he asked, studying her.

"Dana's pregnant." Jack looked away as she changed the subject. "She and Hud are expecting their first child this fall."

That surprised Dillon. He hadn't seen his cousin in years. But Uncle Brick had stopped up to the prison a few times a year to give Dillon a lecture and tell him how glad he was that his brother and sister-in-law weren't still alive to see their son behind bars. Brick had also shared the going-ons with the family. The pregnancy must have been a recent development.

"I'm happy for Hud and Dana," Dillon said, meaning it. "A baby." Hud would make a great father. For the first time, Dillon felt a prickle of envy. Hud with a wife and a baby and living on Dana's family ranch.

Settling down had been the last thing Dillon had imagined doing. He'd always told himself he would be bored to death with that kind of life. He needed excitement, adventure, challenge.

Hell, apparently he needed to be running from the law.

"If you don't buy a ranch in the future, what will you do?" she asked.

He'd had plenty of time to think about what he would do once he was really free. "Can you see me behind a desk, wearing a three-piece suit?"

"Yes."

He laughed. "Liar." This felt good between them. Lighter. Freer. He liked it. He liked her, in spite of everything. That surprised him.

"So I guess you'll ranch, since apparently cattle are in your blood."

"Raising cattle so someone can steal them?" He chuckled to hide how close she'd come to the truth. "But then, you'd be around to catch the rustlers, right?"

She looked away.

"Hey, don't worry about me," he said, moving into her range of vision to smile at her.

"I'd hate to see you go back to rustling," she said quietly.

"I'm sure you're aware that my grandfather left me money," Dillon said. "It's not like I need to find a job."

"Everyone needs a job," she said adamantly. "You need something to occupy your mind. Especially *your* mind."

I have something to occupy my mind, he thought as he looked at her.

"How much farther?" she asked, as if feeling the heat of his gaze.

"I think I know where the calves are buried and how to get there." Dillon had been trying to think like Shade Waters. He regretted to realize that it wasn't that hard. He'd gotten to know the man too well. Maybe had even become too much like him over the years.

"On the other side of the canyon," he said. He'd been mulling over why Waters would be rustling cattle. It made no sense. Especially just to kill them. Was he trying to force out ranchers in the county so he could buy their land like he had Dillon's father?

The W Bar was so huge now that Waters had to be having trouble running it all. Dillon doubted Nate was of any help. Nate had never been much of a cowboy, let alone a rancher. Unlike his brother, Halsey, who had loved ranch life as much as Dillon had.

Also what didn't make sense—if he was right and Waters was dumping some of the stolen cattle on the old Savage Ranch—was why? Sure, he and the big rancher couldn't stand the sight of each other, but Dillon was small potatoes. Waters was too smart to risk everything to try to get even with Dillon after all this time. And hadn't he just offered to give back the ranch if Dillon got Morgan out of his life?

But what really worried him was why Buford Cole would be going to the W Bar. Buford had hated Waters as much as Dillon did. Or at least Dillon had thought so.

Ahead, the rolling prairie rose to rocky bluffs. "The canyon will be hot, but the route is shorter this way."

She glanced over at him. Was that suspicion he saw in her eyes?

"It isn't like we've been followed," he said, looking over his shoulder. He could see for miles. No one knew they were here. And yet he couldn't shake the feeling that Waters was one step ahead of them, laying a trap they were about to walk into.

As they rode between the rocks and into the narrow canyon, rocks and trees towering on each side, Dillon felt even more unease.

"Just a minute," he said, reaching out to touch Jack's hand on the reins.

She brought her horse up. "What's wrong?"

He wished he knew what to tell her. How could he explain this feeling? "Let me go first," he said, adding, "I know the way."

The look she gave him said she doubted there was a

chance of getting lost in the narrow canyon, but she let him ride ahead of her.

He urged his horse among the rocks. There was no breeze in here, only heat. It felt stifling. That and quiet. He was regretting coming this way when a shadow fell over him.

He glanced up in time to see a hawk soar low over the rocks, its shadow flickering over the canyon for a few seconds before it was gone.

Dillon was literally jumping at shadows. What the hell was wrong with him?

As he turned to look back at Jack, he felt his horse stumble and heard a metal ping like the snapping of a guitar string.

"Get back!" he yelled, and jerked his mount's head around, digging his boot heels into its flanks.

He grabbed her reins as his horse rushed past hers, pulling her with him as the first rocks began to fall.

Their horses bounded along the canyon floor as the air filled with dust and the roar of a rockslide.

Chapter 13

Jacklyn bent over her horse as Dillon charged ahead on his, drawing her after him through the tight canyon.

Behind her she could hear the crash of rocks. Dust filled the air, obliterating everything. Then, suddenly, they were riding out of the dust, out of the canyon. The breeze chilled her skin as Dillon brought the horses to a stop in the open.

"Are you all right?" he cried, swinging around to look at her.

She nodded. "What was that back there?" she demanded, knowing it was no accident.

"A booby trap."

She stared at him, not comprehending. "You're telling me someone was waiting for us in the canyon? How is that possible? No one knew we were headed this way."

"The booby trap was wired to set off the rockslide if anyone tried to come up through the canyon."

"Who would do such a thing?"

Dillon gave her a knowing look. "Who do you think?"

"You aren't going to try to tell me that Shade Waters rigged that, are you?"

He gave her a cold stare. "No. I doubt he knows how."

She felt a chill. "But you do." She remembered six years ago almost getting caught in a rockslide when she was chasing him.

"Oh, my God," she said, drawing back from him.

"The difference is that mine was just to slow you down," he said. "There was no chance of you being hurt."

She shook her head, wondering if she would ever really know this man. It was an odd thought, since more than likely he would be going back to prison. Where he belonged.

"I never did it again," he said, his gaze holding hers. "Too many things can go wrong. I didn't want your death on my conscience."

She realized she was still trembling inside at their near tragedy as she glanced back up the canyon. "You know who rigged that, don't you," she said quietly.

"No, but I used to know some men who were acquainted with the technique."

She turned in her saddle to look at him. "You're talking about the men who rode with you. I've never understood why you didn't give up their names. You could have gotten less time in prison if you had."

"Don't you know me better than that?" With a shake of his head, he added, "I made a lot of mistakes before I went to prison."

"You mean like getting caught."

He locked eyes with her, his expression intense even though he was smiling. "No, before that. I started off with what I felt was a damn good reason for what I did. But if prison taught me anything, it was that, while vindicated, I lost more than my freedom. I'm trying to get that back."

"What do we do now?" she asked, glancing at her watch. They had been riding most of the day. They were losing light.

"We'll have to go around the bluffs. It will take longer, but it will be safer."

"You expect other booby traps?"

"No. But I'm not taking any chances. The good news is that the rockslide confirmed what we suspected. They had to have gotten rid of the stolen calves on the other side of the canyon. That's why they booby-trapped it from this side."

"Either that or they were expecting us because they know you," she said.

Dillon's eyes narrowed as he looked toward the canyon. "Yeah, that's another possibility, isn't it?"

The sun had made its trip from horizon to horizon by the time they reached the other side of the canyon. The shadows of the bluffs ran long and dark. The air had cooled. They still had a couple of hours of daylight. Jacklyn hoped they'd find the evidence, then ride out to the road, and avoid being forced to camp tonight.

She'd made sure they had the supplies they needed, just in case. There was no telling how long it would take to find where the calves had been buried. She refused to consider the possibility that Dillon was wrong, that Waters had too much land to hide in, that it might be impossible to find the dead calves—let alone that they didn't exist, that she'd been taken in by Dillon.

She concentrated her thoughts on Shade Waters. As arrogant as the man was, he would feel safe, if he was behind the rustling. This part of the ranch was isolated, far from a public road and all his land. He would feel confident doing whatever he wanted back here, she told herself. No matter what happened in this remote section, no one would be the wiser.

And there would be some poetic justice in dumping the cows on what had been the Savage Ranch.

At the top of a hill, Dillon reined in his horse. She joined him, glad to see that they'd finally made it to the old section road. Jacklyn could make out the hint of tracks, faint as a memory, through the grass.

"They left us a trail," Dillon said.

From this point, they could see for miles to the west. Almost as far as Waters's ranch house, but not quite. The good news was there were no vehicles in sight.

They rode down the hill and followed the faint tracks through the deep grass along what had once been a section road between the Savage and Waters ranches. Someone had definitely been using it lately.

There had been a barbed wire fence along both sides of the road, but Waters had it taken down after he'd bought out Dillon's father.

Jacklyn could feel the change that came over Dillon. The land off to their left had once been his. He would have probably been ranching it now if not for Waters.

She saw him looking ahead to the rocky bluffs, and wished she'd known him before he became a cattle thief.

"There's been more than one rig on this road," Dillon said.

"Can you still get out this way?" she asked, thinking that the road must dead-end a few miles from here.

"You can reach the county road, if you know where you're going," he said, pointing to the southeast.

The road wound through the badlands. To the right ahead was the opening to the canyon they'd tried to come up. To the left were more deep ravines and towering bluffs, then miles of ranch land.

As they rode closer to the canyon entrance, she saw the distinct track through the grass where someone had driven off the road back into the rocks. She could hear a meadowlark's sweet song, feel the day slipping away as the air cooled around her and the light dimmed.

She felt an urgency suddenly and rode out ahead, following the tracks. Along with the urgency was an overwhelming sense of dread. How many cattle had been buried back here? She hated to think.

She reined in in surprise where one set of vehicle tracks veered off to the left, while the other headed to the right, toward the canyon entrance.

As Dillon joined her, he reached over and touched her shoulder. "Look," he said, his voice a low, worried murmur.

She followed his gaze to a rock outcropping and saw the glint of light off a windshield. Her gaze met his as she unsnapped the holster on her weapon. Sliding off her horse to the ground, she whispered, "Wait here."

"Not a chance," he whispered back.

Ground-tying her horse, Jacklyn moved cautiously toward the vehicle hidden among the rocks. Dillon walked next to her, as quietly as a cat. The air that had felt cool and smelled sweet just moments before became stifling as she entered the shadow of the bluffs. Crickets chirped from the nearby grass, overhead a hawk cried out as it soared in a wide circle, and yet there was a deathly quiet that permeated the afternoon.

* * *

"It's Reda Harper's pickup," Jack said as they rounded the rocks and saw where someone had hidden the truck.

Dillon peered inside. Empty. "You don't think Reda is behind the rustling, do you?"

Jack shrugged. She wouldn't have put anything past the ranchwoman, even rustling cattle. "You have to admit she's smart enough to be the leader of the rustling ring. Otherwise, what is her truck doing here?" She glanced up as if the words had just hit her, and shook her head, dread in every line of her face.

"I'll go have a look, and if everything checks out—"

"Not a chance," she said, echoing his words. "I got you into this. I won't be responsible for you getting killed while I stand by."

He smiled at that. "Be careful," he said softly. "You're going to make me think you're starting to like me."

"Don't you wish," she joked as she strode toward her horse.

Yeah, he did wish, he thought as he watched her swing into the saddle. He reminded himself that this was the woman who'd captured him and helped send him to prison. But the memory didn't carry the usual sting. He smiled to himself as he caught his reins and swung up onto his horse. He was starting to like her. More than he should.

"I forgot that you see me only as a means to an end," he said as he looked at her. "I need to keep reminding myself of that."

She didn't glance at him, but he saw color heat her throat. Had he hit a little close to home or had their relationship changed since she'd gotten him out of prison?

He told himself, as he led the way, that he must be

crazy if he thought he might be getting to Jack. True, she wasn't calling him Mr. Savage anymore. She was still ordering him around, but he wasn't paying any attention. And she hadn't sent him back to prison even though they hadn't caught the rustlers. Yet.

All in all, he hadn't made much progress with her. But then, he supposed that depended on what kind of progress he wanted to make. His plans had changed, he realized. He no longer felt any anger toward her. If only he felt the same way about Shade Waters...

The canyon was wider at this end. A few aspens grew in clumps along the sides of the bluffs, their leaves whispering in the breeze as he and Jack rode past.

They hadn't gone far, following the tire tracks in the soft earth, when he spotted the backhoe and the freshly turned earth a dozen yards down a small ravine at one side of the canyon. That the rustlers had used a backhoe to bury the calves didn't surprise him.

It was the pile of rocks that had cascaded down from the canyon wall along one side of the ravine that brought him up short. He let out a curse as Jack rode ahead of him, dismounting near the tumbled heap.

He went after her, already pretty sure he knew what she was about to find when he saw the shotgun lying to one side.

She let out a small cry and dropped to her knees beside the pile. The fallen rocks were shot with color.

"Jack, don't!" Dillon yelled as she frantically began throwing stones to one side. "It's too late."

Jacklyn didn't remember dismounting and rushing to the rocks. Didn't remember falling to her knees beside the pile or reaching out to touch the bright fabric of a shirtsleeve.

All the time, she must have known what was trapped underneath, but it wasn't until she moved one of the rocks and saw first a hand, the nails short but bright red with polish, then a face contorted in pain and death, that she let out a cry and stumbled back.

Dillon grabbed her, pulling her to him. "There's nothing you can do. She's dead."

Jacklyn pressed her face against his chest, his shirt warm, his chest solid. She needed solidity right now. In her line of work, she took chances. She carried a gun. She knew how to shoot it, but she'd never had to use it. Nor was she in the habit of finding dead bodies. Cows, yes. People, no.

She just needed a moment to catch her breath, to get her emotions under control, to stop shaking. That's all it took. A moment listening to Dillon's steady heartbeat, feeling his arms wrapped protectively around her. She stepped back, nodding her thanks, under control again even if she was still shaking inside.

"We have to call someone," she said, as she dug out her cell phone.

Dillon watched, looking skeptical. "I doubt you'll be able to get service—"

She swore. "No service."

He nodded.

She glanced at the pile of rocks, then quickly turned her head away. "What was she doing here? She must have seen the backhoe in here and walked back to investigate."

Dillon shook his head. "What was she doing on Waters's ranch to begin with?"

That was the question, wasn't it. Everyone in the

county knew there was no love lost between the two of them.

"I need to see if I can get the phone to work higher up in the hills," Jacklyn said, reaching for her horse's reins so she could swing up into the saddle. "I'll ride up—" She heard Dillon call out a warning, but it was too late.

She was already spinning her horse around, only half in the saddle, headed for a high spot on the bluffs, when she heard a sound that chilled her to the bone.

Shade Waters looked up from his plate in the middle of dinner and realized he hadn't been listening. He'd insisted they eat early because he had some things to take care of.

"Shade," Morgan said in that soft, phony Southern drawl of hers. "I asked what you thought about my idea."

"What idea is that, Morgan?"

"Redecorating the house. It's so…male. And so…old-fashioned. Don't you think it's time for some changes around here?"

He could well imagine the changes she really meant. "Definitely," he said. "In fact, that's what I was doing, thinking it was high time for some changes around here."

Morgan looked a little surprised. He was taking this all too well. He knew she kept wondering why he wasn't putting up a fight.

"My first suggestion," he said, looking over at his son, "is that you both move into town."

Nate started in surprise. "What?"

"I'm changing my will in the morning," Shade announced. "I'm not going to leave you a dime. Oh, I know you'll spend years fighting it, but I can assure you, the way I plan to change my will, you'll lose. You'll never have the W Bar," he said, his gaze going to Morgan. "Or any of my money."

For once Morgan appeared speechless.

"Dad, you can't—"

"Oh, Nate, I can. And I will. You have no interest in the ranch. You never have. As for your...*wife*—"

"I think your father might be getting senile," Morgan said, glaring at Shade. "Clearly he is no longer capable of making such an important decision."

The rancher laughed. "I wondered how long it would take before you'd try to have me declared incompetent. Understand something, both of you. I will burn this place to the ground, lock, stock and barrel, before either of you will ever have it." He tossed down his napkin. "I have an appointment with my lawyer in the morning. I suggest you find a nice apartment in town to redecorate, Mrs. Waters. And Nate, you might want to find a job."

With that, he left the room, doing his best not to let them see that his legs barely held him up and he was shaking like the leaves on an aspen. The moment he was out of the house, he slumped against the barn wall and fought to control his trembling as he wiped sweat from his face with his sleeve.

He'd done it. There was no turning back now.

Jacklyn's horse shied an instant after she heard the ominous rattle. Both caught her by surprise. She only had one foot in a stirrup as the animal reared. The next thing she knew she was falling backward, her boot caught there.

"Jack!" she heard Dillon yell as he lunged for her and her horse.

She hit the ground hard and felt pain shoot through

her ankle as it twisted. Her horse shied to the side, dragging her with it, the pain making everything go black, then gray.

When her vision cleared she saw Dillon leap from his horse and grab her mount's reins, dragging the mare to a stop before he gently freed Jacklyn's boot from the stirrup.

She would have cried out in pain, but the fall had knocked the air from her lungs. She lay in the dust, unable to breathe, the throbbing in her ankle so excruciating it took her a moment to realize the real trouble she was in.

Out of the corner of her eye, she saw the rattlesnake coiled not a foot from her. The snake's primeval head was raised, tongue protruding, beaded eyes focused on her as its tail rattled loudly, a blur of movement and noise as it lunged at her face.

The air filled with a loud boom that made her flinch.

The snake jerked. Blood splattered on the rocks behind it, then the serpent lay still.

In that split second before she saw the rattler lunge at her, and heard the deafening report of the gun, Jacklyn had seen her life pass before her eyes, leaving her with only one regret.

The boom of her gun startled her into taking a breath. She gasped, shaken, the pain in her ankle making the rest of her body feel numb and disconnected.

Dillon dropped to the ground next to her, her gun still in his hand. Later, she would recall the brush of his fingers at her hip in that instant before the snake struck.

She took deep ragged breaths, eyes burning with tears of pain and relief and leftover fear.

"How badly are you hurt?" Dillon asked as he looked into her beautiful face. There was no doubt that she was hurting, even though she tried to hold back the tears. Her body was trembling, but he couldn't tell if it was from pain or fright.

"I'm fine," she managed to say, lying through her teeth. He could see that she was far from fine. But he let her try to get to her feet, ready to catch her when she gave a cry of pain and was forced to sit back down.

He handed her the gun. "Let's try my question again. How badly are you hurt?"

"It's my ankle," she said, replacing the pistol in her holster with trembling fingers.

"Let me take a look." He gently urged her to lie down, watching her face as he carefully eased her jeans up her leg. "I don't want to take off the boot yet." She wouldn't be able to ride without it. Also, it would keep the swelling down.

As he carefully worked his way down one side of her boot with his warm fingers, tears filled her eyes. She tried to blink them back and couldn't.

"I don't think it's broken. But if it's not, it's one nasty sprain." He looked past her and saw that both horses had taken off, skittish over the rattlesnake or the gun blast.

"I need to go round up the horses. Will you be all right for a few minutes?"

"Of course."

He nodded, glancing around to make sure there were no more rattlers nearby. "I'll be right back."

"Take your time. I'm fine."

He rose to his feet, then leaned back down. "Do not try to walk on that ankle. You'll only make matters worse if you do."

"I'm aware of that." She sounded as if she would have cried if he hadn't been there.

* * *

The moment Dillon was gone, Jacklyn eased herself as best she could away from the dead snake, putting her back to a warm rock. She prayed that her ankle wasn't broken, but the pain of just moving it almost made her black out again.

As Dillon disappeared from view, she felt a sob well up inside her, then surface. She swore, fighting back the urge to give in to the pain, to the despair. How was she going to be able to find the evidence now, let alone ride out of here?

Not only that, the receiver terminal for Dillon's tracking device was on her horse. This would be the perfect opportunity for him to take off. She couldn't very well chase after him. She couldn't even walk, and if he didn't return with her horse...

She looked up to see him leading both horses toward her, and relief made her weak. She was reminded of how gentle he'd been moments before as he'd checked her leg.

"You all right?" he asked, as he knelt down in front of her again.

She nodded, unable to speak around the lump in her throat. He had to have known she'd be worried he might not come back for her.

He reached out and brushed his fingers across her cheek. "Let me help you up on your horse."

She nodded and let him ease her up onto her good leg. His big hands were gentle as he put them around her waist and lifted her up into the saddle.

The cry escaped her lips even though she was fighting to keep it in as she tried to put her injured foot into the stirrup.

"Okay, you aren't going to be able to ride out of here," he said.

"No, I—"

"It's miles to the nearest ranch—and that ranch belongs to Shade Waters. You'd never make it. Anyway, it will be getting dark soon. We'll make camp for the night up there on that hill, and take the road out in the morning," he said, pointing to the southeast.

Clearly, he'd given this some thought already. She shook her head, close to tears. "I can ride. We have to tell someone about Reda."

Dillon pulled off his hat and raked a hand through his hair as he looked up at her. "Won't make any difference to Reda if we tell someone tonight or in the morning."

"You could ride out for help," she said through the pain.

"I'm not leaving you here alone. Tom Robinson is dead. So is Reda. The men behind this have nothing to lose now in killing anyone else who gets in their way."

She met his gaze.

He gave her a slow smile. "Finally starting to trust me? Scary, huh?"

Very. She looked toward the top of the bluff, where he planned to make camp. They would be able to see for miles up there. That's why he was insistent on camping on the spot, she realized. "You think they'll be back, don't you?"

"Let's just say I'm not taking any chances." He swung up into the saddle and looked over at her. "Come on. It's flat up there, with a few trees for shade and wood for a fire."

She wanted to argue, but as her horse began to move and she felt the pain in her ankle, she knew he was right.

She wasn't going far. Nor could she leave here without evidence that would finally bring this rustling ring down.

As she let Dillon lead her up the steep bluff, she had one clear thought through the pain: her life was now literally in his hands.

Chapter 14

The sun had dipped behind the mountains, leaving them a purple silhouette against the sunset. The air smelled of pine and aspens.

After Dillon had set up the tents and taken care of the horses, he made them dinner over a fire.

Jacklyn watched from where he'd settled her. He worked with efficiency, his movements sure, a man at home in this environment.

She felt herself relax as she watched him. The world seemed faraway, almost as if it no longer existed. Plus the pills he'd given her hadn't hurt.

"Looks like you're always prepared," Dillon had said when he'd found pain pills in the first aid kit she'd brought along with the other supplies.

"I try to be," she'd said, but in truth nothing could have prepared her for Dillon Savage.

A breeze stirred the leaves of the aspen grove where he'd chosen to camp. She stared at his broad back, surprised how protective he was.

"I feel so helpless," she said as he handed her a plate.

"It gives me a chance to wow you with my culinary talents, since dancing is out."

She tasted the simple food she'd brought and looked up at him in surprise. "It's wonderful."

He smiled, obviously pleased. "I had a lot of practice cooking over a fire." He sat down beside her with his own plate. She ate as if it had been days since she'd last tasted food.

He laughed. "I love a woman with a good appetite."

The fire crackled softly, filling the air with a warm glow as blackness settled around them. A huge sky overhead began to blink on as, one after another, stars popped out in the great expanse.

"I've lived in town for too long," she said, leaning back to gaze up at them. She found the Big Dipper, the constellation that had always been her guide since her father had first pointed it out to her as a child.

"This was the part I liked best," Dillon said from beside her.

She knew he was talking about his rustling days. He'd stayed in the wilds, seldom going into a town for anything except supplies. Or maybe to see some woman.

Mostly, she knew, he'd killed what he needed for food. Illegally, of course. She'd found enough of his camps, the coals still warm and the scent of wild meat in the air, but Dillon had always been miles away by that time.

"You know when I left here to go away to college, I never thought I'd come back," Dillon said. "Too many bad memories."

"Halsey's death," she said.

He nodded. "I thought I wouldn't miss Montana. But

then, I always thought the ranch would be there if I ever changed my mind."

She glanced over at him, hearing his pain, remembering her own. After she'd left for college, her parents had divorced and gone their separate ways, the life she'd known, her childhood home and her family, dissolving.

She and Dillon fell into a comfortable silence, the fire popping softly, the breeze rustling the pine boughs and carrying the sweet scents of the land below them.

Dillon was surprised when Jacklyn began to tell him about her parents, the divorce, the new families they'd made, how hard it was to accept the changes, to bond with the strangers that were suddenly her family.

He sat quietly as she opened up to him. Then he talked about Halsey, something he never did.

But it was a night for confidences, he decided. A night for clearing the air between them. Here, on this high bluff, they weren't an ex-con rustler and a stock detec tive. They had no shared past. They were just a man and a woman, both with histories they wanted to let go of.

Their talk turned to more pleasant things, like growing up in Montana. Both had spent most of their time as kids wading through creeks, climbing rocks and trees, daydreaming under a canopy of stars.

As the fire burned down, he saw there were tears in Jack's eyes. "How's the ankle?"

"Better."

He couldn't tell if she was lying or not. "Cold?"

She shook her head, her gaze holding his.

"I better check the horses," he said, dragging his eyes away as he got to his feet. She dropped her gaze as well, but he could still feel the warmth of it as he walked down the steep slope to the creek. The horses were fine, just as he knew they would be.

His real reason for coming down here was to make sure the area was secure. Earlier he'd rigged a few devices that would warn him if anyone tried to come up the bluff tonight. He didn't like surprises and he couldn't shake the bad feeling that had settled in his belly the minute he saw Reba Harper's shotgun lying beside the rock pile.

Jacklyn stared into the fire. Sparks rose from the flames, sending fiery light into the air like fireflies. She could feel the effects of the pills Dillon had given her, but she knew they weren't responsible for the way she was feeling about him.

No, just before the rattlesnake had lunged, before Dillon had killed it, before she'd taken the pills, she'd acknowledged she would have only one regret if she were to die at that moment.

When Dillon touched her shoulder, she jumped. She hadn't heard him return.

"Sorry. I didn't mean to scare you." He threw some more wood on the fire.

She gazed into the flames again, too aware of him as he sat down beside her. Her heart was pounding, and all the oxygen seemed to be sucked up by the fire.

"You're trembling," he said softly, his breath stirring the hair at her temple. "Your ankle is worse than you said."

"No, it's not my ankle," she managed to say around the lump in her throat. She turned her face up to the stars, feeling free out here, as if there were no rules. Was that how Dillon had felt? With society so far away, was it as if that life didn't exist? "Dillon…"

"We should get some sleep," he said, rising to his feet.

She grabbed his shirtsleeve and pulled him back down to her, landing her mouth on his.

He let out a soft chuckle. "What do you think you're doing?"

"I'm seducing you," she said, and began to unbutton his shirt.

He placed a hand over hers, stopping her. "I don't think that's a good idea."

"I do." She unbuttoned her own shirt and let it slide off her shoulders.

Shade Waters heard the creak of the barn door. The ranch hands were all in town, a little treat he'd given them for the night. He listened to the soft, stealthy movements and waited.

He'd thought it would take longer. He smiled to himself and felt his eyes flood, the bittersweet rush of being right.

"Dad?" Nate's voice was tenuous. "Shade?" he called a little louder. "We need to talk."

Shade gave himself a little longer.

"Dad, I know you're in here," Nate said, irritation mixing with the anxiety.

Shade was just glad Elizabeth wasn't here to see the kind of man her son had turned into. Or what lengths Nate would go to. Or for that matter, Shade himself.

"I'm back here," he finally called, and waited. He'd purposely sat on the bench next to the tack room. The only light was the overhead one a few yards down the aisle. He liked being in the dark as Nate came toward him, his son's face illuminated in the harsh yellow light, his in shadow.

"We need to talk."

"There isn't anything to talk about. I've made up my mind."

Nate stopped a few yards from him and didn't seem to know what to do with his hands. He finally stuck them into the back pockets of his jeans and shifted nervously from boot to boot. He looked young and foolish. He looked afraid.

"I know you don't want to cut me out of your will."

"No, I don't," Shade admitted. "But I'm going to."

"This is about Morgan, isn't it?"

"No, Nate, it's more about you."

"What can I say to you to make you change your mind?"

Shade shook his head. "You wanted Morgan. You have her. Or did you get her only because she thought that the W Bar would be hers someday?"

Nate glared at him, fury in his eyes. "You think I can't get a woman without buying her with *your* money?"

Shade said nothing. The answer was too obvious.

"Can't we at least talk about this?" Nate's voice broke.

"There's nothing to talk about, Nate. You made your bed. Now lie in it."

"Like you made your bed when you cheated on my mother?" Nate snapped.

Waters saw an image of Reda Harper flash in his mind. She'd been so young, so beautiful and alive, so trusting. He would never forgive himself for what he'd done to her. He'd made her the angry, bitter woman she was today.

"I gave her up for you boys and your mother." He turned away, hoping that was the end of it.

"Do you think monsters are made or born?"

Waters turned back to stare at his son. "Are you crazy?"

Nate laughed. "Crazy? I'm just like you."

"You're nothing like me," Waters snapped.

"Oh, you might be surprised."

"I doubt that," he said. "Nothing you could do would surprise me."

"How could I not be like you? All these years of watching the way you just took whatever you wanted. You didn't think I knew." Tears welled in his eyes. "You made me who I am today."

Shade felt sick just looking at his son.

"I only wanted something of my own. Morgan—" His voice broke and he sounded close to tears.

"For hell's sake, if you wanted something of your own why would you marry a woman who's been with half the men in the county, including Dillon Savage?" Shade demanded.

Nate nodded, smiling through his tears. "I have to ask you since I won't get another chance. If Halsey had died before you hooked up with Reda Harper…"

"What are you trying to say?" Waters demanded, knowing exactly where Nate was going with this.

"You would have left me and Mom, wouldn't you?"

The big rancher rose to his feet. "I've heard enough of this. A man has to make sacrifices in this life. You need to learn that." He couldn't help the bitterness he heard in his voice. How could he explain true love to a man who'd just married a woman like Morgan Landers?

Nor could he tell Nate what giving up Reda had cost him. That he still regretted it every day of his life and would take that regret to his grave with him. And maybe worse, he'd had to let her go on hating him, let her go on believing that he'd only been after her ranch all those years ago, that he'd never loved her.

Nate would never understand that kind of loss. But he would someday, when Shade was dead and couldn't walk up the road to the mailbox to get the letters in the faded lavender envelopes, trying to keep his secrets.

"So what would you like me to sacrifice?" Nate asked. "Morgan? Maybe my life? Because you and I both know that I will never measure up to Halsey, will I, *Dad?* Isn't that what this is about? Halsey."

"I loved Halsey. He was my son." Just saying his son's name made him ache inside.

"Admit it," Nate said, stepping closer. "If you had the choice, if you could wave your hand through the air and change everything, you'd want it to be me who died instead of my brother."

There it was. "Yes," Shade said, and looked away in shame.

She was beautiful, the black lacy bra cupping her perfect breasts, her skin creamy and smooth. Dillon felt an ache in his belly and felt himself go instantly hard.

Leaning down, he brushed his lips across hers. "Jack, do you have any idea what the sight of you half-naked is doing to me?"

She grinned in the firelight. "I noticed, actually."

"Does this mean you trust me?" he had to ask as he looked into her eyes.

"With my life," she said.

He laughed and shook his head. "I just wanted you to believe that I wasn't behind the rustling. I'm not sure you should trust me with your life, Jack," he added seriously.

"Too late. I already have," she said, and he saw naked desire in her gray eyes.

It was the last thing he expected. And, he realized, the only thing he wanted. "Jack——"

She pulled him to her and kissed him. He dropped to his knees in front of her, being careful not to brush against her hurt ankle as he took her in his arms and kissed her the way he'd been wanting to since the first time he'd laid eyes on her.

Damn, but this woman had gotten in his blood. For the past four years he'd told himself he wanted to get even with her. But as usual, he'd been lying to himself.

He just wanted Jacklyn Wilde. Wanted her in his arms. Wanted her in his bed. He drew back from the kiss to trail a finger over her lips as he searched her eyes, his heart beating too fast.

"There's no going back," he said as he unbuckled her gun belt. "Unlike you, I take no prisoners."

Jacklyn felt her blood run hot as he drew his palm down her throat to her breasts. She leaned back, closing her eyes as she felt his fingers slip aside the lace of her bra, his touch warm and gentle.

Her eyes flew open, heat rushing to her center, when he traced around her rock-hard nipple, then bent to suck it through the thin lace, his mouth as hot as the fire he'd started inside her.

She arched against his mouth, wanting him as she had never wanted anything in her life.

He scooped her up in his arms and carried her to one of the small tents, setting her gently down inside it and crawling in after her.

She could see the firelight glowing through the thin

nylon, could still smell the smoke and the pines. It was cold in the tent, but in Dillon's arms she instantly warmed.

He unhooked her bra, baring her breasts to his touch. She hurriedly unbuttoned his shirt, desperate to feel his chest against hers, skin to skin. It was hard and hot, just as she knew it would be.

His hand slipped under her waistband and she gasped as he touched her, finding her wet and ready. Their eyes met. Slowly he unbuttoned her jeans.

"We have to leave your boot on," he said. "I've never made love to a woman wearing her boots. But you know me, I'm up for anything." His smile faded. "Are you sure this won't be too painful?"

She grabbed his shoulders and pulled him down in answer. He wrapped his arms around her and kissed her, teasing her tongue with his, his movements slow and purposeful, as if they had all night. They did.

It was almost daylight when Dillon heard a sound and sat up with a start. They'd left the tent flap open. He could see the cold embers in the fire pit and smell the smoke as a light wind stirred the ashes and rustled the leaves on the nearby trees.

But he knew that wasn't what he'd heard. Someone was out there.

Feeling around in the darkness, he found Jack's weapon and slid it from the holster, careful not to wake her. He could hear her breathing softly and was reminded of their lovemaking. Desire for her hit him like a fist. He would never get enough of her even if he lived to be a hundred.

He edged away from her warm body with reluctance,

not wanting to leave her even for a moment. Stopping at the door, he leaned back to brush a kiss over her bare hip, and then rose and stepped from the tent.

Reaching back in, he withdrew his jeans and boots, then put them on, tucking the pistol into the waistband of his pants as he straightened and listened.

Just as he'd feared, he heard a limb snap below him on the hillside. He'd set up some small snare traps to warn him if anyone approached their camp, and knew that was what had awakened him. Now it sounded as if someone was trying to make his way up the slope.

It would be light soon, but Dillon knew he couldn't wait. The noise he'd heard could have been made by an animal. There were deer and antelope here, and smaller creatures that could have released one of the traps.

But his instincts told him this animal was larger and more cunning. This one would find a way up the steep bluff. Unless Dillon stopped him.

How had someone found them so quickly?

He could only assume that one of Waters's men had seen where they'd driven across the pasture. Once they found the hidden truck, they would tell Waters. And he would know exactly where they were headed.

Dillon heard one of the horses whinny. He thought about waking Jack. All he wanted to do was get back to bed with her as quickly as possible. And maybe he was wrong. Maybe there was nothing to worry about.

Moving through the trees, he headed toward the creek and the horses. If someone had found them, he'd be smart enough to take their mounts. It was much easier to run down a man on foot.

As he neared the creek, Dillon stopped to listen again. Not a sound. Was it possible it had just been the wind in the trees? Moving on down the bluff, he saw both horses were still tied to the rope he'd strung between two tree trunks beside the narrow stream. The animals would be reacting if there were any other horses around. But probably not to a man on foot.

Dillon tried to convince himself that everything was fine. And yet as he started to turn, he felt a rush of apprehension. He couldn't wait to get back to Jack.

"Dillon." The voice was soft. One of the horses whinnied again, moving to one side.

In the dim light of morning, Dillon watched Buford Cole step from the shadows. He'd wondered why Buford was going out to Waters's place when he'd seen him earlier. Now he had a pretty good idea.

"You work for Waters." Dillon's words carried all of his contempt.

Buford chuckled, still keeping one of the horses between him and Dillon. "Put down the gun and we can talk about it."

"Doesn't seem like there is much to say," Dillon commented, his heart in his throat. Had Buford come alone? Not likely. Dillon glanced back up the bluff toward the camp.

"She's fine. I thought you and I should talk."

"Too bad you didn't want to talk in town, where we could have sat down with a beer," Dillon said.

"I'm serious, Dillon. Put down the gun and make this easy on both of us."

The last thing he wanted to do was make things easy for Buford. He brought the gun up fast, knowing he would probably only get one shot. Unless he missed his guess, Buford would be armed.

Dillon fired just a split second before he was struck

from behind. He tumbled headlong toward the creek, out before he even hit the ground.

Jacklyn came awake instantly, sitting up in the tent and reaching for Dillon as she tried to make sense of what she'd just heard. A gunshot?

The bedroll beside her was empty, but still warm. Dillon was gone, but he hadn't been for long.

Her pulse raced as she scrambled in the semidarkness of dawn to find her holster. Her heart fell even though she'd known what she was going to find. The holster was empty.

Where was Dillon? Her pulse took off at a gallop. The gunshot. Oh God. He would have returned to her if he could have. Her heart was pounding so hard in her ears she almost didn't hear it.

A limb cracked below her on the steep bluff. She froze. A squirrel chattered off in the distance. A bird belted out a short song in a tree directly overhead. One of the horses whinnied. Another answered.

Move! Move!

As she hurriedly pulled on her jeans, she was reminded of her injured ankle. Thank God it wasn't broken. But it was badly sprained. She wasn't sure she could walk on it. What was she saying? She had no choice.

She pulled on her shirt and other boot. Dillon. She fought the tears that burned her eyes. She'd gotten him into this.

And if he was still alive, she would get him out. She dug in her saddlebag and found the second gun she always carried, and her knife. Then, as quietly as possible, she cut a slit in the back of the tent and taking the tracking monitor in its case, crawled out. She continued to crawl until she reached the trees before she managed to get painfully to her feet.

Her ankle hurt, but not as much as her heart. She wanted to call to Dillon, except she knew that would only let whoever was out there know exactly where she was. Dillon wouldn't answer, anyway. If he could, he would have returned to the tent for her.

A little voice at the back of her mind taunted that she was wrong about him. That he was the leader of the rustling ring. That he'd gotten her out here for more than a romp in the tent.

She told the voice to shut up, checked the gun and considered her options. They weren't great. Her first instinct was to head in the direction of the horses. She had a pretty good idea that was where whoever had come into camp would be found, given that the horses sounded restless.

That was where she suspected she would find Dillon.

As much as she wanted to find him, she was smart enough to know whoever was out there was counting on her appearing. Waiting down there for her. Figuring she would hear the gunshot and come to investigate.

It would be full light soon. She had to move fast. She worked her way back through the trees, in the opposite direction from the horses. The going was slow and painful, the ground steep.

When she reached the bottom of the bluff, she stopped in a stand of trees. Opening the case, she took out the receiver terminal, listened to make sure she was still alone, and turned it on.

The steady beep of the tracking monitor filled her with relief even as she reminded herself it didn't mean that Dillon was alive.

But at least now she knew where he was.

Chapter 15

Dillon came up out of the darkness slowly. His head hurt like hell and for a moment he forgot where he was. He was so used to waking up in a prison cell that at first he thought he was dreaming. Especially when he saw Buford standing over him.

Dillon groaned and, holding his head, sat up. As he felt his skull and found the lump where someone had hit him, his memory gradually started to come back to him.

"What the hell's going on, Buford?" he demanded, taking in the gun in his old friend's hand—and the fact that the barrel was pointed at his chest.

"You should have stayed in prison."

"I'm getting that," Dillon said. "Look, I don't know who else is with you, but don't hurt Wilde, okay?"

"So it's like that," Buford said with a smirk.

"You know, I misjudged you." Dillon's mind was racing. He knew he'd never be able to get to his feet fast enough to jump Buford before he caught a bullet in the chest. But he had to think of something.

"Misjudged me?" Buford kept looking up toward the camp. Dillon was betting that whoever had hit him had gone there looking for Jack.

"I never figured you for the leader of this rustling ring. Frankly, I never thought you were smart enough. I guess I was wrong." The moment the words were out of his mouth, Dillon saw that Buford *wasn't* the man giving the orders. So did that mean whoever had gone up the bluff was?

"Just shut up," Buford snapped. "Too bad he didn't hit you harder."

"Yeah." Dillon reached back again to rub the bump on his head. "You know, I've always wanted to ask you, were you the one who set me up the day Wilde caught me?"

Buford had always been a lousy poker player. Too much showed in his face. Just like right now.

"Well, that solves that mystery." Dillon kept his voice light, but his heart was pounding. It was all he could do not to lunge at his old friend and take his chances.

"You were always such an arrogant bastard," Buford said.

Dillon nodded in agreement, even though it hurt his head, as everything became clear to him. "It's because I wanted to stop rustling cattle, wasn't it."

"You get us involved and then you want to quit just when we're starting to make some money," Buford said, anger in his voice.

Dillon stared at him, a bad feeling settling in his stomach. "You didn't put all the cattle on the W Bar like I told you to."

"What was the point? No one gave a crap about your warped attempt at your so-called justice. Waters bought out my family's ranch just like he did yours. You didn't see me losing sleep over it. The only reason I'd risk rustling cattle was if there was real money in it and not what you paid us to help."

Dillon let that settle in for a moment. It explained a lot. Buford, Pete Barclay and Arlen Dubois had seemed guilty when he'd seen them. Now he understood why. He'd thought it was because they'd set him up. As it turned out, they'd done that, too—and double-crossed him.

"I've gotta know. Halsey's good-luck coin... I'm betting you took it from his pocket at the funeral."

"You'd lose that bet," Buford said.

Then who? "So who do I have to thank for this lump on my head? Pete?" Buford's expression told him it hadn't been Pete. *"Arlen?"*

"I told you to shut up."

Dillon frowned. If it really hadn't been either of them, who did that leave?

"Where's your girlfriend?" a very familiar voice asked, from directly behind him. Dillon felt his skin crawl, and heard Buford chuckle at his obvious surprise.

As Jacklyn worked her way around the rock bluff, the sun broke over the horizon. She would have less cover and more chance of being seen before she discovered what she had to fear.

The wind in the trees sounded like ocean waves. Past the trees, she spotted a pond, its surface pitching and rolling, the chop cresting white as it beat against the shoreline. The wind whistled past her, too, tossing her hair into her eyes.

Last night Dillon had taken out her braid.... Just the memory made her weak. His fingers in her hair... The two of them had made love through the night with an intimacy that she'd never experienced before. There was only one way she could explain it. Love.

The wind groaned in the pine boughs, whistling through the branches, making it impossible to hear if someone was sneaking up on her.

She pushed on through the tall grass. The sky stretched overhead, a pale blue canvas empty of clouds. But the wind had a bite to it.

She stopped to listen, the wind seeming to be her only companion. Ahead was another stand of pines, dark green. She had to be getting near the creek. Near where she believed Dillon had left the horses. She didn't dare check the monitor again.

Angling down the mountain through the pines, she came across a smaller pond nearly hidden in the trees. There, with the dense pines acting as a windbreak, the surface was slick and calm. She stopped to listen, hearing the wind sigh among the treetops.

A track in the soft mud at the edge caught her eye. She stepped closer, crouching down to study the multitude of animal prints. In the middle of the deer and antelope tracks was the clear imprint of a boot heel.

She froze as she heard something other than wind in pine boughs. The water beside her mirrored the sky, the dark green of the trees towering over her. Something moved in the reflection.

She jerked back, her eyes on the pines, the fallen needles a bed at her feet. Even over the wind, she heard the soft rustle. Not of swaying branches, but something advancing through the grass, moving with purpose.

She unsnapped her holster and rested her palm on

the butt of the pistol as she moved, just as purposefully, around the pond.

The wind whipped through the pines, sending a shower of dust over her. She froze, blinded for one terrifying instant.

Her prey had stopped, as well. A strange silence fell over the landscape. Shadows played at the edge of the water.

She started to take a step toward the cool shade in the pines as it burst from the trees. All she saw was the frantic flutter of wings. She didn't remember pulling the pistol, her heart lurching, her breath catching. The thunder of blood in her ears as the grouse flew past was too much like the heart-stopping buzz of the rattlesnake.

Jacklyn sucked in a breath, then another, her hand shaking as she slid the pistol back in the holster. But she kept her hand on the cool, smooth butt, her eyes on the trees ahead.

He was here. She could feel him. Unconsciously, she lifted her head and sniffed the air. Crickets began to chirp again in the grass. Somewhere off to her left a meadowlark sang a refrain. Closer, the grass rustled again with movement.

Once in the awning of the trees, she saw the game trail. It wound through the pines, disappearing in shadow. She stopped, crouched and touched the soft damp earth.

Another boot print.

Few people ever knew this kind of eerie silence. Solitude coupled with an acute aloneness. A feeling of being far from anything and anyone who mattered to her. Entirely on her own. She'd been here before. Fighting not only a country wrought with dangers, but also men—the most dangerous adversaries of all.

Tracking required stealth, so as not to warn other animals of her presence. She'd walked up on her share of bears, the worst a grizzly sow with two cubs. The mother grizzly had let out a whoof, but the warning came too late. The sow's hair had stood up on her neck as she rose on her hind legs, even as Jacklyn slowly began to back away. Then the sow had charged.

Jacklyn knew that running was the worst thing she could do, but in that instant it was a primal survival instinct stronger than any she'd ever felt. Fortunately, her training had kicked in. She'd dropped to the ground, curled into a fetal position and covered her head with one arm as she slipped her other hand down to the bear spray clipped to her belt.

The spray had saved her life.

Just as she hoped the gun would today, because whoever, whatever, was after her was nearby now.

Morgan Landers moved around to stand in front of Dillon, flashing him one of her smiles. "I lied about hoping I wouldn't see you again."

"It seems that's not the only thing you lied about," Dillon said. He'd always thought he wouldn't put anything past Morgan, but he was having a hard time believing she'd been the one to coldcock him. He had a sizable lump on his head. Morgan must have one hell of a swing. Unless it had been someone else.

He felt a sliver of worry stab into him as he realized that Morgan had just come from the camp on top of the bluff. "See Wilde while you were up there?" he asked, tilting his head toward the camp.

Morgan's gaze said she had guessed how close he was with the stock detective, and didn't like it. Too bad for Morgan. "As a matter of fact, she seems to be missing."

Dillon felt his heart soar. Jack had heard the shot, and being Jack, she'd known what to do.

Buford swore. "So what are you doing here? Go find her."

Morgan sent him a bored look. "It's being taken care of."

Jack was out there somewhere. She would need an advantage, because from what Dillon could see, there were at least three of them, maybe more. And as far as he knew she wasn't armed. But Jack being Jack she'd have a second gun he didn't know about.

What was also clear was that whoever was running this show wasn't going to let them out of this alive.

"Being taken care of by your boss?" Dillon asked Morgan.

"I don't have a boss," she snapped.

"Right. I could believe Buford was running this rustling ring easier than I could you, Morgan."

"You know, Dillon, you always were a bastard," she said, stepping closer.

He grinned at her. "And you, Morgan, were always a greedy, coldhearted bitch."

She lunged at him as if to slap his face. Buford yelled for her to stop, but Dillon was pretty sure she didn't hear him—or didn't care.

He grabbed her arm, using it as leverage as he pulled himself up, then swung her around in front of him for cover as he propelled her into Buford, knocking him off balance.

Buford's gun went off with a loud boom that echoed in the trees as the three of them, locked in a tangle of limbs, went down.

* * *

Jacklyn froze as the sound of the gun report filled the air. Her heart lodged in her throat. Not knowing if Dillon was alive or dead was killing her.

Worse, that little voice in the back of her head kept taunting her, trying to make her lose faith in him, telling her it was him stalking her through the trees.

As the gunshot blast died away, she heard the rustle of grass, the crack of a limb and knew he'd circled around her and was now right behind her.

Jacklyn took a breath and turned, her weapon coming up and her mind screaming: *Who are you about to kill?*

He stood just a few feet from her. She could see both of his hands. He appeared to be unarmed. He looked confused, almost lost.

"Nate?"

"What happened to you?" Nate asked, having apparently noticed her limp.

"I sprained my ankle." This felt surreal, as if she was dreaming all of it. She held the gun on him, but he didn't seem to care.

"Any luck catching those rustlers?" he asked, his voice sounding strange, almost as if he was trying not to laugh.

She tightened her hold on the gun. "Nate, what are you doing here?"

"Looking for you. Dillon told me to find you and bring you back to camp."

"Why didn't he come himself?"

"He's hurt."

Her breath rushed out of her. "How did he get hurt?"

Nate shrugged.

"Is it bad?" she asked, her heart beating so hard her chest hurt.

"You'd have to be the judge of that," he said. She wondered if he'd been drinking. She'd never seen him like this.

"Nate, what's going on?" she pressed, the way she might ask a mental patient.

He tilted his head as if he heard a voice calling him. She heard nothing. "Are you here alone?"

"Who would be here with me?" he asked, as if amused.

"I thought Shade might have come with you," she said.

"Oh, that's right, you haven't heard. My father was murdered last night in his barn."

Dillon rolled over, trying to catch his breath. He felt as if he'd been punched in the chest, all the air knocked from his lungs. His hand went there and came away sticky with blood. He'd been hit.

But after a moment, he realized it wasn't his blood. It was Morgan's.

She lay on her back, staring vacantly up at the morning sky. Her shirt was bright red, soaked with blood.

Dillon tried to get up, but Buford was already on his feet and holding the gun. The cowboy kicked at his head. Dillon managed to evade him, taking only a glancing blow, as he rolled over and came up in a sitting position, his back to a tree.

"You stupid bastard," Buford swore. "You stupid bastard."

Dillon focused on him, hearing the fear in the man's voice. Buford was pacing in front of him, clearly wanting to shoot him. Had whoever Buford took orders from told him not to kill Dillon?

But looking into his old friend's eyes, he saw that change. Buford raised the gun, pointing it into Dillon's face. "You're a dead man."

* * *

Jacklyn stared at Nate in shock. Shade Waters murdered? "That's horrible. Do they know who—"

"Sheriff McCray has put out an APB. I hate to be the one to tell you this, but I saw Dillon Savage running away from the barn right before I found my father's body."

All the air rushed out of her as if she'd been hit. "Nate, that's not possible. Dillon was with me last night."

He shrugged. "I guess you'll have to sell that to Sheriff McCray, but since Dillon made his getaway in your state truck, the sheriff thinks you might have been an accomplice."

"What? Nate…" She felt fear seize her. "Nate, that's crazy. No one will ever believe it."

"No? Well, the sheriff says the only reason you got Savage out of jail is that you have something for him. And everyone knows he's the one who's been headin' up this gang of rustlers. I'm betting the rustling will stop once he's back in prison."

She stared at Nate Waters as if she'd never seen him before. She'd never seen *this* man, and he frightened her more than if he had been holding a gun on her.

"You must be in shock," she said, realizing that had to be what was going on.

He laughed as if that was the funniest thing he'd ever heard. "You know my father always blamed me for Halsey's death. Dillon thought he blamed him, but he was wrong. I was the one holding the rope on that horse that day. I killed Halsey. His luck had finally run out. So I took his good-luck coin after I saw Dillon put it in my brother's suit jacket at the funeral."

The good-luck coin found near where Tom Robinson was attacked. Nate Waters had just implicated himself.

"Nate, why don't you take me to Dillon," she said, trying to keep her voice even.

"Not until you put down your gun, Ms. Wilde."

"I can't do that." Even though Nate didn't appear armed, he was talking crazy. If anything he was saying was true, then he was responsible for the rustling, for the attack on Tom Robinson, the death of Reda Harper and… Jacklyn felt sick. And apparently the death of his father, Shade Waters.

"The thing is, if you don't drop the gun, I'm going to give my men orders to kill Dillon," Nate said. "His blood will be on your hands."

His men? How many were there? "Nate, why would you do that?"

The smile never reached his eyes. "I think you already know the answer to that. The gun, Ms. Wilde. Drop it and step away."

She didn't move. She had to get to Dillon. But without a weapon, she knew they were both dead.

"Buford?" Nate called.

"Yeah." The answer came from the trees behind Nate.

"Everything all right over there?" Nate asked.

"Yeah. Just a little accident, but everything's okay."

Jacklyn recognized Buford Cole's voice and could tell that things were definitely not all right. She hated to think what that last gunshot was about.

"Well?" Nate asked her with an odd tilt of his head. "You want me to give the order?"

"How do I know Dillon isn't already dead?"

"Dillon?" Nate called.

Silence, then a surprised-sounding Dillon said, "Nate?" as if he'd been trying to place the voice, since it had to be the last one he'd expected to hear out here.

"Dillon," Jack called to him.

"Jack!" His response came back at once.

She heard so much in that one word that tears burned her eyes. "Are you all right?"

"He won't be if you say one more word to him," Nate said in that calm, frightening voice.

Dillon took a deep breath, weak with relief. Jack was alive and Buford seemed to be using every ounce of his self-control not to pull the trigger on the gun he was holding on him.

The overwhelming relief was quickly replaced with the realization that Jack was with Nate. And Buford seemed to be losing it by the minute.

So Shade Waters was behind the rustling, just as Dillon had thought. He found little satisfaction in being right though. Shade was dangerous enough. But apparently, he'd sent Nate to tie up some loose ends. Nate was unpredictable. Maybe even a little unstable. No way was this going to end well.

"Oh man, I can't believe this," Buford said again as he began to pace back and forth again, always keeping the gun aimed in Dillon's direction. He looked more than nervous; he looked scared to death. Unfortunately, it only made him more dangerous.

"I can't believe she's dead," he said, raking his free hand through his hair. His hat had fallen off during the skirmish, but he didn't seem to have noticed.

"I think you'd better tell me what's going on," Dillon said, trying to keep his voice calm. "What's Nate doing with Jack?"

"You've messed everything up," Buford said, sounding as if he might break down at any minute. "You killed

Morgan. What's Nate going to do when he sees that you killed Morgan? Hell, man, he married her. They were going to go on their honeymoon."

"*You* pulled the trigger," Dillon said. "I didn't kill her. You did."

Buford stopped pacing. His eyes had gone wild, and he looked terrified of what Nate Waters was going to do to him. Nate Waters, a kid they'd all teased because he'd been such a big crybaby.

Dillon felt bad about that now. Worse, because he had a feeling that Nate Waters was going to kill him. He just didn't want the same thing to happen to Jack. He tried to think fast, but his head ached and Buford was standing over him with a gun, acting like a crazy person.

"You'd better let me help you," Dillon said. "Nate's obviously going to be upset about his wife." Dillon avoided looking at Morgan, lying dead on the ground. Even though she was obviously in this up to her sweet little neck, she didn't deserve to die like this.

Buford was right about one thing. Things were messed up big time.

"I'm telling you, Buford, for old times' sake, let me help you."

The man looked as if he might be considering it, so Dillon rushed on. "Come on, old buddy. Things are messed up if you're taking orders from Nate Waters, anyway. Whatever he's gotten you into, Jack and I can help cut you a deal. But if you wait and he kills anyone else—"

"There a problem here, Buford?" Nate asked as he came out of the trees, holding a gun on Jack.

Dillon groaned inwardly. A few more minutes and he might have been able to turn Buford. Now there was no hope of that.

"It was an accident," Buford said. "Man, I'm so sorry. I…"

Nate pushed Jack over by Dillon. She dropped to the ground next to him and he put his arm around her. He could see that she was scared, and her ankle had to be killing her. But he knew Jack, knew she was strong and determined. And with her beside him, he told himself, they had a chance of surviving this. She owed him a dance. Kind of.

Mostly, he couldn't bear the thought that they'd found each other, two people from worlds apart, only to have some jackass like Nate Waters kill them.

Nate walked over to where Morgan lay dead on the ground.

Dillon heard a small wounded sound come out of Jack. He pulled her closer and whispered, "It's going to be okay."

Buford was pacing again, swinging the gun around. "Oh man, Nate, I'm so sorry. It was an accident. Dillon, man, it's his fault. You told me not to shoot him, but he jumped me. Morgan… Oh man."

"Shut up," Nate said, sounding close to tears. "She was just a greedy bitch who slept with anyone and everyone."

"She was your *wife*," Buford said, obviously before he could think.

Nate turned to glare at him. "She tricked me into marrying her. I don't want a woman who's been with Dillon Savage."

Oh, boy, here it comes, Dillon thought, as Nate swung the gun in his hand toward Dillon's head. Next to him, he felt Jack press something hard against his thigh. Apparently she'd taken it from one of her boots.

A knife.

He slipped his arm from around her. "What? This is about Morgan Landers?" He shook his head and sat up a little, dropping his hands to the ground next to him. "Come on. There has to be more to it than that."

Nate stepped closer. "What would you know about it? You have any concept what it's like to grow up with Shade Waters as a father? To live your whole life in the shadow of the great Halsey Waters? You have no idea."

"So all this is to show your father," Dillon said, closing his hand around the knife handle hidden beneath his thigh. If Nate came any closer…

"It was bad enough that he idolized Halsey but when you started rustling cattle to pay back the ranchers who you felt had wronged you…" Nate took a breath and let it out on a sigh. "The bastard actually admired you the way you slipped those stolen cattle in among his." Waters's laugh held no humor. "You were a damn hero. Even the great stock detective here couldn't catch you. I was the one who put up the hundred thousand dollar reward for your capture from the money my mother left me. He never knew."

"Damn, I wish I had known that. I would have had my friend Buford here collect it." He looked past Nate. "But then he already had, huh?" Dillon remembered the truck Buford had been driving when he passed them, headed for the W Bar. It had been an expensive ride—not the kind of vehicle a man who works at the stockyards could afford. "So it really was you, Buford, who betrayed me."

Buford Cole had looked frightened before. Now he looked petrified. "Kill him. Just get it over. You said nobody knows where they are. We can bury them with the cattle. Morgan, too. No one will ever have to know."

Nate raised his gun, pointed it at Dillon's head. Unfortunately, Dillon wasn't close enough to reach him with the knife. Nor could he launch himself faster than a speeding bullet. He hoped his life didn't pass before his eyes before he died. He wasn't that proud of the things he'd done.

It happened so fast that Jacklyn never saw it coming.

She'd buried the hand farthest away from Nate's view, grabbing a handful of fine dirt. She was planning to throw it in Nate's face, anything to give Dillon a chance to use the knife.

But as she raised her balled fist holding the dirt, Nate swung around and fired. He couldn't have missed in a million years. Not with Buford standing just feet behind him.

The bullet caught Buford Cole in the face. He went down with a thump.

But before he hit the ground Dillon was on his feet. He drove the knife into Nate's side.

It took Jacklyn a little longer to get to her one good foot. She hit Nate in the face with the dirt and wrestled her weapon from him.

"Nate Waters? You're under arrest for the murders of Buford Cole, Reda Harper, Morgan Landers—"

"Morgan *Waters*," he corrected, holding his side and looking down at the blood leaking between his fingers, as if he'd never seen anything quite so interesting.

"Shade Waters and the attack on Tom Robinson."

Nate looked up at her. "Tom died earlier this morning."

"The murder of Tom Robinson," she said, her voice breaking.

Nate looked up, his head tilted, as if again listening to something she couldn't hear.

After a moment, he smiled. "Halsey said to make sure they spell my name correctly in the paper. Too bad Shade isn't around to see it."

Epilogue

Jacklyn hesitated at the door. She could hear the band playing. Glancing at her reflection in the window, she ran a hand over her hair, feeling a little self-conscious.

Her hair was out of its braid and floating around her shoulders. She so seldom wore it down that her image in the glass looked like that of a stranger. A stranger with flushed cheeks and bright eyes. A stranger in love.

She felt like a schoolgirl as she pushed open the door to the community center. The dance was in full swing, the place crowded.

For a while there'd been shock, then sadness, then slowly, the community rallied, and pretty soon even the talk had died down. And there had been plenty of talk. The gossips kept the phone lines buzzing for weeks.

The first shock was Shade Waters's murder, followed by the news that his son Nate had confessed not only to killing him and the others, but also to having been behind all the cattle rustling.

Buford had been one of the rustlers Nate had hired but

it was suspected that Pete Barclay and Arlen Dubois were also involved. Nate took full responsibility, though, for all the deaths and thefts, posing for reporters.

Jacklyn had wondered if he'd wished his father was alive to see it. Or had Nate told Shade everything before he killed him? She would never know.

On the heels of all the publicity came word that Shade Waters had been dying of cancer and had had but a few months to live, anyway. Everyone loved the irony of that, since few people had liked either Waters much.

The community had also taken Reda's death fairly well—especially when it came to light that she'd been blackmailing nearly half the county, including Shade Waters. For years, the sinners in the county had lived in fear of getting one of her letters, letting them know she knew their secrets and what it would take to keep her quiet.

But probably the news that had tongues wagging the most was Shade Waters's will. He'd changed it, unknown to Nate, about the time that Nate had taken up with Morgan Landers. In the will, Shade left everything to the state except for one ranch—the former Savage Ranch. That he left to a boys' ranch for troubled teens, in his son Halsey's name.

"I thought you might not come," Dillon said behind Jacklyn, making her jump as the band broke into another song.

She turned slowly, feeling downright girlie in the slinky dress and high heels. She'd even put on a little makeup.

"Wow," he said, his blue eyes warming as he ran his fingers up her bare arms. "You look beautiful, Jack. But then I think you always look beautiful."

She smiled, pleased, knowing it was true. Dillon liked

her in jeans and boots as much as he liked her in a dress. Mostly he liked her naked.

"You know, I didn't exactly win the bet," he said, feigning sheepishness.

"You said Waters was guilty. True, it wasn't the Waters you meant, but I'm not one to haggle over a bet," she said. "I just had to wait until my ankle was healed before I could pay up."

"Well, in that case, I guess you owe me a dance," he said as the band broke into a slow song.

She stepped into his arms, having missed being there even for a few hours. She looked up into his handsome face, wondering how she'd gotten by as long as she had without Dillon Savage in her life. The diamond ring he'd bought her glittered on her finger, his proposal still making her warm to her toes.

He'd bought a ranch up north, near a little town called Whitehorse, Montana. "I'm thinking we'll raise sheep. Nobody rustles sheep," he'd joked when he showed her the deed. "And babies. Lots of babies. I promise you I'm going to make you the happiest woman in northeastern Montana."

She'd laughed. But she was learning that Dillon Savage was good as his word. The man could dance. And he'd already made her happier than any woman in central Montana. She didn't doubt he'd live up to all his promises.

As he spun her around the room, she thought of the babies they would have, hoping they all looked like him. Except maybe the girls.

"You sorry?" he asked, his breath tickling her ear.

"About what?" She couldn't think of a single thing to be sorry for.

"I just thought you might be having second thoughts about settling down with me instead of chasing rustlers."

She smiled. "Darlin', there's only one rustler I want to be chasing."

"We can both stop running then. Because, Jack, you already caught him. The question now," he said with a grin, "is what you're going to do with him."

* * * * *

Delores Fossen, a *USA TODAY* bestselling author, has sold over fifty novels with millions of copies of her books in print worldwide. She's received a Booksellers' Best Award and an RT Reviewers' Choice Best Book Award. She was also a finalist for a prestigious RITA® Award. You can contact the author through her website at deloresfossen.com.

Books by Delores Fossen

Visit the Author Profile page at Harlequin.com for more titles.

BRANDED
BY THE SHERIFF

DELORES FOSSEN

To Debbie Gafford,
thanks for always being there for me.

Chapter 1

LaMesa Springs, Texas

A killer was in the house.

Sheriff Beck Tanner drew his weapon and eased out of his SUV. He hadn't planned on a showdown tonight, but he was ready for it.

Beck stopped at the edge of the yard that was more dirt than grass. He listened for a moment.

The light in the back of the small Craftsman-style house indicated someone was there, but he didn't want that someone sneaking out and ambushing him. After all, Darin Matthews had already claimed two victims, his own mother and sister. Since this was Darin's family home, Beck figured sooner or later the man would come back.

Apparently he had.

Around him, the January wind whipped through the bare tree branches. That was the only sound Beck could hear. The house was at the end of the sparsely populated

County Line Road, barely in the city limits and a full half mile away from any neighboring house.

There was a hint of smoke in the air, and thanks to a hunter's moon, Beck spotted the source: the rough stone chimney anchored against the left side of the house. Wispy gray coils of smoke rose into the air, the wind scattering them almost as quickly as they appeared.

He inched closer to the house and kept his gun ready.

His boots crunched on the icy gravel of the driveway. No garage. No car. Just a light stabbing through the darkness. Since the place was supposed to be vacant, he'd noticed the light during a routine patrol of the neighborhood. Beck had also glanced inside the filmy bedroom window and spotted discarded clothes on the bed.

The bedroom wasn't the source of the light though. It was coming from the adjacent bathroom and gave him just enough illumination to see.

Staying in the shadows, Beck hurried through the yard and went to the back of the house. He tried to keep his footsteps light on the wooden porch, but each rickety board creaked under his weight. He knew the knob would open because the lock was broken. He'd discovered that two months earlier when he checked out the place after the murder of the home's owner.

Beck eased open the door just a fraction and heard the water running in the bathroom. "A killer in the shower," he said to himself. All in all, not a bad place for an arrest.

He made his way through the kitchen and into the living room. All the furniture was draped in white sheets, giving the place an eerie feel.

Beck had that same eerie feeling in the pit of his stomach.

He'd been sheriff of LaMesa Springs for eight years,

since he'd turned twenty-four, and he'd been the deputy for the two years before that. But because his town wasn't a hotbed for serious crime, this would be the first time he'd have to take down a killer.

The thought had no sooner formed in his head when the water in the bathroom stopped. He had to make his move now.

Beck gripped his pistol, keeping it aimed.

He nudged the ajar bathroom door with the toe of his boot, and sticky, warm steam and dull, milky light spilled over him.

Since the bathroom was small, he could take in the room in one glance. Outdated avocado tile—some cracked and chipped. A claw-footed tub encased by an opaque shower curtain. There was one frosted glass window to his right that was too small to use to escape.

Beck latched on to the curtain and gave it a hard jerk to the left. The metal hooks rattled, and the sheet of yellowed vinyl slithered around the circular bar that supported it.

"Sheriff Beck Tanner," he identified himself.

But his name died on his lips when he saw the person standing in the tub. It certainly wasn't Darin Matthews.

It was a wet, naked woman.

A scream bubbled up from her throat. Beck cursed. He didn't know which one of them was more surprised.

Well, she wasn't armed. That was the first thing he noticed after the "naked" part. There wasn't a gun anywhere in sight. Just her.

Suddenly, that seemed more than enough.

Water slid off her face, her entire body, and her midnight-black hair clung to her neck and shoulders. Because he considered himself a gentleman, Beck tried not to notice her small, firm breasts and the triangular patch of hair at the juncture of her thighs.

But because he was a man, and because she was there right in front of him, he noticed despite his efforts to stop himself.

"Beckett Tanner," she spat out like profanity. She swept her left hand over various parts to cover herself while she groped for the white towel dangling over the nearby sink. "What the devil are you doing here?"

Did he know her? Because she obviously knew him.

Beck examined her face and picked through all that wet hair and water to see her features.

Oh, hell.

She was obviously older than the last time he'd seen her, which was…when? Just a little more than ten years ago when she was eighteen. Since then, her body and face had filled out, but those copper brown eyes were the same.

The last time he'd seen those eyes, she'd been silently hurtling insults at him. She was still doing that now.

"Faith Matthews," Beck grumbled. "What the devil are *you* doing here?"

She draped the towel in front of her and stepped from the tub. "I own the place."

Yeah. She did. Thanks to her mother's and sister's murders. Since her mother had legally disowned Faith's brother, the house had passed to Faith by default.

"The DA said you wanted to keep moving back quiet," Beck commented. "But he also said you wouldn't arrive in town until early next month."

Beck figured he'd need every minute of that month, too, so he could prepare his family for Faith's return. It was going to hit his sister-in-law particularly hard. That, in turn, meant it'd hit him hard.

What someone did to his family, they did to him.

And Faith Matthews had done a real number on the Tanners.

"I obviously came early." As if in a fierce battle with the terry cloth, she wound the towel around her.

"I didn't see your car," he pointed out.

She huffed. "Because I took a taxi from the Austin airport, all right? My car arrives tomorrow. Now that I've explained why I'm in my own home and how I got here, please tell me why you're trespassing."

She sounded like a lawyer. And was. Or rather a lawyer who was about to become the county's new assistant district attorney.

Beck had tried to convince the DA to turn down her job application, but the DA said she was the best qualified applicant and had hired her. That was the reason she was moving back. She wasn't moving back alone, either. She had a kid. A toddler named Aubrey, he'd heard. Not that motherhood would change his opinion of her. That opinion would always be low. And because LaMesa Springs was the county seat, that meant Faith would be living right under his nose, again. Worse, he'd have to work with her to get cases prosecuted.

Yeah, he needed that month to come to terms with that.

"I'm *trespassing* because I thought your brother was here," he explained. "The clerk at the convenience store on Sadler Street said he saw someone matching Darin's description night before last. The Rangers are still analyzing the surveillance video, and when they're done, I figure it'll be a match. So I came here because I wanted to arrest a killer."

"An *alleged* killer," she corrected. "Darin is innocent." The towel slipped, and he caught a glimpse of her right breast again. Her rose-colored nipple, too. She quickly righted the towel and mumbled something under her breath. "Before I got in the shower, I checked the doors and windows and made sure they were all locked. How'd you get in?"

"The back lock's broken. I noticed it when I came out here with the Texas Rangers. They assisted me with the investigation after your mother was killed."

Her intense stare conveyed her displeasure with his presence. "And you just happened to be in the neighborhood again tonight?"

Beck made sure his scowl conveyed some displeasure, too. "As I already said, I want to arrest a killer. I figure Darin will eventually come here. You did. So I've been driving by each night on my way home from work to see if he'll turn up."

She huffed and walked past him. Not a good idea. The doorway was small, and they brushed against each other, her butt against his thigh.

He ignored the pull he felt deep within his belly.

Yes, Faith was attractive, always had been, but she'd come within a hair of destroying his family. No amount of attraction would override that.

Besides, Faith had been his brother's one-night stand. She'd slept with a married man, and that encounter had nearly ruined his brother's marriage.

That alone made her his enemy.

Faith snatched up her clothes from the bed. "Well,

now that you know Darin's not here, you can leave the same way you came in."

"I will. First though, I need to ask some questions." In the back of his mind, he wondered if that was a good idea. She was only a few feet away…and naked under the towel. But Beck decided it was best to put his discomfort aside and worry less about her body and more about getting a killer off the streets.

"When's the last time you saw your brother?" he asked, without waiting to see if she'd agree to the impromptu interrogation.

With a death grip on the towel, she stared at him. Frowned. The frown deepened with each passing second. "Go stand over there," she said, pointing to the pair of front windows that were divided by a bare scarred oak dresser. "And turn your back. I want to get dressed, and I'd rather not do that with you gawking at me."

It was true. He had indeed gawked, and he wasn't proud of it. But then he wasn't proud of the way she'd stirred him up.

"Strange, I hadn't figured you for being modest," he mumbled, strolling toward the windows. He could see his SUV parked out front. It was something to keep his focus on, especially since he didn't want to angle his eyes in any direction in case he caught a glimpse of her naked reflection in the glass.

"Strange?" she repeated as if this insult had actually gotten to her. "I'd say it's equally *strange* that Beckett Tanner would still be making assumptions."

"What does that mean?" he fired back.

Her response was a figure-it-out-yourself grunt. "To answer your original question, I haven't seen Darin in nearly a year." Her words were clipped and angry. "That's in the statement I gave the Texas Rangers two months ago. I'm sure you read it."

Heck, he'd memorized it.

The part about her brother. Her sister's ex. Her estranged relationship with all members of her family. When the Rangers had asked her if Aubrey's father, Faith's own ex, could have some part in this, she'd adamantly denied it, claiming the man had never even seen Aubrey.

All of that had been in her statement, but over the years he'd learned that a written response wasn't nearly as good as the real thing.

"You haven't seen your brother in a long time, yet you don't think he's guilty?"

Silence.

Beck wished he'd waited to ask that particular question because he would have liked to have seen her reaction, but there wasn't any way he was going to turn around while she was dressing.

"Darin wouldn't hurt me," she finally said.

He rolled his eyes. "I'll bet your mother and sister thought the same thing."

"I don't think he killed them." Her opinion wasn't news to him. She had said the same in her interview with the Texas Rangers. "My sister's ex-boyfriend killed them."

Nolan Wheeler. Beck knew him because the man used to live in LaMesa Springs. He was as low-life as they came, and Beck along with the Texas Rangers had been looking for Nolan, who'd seemingly disappeared after giving his statement to the police in Austin.

Well, at least Faith hadn't changed her story over the

past two months. But then Beck hadn't changed his theory. "Nolan Wheeler has alibis for the murders."

"Thin alibis," Faith supplied. "Friends of questionable integrity who'll vouch for him."

"That's more than your brother has. According to what I read about Darin, he's mentally unstable, has been in and out of psychiatric hospitals for years, and he resented your mom and sister. On occasion, he threatened to kill them. He carried through on those threats, though I'll admit he might have had Nolan Wheeler's help."

"Now you think my brother had an accomplice?" Faith asked.

He was betting she had a snarky expression to go along with that snarky question. "It's possible. Darin isn't that organized."

Or that bright. The man was too scatterbrained and perhaps too mentally ill to have conceived a plan to murder two women without witnesses or physical evidence to link him to the crimes. And there was plenty of potential for physical evidence since both victims had been first shot with tranquilizer darts and then strangled. Darin didn't impress him as the sort of man who could carry out multistep murders or remember to wear latex gloves when strangling his victims.

Beck heard an odd sound and risked looking in her direction. She was dressed, thank goodness, in black pants and a taupe sweater. Simple but classy.

The sound had come from her kneeling to open a suitcase. She pulled out a pair of flat black shoes and slipped them on. Faith also took out a plush armadillo before standing, and she clutched onto it when she faced him head-on. She was about five-six. A good eight inches shorter than he was, and with the flats, Beck felt as if he towered over her.

"My brother has problems," she said as if being extra mindful of her word choice. "I don't need to tell you that we didn't have a stellar upbringing, and it affected Darin in a negative way."

It was the old bad blood between them that made him want to remind her that her family was responsible for the poor choices they'd made over the years.

Including what happened that December night ten years ago.

Even now, all these years later, Beck could still see Faith coming out of the Sound End motel with his drunk brother and shoving him into her car. She, however, had been as sober as a judge. Beck should know since, as a deputy at that time, he'd been the one to give her a Breathalyzer. She'd denied having sex with his brother, but there'd been a lot of evidence to the contrary, including his own brother's statement.

"You got something to say to me?" Faith challenged.

Not now. It could wait.

Instead, he glanced at the stuffed baby armadillo. It had a tag from a gift shop in the Austin airport and sported a pink bow around its neck. "I heard you had a baby." Because he was feeling ornery, he glanced at her bare ring finger.

"Yes." Those copper eyes drilled into him. "She's sixteen months old. And, no, I'm not married." The corner of her mouth lifted. Not a smile of humor though. "I guess that just confirms your opinion that I have questionable morals."

He lifted a shoulder and let it stand as his response

about that. "You think it's wise to bring a child to LaMesa Springs with a killer at large?"

She mimicked him by lifting her own shoulder, and she let the seconds drag on several moments before she continued. "I have a security company rep coming out first thing in the morning to install some equipment. Once he's finished, I'll call the nanny and have her bring my daughter. We'll stay at the hotel until I have some other repairs and updates done to the house." She glanced around the austere room before her gaze came back to his. "I intend to make this place a home for her."

That's what Beck was afraid she was going to say. This wasn't just about her new job. It was Faith Matthews's homecoming. Something he'd dreaded for ten years. "Even with all the bad memories, you still want to be here?"

Her mouth quivered. "Ah. Is this the part where you tell me I should think of living elsewhere? That I'm not welcome here in *your* town?"

He took a moment with his word selection as well. "You being here will make it hard for my family."

She had the decency to look uncomfortable about that. "I wish I could change that." And she sounded sincere. "But I can't go back and undo history. I can only move forward, and being assistant DA is a dream job for me. I won't walk away from that just because the Tanners don't want me here."

He could tell from the resolve in her eyes that he wasn't going to change her mind. Not that he thought he could anyway. At least he'd gotten his point across that there was still a lot of water under the bridge that his brother and she had built ten years ago in that motel.

But there was another point he had to make. "Even

with security measures, it might not be safe for you or your daughter. The man who killed your mother and sister is still out there."

Oh, she was about to disagree. He could almost hear the argument they were about to have. Maybe that wasn't a bad thing. A little air clearing. Except the old stench was so thick between them that it'd take more than an argument to clear it.

She opened her mouth. At the exact moment that Beck caught movement out of the corner of his eye.

Outside the window.

Front yard.

Going on gut instinct, Beck dove at Faith and tackled her onto the bed. He lifted his head and saw the shadowy figure. And worse, it looked as if their *visitor* had a gun pointed right at Faith and him.

Chapter 2

Faith managed a muffled gasp, but she couldn't ask Beck what the heck was going on. The tackle onto the bed knocked the breath from her.

She fought for air and failed. Beck had her pinned down. He was literally lying on her back, and his solid weight pushed her chest right into the hard mattress.

"Someone's out there," Beck warned. "I think he had a gun."

Just like that, she stopped struggling and considered who might be out there. None of the scenarios that came to mind were good. It was too late and too cold for a neighbor to drop by. Besides, she didn't have any nearby neighbors, especially anyone who'd want to pay her a friendly visit. Plus, there was Beck's reaction. He obviously thought this might turn dangerous.

She didn't have to wait long for that to be confirmed.

A sound blasted through the room. Shattering glass. A split-second later, something thudded onto the floor.

"A rock," Beck let her know.

A rock. Not exactly lethal in itself, but the person who'd thrown it could be a threat. And he might have a weapon.

Who had done this?

Better yet, why was Beckett Tanner sheltering her? He had put himself in between her and potential danger, and once she could breathe, Faith figured that maneuver would make more sense than it did now.

Because there was no chance he'd put himself in real harm's way to protect her.

"Get under the bed," Beck ordered. "And stay there."

He rolled off her, still keeping his body between her and the window. Starved for air, Faith dragged in an urgent breath and scrambled to the back side of the mattress so she could drop to the floor. She crawled beneath the bed amid dust bunnies and a few dead roaches.

Staying here tonight, alone, had obviously not been a good idea.

Worse, Faith didn't know why she'd decided at the last minute to stay. Her plan had been to check in to the hotel, to wait for the renovations to be complete and for the new furniture to arrive. But after stepping inside, she thought it was best to exorcise a few demons before trying to make the place "normal." So she'd sent the cab driver on his way, made a fire to warm up the place and got ready for bed.

Now someone had hurled a rock through her window.

There was another crashing sound. Another spray of glass. Another thud. Her stomach tightened into an acidy knot.

Beck got off the bed as well. Dropping onto the floor and staying low, he scurried to what was left of the window and peeked out.

"Can you see who's out there?" she asked.

He didn't answer her, but he did take a sliver-thin cell phone from his jeans pocket and called for backup. For some reason that made Faith's heart pound even harder. If this was a situation that Beck Tanner believed he couldn't handle alone, then it was *bad*.

She thought of Aubrey and was glad her little girl wasn't here to witness this act of vandalism, or whatever it was. Faith also thought of their future, how this would affect it. *If* it would affect it, she corrected. And then she thought of her brother. Was he the one out there in the darkness tossing those rocks? It was a possibility— a remote one—but Beck wouldn't believe it to be so remote.

Her brother, Darin, was Beck's number one murder suspect. She'd read every report she could get her hands on and every newspaper article written about the murders.

She didn't suspect Darin, though. She figured her sister's ex, Nolan Wheeler, was behind those killings. Nolan had a multipage arrest record, and her sister had even taken out a temporary restraining order against him.

For all the good it'd done.

Even with that restraining order, her sister, Sherry, had been murdered near her apartment on the outskirts of Austin. Their mother's death had happened twenty-four hours later in the back parking lot of the seedy liquor store where she worked in a nearby town. The murder had occurred after business hours, within minutes of her mother locking up the shop and going to her car. And even though Faith wasn't close to either of them and hadn't been for years, she'd mourned their loss and the brutal way their lives had ended.

Still staying low, Beck leaned over and studied one

of the rocks. It was smooth, about the size and color of a baked potato, and Faith could see that it had something written on it.

"What does it say?" she asked when Beck didn't read it aloud.

His hesitation seemed to last for hours. "It says, 'Leave or I'll have to kill you, too.'"

Mercy. So it was a threat. Someone didn't want her moving back to town. She watched Beck pick up the second rock.

Beck cursed under his breath. "It's from your brother."

Faith shook her head. "How do you know?"

"Because it says, 'I love you, but I can't stop myself from killing you. Get out,'" Beck grumbled. "I don't know how many people you know who both love you and want you dead. Darin certainly fits the bill. Of course, maybe he just wrote the message and had Wheeler toss it in here for him."

She swallowed hard, and the lump in her throat caused her to ache. God. This couldn't be happening.

Faith forced herself to think this through. Instead of Nolan being Darin's accomplice, Nolan himself could be doing this to set up her brother. Still, that didn't make it less of a threat.

"Listen for anyone coming in through the back door," Beck instructed.

There went her breath again. If Beck had been able to break in, then a determined killer or vandal would have no trouble doing the same.

Because she had to do something other than cower and wait for the worst, Faith crawled to the end of the bed where she'd placed her suitcase. After a few run-ins with

Nolan Wheeler, she'd bought a handgun. But she didn't have it with her. However, she did have pepper spray.

She retrieved the slender can from her suitcase and inched out a little so she could see what was going on. Beck was still crouched at the window, and he had his weapon ready and aimed into the darkness.

With that part of the house covered, she shifted her attention to the bedroom door. From her angle, she could see the kitchen, and if the rock thrower took advantage of that broken lock, he'd have to come through the kitchen to get to them. Thankfully, the moonlight piercing through the back windows allowed her to see that the room was empty.

"You don't listen very well," Beck snarled. "I told you to stay put."

She ignored his bark. Faith wouldn't make herself an open target, but she wanted to be in a position to defend herself.

"Do you see anyone out there?" she barked back.

She clamped her teeth over her bottom lip to stop the trembling. Not from fear. She was more angry than afraid. But with the gaping holes in the window, the winter wind was pushing its way through the room, and she was cold.

"No. But if I were a betting man, I'd say your brother's come back to eliminate his one and only remaining sibling—you."

"Maybe the person outside is after you?"

He glanced back at her. So brief. A split-second look. Yet, he conveyed a lot of hard skepticism with that glimpse.

"You're the sheriff," she reminded him. "You must have made enemies. Besides, my mother and sister have been dead for over two months. If that's Darin or their real killer out there, why would he wait this long to come after me? It's common knowledge that I was living in Oklahoma City and practicing law there for the past few years. Why not just come after me there?"

"A killer doesn't always make sense."

True. But there were usually patterns. Her mother and sister's killer had attacked them when they were alone. He hadn't been bold or stupid enough to try to shoot them with a police officer nearby. Of course, maybe the killer didn't realize that the car out front belonged to Beck, since it was his personal vehicle and not a cruiser. Therefore he wouldn't have known that Beck was there. She certainly hadn't been aware of it when she had been in that shower. Talk about the ultimate shock when she'd seen him standing there.

Her, stark naked.

Him, combing those smoky blue eyes all over her body.

"Dreamy eyes," the girls in school had called him. Dreamy eyes to go with a dreamy body, that toast-brown hair and quarterback's build.

Faith hadn't been immune to Beck's sizzling hot looks, either. She'd looked. But the looking stopped after the night he'd given her a Breathalyzer test at the motel.

A lot of things had stopped that night.

And there was no going back to that place. Even if those dreamy looks still made her feel all warm and willing.

"I hope you're having second and third thoughts about bringing your daughter here," Beck commented. He still had his attention fastened to the front of the house.

She was. But what was the alternative? If this was

Darin or her sister's slimy ex, then where could she take Aubrey so she'd be safe?

Nowhere.

That was a sobering and frightening thought.

But Beck was right about one thing. She needed to rethink this. Not the job. She wasn't going to run away from the job. However, she could do something about making this a safe place for Aubrey. And the first thing she'd do was to catch the person who'd thrown those rocks through her window.

She could start by having the handwriting analyzed. Footprints, too. Heck, she wanted to question the taxi driver to see if he'd told anyone that he'd dropped her off at the house. Someone had certainly learned quickly enough that she was there.

"I think the guy's gotten away by now," Faith let Beck know.

He didn't answer because his phone rang. Beck glanced at the screen and answered with a terse, "Where are you right now?" He paused, no doubt waiting for the answer. "Someone in front of the house threw rocks through the window. Check the area and let me know what you find."

Good. It was backup. If Nolan Wheeler or whoever was still out there, then maybe he'd be caught. Maybe this would all be over within the next few minutes. Then she could deal with this adrenaline roaring through her veins and get on with her life.

Faith waited there with her fingers clutched so tightly around the pepper spray that her hand began to cramp. The minutes crawled by, and they were punctuated by silence and the occasional surly glance from Beck.

He still hated her.

She could see it in his face. He still blamed her for that night with his brother. Part of her wanted to shout the truth of what'd happened, but he wouldn't believe her. Her own mother hadn't. And over the years she'd convinced herself that it didn't matter. That incident had given her a chip on her shoulder, and she'd used that chip and her anger to succeed. Coming back here, getting the job as the assistant district attorney, that was her proof that she'd risen above the albatross of her family's DNA.

"It's me," someone called out, causing her heart to race again.

But Beck obviously wasn't alarmed. He got to his feet and watched the man approach the window.

"I see some tracks," the man announced. "But if anybody's still out here, then he's freezing his butt off and probably hiding in the bushes across the road."

The man poked his face against the hole in the window, and she got a good look at him. It was Corey Winston. He'd been a year behind her in high school and somewhat of a smart mouth. These days, he was Beck's deputy. She'd learned that during her job interview with the district attorney.

Corey's insolent gaze met hers. "Faith Matthews." He used a similar tone to the one Beck had used when he first saw her. "What are you doing back in LaMesa Springs?"

"She's going to be the new assistant district attorney," Beck provided.

That earned her a raised eyebrow from Corey. "Now I've heard everything. You, the ADA? Well, you're not off to a good start. You breeze into town, your first night back, and you're already stirring up trouble, huh?"

The *huh* was probably added to make it sound a little

less insulting. But it only riled her more. She'd let jerks like Corey, and Beck, run her out of town ten years earlier, but they wouldn't succeed this time.

She would continue full speed ahead, and if that included arresting her own brother, she'd do it and carry out her lawful duties. Of course, because of a personal conflict, the DA himself would have to prosecute the case, but she would fully cooperate. It helped that she had been estranged from her mother and sister. That wouldn't help with Darin. It would hurt. But duty had to come first here.

Beck reholstered his gun and glanced around at the glass on the floor. "Secure the scene," he told Corey. "Cast at least one of the footprints, and I'll send it to the lab in Austin. We might get lucky."

"You think it's worth it?" Corey challenged. But his defiance went down a notch when Beck stared at him. "It just seems like a lot of trouble to go through considering this was probably done by those Kendrick kids. You know those boys have too much time on their hands and nobody at home to see what they're up to."

"There's a killer on the loose," Beck reminded him.

That reminder, however, didn't stop Corey from scowling at Faith before he turned from the window and got to work. He grumbled something indistinguishable under his breath.

Beck looked at her then. He wasn't exactly sporting a scowl like Corey, but it was close. "I need you to come with me to my office so I can take a statement."

It was standard operating procedure. Something that needed to be done, just in case it had been the killer outside that window. Besides, she didn't want to be alone in the house. Not tonight. Maybe not ever. She would truly have to rethink making this place a home for Aubrey.

Faith grabbed her purse and got ready to go.

"I don't believe it was the Kendrick kids who threw those rocks," Beck said to her.

That stopped her in her tracks. "You think it was Darin?" she challenged.

"If not Darin, then let's play around with your assumption, that your mom and sister's killer was Sherry's ex, Nolan Wheeler." He hitched his thumb toward the broken glass. "If Nolan was outside that window tonight, he could want to do you harm."

She shook her head. "Stating the obvious here, but if that's true, why wait until now?"

"Because you were here, alone. Or so he thought. You were an easy target."

Faith zoomed in on the obvious flaw in his theory. "And his motive for wanting me dead?"

"Maybe Nolan thinks you'll use your new job to come after him for the two murders. He might even think that's why you've come back."

She opened her mouth to deny it, but she couldn't. In fact, that's exactly the way Nolan would think.

Other than in confidence to her boss, Faith hadn't announced to anyone in Oklahoma that she had accepted the job in LaMesa Springs.

Not until this morning.

This morning, she'd also called LaMesa Springs' DA to tell him she would be arriving. She had arranged for renovations and a security system for the house. She'd made lots and lots of calls, and anyone could have found out her plans.

Anyone, including Nolan.

"Where's your daughter right now?" Beck asked. His tone alone would have alarmed her, but there was more than a sense of urgency in his expression.

"Aubrey's still in Oklahoma with her nanny. Why?"

"Because I was just trying to put myself in Nolan's place. If he came here to scare you off and it didn't work, then what will he do next?" His stare was a warning. "If he's got an accomplice or if it was his accomplice who just tossed those rocks, that means one of them could be here in LaMesa Springs and the other could be in Oklahoma."

Her heart dropped to her knees.

Beck took a step toward her. "Either Darin or Nolan might try to use your daughter to get to you."

"Oh, God."

Faith grabbed her phone from her purse and prayed that it wasn't too late to keep Aubrey safe.

Chapter 3

By Beck's calculation, Faith had been pacing in his office for three hours while she waited for her daughter to arrive. Even when she'd been on the phone, which was a lot, or while giving her official statement to him, she still paced. And while she did that, she continued to check her delicate silver watch.

The minutes were probably dragging by for her.

They certainly were for him.

Beck tried to keep himself occupied with routine paperwork and notes on his current cases. Normally he liked keeping busy. But this wasn't a normal night.

Faith Matthews was in his office, mere yards away, and sooner or later he was going to have to break the news to his family that she'd returned. Since it was going on midnight, Beck had opted for later, but he knew, with the gossip mill always in full swing, that if he didn't tell his father, brother and sister-in-law by morning—early morning, at that—then they'd find out from some other source.

As if she knew what he was thinking, Faith tossed him a glance from over her shoulder.

Despite the vigor of her pacing, she was exhausted. Her eyes were sleep-starved, and her face was pale and tight with tension. On some level he understood that tension.

Her daughter might be in danger, and she was waiting for the little girl to arrive with her nanny and the Texas Ranger escort from the Austin airport. Beck hadn't had the opportunity to be around many babies, but he figured the parental bond was strong, and the uncertainty was driving Faith crazy.

"You're staring at me," she grumbled.

Yeah. He was.

Beck glanced back at his desk, but the glance didn't take. For some stupid reason, his attention went straight back to Faith. To her tired expression. Her tight muscles. The still damp hair that she hadn't had a chance to dry after her shower.

Noticing her hair immediately made him uncomfortable. But then so did Faith. Dealing with a scrawny eighteen-year-old was one thing, but Faith was miles away from being that girl. She was poised and polished, even now despite the damp hair. A woman in every sense of the word.

Hell. That made him uncomfortable, too.

"I figure you're having second thoughts about accepting the ADA job," he grumbled, hoping conversation would help. It was a fishing expedition since she'd kept her thoughts to herself the entire time she had been waiting for her daughter and the nanny to arrive.

"You wish," she tossed at him. "The DA and the city

council want me here, and I have to just keep telling myself that not everyone in town hates me like the Tanners."

Okay. No second thoughts. Well, not any that she would likely voice to him. She had dug in her heels, unlike ten years ago when she'd left town running. Part of him, the part he didn't want to acknowledge, admired her for not wavering in her plans. She certainly hadn't shown much backbone or integrity ten years ago.

She flipped open her cell phone again and pressed redial. Beck didn't have to ask who she was calling. He knew it was the nanny. Faith had called the woman at least every half hour.

"How much longer?" Faith asked the moment the woman apparently answered. The response made her relax a bit, and she seemed to breathe easier when she added, "See you then."

"Good news?" he asked when she didn't share.

"They'll be here in about fifteen minutes." She raked her hair away from her face. "I should have just gone to the airport to meet them."

"The Texas Rangers didn't want you to do that," Beck reminded her, though he was certain she already knew that. The Ranger lieutenant and her new boss, the DA, had ordered her to stay put at the sheriff's office.

The order was warranted. It was simply too big of a risk for her to go gallivanting all over central Texas when there might be a killer on her trail.

"So what's the plan when your daughter arrives?" Beck asked.

"Since the Texas Rangers said they'll be providing security, we'll check in to the hotel on Main Street." She didn't hesitate, which meant, in addition to the calls and pacing, she'd obviously given it plenty of thought.

"Then tomorrow morning, I can start putting some security measures in place."

He'd overheard her conversations with the Rangers about playing bodyguard and the other conversation about those measures. She was having a high-tech security system installed in her childhood home. In a whispered voice, she'd asked the price, which told Beck that she didn't have an unlimited budget. No surprise there. Faith had come from poor trash, and it'd no doubt taken her a while to climb out of that. She probably didn't have money to burn.

She made a soft sound that pulled his attention back to her. It was a faint groan. Correction, a moan. And for the first time since he'd seen her in the shower, there was a crack in that cool composure.

"I have to know if you're a real sheriff," she said, her voice trembling. "I have to know if it comes down to it that you'll protect my daughter."

Because the vulnerable voice had distracted him, it took him a second to realize she'd just insulted the hell out of him.

Beck stood and met her eye-to-eye. "This badge isn't decoration, Faith," he said, and he tapped the silver star clipped to his belt.

She just stared at him, apparently not convinced. "I want you to swear that you'll protect Aubrey."

Riled now, Beck walked closer. Actually, too close. No longer just eye-to-eye, they were practically toe-to-toe. "I. Swear. I'll. Protect. Aubrey." He'd meant for his tone to be dangerous. A warning for her to back down.

She didn't. "Good."

Faith actually sounded relieved, which riled him even

more. Hell's bells. What kind of man did she think he was if he wouldn't do his job and protect a child?

Or Faith, for that matter?

And why did it suddenly feel as if he wanted to protect her?

Oh, yeah. He remembered. She was attractive, and mixed with all that sudden vulnerability, he was starting to feel, well, protective.

Among other things.

"Thank you," she added.

It was so sincere, he could feel it.

So were the tears that shimmered in her eyes. Sincere tears that she quickly blinked back. "For the record, I'm a good lawyer. And I'll be a good ADA." Now she dodged his gaze. "I have to succeed at this. For Aubrey. I want her to be proud of me, and I want to be proud of myself. I'll convince the people of this town that I'm not that same girl who tried to run away from her past."

She turned and waved him off, as if she didn't want him to respond to that. Good thing. Because Beck had no idea what to say. He preferred the angry woman who'd barked at him in the shower. He preferred the Faith that'd turned tail and run ten years ago.

This woman in front of him was going to be trouble.

His brother had once obviously been attracted to her. Beck could see why. Those eyes. That hair.

That mouth.

His body started to build a stupid fantasy about Faith's mouth when thankfully there was a rap at his door. Judging from Corey's raised eyebrow, he hadn't missed the way Beck had been looking at Faith.

"What?" Beck challenged.

Corey screwed up his mouth a moment to indicate his

displeasure. "I took a plaster of one of the footprints like you said. It's about a size ten. That's a little big for one of the Kendrick kids."

Beck had never believed this was a prank. Heck, he wasn't even sure it was a scare tactic. Those rocks had been meant to send Faith running, and Beck didn't think the killer was finished.

"I'll send the plaster and the two rocks to the Rangers lab in Austin tomorrow morning." With that, Corey walked away.

Realizing that he needed to put some distance between him and Faith, Beck took a couple of steps away from her.

"My brother wears a size-ten shoe," Faith provided.

He stopped moving away and stared at her again. "So does your sister's ex, Nolan."

She blinked, apparently surprised he would know that particular detail.

"Even though the murders didn't happen here in my jurisdiction, I've been studying his case file," Beck explained.

Another blink. "I hope that means you're close to figuring out who killed my mother and sister."

"I've got it narrowed down just like you do." He shrugged. "You think it's Nolan. I think it's your brother, Darin, working with Nolan. The only other person I need to rule out is your daughter's father."

She folded her arms over her chest. Looked away. "He's not in the picture."

"So you said in your statement to the Rangers, but I have to be sure that he's not the one who put those rocks through the window."

"I'm sure he has no part in this," she snapped. "And

that brings us back to Darin and Nolan. Darin really doesn't have a motive to come after me—"

"But he does," Beck interrupted. "It could be the house and the rest of what your mother owned."

Faith shook her head. "My mother disowned Darin four years ago. He can't inherit anything."

"Does your brother know that?"

"Darin knows." There was a lot emotion and old baggage that came with the admission. The disinheritance had probably sparked a memorable family blowup. Beck would take her word for it that Darin had known he couldn't benefit financially from the murders.

"That leaves Nolan," Beck continued. "While you were on the phone, I did some checking. Your sister, Sherry, lived with Nolan for years, long enough for them to have a common-law marriage. And even though they hadn't cohabited in the eighteen months prior to her death, they never divorced. That means he'd legally be your mother's next of kin…if you and your daughter were out of the way."

Her eyes widened, and her arms uncrossed and dropped to her sides. "You think Nolan would kill me to inherit that rundown house?"

"Not just the house. It comes with three acres of land and any other assets your mother left. She only specified in her will that her belongings would go to her next of kin, with the exclusion of Darin."

"The land, the house and the furniture are worth a hundred thousand, tops," she pointed out.

"People have killed for a lot less. That's why I alerted every law-enforcement agency to pick up Nolan the moment he's spotted. I want him in custody so I can question him."

That caused her to chew on her bottom lip, and Beck wondered if she was ready to change her mind about staying in town. "I have to draw up my will ASAP. I can write it so that Nolan can't inherit a penny. And then I need to let him know that. That'll stop any attempts to kill me."

Maybe.

Unless there was a different reason for the murders.

The front door opened, and just like that, Faith raced out of his office and into the reception area. Corey was at the desk, by the dispatch phone, and Faith practically flew right past him to get to the three people who'd just stepped inside.

A Texas Ranger and a sixtysomething-year-old Hispanic woman carrying a baby in pink corduroy overalls and a long-sleeved lacy white shirt. Aubrey.

Faith pulled the little girl into her arms and gave her a tight hug. Aubrey giggled and bounced, the movement causing her mop of brunette hair to bounce as well.

Beck hadn't really known what to expect when it came to Faith's daughter, but he'd at least thought the child would be sleeping at this time of night. She wasn't. She was alert, smiling, and her brown eyes were the happiest eyes he'd ever seen.

"Sgt. Egan Caldwell," the Ranger introduced himself first to Beck and then to Faith.

"Sheriff Beck Tanner."

"Marita Dodd," the nanny supplied. Unlike the little girl, this woman's dark eyes showed stress, concern and even some fear. She was petite, barely five feet tall, and a hundred pounds, tops, but even with her demure size and sugar-white hair, she had an air of authority about her. "Aubrey's obviously got her second wind. Unlike the rest of us."

"Ms. Matthews," the Ranger said to Faith. "Could I have word with you?" He didn't add the word *alone,* but his tone certainly implied it.

"Of course." After another kiss on the cheek, Faith passed the child back to the nanny, and she and Sgt. Caldwell went to the other side of the reception area to have a whispered conversation.

Beck watched Faith's expression to see if she was about to get bad news, but if her brother had been caught or was dead, then why hadn't the Ranger told Beck as well? After all, Beck was assisting with the case.

"I really have to go the ladies' room," Marita Dodd said. That brought Beck's attention back to her.

"Down the hall, last room on the right," Beck instructed.

But Marita didn't go. She glanced at Aubrey, then at Faith, and finally thrust Aubrey in his direction. "Would you mind holding her a minute?"

Beck was sure his mouth dropped open. But if Marita noticed his stunned response, she didn't react. Aubrey reacted though. The little girl went right to him. Straight into his arms.

And then she did something else that stunned Beck.

Aubrey grinned and planted a warm, sloppy kiss on his cheek.

That rendered him speechless and cut his breath. Man. That baby kiss and giggle packed a punch. In that flash of a moment, he got it. He understood the whole parent thing and why men wanted to be fathers.

He got it, and he tried to push it aside.

This was the last child on earth to whom he should have an emotional response.

Aubrey babbled something he didn't understand and cocked her head to the side as if waiting for him to reply. She kept those doe eyes on him.

"I don't know," Beck finally answered.

That caused her to smile again, and she aimed her tiny fingers at the Ranger vehicle parked just outside the window. "Tar," she said as if that explained everything.

"Car?" Beck questioned, not sure what he was supposed to say.

"Tar," she repeated. Then added, "Bye-bye."

Another smile. Another kiss that left his cheek wet and smelling like baby's breath. And she wound her plump arms around his neck. The child obviously wasn't aware that he was a stranger at odds with her mother.

Beck was having a hard time remembering that, too.

Well, he was until he heard Faith storming his way. Her footsteps slapped against the hardwood floor. "Aubrey," she said, taking the child from his arms.

While Beck understood Faith's displeasure at having him hold her baby, Aubrey showed some displeasure, too.

"No, no, no," Aubrey protested and reached for Beck again. She waggled her fingers at him, a gesture that Beck thought might mean "come here."

"This won't take but another minute," the Ranger interjected. He obviously wasn't finished talking to Faith.

Faith huffed. Aubrey continued to struggle to get back to Beck, and she clamped her small but persistent hand onto the front of his shirt. They were still in the middle of the little battle when the phone rang. The deputy, Corey, answered it, but immediately passed the phone to Beck.

"It's your brother," Corey announced.

Great. This was not a conversation Beck wanted to have tonight.

Faith practically snapped to attention, and despite Aubrey's protest, she carried the child back across the room and resumed her conversation with the Ranger.

"Pete," Beck greeted his brother. "What can I do for you?"

"You can tell me if what I heard is true," Pete stated. "Is Faith Matthews back in town?"

Because he was going to need it, Beck took a deep breath. "She's here."

With that, Faith angled her eyes in his direction. Hearing his brother's voice and seeing Faith was a much-needed reminder of the past.

"Why did she come back?" Pete didn't ask in anger. There was more dread in his voice than anything else.

"She's the new assistant district attorney. I didn't tell you sooner because I didn't think she was coming until next month. It wasn't my decision to hire her. It was the DA's."

"It's for sure? The DA actually hired her?"

"Yeah. It's for sure."

"Then I'll have a chat with him," Pete insisted.

Beck had already had that chat, and the DA wouldn't budge. Pete wouldn't, either. His brother would talk and argue with the DA, too, but in the end the results would be the same—Faith would still be the new ADA.

"In the meantime, you do whatever it takes to get Faith Matthews away from here," Pete continued. "I don't want her upsetting Nicole."

Nicole, Pete's wife of nearly a dozen years. This would definitely upset her. Nicole was what his grandmother would have called high-strung. An argument would give

Nicole a migraine. A fender bender would send her running to her therapist over in Austin.

This would devastate her.

"There's a lot to be resolved," Beck told his brother.

"What does that mean?"

Heck, he was just going to say it even though he knew Faith would overhear it. "It means Faith might change her mind about staying."

Yeah, that earned him a glare from her. He hadn't expected anything less. But then she glared at whatever the Ranger said, too. Her glare was followed by a look of extreme shock. Wide eyes. Drained color from her cheeks. Her mouth trembled, and he wasn't thinking this was a fear reaction. More like anger.

"I'll call you back in the morning," Beck continued with his brother. "In the meantime, get some sleep."

"Right." With that final remark, Pete hung up.

Beck hung up, too, and braced himself for the next round of battle he was about to have with Faith. But when he saw her expression, he rethought that battle. No more shock. Something had taken the fight right out of her.

Sgt. Caldwell stopped talking to Faith and made his way back to Beck. "I got a call on the drive over here. The crime lab reviewed the surveillance disk you sent us. The one from Doolittle's convenience store. They were able to positively identify your suspect."

Beck let that sink in a moment. Across the room while holding a babbling happy baby, Faith was obviously doing the same.

"So Darin Matthews was in LaMesa Springs?" Beck clarified.

The Ranger nodded. "We can also place him just five

miles from here. About four hours ago, he filled up at a gas station on I-35."

Everything inside Beck went still. "Any reason he wasn't arrested?"

"The clerk thought Darin looked familiar, but he didn't make the connection with the wanted pictures in the newspaper until Darin had already driven away. But the store had auto security feeds to the company that monitors them, and that means we had fast access to the surveillance video. That's how we were able to make such a quick ID."

So Darin had come back, and he might have thrown those rocks with the threatening messages through Faith's window. "You didn't see Nolan Wheeler on either surveillance feed?" Beck asked.

"No. But that doesn't mean he wasn't there. He could have been out of camera range."

Beck snared Faith's gaze. "Does this mean you're leaving?"

She didn't jump to defend herself. Her mouth tightened, she kissed the top of Aubrey's head and looked at Sgt. Caldwell. "They want me to be bait."

Beck repeated that, certain he'd misunderstood. "Bait?"

"An enticement," the Ranger clarified. "We believe there's only one person who can get Darin Matthews to surrender peacefully, and that's his sister."

True. But Beck could see the Texas-size holes in this so-called plan. "She's got a kid. Being bait isn't safe for either of them."

Sgt. Caldwell nodded. "We're going to minimize the risks."

"How?" Beck demanded.

"By making her brother think he can get to her. No matter where she goes, she'll be in danger. Her baby, too. My lieutenant thinks it's best if we make a stand. Here. Where we know Darin is."

Beck cursed under his breath, but he bit off the rest of the profanity when he realized Aubrey was smiling at him. "So what's the plan to keep her and that little girl safe?"

"The lieutenant wants to set up a trap to lure Darin back. We'll alert all the businesses in town and the surrounding area to be on the lookout for Matthews. Meanwhile, we'll put security measures in place for Ms. Matthews's house while she's at the hotel tonight."

"Her house?" Beck questioned. He didn't like anything about this plan. "You honestly expect her to stay there after what happened tonight? Someone threw rocks through her window."

Another nod. "She won't actually be staying at the house. She'll just make an appearance of sorts, but we'll tell everyone in town that's where she'll be staying."

Beck felt a little relief. "So Faith and her daughter will be going to a safe house?"

The sergeant glanced back at Faith, and it was she who continued. "Not exactly. I can't live in a safe house for the rest of my life, and Darin won't be able to find me if I'm hidden away. So the Rangers want to set up a secure place for Aubrey and the nanny. I'll be there, too, while making appearances at my house to coax out Darin. Obviously, we can't have Aubrey in harm's way, but my brother would know something was up if Aubrey's in one location and I'm in another. So we have to make it look as if she's with me even though she'll be far from danger." She paused, moistened her lips. "I'm hoping it won't take long for my brother to show, especially since he's already in the area."

So she agreed with this plan. But for someone in agreement, she certainly didn't seem pleased about it.

"If it weren't for Aubrey, I would have never gone along with this," she stated.

Confused, Beck shook his head. "Excuse me?"

"She means the protective custody issue," Sgt. Caldwell explained.

Beck sure didn't like the sound of this. "What about it? She doesn't want to be in the Rangers' protective custody?"

"No." Faith hesitated after her terse answer. "I don't want Aubrey to be in yours."

"Mine?" Beck felt as if someone had slugged him.

"Yours," Caldwell verified. "The Rangers will continue to provide you assistance on the case, but with a possible suspect in your jurisdiction, this is now your investigation, Sheriff Tanner."

"What are you saying exactly?"

The Ranger looked him straight in the eyes. "I'm saying we'll need your help. We can't risk it being leaked that Ms. Matthews really isn't staying at her place. And we can't keep her real whereabouts concealed if she's in the hotel for any length of time. There are too many employees there who could let it slip."

Beck's hands went on his hips. "So where do you propose her daughter and she go?"

"First, to the hotel to give us time to set up some security. Then, when everything's in place, they can go to your house. Her daughter will be in your protective custody." The Ranger didn't even hesitate.

It took Beck a moment to get his jaw unclenched so

he could speak. "Let me get this straight. I'll become a bodyguard and babysitter in my own home?"

Sgt. Caldwell gave a crisp nod. "Protecting the child will be your primary task." The Ranger glanced at Faith again. Frowned. Then turned back to Beck. "Ms. Matthews has refused to be in your protective custody."

Her left eyebrow lifted a fraction when Beck's attention landed on her. "Yet you'd trust me with your daughter?" Beck asked.

"This wasn't her idea," Sgt. Caldwell interjected, though Faith had already opened her mouth to answer. "I had to convince her that this was the fastest and most efficient way to keep the child safe. And as for her not being in your protective custody, well, you can call it what you want, but it won't change what you have to do."

Beck stared at the Ranger. "And what exactly do I have to do?"

Sgt. Caldwell stared back. "Once we have this plan in place, Faith and her daughter's safety will be *your* responsibility."

Chapter 4

This was not the homecoming Faith had planned.

From the window of the third-floor "VIP suite" of the Bluebonnet Hotel, she stared down at the town's equivalent of morning rush hour. Cars trickled along the two-lane Main Street flanked with refurbished antique streetlights. The sidewalks were busy but not exactly bustling as people walked past the rows of quaint shops and businesses. Many of the townsfolk stopped to say "Good morning."

There were lots of smiles.

She wanted to be part of what was going on below. She wanted to dive right into her new life. But instead she was stuck inside the hotel, waiting for "orders" from Beck and the Texas Rangers, while one of Beck's deputies guarded the door to make sure no one got in.

The three-room suite was a nice enough place with its soothing Southwest decor. Her and Aubrey's room was small but tastefully decorated with cool aqua walls and muted coral bedding. Marita's room was similar, just slightly smaller, and the shared sitting room had a functional, golden-pine desk and a Saltillo tile floor.

It reminded Faith of a gilded cage.

Of course, anything less than getting on with her new life would feel that way.

She forced herself to finish the now cold coffee that room service had delivered an hour earlier. She already had a pounding headache, and without the caffeine, it would only get worse. She had to be able to think clearly today.

What she really needed was a new plan.

Or a serious modification of the present one.

Aubrey was now in Beck's protective custody and he was responsible for her safety. Right. What was wrong with this picture?

She went back to the desk, sank down onto the chair and glanced at the notes she'd made earlier. It was her list of possible courses of action. Unfortunately, the list was short.

Option one: she could immediately leave LaMesa Springs, and go into hiding. But that would be no life for Aubrey. Besides, she had to work. She couldn't live off her savings for more than six months at most.

Faith crossed off option one.

Option two: she could arrange for a private bodyguard. Again, that would eat into her savings, but it was a short-term solution that she would definitely consider. Plus, she knew someone in the business, and while things hadn't worked out personally between them, she hoped he could give her a good deal.

And then there was option three, and it would have to be paired with option two: try to speed up her brother's and Nolan's captures. The only problem was that other than making herself an even more obvious target, she wasn't sure how to do that. Maybe she could make an appeal on the local TV or radio stations? Or maybe she could just step foot inside her house a few times.

She already felt like a target anyway.

Frustrated, she set her coffee cup aside and grabbed a pen, hoping to add to the meager list. She sat, pen poised but unmoving over the paper, and she waited for inspiration to strike. It didn't.

The bedroom door opened, and Marita came out. Behind her toddled Aubrey, dressed in a pink eyelet lace dress, white leggings and black baby saddle oxfords. Just the sight of her instantly lightened Faith's mood.

"'i," Aubrey greeted her. It was her latest attempt at "hi" and she added a wave to it.

"Hi, yourself." Faith scooped her up in her arms and kissed her on the cheek.

"She ate every bite of her oatmeal," Marita reported. "And getting to bed so late doesn't seem to have bothered her." Marita patted her hand over a big yawn. "Wish I could say the same for my old bones."

"Yes. I'm sorry about that."

"Not your fault." Marita went to the window and looked out. "You warned me that some folks in this town wouldn't open their arms to you." She paused. "Guess Sheriff Tanner is one of those folks."

It wasn't a question, but Faith knew the woman wanted and deserved answers. After all, Marita had essentially been part of her family since Faith had hired her fifteen months ago as Aubrey's nanny. Faith had gotten Marita through an employment agency, but their short history together didn't diminish her feelings and respect for Marita.

"I left town ten years ago because of a scandal," Faith said, hoping she could get this out without emotion straining her voice. "Beck saw me coming out of a motel with his brother, Pete. His married brother. Word quickly got around, and his brother's wife attempted suicide because she was so distraught. Beck blames me for that."

Marita turned from the window, folded her arms over her chest and stared at Faith. "You *were* with the sheriff's married brother?"

Aubrey started to fuss when she spotted the stuffed armadillo on the settee, and Faith eased her to the floor so she could go after it.

"I was with him at the hotel." But Faith shook her head. She wasn't explaining this to Beck, who would challenge her every word. Marita would believe her. "But I didn't have sex with him. It didn't help that I couldn't tell the whole truth." She lowered her voice so that Aubrey wouldn't hear, even though she was much too young to understand. "It also didn't help that there were used condoms in the motel room. And when Beck found us, Pete was groping at me."

Marita made a sound of displeasure. "Beck was an idiot not to see what was really going on. You're not the sort to go after a married man." She glanced at the papers on the desk and frowned again. "Is that what I think it is?" Marita pointed to the document header, Last Will and Testament.

"I wrote it this morning." She noted the shocked look on Marita's face. "No, I'm not planning to die anytime soon. I just need to let someone know that he won't inherit anything in the event of my demise."

Faith didn't have time to explain that further because

her cell phone rang. Since she was expecting several important calls, she answered it right away.

"Zack Henley," the caller identified himself. "I'm the driver who took you from the airport to LaMesa Springs last night. You left a message with my boss saying to call you, that it was important."

"It is. I need to know if you told anyone that you'd taken me to my house."

"Told anyone?" he repeated. He sounded not only surprised but cautious.

Faith rephrased it. "Is it possible that someone in LaMesa Springs learned that you had driven me to my house?"

He stayed quiet a moment. "I might have mentioned it to the guy at the convenience store."

That grabbed her attention. "Which guy and which convenience store?"

"Doolittle's, I think is the name of it."

The same store where her brother had been sighted. "And who did you tell about me?"

"I didn't tell, exactly. I mean, I didn't go in the place to blab about you, but the guy asked me what a cab driver was doing in LaMesa Springs, and I told him I'd dropped someone off on County Line Road. He asked who, and I told him. I knew your name because you paid with your credit card, and you didn't say anything about keeping it a secret."

No. She hadn't, but she also hadn't expected to be threatened with those tossed rocks. Or with the possibility that her brother had been the one to do the threatening. "Describe the person you spoke to."

"What's this all about?" he asked.

"Just describe him please." Faith used her courtroom voice, hoping it would save time.

"I don't remember how he looked, but he was the clerk behind the counter. A young kid. Maybe nineteen or twenty. Oh, yeah, and he had a snake tattoo on his neck."

She released the breath she didn't even know she'd been holding and jotted down the description. That wasn't a description of her brother. But it didn't mean this clerk hadn't said something to anyone else. Or her brother could have even been there, listening.

"Thank you," she told the cab driver.

Faith hung up and grabbed the Yellow Pages so she could find the number of the convenience store. She had to talk to that clerk. But before she could even locate the number, there was a knock at the door. Faith reached for her pepper spray, only to remind herself that there was a deputy outside and that a killer probably wouldn't knock first.

"It's me, Beck," the visitor called out.

Faith groaned, unlocked the door and opened it. It was Beck all right. Wearing jeans, a blue button-up and a walnut-colored, leather rodeo jacket. The jacket wasn't a fashion statement, though on him it could have been. It was as well-worn as his jeans and cowboy boots.

"My deputy needed a break," Beck explained. He didn't move closer until Aubrey came walking his way.

"'i,'" Aubrey said, grinning from ear to ear. It was adorable. But in Faith's opinion that cuteness was aimed at the wrong person.

Beck, however, obviously wasn't able to resist that grin either because he smiled and stepped around Faith to come inside the suite.

"Is she ever in a bad mood?" he asked, keeping his focus on Aubrey.

"Wait 'til nap time," Marita volunteered. Unlike Aubrey's cheerfulness, Marita's voice had an unfriendly edge to it.

When Aubrey began to babble and show Beck the armadillo, he knelt down so that he'd be at her eye level. "That's a great-looking toy you got there."

"Dee-o," Aubrey explained, giving him her best attempt to say "armadillo." She put the toy right in Beck's face and didn't pull it back until he'd kissed it.

Aubrey giggled and threw her arms around Beck's neck as if she'd known him her entire life. The hug was brief, mere seconds, before she pulled back and pointed to the silver badge he had clipped to his belt.

"See?" Aubrey said. "Wanta see."

And much to Faith's surprise, Beck unclipped it and handed it to her so she could "see."

Frustrated with the friendly exchange, Faith shut the door with more force than necessary. Beck seemed to become aware of the awkward situation, and he stood.

"We need to talk," he told her, suddenly sounding very sherifflike.

That was obviously Marita's cue to give them some privacy, so she came across the room and picked up Aubrey. However, she stopped and looked at Beck. "Maybe this time you'll be willing to see the truth," she snarled. She took the badge from Aubrey and handed it back to him.

"What does that mean?" Beck asked, volleying confused glances between Faith and Marita.

"Nothing," Faith said at the same time that Marita

said, "She wasn't with your brother that night. Faith's not like that."

And with that declaration which would be hard to explain, Marita started walking. Aubrey waved and said, "Bye-bye," before the two disappeared into the bedroom.

"Don't ask," Faith warned him.

"Why not?"

"Because you won't believe me."

He lifted his shoulder. "What's not to believe? Didn't you tell me the truth ten years ago?"

"I told you I hadn't slept with your brother. That's the truth."

"He said otherwise."

She huffed and wondered why she was still trying to explain this all this time later. "Pete was drunk, and he lied, maybe because he was too drunk to know the truth. Or maybe because he didn't want you to know what'd really happened. I didn't seduce him, and I didn't take him to that motel. The only thing I tried to do was get him out of there."

Faith stopped when she noted his stony expression. "You know what? Enough of this. I don't owe you anything." To give herself a moment to calm down, she went to the desk and glanced at the notes she'd taken earlier. "I need to question a clerk at Doolittle's convenience store. The cabbie who drove me home told this clerk that I was in town. I want to find out who else knew so I can figure out who threw those rocks."

Beck just stared at her.

Unnerved and still riled, Faith continued, "You said we had something to discuss, and I don't think you meant personal stuff."

"Why would Pete lie about being with you?" He walked closer, stopping just a few inches away.

Why didn't he just drop this? "Ask him. For now, stick to business, *Sheriff*."

"The personal stuff between us keeps interfering with the business."

He caught her arm when she started to move away. Faith looked down at his grip, but he didn't let go of her. He kept those gunmetal-blue eyes nailed to her, and though she hadn't thought it possible, he got even closer. So close that she could smell coffee and sugar on his breath.

Faith hiked up her chin and met his gaze. "Be careful," she warned. She meant her voice to sound sharp and stern. It didn't quite work out that way.

Because something changed.

With his hand on her, with him so close, old feelings began to tug at her. She'd once been hotly attracted to him. A lifetime ago. But those years suddenly seemed to melt away.

She was still attracted to him. And this time, she didn't think it was one-sided.

She was toast.

"The Rangers installed some security equipment at your house," Beck said. His voice wasn't strained. Nor angry. He sounded confused, and the subject didn't fit the slow simmer in the air.

"Good," she managed to answer. She tried to step away, but he held on. And she didn't fight him.

She was obviously losing her mind.

"The Rangers dressed like security technicians so anyone looking wouldn't realize the authorities had staked out the place." He paused. His jaw muscles stirred.

"There. That's what I came to say. Now, let's finish this." He shook his head. Cursed. Shook his head again. And finally, he let go of her and took a step back. "This can't happen between us."

"You're right. It can't."

Neither of them looked relieved.

And neither of them looked as if they believed it.

That tug inside her pulled harder. So hard that she moved away and returned to the window. She needed a few deep breaths before she could continue. "I want a different plan than the one the Rangers came up with."

He paused. Nodded. Nodded again. "I'm listening."

It took her a moment to realize that was all he was going to say. "Well, I don't *have* a different plan," she admitted. "I just *want* one."

"Welcome to the club. I sat up most of the night trying to make a list of options."

She huffed and glanced at her list. "Since Sgt. Caldwell made it clear that the Rangers don't have the manpower to provide protection for Aubrey, Marita and me, I was thinking of hiring a private bodyguard from Harland Securities in San Antonio. A friend owns the company."

"Ross Harland," Beck provided. "I've heard of him. He's your friend?"

"We used to date." Though she had no idea why she'd just told him that, especially since things hadn't ended that well between Ross and her. Ross might not even want to talk to her, but that wouldn't stop her from trying. "I plan to call him this morning and ask if he can help."

"You mean so that Aubrey and you won't be in my protective custody?"

Suddenly, that made her feel a little petty, but she

pushed the uncomfortable feeling aside. Who cared if he was insulted that she would look elsewhere for protection? "You said yourself the personal stuff keeps getting in the way."

His jaw muscles went to war. "I swore I'd protect Aubrey, and I will. I'll protect you and Marita, too. There's not enough personal stuff in the world to ever stop me from doing my job."

She believed him. More than she wanted to.

Their eyes met again, and something circled around them. A weird intimacy. Something forged with all the emotion of the bad blood. And this bizarre attraction that had reared its hot, ugly head.

Faith forced herself to look away. To move. She shook off the Beck Tanner hypnotic effect and reached for the phone to call Ross Harland. She pressed in the number to his office, hoping she remembered it correctly, and the call went straight to voice mail. It was still before normal duty hours.

"Ross, this is Faith," she said. "Please call me. I'm in LaMesa Springs, and my cell-phone service is spotty so if you can't get through, you can reach me at the Bluebonnet Hotel."

She read off the number of the hotel phone and her room number and clicked the end call button just as the door to the suite burst open. The movement felt violent. And suddenly so did the air around them.

The woman who rushed into the room was Nicole Tanner.

Beck's sister-in-law. Pete's wife.

Faith hadn't seen the woman since the night of the motel incident, but Nicole hadn't changed much. Sleek and polished in her high-end, boot-length, black duster,

London blue pants and matching top. Her shoulder-length honey-blond hair was perfect. Not a strand out of place. She looked like the ideal trophy wife.

Except for her eyes and face.

The tears had cut their way through her makeup, leaving mascara-tinged streaks on her porcelain cheeks.

"Nicole, what are you doing here?" Beck demanded.

"Taking care of a problem I should have taken care of years ago."

And with that, Nicole took her hand from her coat pocket and aimed a slick, silver handgun right at Faith.

Chapter 5

*H*ell.

That was Beck's first thought, right after the shock registered that his sister-in-law had obviously gone off the deep end. Now he had to defuse this situation before it turned deadly.

Beck stepped in front of Faith. He didn't draw his weapon, though that was certainly standard procedure. Still, he couldn't do that to Nicole.

Not yet anyway.

He lifted his hands, palms out, in a backup gesture. "Nicole, put down that gun."

Nicole shook her head and swiped away her tears with her left hand. "I can't. I have to make her leave."

Beck could hear Faith's raw breath and knew she was afraid, but that didn't stop her from leaving the meager cover he'd provided her. She stepped out beside him.

"Get back," he warned her. "Nicole's not going to shoot me," he added. But he couldn't say the same about what she might do to Faith. He didn't want his sister-in-

law to do anything stupid, and he didn't want bullets flying with Aubrey just in the next room.

He didn't want Faith hurt, either.

"I'm not leaving," Faith said, though her voice trembled slightly.

Man, it took courage to say that to an armed woman.
Ill-timed courage.

"Let me handle this," he insisted. He then fastened
his attention to Nicole. "You have to put the past behind
you. Faith won't cause you any more trouble."

Nicole's hysteria increased. "She already has caused
more trouble. Pete's been up all night talking about her.
You know how he is when he gets upset. He shuts me
out, and he drinks too much."

Beck did know. Like Nicole, Pete had a low tolerance
for certain kinds of stress, and Faith's return would have
set him off.

"Put down the gun, Nicole," Beck tried again. "And
I'll talk to Pete."

"It won't do any good. I have to make Faith leave before it destroys my marriage."

"Your marriage?" Faith spat out. She obviously didn't
intend to let him handle this in his own way. "You have
a gun pointed at me, and my daughter is just one room
away. You're endangering her as well as Beck, and yet
your top priority is saving your marriage?"

Nicole blinked. She probably hadn't expected this.
Faith hadn't stood up for herself ten years ago. "My marriage is in trouble because of you."

"No," Faith countered. "Your marriage is in trouble
because of your cheating husband. Now, put down that
gun, or I'll take it away from you myself."

Since this was quickly getting out of hand, Beck

moved in front of Faith again. The new position wouldn't last long. Faith was already trying to maneuver herself to his side, but Beck didn't let that happen. It was a risk. He didn't want to push Nicole into doing something even more stupid.

"Give me the gun," he insisted. Beck didn't bolt toward her. He kept his footsteps even and unhurried. No sudden moves.

But Beck was just about a yard away when there was movement in the hall, just outside the suite. Nicole automatically glanced over her shoulder, and that split-second distraction was all Beck needed. He lunged at Nicole, snagged her by the wrist and latched on to the gun. The momentum sent them flying, and they landed against the two men who'd just arrived.

His brother, Pete, and his father, Roy.

"What the hell's going on here?" Pete shouted.

"I'm disarming your wife," Beck snarled. He took control of the gun and stepped back just in case anyone else decided to try to make a move toward Faith.

Pete shot Nicole a glance. Not of disapproval, either. The corner of his mouth actually lifted as if he were pleased that Nicole was in the process of committing a felony.

"I tried to get her to leave," Nicole volunteered.

"Well, this probably wasn't the way to go about it," her father-in-law interjected.

Good. Father was being reasonable about this. Beck needed another voice of support since Faith's and his didn't seem to be enough.

He checked Nicole's gun and discovered that it wasn't loaded. Beck showed Faith the empty chamber, causing her to groan again.

"I wanted to scare her into leaving," Nicole explained. "I didn't want to actually hurt her."

Well, that was something at least, but it didn't make this situation less volatile.

With emotion zinging through the air, his father and Pete stood side by side, and Pete glared at Faith. Roy only shook his head and mumbled something under his breath. The men were the same height, same weight, and with the exception of some threads of gray in Roy's hair, they looked enough alike to be brothers. That probably had something to do with the fact that Roy had only been eighteen years old when Pete was born.

Beck glanced back at Faith. He could tell she wasn't about to back down despite being outnumbered.

"Before this gets any worse, I want everyone to know that I'm not Beck right now. I'm *Sheriff* Tanner, and this is not going to get violent."

"Then she's leaving." That from Pete, and it was a threat aimed at Faith. Their father caught onto Pete's arm and stopped him from moving any closer.

"No. I'm not," Faith threatened right back. "Maybe it is time for an air clearing. For the truth. I'd planned to do it anyway, just not this soon."

That got everyone's attention, and the room fell silent.

Faith pointed to Pete. "I didn't sleep with you ten years ago. Or any other time."

There it was. The finale to the conversation that Faith and he were having shortly before Nicole arrived.

Beck pushed aside his own surprise and checked out the responses of the others. Nicole went still, the muscles in her arms going slack. The reactions of his father and brother, however, went in different directions. Pete's face flushed with anger, and it seemed as if Father had been expecting her to say just that. He didn't look surprised at all.

"You were drunk," Faith reminded Pete. "All the years I've told myself that maybe you actually didn't lie about what happened, that you simply couldn't remember what you'd done, but now I'm not so sure."

"I didn't lie." Pete's voice was low and tight. Dangerous.

Faith walked closer. "Well, it wasn't me in that motel room with you. It was my sister, Sherry."

"Sherry," Beck mumbled. Since Sherry had been the town's wild child, he didn't have any trouble believing that, but apparently two members of his family did: Pete and Nicole. His father was still just standing there as if all of this was old news.

And maybe it was to him.

Had his father known the truth this whole time?

Nicole shook her head. "If that's true, why didn't you say so sooner? No one put a gag on you when you were outside the motel."

All attention turned back to Faith.

She pulled in a long breath. "I didn't say anything because Sherry's boyfriend, Nolan, would have killed her if he'd found out she cheated on him with your husband or with any other man, for that matter."

That made sense, and it also made Beck wonder why he hadn't thought of it sooner. But he knew why—he'd believed his brother.

"So why were you even there that night?" Nicole questioned Faith again. Judging from her expression, she wasn't buying any of Faith's account.

Faith took another breath. "When you came to the motel and started pounding on the door, Sherry called me. She was terrified word would get out that she'd been with Pete. I came over, hid on the side of the building and waited for you to leave. Then I took Sherry out of there. I was trying to get your husband out, too, when you and Beck showed up and accused me of seducing Pete."

"That's not the way I remember things," Pete insisted.

"Then your memory is wrong," Faith insisted right back.

Pete rammed his finger against his chest. "Why would I lie about which Matthews sister I'd slept with when I was drunk?"

"Only you can answer that, Pete." Faith volleyed glares at each one of them. "I want you all out of here. Now. If not, I intend to call the Texas Rangers and have you arrested."

He understood Faith's desire to be rid of his kin, but that riled Beck. Of course, he was already riled about this entire situation, so that was only frosting on the cake. "I don't need the Rangers to handle this," he assured Faith. "Do you want to file charges against Nicole?"

That earned him a fierce look from Pete, a raised eyebrow from his father and a surprised gasp from Nicole. Why, Beck didn't know. Nicole couldn't have possibly thought brandishing a gun, even an unloaded one, wouldn't warrant at least a consideration of arrest.

"I won't file charges at the moment," Faith said, pointing at Nicole. "But let's get something straight. I won't have you anywhere near my daughter or me with a weapon again. Understand?"

"But you ruined my life. *You.* It wasn't Sherry in that motel room. If it'd been your sister, my husband would have said so."

"Get them out of here," Faith mumbled, and she turned and walked into the adjoining room.

She didn't slam the door. She closed it gently. But Beck figured if she'd been wrongly accused and run out of town, that had to be eating away at her. Now add this latest incident with Nicole, and, oh, yeah, Faith was no doubt stewing.

"Go home, Nicole," Pete told his wife.

When Nicole didn't move, Roy caught onto his daughter-in-law's arm and led her toward the door. "I'm sorry about this, Beck. We'll talk later."

Beck nodded his thanks to his father and turned back to unfinished business. "Did you sleep with Faith or not?"

Pete glanced away. "What does it matter?"

Beck cursed under his breath. "That's not an answer to my question."

"Because it's not a question you should be asking. I'm your brother, for heaven's sake."

"Being my brother doesn't mean I'll gloss over your indiscretions. Especially if that indiscretion has put the blame on the wrong woman for all these years."

Pete looked him straight in the eye. "I was with Faith that night, not Sherry."

For the first time, Beck was seriously doubting that his brother had told the truth. But if he was lying, why? What could be worse than letting everyone, especially Nicole, believe he'd had sex with Faith? Unless fear of Nolan did play some part of this. The problem was his brother wasn't usually the sort to fear anyone.

"So what happens now?" Pete asked. "Faith just stays in town like nothing ever happened?"

Beck didn't want to mention that Faith, Aubrey and the nanny would soon be going to his house. And that they were in his protective custody. Besides, he didn't want anyone to know that his place was now essentially a safe house for the three. He wanted to get Faith, Aubrey and Marita in there without anyone else noticing. Or knowing about it. That would mean hiding them in the backseat of his car, parking in his garage and getting them inside only after the garage door was closed.

Of course, there was the other part to the plan. The part he could tell Pete since he needed the gossip mill working for the bait plan to succeed.

"Faith plans to stay at her mother's old house," Beck informed him, and he watched carefully for his brother's reaction. There wasn't much of one, just a slight shift in his posture. "I tried to talk her out of it, but she insisted on staying there."

"Then she's an idiot," Pete declared. "Her brother's a killer, and he's out on the loose. Anything could happen to her at that house."

And it wasn't a surprise that Pete didn't seem torn up about that. He probably wanted Darin to go after Faith.

Beck nodded and tried to appear detached from the situation. He realized, much to his disgust, that he wasn't detached. He didn't like this plan, and he didn't like that he'd just used his brother to set it into motion.

"You need to leave," Beck said, unable and unwilling to keep the anger from his voice. "See to your wife and make sure she doesn't come anywhere near Faith again."

Beck practically shoved his brother out the door, and he locked it. He made a mental note to keep it locked in case Nicole or Pete returned for round two. He needed to do some damage control from round one first.

Because once Faith gave it some thought, she just might file those charges against Nicole.

And if so, he'd have to arrest his own sister-in-law. Beck didn't want to speculate what kind of powder keg that would create between Pete, Nicole and Faith.

The phone on the desk rang. Figuring that Faith was still too shaken to answer it, Beck snatched it up. "Sheriff Tanner," he answered.

He was greeted with several seconds of silence, and for a moment Beck thought this might be another threat, similar to the rocks.

"Ross Harland," the caller finally said. "I'm returning Faith's call."

Beck glanced at the closed bedroom door. "She's, er, indisposed at the moment."

"Is she okay?" It didn't sound like a casual question, which might mean this guy, this former boyfriend, still had feelings for her.

"Faith's fine, but she had a rough morning. And a rough night, too."

"What happened?" Another noncasual question.

Beck didn't intend to get into specifics, but for anyone who knew Faith, her background was no doubt common knowledge. "Faith's brother is suspected of murder and is still at large. Aubrey and Faith might be in danger because of him."

"Who's Aubrey?"

That caused Beck to pause a moment. "Faith's daughter."

"A daughter?" He sounded shocked.

"I figured you knew."

"No. Faith and I dated for a year or so, but we stopped seeing each other nearly two years ago."

He didn't want to, but Beck quickly did the math. Aubrey was sixteen months old, which meant she'd been conceived a little over two years ago.

Right about the time Faith had been with Ross Harland.

Beck mentally groaned. Had Faith kept it from this man that he'd fathered a child?

"How can I help Faith?" Harland asked.

The question stunned Beck. Here, Beck had just told him in a roundabout way that he likely had a daughter, and Harland hadn't even asked about Aubrey. Certainly Harland could do the math as well. And that riled Beck to the core. If Aubrey had been his child, he'd sure as hell want to know, and he'd want to be part of her life.

"I'm not sure you can help," Beck answered, trying not to launch into a rant about how Harland should step up to the plate and be a man. "But Faith wanted to ask about getting a bodyguard for Aubrey."

Harland made a sound of understanding. "Well, I do have someone on staff who might work. Her name is Tracy Collier, and she's trained as both a nanny and a bodyguard. How old is Faith's daughter?"

Now the guy might finally get it. "Sixteen months."

"Good. I was hoping we weren't dealing with a newborn here."

"No. Not a newborn." Beck hesitated, wondering how much he should say and knowing he couldn't stop himself. He had to know, because despite Faith's denial, her past lover could have a part in this. "I thought you might be Aubrey's father."

"Me? Not a chance."

Beck had to hesitate again. This conversation was getting more and more confusing. "But you were with Faith about the time Aubrey was conceived."

"Look, I don't know what Faith told you about our relationship, and I'm not even sure it's any of your business, but there's no way that child could be mine."

"Birth control isn't always effective," Beck pointed out.

He cursed. "I want to talk to Faith."

"Like I said, she's indisposed. She'll have to call you back. And for the record, she never said you were Aubrey's father. I just put one and one together."

"Well, you came up with the wrong answer. Faith and I weren't lovers."

Beck nearly dropped the phone. "Not lovers? And you were together for a year?"

"Her choice. Not mine. Now, what the hell does this have to do with your investigation, Sheriff?"

Maybe nothing. Maybe everything. "Faith doesn't believe her brother is trying to kill her, and it's possible the danger is linked to someone in her past. When relationships go bad, situations can turn dangerous. Aubrey's father might have some part in this."

"Well, I don't know who he is, but he must be someone pretty damn special."

"What do you mean?"

Harland cursed again, and he stayed silent so long that Beck thought maybe the call had been dropped. "Ask Faith why we never slept together," Harland finally said.

"Excuse me?" Beck said because he didn't know what else to say.

"You heard me. If you want answers, ask her." And with that, Harland hung up.

Beck glanced at the phone and then at Faith's bedroom door. He didn't know what the devil was going on, but he intended to find out.

Chapter 6

"Beck Tanner asked you *what?*" Faith demanded.

There was a groan from the other end of her cell-phone line. "He thought I was your daughter's father," Harland explained.

Faith slowly got up from the bed where she'd been sitting and started to pace across the guest room in Beck's house. "What did you say?"

"The truth, that the child couldn't be mine because we were never lovers."

Faith didn't groan, but she squeezed her eyes shut a moment and silently cursed a blue streak.

"The sheriff said this was pertinent to the investigation," Ross added. "He said he wanted to be certain that none of your previous relationships could have a part in you being in danger."

"Maybe, but he had no right to ask you about our sex life." Or the lack thereof. Mercy, she did not want to explain this to Beck.

The truth could ultimately put Aubrey in danger.

"Anyway, the bodyguard I'm sending over is Tracy Collier," Ross continued, obviously opting for a less volatile subject. "She's one of my best. She should be there any minute, and she's yours for as long as you need her."

"Thanks, Ross," Faith managed to say. She did appreciate this, truly, but it was hard to be thankful when Beck might learn the truth.

"I'm sorry I told Sheriff Tanner anything about our relationship," Ross continued. "Should I phone him and have a little chat with him?"

It wouldn't be a chat. More like a tongue-lashing. "No. I'll do that myself." She thanked her old friend again and ended the call.

How dare Beck ask Ross a question like that, and he hadn't even had the nerve to tell her. But then he hadn't exactly had a chance, she reluctantly admitted. Like her, he'd been tied up all day planning to make Aubrey as safe as possible.

And they had succeeded. For now, anyway.

She, Marita and Aubrey were at Beck's house on the edge of town, and it appeared that no one had been aware of the move. Beck had literally sneaked them out the back of the hotel and into his place. Once the bodyguard arrived, then the plan was for a Texas Ranger to pull backup bodyguard duty while she and Beck made an appearance at her own house.

But first, she wanted to let Beck have it for that phone conversation with Ross.

Faith jerked open the guest-room door and stormed toward the family room, where she could hear voices. Beck's house was large, especially for a single guy: three bedrooms, three baths and an updated gourmet kitchen. A real surprise. When Beck had given them the whirlwind tour, she'd wanted to ask if he actually used the brick-encased, French stove or the gleaming, stainless cookware on the pot rack over the butcher's block island. But she hadn't said a word, because she hadn't wanted to intrude on his personal life.

He obviously hadn't felt the same about hers.

She nodded to Sgt. Sloan McKinney, a Texas Ranger who was sipping coffee while he stood by the kitchen door. Faith went straight to the family room and stopped dead in her tracks. Her temper didn't exactly go cold, but it did chill a bit when she saw what was going on. Marita was talking to a tall brunette. The bodyguard, no doubt. But it wasn't the bodyguard who snared her attention. Aubrey was on the floor, sitting in Beck's lap while he read *Chicka Chicka Boom Boom* to her.

Beck looked up at Faith, and his smile dissolved. Maybe because she looked angry. And was. And maybe because he knew the reason for her anger.

He'd changed clothes since they'd arrived and was now wearing black jeans and a white, button-up, long-sleeve shirt. Anything he could have worn would have made him look hot. But sitting there with Aubrey made him look hot and...extraordinary. It wasn't just his good looks now. It was that whole potential fatherhood thing. Beck seemed totally natural holding a child. Her child. And that created a bizarre ripple of emotions.

She had to remind herself to hang on to the anger.

"We'll go to your house when I'm done with the story," Beck let her know. Aubrey didn't take her eyes off the brightly colored pages.

"Faith, this is Tracy Collier," Marita said.

Faith shook the woman's hand. "Thank you for coming."

"No problem. Ross said it was important."

Yes, and Faith owed him for that. But not for what he'd volunteered to Beck.

"Sheriff Tanner checked my ID," Tracy volunteered. "And he ran a background check on me before I arrived." She didn't sound upset. More amused.

"She checked out clean," Beck informed Faith.

Though she was upset with him, she couldn't find fault with the extra security steps he'd taken with Tracy. But how could any man look that hot while jabbering nonsensical words like *chicka, chicka?*

Marita and Tracy resumed their conversation about sleeping arrangements. Apparently, Tracy had decided to take the sofa in the family room since it was near the front door. The Ranger would have a cot near the back door. Good. The arrangement gave Faith a little reassurance about leaving Aubrey, but it would still be tough.

Babbling, Aubrey tried to repeat the last line of the book that Beck read. He then did something else that shocked Faith. He brushed a kiss on Aubrey's forehead. There was genuine affection in his eyes. Aubrey's eyes, too.

Aubrey gave Beck a hug.

Beck's gaze met Faith's again, and he went from affection to a little discomfort. With Aubrey in his arms, he stood and walked to Faith.

"Ready to go to your house?" he asked.

No, but she was ready for that conversation. And ready to get her mind off Beck as a potential father.

Marita came to take Aubrey, and Faith gave the little girl a kiss. "Mommy won't be long."

Aubrey babbled something, reached for Beck again,

but Marita moved her away. Faith gave her a nod of thanks.

"You don't want me reading to Aubrey," Beck mumbled.

"Yes. I mean, no." Since she was starting to feel petty again, she headed toward the garage. "I'm just surprised, that's all."

"Me, too. But it's hard not to get attached to her."

"Oh, that should make your family really happy," she snarled.

He didn't respond to that. They went into the garage, got into his SUV. Even though the windows were tinted and it was dusky dark outside, he still had her slip down low in the seat so that none of his neighbors, or a killer, would spot her coming out of his place.

On the backseat, there was a doll wrapped in a blanket. Faith already knew what she would do with that doll. She'd carry it into her house so that anyone watching would think it was Aubrey. The little detail had been Beck's idea because he said he didn't want anyone questioning why Faith wouldn't have her daughter with her at her house, especially since everyone in town likely knew about the child's arrival the night before.

Beck looked down at her. "You talked to Ross Harland," he said. Apparently, that was an invitation to start the argument he guessed they were about to have.

"You had no right to ask him those questions," Faith accused.

"I beg to differ. You don't think your brother is guilty. But I'm trying to figure out the identity of a killer. Your previous relationships are relevant." He pulled out of the garage and immediately hit the remote control clipped to his visor to shut it. He didn't pull away from the house until the door was fully closed.

Faith just sat there. Stewing. And waiting. She didn't have to wait long.

"Harland said he couldn't possibly be Aubrey's father," Beck continued. "I don't guess you intend to tell me who is."

"No." She didn't even have to think about her answer.

"That's what I figured you'd say, though I don't have a clue why you'd keep something like that a secret. I'm repeating myself here, but I'm trying to find a killer, Faith."

"And knowing Aubrey's father won't catch that killer."

He cursed under his breath. "I had a friend at the FBI fax me a copy of Aubrey's birth certificate. The father's name isn't listed. Just yours."

That had been intentional, and it would stay that way. Her silence must have let him know that because he didn't say anything else about it. Silently, he drove through LaMesa Springs and down Main Street—Faith could tell from the tops of the streetlights, but she was too low in the seat to actually see anything.

"No one seems to be following us," he explained, checking the rearview and side mirrors. He made the turn into the hotel and went to the back parking lot. Beck glanced all around them. "You can sit up now. I want people to think I picked you up here."

"But what if someone on the hotel staff blabs that I wasn't here all afternoon?"

"No one knows. There's been a Do Not Disturb sign on the door and strict orders that no one goes into the room. Later, I'll phone the manager and tell him that I've moved you guys to your house."

Even though it was the plan, it still sent a chill over her. After that call, she'd officially be bait.

"So it was really Sherry in the motel with Pete?" Beck asked as he drove away from the parking lot. Except it didn't sound like a question.

But Faith answered it as if it'd been one. "What did your brother say?"

"He lied."

She glanced at him, and even in the darkness she had no trouble seeing his expression. A mixture of emotions. "How do you know that?"

"Because I could see it in his eyes."

Faith blew out a long breath. "Why didn't you see it ten years ago?"

"Because I wasn't looking. I just accepted what he told me as gospel."

"You accepted it because you already believed the worst about me."

He took a moment to answer. "Yes, and it's probably too little, too late, but I'm sorry."

She nearly laughed. For years, she'd wanted that apology. She'd wanted Beck to know the truth. But it seemed a hollow victory since she couldn't enjoy it. Well, not now anyway. But once the danger had passed it would no doubt sink in that this moment had been monumental.

Faith frowned.

She certainly hadn't expected an apology from Beck to feel so darn good. Maybe because she'd already written him off. She hoped it had nothing to do with this crazy attraction between them

"I'll work on my father and Nicole," he continued, taking the final turn to her house. Even though the curtains all appeared to be closed, some lights were on.

"Pete, too, eventually. Once they've accepted that you were the scapegoat in this, then your life here should be a little smoother."

"Thank you." That was a gift she certainly hadn't expected so soon. Then it hit her. "You're doing this for Aubrey."

"In part," he readily admitted. "I don't want her to feel any resentment from anyone. But I'm doing it for me, too. Because it's the right thing to do, and since Sherry is dead, I think this will help my family get past the hurt. You know that old saying—the truth will set you free."

"Not always," she said under her breath.

They came to a stop outside her house, directly in front of the porch. All she had to do was go up the steps, and she'd be inside.

Beck glanced at her again, and for a moment she thought he might have heard her and was going to question it. He didn't. He just looked at her.

He opened his mouth. Closed it. Shook his head. But he didn't explain why he was suddenly speechless. Instead, he picked up the doll, handed it to her and motioned for her to get out.

"Make it quick but not too obvious that you're trying to hurry," he instructed.

Faith did. While clutching the doll, she got out of the SUV and went inside to find Sgt. Caldwell waiting for them.

Beck and he exchanged handshakes. "Let's hope we catch a killer tonight," Beck greeted him.

"We'll do our best." The Ranger pointed to the security keypad by the door. "Before I leave, I want to go over the updates. There are external motion detectors that'll alert you if anyone comes within twenty feet of the house."

"What about windows?" Beck asked.

"All doors and windows are wired for security, and if anything's tripped, the alarm will go off, and the keypad will light up the problem area."

Faith was certain she looked confused. "But won't the alarm scare off Darin if he shows?" She propped the doll against the wall.

"No. The alarm will be a series of soft beeps. You shouldn't have any trouble hearing them, but they won't be loud enough to be heard from outside."

Beck's cell phone rang, and he stepped aside to answer it.

"The keypad's easy to work," Sgt. Caldwell continued. "Just press in the numbers one, two, three and four to arm it after I leave. Oh, and don't stand directly in front of any windows."

She had no plans for that. "If Darin shows, how fast can you respond?"

"Less than two minutes. I'll be nearby, parked several streets over. I don't want to be any closer, because if he sees me, it might scare him off."

"Two minutes," she repeated. "I hope that's fast enough to catch him."

Sgt. Caldwell lifted his shoulder. "Best case scenario is that your brother will call you first before he shows up. If that happens, just stay on the line with him and have Beck contact us so we can make a trace."

Faith nodded. "I don't want Darin hurt."

"We'll try our best. But it might not be possible. For that matter, it might not even be your brother who shows up."

"Nolan Wheeler," she provided.

Yes, he might have tossed those rocks through the window. And if so, if he was the one who arrived on her doorstep, then he could be arrested and questioned. It wouldn't tie up the loose ends with her brother, but she believed it would get a killer off the street.

Beck ended his call and rejoined them. One glance at him, and Faith knew something was wrong.

"That was the manager of the convenience store," Beck explained.

She held her breath, waiting for him to say her brother had been spotted again.

"Not Darin," Beck clarified, obviously understanding the concern in her body language. "This is about the taxi driver who stopped there after dropping you here at your house. When the clerk asked him what he was doing in LaMesa Springs, the driver told him."

Which confirmed what the taxi driver told Faith. "Let me guess—Nolan Wheeler was in the store?"

Beck shook his head. Paused. "No, but my father was."

"Your father?" she mumbled.

She didn't have to clarify what that meant. If his father knew, then so had Nicole and Pete. And after that stunt Nicole had pulled in her hotel room, Nicole could have been the one who'd thrown those rocks.

Beck looked away from her and handed Sgt. Caldwell his car keys. "I turned off the porch light. Figured it'd help in case someone's already watching the place."

And that person would believe it was Beck leaving. That's why Beck had changed his clothes, so that he would be dressed like the Ranger. Since no one knew the Ranger was there, the killer or her brother would think Faith was alone and vulnerable. Well, she wouldn't be alone, but the vulnerable part still applied.

"This could end up lasting all night," the Ranger reminded him.

Faith had considered that, briefly. What she hadn't considered was staying in the house alone with Beck. That suddenly didn't seem like a smart idea. But she couldn't let something like attraction get in the way of catching the person responsible.

"Good luck," Sgt. Caldwell said, heading for the door. He turned off the light in the entry as well and waited until Beck and Faith stepped into the shadows before he walked out. She immediately went to the door, locked it and set the security alarm.

"I'll talk to my dad," Beck promised. "I'll see if he repeated any information he got from the taxi driver. Plus, the rocks and foot casting are still at the crime lab. Either might give us some evidence."

"If it's Nicole who threw those rocks, I intend to file charges for that and the empty gun incident." Faith couldn't let the woman continue her harassment. Of course, if it was Nicole, there was a problem with the size-ten shoeprint that'd been found. Though maybe that print had been left earlier by someone not involved in this.

"If it's Nicole, I'll arrest her."

Faith caught his gaze. And saw the determination there. The pain, too. She also saw concern for her, so she thought it best if she stepped away from him.

Keeping in the shadows, she walked into the living room. Someone had taken the sheets from the furniture, and the sofa and recliner had a stack of bedding and pillows on them. This was where she and Beck were supposed to sleep. If sleep was even possible.

Beck would only be a few feet away from her.

With that overdue apology out of the way, there didn't seem to be so many old obstacles standing between them. Too bad. Because it made her remember a time when she'd lusted after him.

Who was she kidding?

She was still lusting after him. At least she was when she wasn't riled at him.

He followed her into the living room and caught onto her arm. The contact surprised her so much that she jumped. Faith reeled around, expecting him to do God knows what, but he merely repositioned her farther away from the window. He let go of her quickly, but then looked down at his hand as if that brief touch had caused him to feel something more.

"You might as well just go ahead and slap me," he said.

"For what?" she asked cautiously.

"For what I'm about to say."

Oh. With both curiosity and some fear, she considered the possibilities of what he might say. Maybe he wanted a discussion about the attraction. Or to discuss something about the touch that was still tingling her arm. Maybe he even intended to kiss her. Could that have been wishful thinking on her part?

"What?" she prompted when he didn't continue. Mercy. Her voice had way too much breath in it. She sounded like a lovesick schoolgirl.

"It has to do with the conversation I had with Ross Harland."

Oh, that. Faith hated that she'd anticipated anything not dealing with the case.

Beck moved closer to her again. Too close. "He was so adamant about not being Aubrey's father that I figured he was telling the truth about you two not having had sex." His voice was smooth and easy. No pressure, no expectations. He shrugged. "You can slap me for asking, and I doubt you'll answer, but at least tell me if Ross Harland might have anything to do with the murders."

That easy drawl took away some of the sting. "He doesn't."

He nodded. That was it. Beck's only reaction. He even seemed to believe her, which he should, since it was the truth.

The silence came. It was suddenly so quiet she could hear her own heartbeat in her ears. Seconds passed. Very slowly. While Beck and she just stood there and stared at each other.

"Is Ross Harland gay?" Beck finally asked.

She had no idea why that made her laugh, but it did. Maybe because Beck had lost the battle with curiosity after all. "No. He's not gay. And I don't know whether to be angry or flattered that you'd want to know so much about my sex life."

"Be flattered," he said, his voice all sex and sin.

She was. Flattered and suddenly very warm.

He leaned in, letting his mouth come very close to hers. Breath met breath. Her heart kicked into overdrive. So did her body.

She knew she should say something flippant and move away. But she didn't. "Beck," she warned.

But it sounded more like an invitation than anything else.

He didn't back away. Didn't heed her warning. He moved in for the kiss. His mouth brushed against hers. It was gentle. Nonthreatening. No demands.

It hit her like a boulder.

Faith felt the jolt. New sensations mixed with old ones that she thought she would never feel again. Leave it to Beck and his mouth to accomplish the impossible.

She leaned into him. Deepening the kiss with the pressure. He slid his hand around her neck, easing her closer. Inch by inch. Slowly, as if to give her a chance to escape. Beck was treating her like fine crystal.

And that kiss was melting her.

Faith heard herself moan. She felt the strength of his body. The fire was instant. The impact was so hard that she nearly lost her breath. She'd apparently already lost her mind. But then she broke the intimate contact and stepped back.

"I don't kiss a lot," she said, the words rushing out.

He cocked his head to the side. "Well, you should because you're good at it."

"No. I'm not." She didn't know what to do with her hands so she folded them over her chest.

His easy expression faded a bit. By degrees. Until it was replaced by confusion.

"I like to kiss," she clarified. Well, she liked to kiss Beck, anyway. "But kissing leads to other things. Like sex. Which we aren't going to have."

He lifted his left eyebrow. "You're right. Our relationship is too complicated for sex."

"Yet you still kissed me."

He shook his head, cursed under his breath and dragged his hand through his hair. "I don't know why. Maybe because I haven't been able to get you out of my mind since I saw you naked in the shower. But I know that kiss can't go any further than it just did."

She blinked. "You honestly believe that?"

"I have to believe it. We can't deal with the alternative right now. Aubrey's safety has to come first. Then this investigation. Once we catch this killer, then we can…talk. Or kiss. Or do something we'll really regret like have great sex."

But he waved off that last part. Too bad she couldn't wave off the effect it had on her body. The image of them having sex sizzled through her.

"So *this* is on hold," he continued. "Unless there's something you want to tell me now."

She wanted to. But it wasn't that easy. The truth would give him some answers. More questions, too. And it would open Pandora's box.

Beck was right. Aubrey's safety came first.

Faith was about to repeat that, but a blast tore through the room.

Chapter 7

Someone had fired a shot at them.

The moment the sound of the bullet registered, Beck reacted.

He hooked his arm around Faith's waist and dragged her to the floor. She was already headed in that direction anyway, and they landed on the pile of sheets that'd been removed from the furniture. That cushioned their fall a little, but the new position didn't take them out of the line of fire.

Another bullet came at them and slammed into the wall just above their heads.

Hell.

Beck drew his weapon. "We have to move."

But where and how?

His initial assessment of the situation wasn't good. There'd been no broken glass, and that meant no broken windows. And no tripped motion detector, either. So the shooter had to be more than twenty feet away from the house and was literally shooting through the wall.

Probably with a high-powered rifle.

But it was the accuracy of the shot that caused Beck's stomach to knot. Both bullets had come entirely too close, especially considering there was no way the shooter could have a visual on them.

So, was the guy pinpointing them through some kind of eavesdropping device or had he managed to rig surveillance cameras that had given him an inside view of the house?

The third shot slammed into the wooden floor next to them and sent splinters flying. That was it. They couldn't stay there any longer.

"Let's go." Beck latched on to Faith's arm and got them running out of the living room. He needed to put another wall between them and the shooter.

Staying low, they raced toward the kitchen, the nearest room, but the shooter stayed in pursuit, and the bullets continued. Each blast followed them, tracking them as they made their way across the living room.

Beck shoved Faith ahead of him so that his body would give her some small measure of protection. It wasn't enough. They needed a barrier, something wide and thick. He spotted the fridge. It was outdated and fairly small, but he hoped the metal would hold back those bullets. He hauled Faith in front of it and shoved her to the linoleum floor.

The bullets didn't stop.

They tore through the kitchen drywall and shattered the tiny window over the kitchen sink. That set off the alarm, and the soft beeps began to pulse through the room. If the shooter moved to the back of the house, they'd be sitting ducks with that broken window.

"Call Sgt. Caldwell," Beck instructed Faith. He

handed her his cell phone and kept his gun ready just in case the shooter decided to bash through a window or door and try to come into the house.

Beside him, he felt Faith trembling, and her voice trembled, too, as she made the call to the Ranger and told him that someone was shooting at them from the front of the house. She asked him to come immediately.

Faith had no sooner made that request when the angle of the shots changed.

The next two rounds came right at the refrigerator. The bullets slammed into the metal but thankfully didn't exit out the front. The accuracy of the shots, however, told Beck that the gunman wasn't just using a high-powered, long-range rifle but that it was likely equipped with some kind of thermal scope or camera.

That thermal device could be a deadly addition.

It was no doubt picking up their body heat, and that heat had given away their exact location. That's why the shots were aimed so closely at them.

Faith ended her call with the Ranger. Even though the overhead light wasn't on, there was enough moonlight for Beck to see the terror on her face.

"Aubrey," she said, flipping open the phone again. She frantically stabbed in the numbers, and a moment later over the deafening blasts, she said, "Marita, is Aubrey okay?"

Beck hadn't been truly afraid until that moment. Faith was silent, and he watched her expression, praying that the gunfire had been only for them and a second shooter hadn't gone to his house to make a simultaneous attack there.

"They're fine," she finally said. Faith let out a hoarse sob. Fear mixed with relief.

Beck shared that relief. For just a moment. And then the anger took over. How dare this shooter put Faith through this. This was a blatant attempt to kill her, but the fear of harm to her child was far, far worse.

"I'll get this guy," Beck promised her.

The shots stopped.

Just like that, there were no more blasts. The only sounds were their sawing breaths, the hum of the central heating and the beeps from the security alarm.

"Is it over?" Faith asked.

He caught onto her arm to stop her from trying to get up. "Maybe."

Beck left it at that, but her widened eyes let him know that she understood. This could be a temporary cease-fire, a lure to draw them out away from the fridge.

Or it could mean the shooter was moving to the back of the house.

Where he'd have a direct shot to kill them.

"We'll stay put," he said, not at all sure of his decision. It was a gamble either way.

"I want to go to Aubrey," Faith mumbled.

"I know. So do I."

Waiting was hell, but this was the best way he knew to keep Faith alive.

His cell phone rang, the sound slicing through the room. Faith quickly answered it.

"Sgt. Caldwell's nearby," she relayed to him a moment later. "He'll turn on his sirens and an infrared scanner."

The sirens started to sound almost immediately. They would almost certainly scare off a shooter, if the shooter was still around, that is. But maybe, just maybe, the infrared would help Caldwell spot the shooter so he could be apprehended and arrested.

Beck wanted to be outside, to help with the search. He wanted to be the one to catch this piece of slime. But he couldn't leave Faith because the shooter could use that opportunity to go after her.

So he waited. It seemed endless. But it was probably only a couple of minutes before the phone rang again. This time, Beck grabbed it and answered it.

"It's Caldwell," the Ranger said.

"Did you get him?" Beck snapped.

"No. Nothing showed up on the infrared."

Beck groaned. This couldn't happen. They couldn't let this guy get away.

"I'm taking Faith back to my house to stay with the Ranger there and the bodyguard," he told the Ranger. "And then I'm going after this SOB."

Faith checked the time on the screen of her cell phone. It was ten o'clock. Not that late, but Beck had been out looking for the shooter for well over an hour.

Each minute had seemed like an eternity.

She paced in the family room but kept her movements light so she wouldn't disturb Marita and Aubrey, who were already in bed and hopefully sleeping. Aubrey certainly was. Faith had verified that just five minutes earlier when she peeked in on them in the guest room. Marita had her eyes closed, but Faith doubted the woman was truly asleep.

The shooting had put them all on edge.

Tracy was on the sofa, reading. The Ranger, Sgt. McKinney, was standing guard in the kitchen. Everything was quiet, but the tension was thick enough to taste.

Where was Beck? And why hadn't he checked in?

The silence was driving her crazy. She was imagining

all sorts of things. Like he was lying somewhere shot. Or that he was being held hostage.

Because she was so caught up in those nightmarish thoughts, the sound of the phone ringing caused her to jump. "Hello?" Faith said as quickly as she could get the phone to her ear.

Silence.

That brought on some more horrible thoughts, and then she checked the caller ID. The person had blocked their number, and there was no reason for Beck to have done that.

"Who is this?" she asked.

Her alarmed tone obviously alerted Tracy, who got to her feet. She put her hand on the butt of the pistol that rested in her shoulder holster.

"It's me," the caller finally said.

Faith had no trouble recognizing that voice.

Nolan Wheeler.

Her stomach dropped to her knees from the shock of hearing him, but she welcomed this call. It was the first contact she'd had in years with a man she thought was a cold-blooded killer.

"Nolan," Faith said aloud so that Tracy would know what was going on. Tracy reacted. She went racing into the kitchen to tell Sgt. McKinney. Hopefully, they could do something to trace this call and pinpoint Nolan's location. "Did you take shots at me tonight?"

"Me? Of course not." He used his normal cocky tone, but that didn't mean he was telling the truth. "I called about Sherry."

"What about her? She's dead. And I think you might be responsible."

"Not a chance. I didn't want her dead. She owed me money. Lots of it."

Faith was instantly skeptical. "How did that happen? You've never been one to have extra cash to lend anyone."

"I didn't exactly lend it to her. She stole my car and left a note, saying she was in a bind. She needed cash and needed it fast."

"Did she say why she needed money?" Faith asked.

"To gussy up." Nolan snickered. "Said she had to impress somebody, and she needed to look her best and that she'd pay me back. Killing her wouldn't get me the money so I've got no motive."

"What about the house? Did you think you could inherit it? Because you can't. I made a will, and there's no way you can ever inherit anything that's mine."

He made a tsk-tsk sound. "But I can inherit what's mine. Well, what was Sherry's anyway. Half of the place should have been hers after your mother was killed. Guess what, Faith? I want that half."

She fought to hang on to her temper. Flying off the handle now wouldn't solve anything. Besides, she wanted to give the Ranger more time to locate Nolan.

"Sherry and you separated eighteen months before her death," Faith reminded him. Even though their marriage was common law, Nolan probably did have a right to half of whatever Sherry owned. "And after the hell you put her through, you don't deserve anything from her estate."

"In the eyes of the law, I do. And you know the law, don't you?"

"I know it well enough that you won't see a penny."

"Oh, I want more than pennies," Nolan gloated. "A lot more. So here's the deal. You give me a hundred thousand dollars, and I'll go away."

Oh, mercy. "That's more than the place is worth, and besides, I don't have that kind of money."

"Then get it. Bye, Faith."

"Wait!" she said in a louder voice than she'd antici-pated. This call couldn't end yet. "I need to know about Darin. Have you seen him?"

Nolan took his time answering. "He's around."

That was chilling, and despite the simple answer, it sounded like some kind of threat. "Where?"

"Don't worry about your brother. He can take care of himself."

"I'm not so sure of that, especially if you're manipu-lating him in some way." And if Nolan was in contact with her brother, then he was almost certainly manipu-lating him. "Where are you, Nolan?"

"Just get me that money," he said, ignoring her ques-tion.

Faith tried again. "Where are you?"

"I'm closer than you think, sweet cakes."

With that, Nolan hung up.

Faith looked in the doorway of the family room, where Tracy and the Ranger were standing. Sgt. McKinney took her phone and relayed the numbers to someone on the other end of his own cell-phone line.

A moment later, the sergeant shook his head. "The guy was using a prepaid cell phone. We couldn't trace it."

Faith didn't have time to groan because she heard the garage door open. Beck was home. And she raced to meet him. One look at his face, however, told her that he didn't have any better news than she did.

Beck took off his muddy cowboy boots and dropped them on the laundry-room floor. "I couldn't find the shooter."

Because he looked exhausted and beyond frustrated, Faith motioned for him to go into the family room so he could sit down. He smelled like the woods and sweat, and there were bits of dried leaves and twigs on his clothes.

"What about the shell casings?" Sgt. McKinney asked. "Caldwell called and said you'd found some at the scene."

"We did. They're Winchester ballistic silver tips." Beck looked at her. "They're used for long-range shooting. Coupled with what was probably a thermal camera or scope, I'm guessing the shooter had what we call a hog rifle. It's used for hunting wild hogs or boars at night."

"This type of weapon is rare?" she asked hopefully.

"Not around here. I know of at least a half dozen people who own one. Wild boars can be dangerous to people and livestock so they're usually hunted when they show up too close to the ranches."

Maybe Nolan had gotten his hands on one of these rifles. "Nolan Wheeler called a few minutes ago," she filled him in. "We couldn't trace the call."

The fatigue vanished. The concern returned. "What did he want?"

"Money. A hundred grand to be exact. He wants me to give him more than half of my inheritance. But he didn't tell me how I could find him."

I'm closer than you think.

She pushed aside the chill from remembering Nolan's final remark. "He'll call back." Faith was certain of that. "He'll want that cash. And maybe we can use it to draw him out."

Beck hesitated a moment. Then nodded. "But you won't be the one who's drawing him out. No more playing bait."

Faith was still too shaky to argue with him. Nor did

she argue when Beck reached out and pulled her closer. That was all it took. That bit of comfort. And Faith felt the tears well up in her eyes.

"I could use a cup of coffee," Tracy said, and she hitched her shoulder toward the kitchen. "Why don't you join me?" she asked Sgt. McKinney.

Faith didn't mind the obvious ploy to leave her and Beck alone because the tears started to spill down her cheeks.

"I'm sorry," she mumbled.

Beck pulled her even closer to him and closed his arms around her. She took everything he was offering her, even though it was wrong. Beck had been through that shooting, too, and he wasn't falling apart.

"I'm not ashamed of crying," she said, wiping away the tears with the back of her hand. Beck wiped the other cheek. "But I wish I wasn't doing this in front of you."

"Why?" With his fingers still on tear-wiping duty, he caught her gaze, and the corner of his mouth hitched. "Because I'm the enemy?"

"No. Because you're Beckett Tanner."

The smile didn't fully materialize, and his fingers stayed in place. Warm on her cheek. "What would that have to do with it?"

"I always wanted to impress you. Or at least get your attention in a good way." She blamed the confession on the adrenaline crash and the fatigue.

"You succeeded. You got my attention. Even back then, before you left town." He slid his fingers down her cheek to her chin and lifted it slightly. As if he were readjusting it for a kiss. "You were about sixteen, and I saw you coming out of the grocery store on Main. You were wearing this short red dress. Trust me, I noticed."

Faith was stunned. "So why didn't you ask me out or something?"

"Because you were sixteen and I was twenty. The term *jailbait* comes to mind. I decided it'd be best to wait a couple of years."

For a moment, she got a glimpse of what life could have been if there hadn't been the incident at the motel. Of course, Beck's family would have never accepted her, and besides, the attraction would have run its youthful course and burned out.

She looked at him again.

Maybe not.

His mouth came to hers. Just a brush of his lips, and then he pulled back. When his gaze met hers again, the trip down memory lane was over. He drew her into his arms again. But it had nothing to do with kisses or sex. He eased her onto the sofa and simply held her.

For some reason, it seemed more intimate than a real kiss.

"I'm a good cop," he said, his voice hardly more than a whisper. "But I've made mistakes. I nearly let you get killed tonight."

So he was feeling guilty, too. "You couldn't have known that was going to happen."

"Yes, I did. I should have nixed that bait plan right from the start."

"It worked out all right," she assured him. Though they both knew that was a lie. They'd have nightmares about this for years. "I would just leave town, but I'm afraid this monster will follow me."

He made a sound of agreement.

Faith's phone rang again. She jolted. Her body was still on full alert. The caller had blocked the number.

"Nolan again," she mumbled. She answered the call and held the phone between Beck and her so he could hear as well.

"Hello, Faith."

It was a man all right. But not Nolan.

"Darin?" Though it wasn't a question. She knew it was her brother's voice. "God, I've been so worried about you. Where are you?"

"I can't say." He sounded genuinely sad about not being able to tell her that detail. "I called to warn you. You're in danger."

"Yes. From Nolan." She moved to the edge of the sofa. "I think he tried to kill me tonight."

"Maybe. But watch out for the Tanners. You can't trust them, Faith. They want to hurt you."

She wasn't exactly surprised after what had happened at the hotel. "Who, Nicole Tanner?"

"All of them. The whole family. If Sherry was alive, she'd tell you the same. It's about those letters. Something went wrong with the letters."

Now she was surprised. "Darin, I don't understand—what letters? What do you mean?"

He stayed silent for several long moments. "Just be careful."

"Don't go," she said when she thought he was about to hang up. "I want to see you. Can we meet somewhere?"

That earned her a sharp look from Beck.

"No meeting," Darin insisted. "Not yet. It isn't safe. Not for you. Not for Aubrey."

"Aubrey?" Her breath practically froze in her throat.

Beck had a slightly different response. She saw the anger wash over him, and he tried to take the phone. She shook her head and eased her hand over the receiver. "He'll hang up if he knows you're listening," she mouthed.

"Aubrey's in danger because of the letters," Darin continued a moment later.

"Who has these letters?" Faith asked. "Nolan?"

"I don't know. Maybe."

If those letters contained something sinister, then Nolan was almost certainly involved. "Then I need to find him. Where is he?"

"He's here in LaMesa Springs."

Here.

I'm closer than you think.

And that meant Darin was probably in town, too.

"Yes, but where in LaMesa Springs?" Faith pressed.

"He's in the attic."

Faith flattened her hand over her chest to steady her heart. *Mercy, was Nolan here at Beck's house?* "What attic?" And she held her breath, waiting.

"At the house. Your house. He said the lock on the back door was broken so he went inside and climbed into the attic so he could wait for you. He got there before the cops and Rangers and then stayed quiet so they wouldn't hear him moving around."

"Darin?" Faith forced herself to talk. Nolan could be dealt with later. "I want to see you. Please."

But she was talking to herself. Her brother had already hung up.

Beck pulled out his own phone and jabbed in some numbers. Since the room was so quiet, Faith had no trouble hearing the man who answered. It was Sgt. Caldwell.

"Are you still at the Matthews house?" Beck asked the Ranger.

"Yeah. Why?"

"Check the attic. But be careful. One of our suspects, Nolan Wheeler, might be up there."

"I'll call you back," Caldwell let him know.

Beck hung up and looked at her. "Do you know anything about those letters Darin mentioned?"

She shook her head. This wasn't something she wanted to discuss right now. She wanted to know what was going on in that attic. But at least the conversation would keep her mind off the wait. Plus, this was important. "It sounded as if he believed they were connected to your family."

"Yeah, it did. But this is Darin, remember? He might not be mentally stable right now. Still," Beck continued before she could say anything, "I'll call my father in the morning and set up a meeting. I want to ask him about the convenience store anyway."

With everything else that was going on, she'd nearly forgotten about that. "I think it's pretty clear that he told Pete and maybe even Nicole that I was back in town. After all, your brother called you when I was still at your office. That was only a couple of hours after the rock throwing incident."

He mumbled another "yeah" and checked his watch.

"Sgt. Caldwell will be careful," she said more to herself than Beck.

But she prayed nothing went wrong and that the Ranger didn't get hurt. Besides, her brother could have been wrong. Beck was right about Darin possibly being delusional. God knows how much of what he said was real or a product of his mental illness.

Beck's phone rang, and he answered it immediately. He clicked on the speakerphone function.

"There's no one in the attic," Sgt. Caldwell explained.

"But someone's been here. There's a discarded fast-food bag and graffiti."

"Kids maybe?" Beck asked.

"I don't think kids did this." His comment and tone upped the chill coursing through her. "I used my camera phone to take some pictures of the walls. I'm sending four of them to you now."

Beck went to the phone menu and pressed a few buttons. The first picture started to load on the screen.

Yes, it was definitely the attic. And though she couldn't see the fast-food bag the sergeant had described, she could see the wall that he'd captured in the photograph. Someone had taken red paint—at least she hoped it was paint—and written on the rough wood planks.

It was a calendar of sorts, crudely drawn squares, some blank, some with writing inside. The dates went back to a month earlier. She couldn't make out the writing and motioned for Beck to go to the next picture. It was the square with the date November 11th.

Inside the box someone had written:

Sherry dies.

Faith swallowed hard. That was indeed the day Sherry had been killed. But anyone who knew her sister would have had that information.

The next picture showed the date. November 12th. The caption inside:

Annie dies.

Her mother's name was Annie, and like the previous caption, it was correct. Her mother had been murdered then.

Picture three was dated January 12th with the words:

Faith's homecoming.

Yes, she had come home then. And someone had thrown rocks through her window.

God, had Nolan been there that whole time, waiting for her, watching her? The security had been set up to keep anyone from getting in, but what if he was already inside?

Beck clicked another button and the final picture loaded. There was a date: January 14th.

Tomorrow's date.

And beneath it were two words that caused her to gasp.

Faith dies.

Chapter 8

Faith was not going to die today.

Beck wouldn't let that happen.

It riled the hell out of him to think of the death threat that'd been left in her attic. It had shaken Faith to the core. Immediately after seeing those pictures on the phone, she'd sat motionless in his arms while he rattled off how he was going to put an end to this.

The handwriting and fast-food bag would be analyzed. That was a given. As would the shell casings collected from the attack the night before. But there was something else Beck could do. He could keep Faith away from her house. If he didn't let her out of his sight, he could protect her.

He hoped that'd be enough.

So, after giving her all the assurance he could, he'd sent her off to bed, where he was sure she hadn't gotten any sleep. He certainly hadn't. But that didn't matter. He could sleep later. Right now, he had to solve the case.

The devil was in the details, and there was one detail he could further investigate.

He'd already called his father at the family ranch and asked about the encounter with the taxi driver at the convenience store and the mysterious letters that Darin had mentioned to Faith. His father had become defensive, saying that it wasn't a good time to talk, but Beck didn't think it was his imagination that his dad was confused about those letters. Surprised, even. Maybe that meant his family had nothing to do with any potential evidence.

Maybe.

Since Pete and Nicole also lived on the grounds of the ranch, Beck would extend his questions to them and have that chat about giving Faith a much-needed break.

Beck got up from the kitchen table and poured himself another cup of coffee. He could hear the TV in the family room, where Tracy was having her breakfast. She was alone since the Ranger had left to assist with the processing of the crime scene at Faith's house. Beck had wanted to be part of that, but not at the expense of leaving Faith and Aubrey.

Before he could return to his seat and his case notes, he heard soft uneven footsteps. A moment later, Aubrey appeared. She was wearing a yellow corduroy dress and no shoes, just socks with lace at the tops.

She smiled and waved at him.

Just like that, the weight of the world seemed to leave his shoulders. "Good morning," he told her.

She babbled something with several syllables and went straight to him. "Up, up," she said.

Beck set his coffee aside and out of her reach, and he picked her up Aubrey rewarded him with a hug and kiss on the cheek.

"She's faster than she used to be," Marita said, hurrying in. The nanny stopped and eyed them. "And she seems to think you're her new best friend."

There was worry in the woman's tone. Beck understood that. Faith had probably told her about their bitter past, but as far as Beck was concerned, that wasn't going to play a part in how he felt about his new best friend.

"Anything come back on that stuff you found in her attic?" Marita asked, helping herself to a cup of coffee. "Faith just told me about all of that while she was getting dressed."

So that's where she was. Beck had hoped she was still in bed. "We'll try to link the writing to Nolan Wheeler."

Marita flexed her eyebrows and had a sip of coffee. "Or Faith's brother."

Beck nodded and realized that Aubrey was studying him with those intense, cocoa-brown eyes. The little girl finally reached out and pinched his nose. She giggled. And Beck wondered how anyone could be in a bad mood around this child.

From the doorway, Faith stepped into view, studying him. She'd put on a pair of dark brown pants and a coppery top that was nearly the same color as her eyes. She'd pulled her shoulder-length hair into a ponytail, a style that made him think of fashion models.

And kissing her neck.

He frowned, hating how he couldn't control those thoughts that kept popping into his head.

"I fixed some eggs," Beck let Marita and Faith know. He considered asking Faith how she was, but he knew the answer. Her eyes said it all. She was troubled and weary. Fear and adrenaline could do that.

Marita went to the stove and lifted the lid to a terra-cotta server. "This looks good. Really good."

"I put in a little smoked sausage and Asiago cheese." He got a little uncomfortable when both women stared at him. "I left some plain for Aubrey. If she can eat eggs, that is. I wasn't sure."

Great. Now he was babbling and sounding like a contestant on some cooking or parenting show.

Thankfully, Marita quit staring at him as if he had a third eye. She dished up some eggs and sampled them. "Mmm. A man who can cook. I think I'm in love," she joked.

"It's a hobby," Beck explained.

Faith smiled. An actual real smile. And that made all of his discomfort worth it. He wasn't embarrassed about his hobby, but it wasn't exactly something a man with his true Texas upbringing liked to brag about. Barbecuing steaks was one thing, but stove cooking and a cowboy image didn't always mesh.

It didn't take long, however, for Faith's smile to fade. "Anything new on the investigation?"

Yeah. And it was news she wasn't going to like. "There were no prints on the rocks and no match on the shoe impression. The sole was too worn to come up with anything distinguishable. Also, the track could have been there a day or two. It wasn't necessarily made by the rock thrower."

Faith stayed quiet, processing that information.

Aubrey pointed to the window, obviously wanting to go closer and look out, but Beck moved her farther away from it. The danger was just too great to do normal things, and if a gunman could shoot into Faith's house, he could do the same to Beck's if he found out Faith and Aubrey were there. He couldn't let that happen.

Marita dished up a small plate of plain eggs, took a spoon from the drawer and reached for Aubrey. "Why don't I feed this to her in the family room so you two can talk?"

When the nanny took Aubrey from him, Beck immediately felt the loss. So did Aubrey—her mouth tightened into a rosebud pout as Marita carted her away.

"You look…disappointed," Faith commented.

"I think being around Aubrey makes me think about being a father. I'm thirty-two. Guess this weird, gut feeling is the equivalent of my biological clock ticking."

Great. Now he was talking biological clocks after his cooking babble. He might have to go wrestle a longhorn to get back his manly image.

Faith lifted an eyebrow. "You want to be a father?"

Her astonished expression and tone stung. "You don't think I'd be a good dad?"

"No. I think you'd be very good at it." Faith walked closer and poured some coffee. She smelled like peach-scented shampoo. "I'm just a little surprised, that's all."

Another shrug. He tipped his head to the family room where he could hear Aubrey babbling. "What can I say? I've decided I want a child."

Actually, he wanted Aubrey.

Why did he feel such a strong connection to that little girl? Maybe because he was starting to feel a strong connection to Aubrey's mother.

Beck looked at Faith then, just as her gaze landed on him. Uh-oh. There it was again. The reminder of that kiss.

She moistened her lips, causing his midsection to

clench. He had to move away from her, or he was going to kiss her again. But Faith beat him to it. She leaned in and brushed her mouth over his.

"Mmm," she mumbled. That sound went straight through him. "I shouldn't want you."

He smiled. God knows why. There wasn't anything to smile about. He was getting daddy fever, and he wanted Faith in his bed. Or on the floor.

Location was optional.

Because he was crazed with lust, Beck did something totally stupid. He hooked his arm around her waist and eased her to him. Body against body. It was a good fit. The heat just slid right through him.

"Does saying 'I shouldn't want you' make you want me less?" he asked, making sure it sounded like a joke.

"No." That wasn't a joking tone. A heavy sigh left her mouth. "It's complicated, Beck."

He was aware of that. But something was holding her back other than what'd happened in their past. "Want to tell me about it?"

He saw the hesitation in her eyes. "You'll want to sit down for this," she finally said.

Beck silently groaned. This sounded like trouble.

Before either of them could sit at the kitchen table, he heard the doorbell. It was almost immediately followed by a knock.

Beck snatched his gun from the top of the fridge. "Take Marita and Aubrey and go into the bedroom," he instructed.

Faith gave a shaky nod and started toward the family room. She didn't have to go far. Marita was carrying Aubrey, and she was headed back into the kitchen. Tracy was right on their heels.

"Try to keep Aubrey quiet," Faith told them. She began to pick up the toys that'd been left in the room.

There was another ring of the doorbell. Another knock. Beck hurried to see who his impatient visitor was, but before he could get to the door, the key slid into the lock. He took aim. The door flew open.

His father was standing there.

Pete was behind him.

"Hell." Beck lowered his gun and cursed some more. His father had obviously not waited and used his emergency key to get in. "It's not a good time for a visit. We'll have to get together later."

His father eyed the gun. Then Beck. But Pete looked past Beck, and his attention landed on Faith. She had various toys clutched in her hands and was apparently headed to the bedroom. She froze.

"What's she doing here?" Pete demanded.

His father didn't let Beck answer, and he gave Pete a sharp warning look. "Maybe this is a good thing. She can probably clear up some of this mess."

Beck had no idea what *mess* his father was talking about, but he had a massive problem on his hands. His family now knew Faith's whereabouts, and unless he could convince them to keep quiet—and trust them to do so—then he was going to have to find a new location to use as a safe house. But he'd have to do that later. Right now, he needed to deal with the situation.

"What's this about?" Beck asked.

His father and brother stepped in and shut the door. "When you called earlier, you wanted to know if I knew anything about some letters that had to do with Sherry Matthews," Roy said. "Well, I do."

Beck was poleaxed. This was another unwanted surprise. Beck had expected his father to have no idea about that particular subject. "What do you mean?"

Roy pulled out a large manila envelope he had tucked beneath his arm. "These letters."

Beck placed his gun on top of the cabinet that housed the TV. Hoping this wasn't something that would lead to his father's arrest, he grabbed a Kleenex from the box on the end table, and he used a tissue so that he wouldn't get his prints on what might be evidence.

Still clutching the toys, Faith walked closer and watched as Beck took out the letters.

"Two and a half months ago, Sherry came out to the ranch to see Pete and me," Roy explained. "He wasn't there so I talked to her alone. She wanted money."

"Two and a half months ago?" Beck repeated. "That was just a couple of weeks before she was murdered."

"A week," Roy corrected. "She was very much alive when she left, but she said she was in big trouble. That she owed someone some money."

"Nolan," Faith supplied. "She called me about that same time, and I told her I couldn't lend her any more. I told her to work it out with Nolan."

"She didn't," Roy informed her. "Sherry said if Pete didn't give her ten grand in cash, then she was going to tell Nicole that she was having an affair with him. She said she'd tell Nicole she was having an affair with me, too."

Beck felt every muscle in his body go stiff. He waited for his father to deny it. He didn't. But Pete did.

"They were bald-faced lies," Pete volunteered. "Sherry didn't wait around to say those lies to my face. She left, and a day later, the first letter arrived."

Roy nodded. "When I came out of the grocery store,

it was tucked beneath the windshield wiper of my truck." He pointed to the letter in question.

The envelope simply had "Pete and Roy" written on it. No "to" or "from" address. Still using the tissue as a buffer, Beck took out the letter itself. One page. Typed. No handwritten signature. No date. No smudges or obvious fingerprints.

However, the envelope had obviously been sealed at one time, and since it was the old-fashioned, lick-and-press kind, he might be able to have that tested for DNA to prove if Sherry had indeed sent it. At this point, he had no reason to doubt that she was the sender, but it was standard procedure to test that sort of thing.

Not that his family had followed procedure.

They should have brought the letters to him, and maybe he could have prevented the murders.

"I need that money," Beck read aloud. "You two owe it to me, and if I don't have that ten thousand dollars by Friday, I'm calling Nicole. Miss Priss won't be happy to hear you're both sleeping with me again, and this time I have proof. Sherry."

Again.

That word really jumped out at him. Maybe it was a reference to the motel incident. Or maybe this was something more recent. If his brother could lie about the first, he could probably lie about the second. But where did that leave his father? Had he slept with Sherry, too?

"Sherry called after the first letter," Pete explained. "I told her I wasn't going to give her a dime. The next day, the second letter was in the mailbox."

The second letter was typed like the first, but this one contained a copy of a grainy photo. It appeared to be Pete, sleeping, his chest bare and a sheet covering his lower body. Sherry was also in the shot, and it was a photo she'd obviously taken herself since Beck could see her thumb in the image. She was smiling as if she knew that this photo would be worth big bucks.

"That's not me in the picture," Pete insisted. "It's some guy she got who looks like me."

Maybe. It wasn't clear. It, too, would have to be tested and perhaps could be enhanced to get a better image.

"This is your last chance," Beck read aloud from the second letter. "If I don't have the money by tomorrow at six o'clock, a copy of this picture will go to Nicole. Leave the cash with my mom at the liquor store."

"When he got the second letter, I told Pete that maybe we should just pay Sherry off," his father explained. "I didn't care what people thought about me, but I just didn't want Nicole involved in this."

Since blackmailers were rarely satisfied with one pay-off, Beck ignored that faulty reasoning and went on to the third letter. It was similar to the others, but this time Sherry demanded fifty thousand dollars, not ten. There was no copy of a photo, only the threat to spill all to Nicole.

"Why didn't you tell me about these letters before?" Beck asked.

"Because I wouldn't let him," Pete spoke up. "I wanted to handle it myself. And I didn't want anyone to know. I didn't want this to get back to Nicole. All it would have taken is for one of your deputies to let it slip, and this wouldn't have stayed private very long."

"I wouldn't have shown this to my deputies." His family must have known that was true, which made Pete's excuse sound even less plausible. But Beck couldn't doubt Pete's motives completely. He would have done anything to prevent Nicole from knowing. His brother might have a loose zipper, but he was obsessed enough with his wife that he would do anything to keep her from being hurt.

Pete pointed to Faith. "I think she was in on this blackmail scheme of her sister's. I think she knew all about it."

"I didn't," Faith said at the same moment that Beck said, "She didn't."

His comment got him stares from all three. "Faith's been up-front with me about this case. Unlike you two," Beck added. "You should have come forward with these and told me about Sherry's visit."

Not that it would have helped him catch the killer. But it would have given Beck the whole picture. Of course, it would have also made his brother and father suspects in Sherry's and her mother's murders.

Hell.

First that gun incident with Nicole. Now this. He might have to arrest a Tanner or two before this was over.

"Faith's brainwashed you," his father decided.

"That's not brainwashing," Pete piped in. "She's using her body to blur the lines. It's what the Matthews women are good at."

Beck slowly laid the letter aside and stared down his brother. "How do you know that?"

"What the hell does that mean?" Pete's nostrils flared.

"Were you having an affair with Sherry?"

Pete cursed. "I won't dignify that with an answer."

"Why, because it's true?"

Roy caught onto Pete's arm when his son started to bolt toward Beck. "If your brother says he wasn't sleeping with that woman, then he wasn't."

The denial didn't answer the questions. "Then why

would Sherry say it? Why would she have that picture? And why would she try to blackmail you?"

"Because she's a lying tramp, just like her sister." Pete jabbed his finger at Faith again.

That did it. Beck was tired of this. He put the letters aside, went to the door and opened it. "Both of you are leaving now. Once I've processed these letters, I'll let you know if I'm going to file any charges against you."

"Charges?" his father practically yelled. "For what, trying to be discreet? Trying to protect my family from a liar and schemer?"

Beck reminded himself that he was speaking to his father and tried to keep his voice level. "The Rangers could construe this as obstruction of justice."

Roy looked as if he'd slugged him. "Don't do this, son. Don't choose this woman over your own family."

"It's not about Faith. I'm the sheriff. It's my job to investigate all angles of a double murder." He ushered them out, closed the door and locked it.

Faith dropped Aubrey's toys onto the floor. She blew out a long breath and rubbed her hands against the sides of her pants. "I always say I'm not going to let your family get to me."

But they had. And Beck hated that.

Even though she had her chin high and was trying to look strong, Beck went to her and pulled her into his arms. He brushed a kiss on her forehead.

"I didn't know Sherry tried to blackmail Pete and Roy," she volunteered. "I didn't know anything about the letters until Darin mentioned them last night."

"I believe you. If you'd known, you would have told me."

He felt her go stiff, and she eased back to meet his

gaze. She shook her head, and he got the sinking feeling that he was about to hear another confession that would cause his blood pressure to spike.

"I have to move Aubrey," she said. "Now that your father and brother know she's here, she can't stay."

She was right. Keeping Aubrey safe had to be at the top of their list.

He nodded. "I have a friend who's the sheriff over in Willow Ridge. I'll call him and see if he can set up a place for all of you there."

"No. Not me. I can't go with her. The danger is tied to me, not her. If I get her away from me, then she'll be safe. But if she stays with me, she could be hurt."

Beck wanted to shoot holes in that theory, but he couldn't. "Are you sure you can be away from her?"

"No. I'm not. I'll miss her. But I can't risk another shooting with her around." She blinked back tears. "You can trust this friend?"

"I can trust him," Beck assured her.

He let go of her so he could start making the necessary arrangements. Beck walked toward his office, and Faith went into the bedroom to tell the others that they'd be moving.

She was keeping something from him.

Damn it.

Here, he'd just blasted his family for withholding evidence and information. He'd given Faith a *carte blanche* approval when defending her. But she obviously had some kind of secret. Was it connected to the murders?

It must at least be connected to Sherry or Darin.

And that meant he'd have to deal with it as soon as he made arrangements for the safe house. He also needed to call the bank and find out if his father or brother had recently withdrawn a large sum of money. Beck hated to doubt them, but he had to think like a lawman.

It was possible that one of them had taken the cash to Sherry to pay her off. Maybe an argument had broken out. Maybe one of them had accidentally killed Sherry. Then maybe Sherry's mother had been killed because she suspected the truth. Or might she have been a witness to her daughter's murder?

Beck groaned and scrubbed his hand over his face. Oh, man. He hated to even consider that, but it was possible. He only hoped it didn't turn out to be the truth.

His phone rang, and when he checked the caller ID screen, he saw that it was from the sheriff's office.

"It's me, Corey," his deputy greeted him when Beck answered. "You're never going to guess who just showed up here at your office."

After the morning from Hades that he'd just had, Beck was almost afraid to ask. "Who?"

"Our murder suspect, Nolan Wheeler. And he's demanding to see you and Faith. Now."

Chapter 9

Faith could feel her heart breaking. Letting her daughter go was not what she wanted to do. She wanted Aubrey with her.

But more than that, she needed her child to be safe.

For that to happen, she had to say good-bye, even if it made her ache.

"It'll be okay," Beck assured her. Again. He'd been saying that and other reassuring things for the past three hours, since they'd started the preparations to move Aubrey and Marita to a safer location.

Faith wanted to believe him, especially since she didn't feel as if she had a choice. The killer had seen to that.

She kissed Aubrey again and strapped her into the car seat in Beck's SUV. Marita and Tracy were already seated, as was Sgt. Caldwell, who would be driving them to the sheriff's house in Willow Ridge. The Ranger had already promised her that he would take an indirect route to make sure no one followed. Every precaution would be taken. And he'd call her as soon as they arrived.

Faith's heart was still breaking.

Aubrey waved, first to Faith. Then to Beck, who was standing behind her. The little girl gave them both a grin, looked at Beck and said, "Dada."

Her words were crystal clear.

Faith stepped back and met Beck's gaze. "I have no idea why she said that."

He shrugged. "One of the books I read her yesterday had the word *daddy* in it. Guess she picked it up from there."

Relief washed through Faith. She didn't want Beck to think she'd coached Aubrey into saying that. Their lives were already complicated enough without adding those kind of feelings to the mix. But it was clear that her little girl was very fond of Beck.

Beck leaned in, kissed Aubrey's cheek. Faith added another kiss of her own, and Beck shut the door. They backed into the mudroom, and only then did the Ranger open the garage door.

Somehow, Faith managed not to cry when they drove away.

"We need to go to the station and deal with Nolan," Beck reminded her.

As much as she loathed the idea of seeing Nolan Wheeler, it'd get her mind off Aubrey, and would keep Nolan occupied while Aubrey was being transported to the new safe house.

"You don't have to see him," Beck said, heading toward the other vehicle, a police cruiser, that one of his deputies had driven over earlier. He had the manila envelope with Sherry's blackmail letters tucked beneath his arm, and he laid it on the console next to him. "You can wait in my office while I interrogate Nolan."

"Right," she mumbled. Faith got into the passenger's seat and strapped on the belt. "I'm doing this."

"You're sure?" Beck started the cruiser, drove out and closed the garage door behind him. "I told Corey to put Nolan in a holding cell and test him for gunshot residue. That was three hours ago. Nolan will be good and steamed by now that we didn't jump at his invitation to meet with him immediately."

Yes, but there was an upside to that. "With his short temper, maybe he'll be angry enough to tell us what we want to know."

And maybe that info would lead to an arrest. Preferably Nolan's. Faith wanted there to be enough physical evidence to prove Nolan had murdered her mother and sister. Then she could bring her little girl home and get on with her life.

Part of that included coming clean with Beck.

She needed to do that as soon as this meeting with Nolan was over and they had some downtime. She'd told Beck lies, both directly and by omission. He wouldn't appreciate that—it would put a wedge between them, just when they were starting to make some headway.

Faith touched her fingertips to her lips and remembered the earlier kiss. That kiss wasn't ordinary, but the truth was, it couldn't mean anything. It couldn't lead to something more serious. Still, she fantasized about the possibilities. What if all their problems were to magically disappear? And what if Beck could forgive her for lying to him?

Would they have a chance?

She silently cursed. She had enough on her plate without complicating things with a relationship.

"Having second thoughts?" Beck asked.

Faith looked at him. He glanced at her with those sizzling blue eyes and gave her a quick smile. He was very good with those smiles. They were part reassurance, all sex.

Wishing the attraction would go away wasn't working, and that meant she was fast on her way to a broken heart. She hadn't returned to town for that, but it seemed as inevitable as the white-hot attraction between them.

Beck pulled into a parking space directly in front of the back entrance to the sheriff's office. But he didn't reach for the door. He glanced around the parking lot before his eyes came back to her.

"I need to talk to you when we're done here," she said.

He stared at her, and for a moment she thought he was going to insist that conversation happen now. But he didn't. He glanced around the parking lot again and nodded. "Let's go inside. We'll talk later."

Beck ushered her into the break room and through the hall that led to the offices and the front reception.

Deputy Winston met them. "Glad you're here. Our *guest* is complaining."

"I'll bet he is," Beck commented. "What about the GSR test?"

"It was negative." Corey looked at her. "Probably means he wasn't the one who shot at you."

"Or it could mean he washed his hands in the past twelve hours," Beck disagreed.

Corey shrugged and hitched his thumb to the right. "I was watching the security camera and saw you drive up. I just took Nolan to the interview room. He's waiting for you."

Beck handed Corey the manila envelope. "I need you to process this as possible evidence in the Matthews murders. There are three letters inside. Use latex gloves when you handle them, then copy them and send the originals to the crime lab. I want the DNA analyzed and all the pages and envelopes processed for prints and trace."

Corey studied the envelope. "Where'd you get this?"

A muscle flickered in Beck's jaw. "My father and my brother. Once the letters are processed, I'll have them make official statements."

So there might be charges against his family members after all. Faith hated that Beck had to go through this and hated even more that she had to meet with Nolan. He wouldn't willingly give up anything that would incriminate himself. Still, a long shot was unfortunately their best shot.

Faith was familiar enough with the maze of rooms and offices that constituted the LaMesa Police Department. When she was sixteen, she'd had to come and pick up her mother after she'd been arrested for public intoxication. The holding cell had been in the center of the building, but this was Faith's first trip to the west corridor. The walls were stone-gray and bare, unlike Beck's office, which was dotted with colorful Texas landscapes, photos and books.

There were no books or photos in the interview room, either. Just more bare, gray walls and a heavy, metal table where Nolan was seated. Waiting for them.

Nolan stood when they entered, and Faith caught just a glimpse of his perturbed expression before it morphed into a cocky smile. The man hadn't changed a bit. His overly highlighted hair was too long, falling unevenly on his shoulders, and his stubble had gone several days past being fashionable. Ditto for his jeans, which were ripped at the knees and flecked with stains.

"You're looking good there, sweet cakes," he greeted her. Nolan's oily gaze slid over her, making her feel the urgent need to take a bath.

Faith didn't return his smile. "You're looking like the scum you are."

"Oh, come on." He pursed his mouth, bunched up his forehead and made a show of looking offended. "Is that any way to talk to your own brother-in-law?"

"My sister's abusive ex-live-in," she corrected. "You left a death threat for me in the attic of my house."

"It wasn't me. It was your brother." Nolan put his index finger near his right temple and made a circling motion. "Darin's loco."

Beck walked closer and stood slightly in front of her. Protecting her, again. Nolan didn't miss the little maneuver either. His cat green eyes lit up as if he'd witnessed something he might like to gossip about later.

"Have you two buried the hatchet?" Nolan asked.

"I rechecked your alibis for the nights of the murders," Beck said, ignoring Nolan's too-personal question. "They're weak."

Nolan shrugged and idly scraped his thumbnail over a loose patch of paint on the table. "I was at the Moonlight Bar in downtown Austin both times, nearly twenty miles from where Sherry lived. People saw me there."

"Yes, but those same people can't say exactly when you left. You had time to leave the Moonlight and get to both locations to commit both murders." Beck met him eye-to-eye. "So did you kill Sherry and Annie Matthews?"

"No." Nolan smiled again and sank back down onto the chair. "And you must believe that or I would have been arrested, not just detained."

"The day's not over," Beck grumbled. He pulled out a chair for Faith and one for himself. Both of them sat across from Nolan. "Where were you last night?"

"Any particular time that interests you?" Nolan countered.

"All night."

"Hmm. Well, I got up around noon, ate and watched some TV. Around six, I dropped by the Moonlight and hung out with some friends. I left around midnight."

Beck shook his head. "Can anyone confirm that?"

"Probably not." Nolan winked at her. "You really think I'd want to put a bullet in you? I've always liked you, Faith." Again, he combed that gaze over her.

The glare that Beck aimed at the man could have been classified as lethal. "I want your clothes bagged. My deputy will give you something else to wear."

Nolan lifted his left eyebrow. "And if I say no?"

"I'll make a phone call to Judge Reynolds and have a warrant here in ten minutes. Then I'll have you stripped and searched—thoroughly. Ever had a body cavity search, Nolan?"

For the first time since they'd walked into the room, Nolan actually looked uncomfortable.

"I also want a DNA sample," Beck added.

Faith felt her stomach tighten.

"Why?" Nolan challenged. "I heard there was no unidentified DNA at the crime scenes."

There wasn't, but there might be DNA in her attic

However, it wasn't the prospect of that match that was making her squirm.

"I want to make some DNA comparisons." Beck made it seem routine. "If you're innocent, you have nothing to worry about."

Nolan shifted in the chair. "Are you taking Darin's DNA and his clothes to test them for *comparisons?*"

"I would if I could find him."

"Maybe I can help you with that." Nolan let that hang in the air for several snail-crawling seconds. "He calls me a lot. And, no, you can't trace the number. He bought one of those cheapskate disposable phones. But when he calls again, I think I can talk him into meeting with you." Nolan was looking at her, not Beck, when he said that.

"If you believed you could arrange a meeting, then why haven't you already done it?" Faith asked.

"No good reason to."

"He's a murder suspect," Beck pointed out. "The police and the Rangers have been looking for Darin for two months."

"No skin off my nose." Nolan turned to her again. "But I'll do it. I'll set up a meeting, as a favor to you."

He probably thought this would make her more amicable about splitting the inheritance with him. And maybe she would be. If her brother was guilty. And if it got Darin off the street. But Faith wasn't at all convinced that Darin had committed these crimes.

"Set up the meeting if you can," Faith finally said. She stood. "Once I've talked with Darin, then and only then will I discuss anything else with you."

"Deal," Nolan readily agreed. "But one way or another, I'm getting that money. I don't care who I have to turn over to our cowboy cop friend here." Nolan flashed another smile before turning to Beck. "So am I free to go, after you get my clothes and my DNA?"

"Not just yet. Why don't you hang around for a while." It wasn't exactly a request.

Nolan's smile went south. "You can't hold me, Beckett Tanner. I got myself a lawyer, and she said there's not enough evidence for an arrest."

"Then I'll hold you here until your lawyer shows up," Beck informed him.

Faith didn't say anything until they were outside the room. "A good lawyer will have him out in just a few hours," she whispered.

"Well, that's a few hours that he won't be free to roam around and terrorize you." Beck walked to the reception, where Corey was waiting. "I want his clothes and his DNA, and I want it all sent to the crime lab ASAP."

"Will do. Are we locking him up?"

Beck nodded. "Until his lawyer shows. Maybe by then one of his alibis will fall through. The Rangers have put out feelers to see if anyone noticed Nolan leaving the bar in time to commit the murders. Or the shooting last night."

Corey grabbed an evidence kit from the supply cabinet behind him, and he strolled in the direction of the interview room.

Beck turned to Faith. "You really think Nolan can set up a meeting with your brother, or was that all hot air?"

"Maybe. Darin and Nolan aren't friends, but they did get along. Well, better than Nolan got along with the rest of us."

"Then maybe the meeting will pan out." Beck paused. "You flinched when I told Nolan I wanted a DNA sample."

"Did I?" Though she knew she had.

"You did." He blew out a deep breath and put his hands on his hips. "Nolan flirted with you in there. I thought there'd be more animosity. I thought I'd see more hatred in his eyes. But there wasn't any."

It took a moment for all that to sink in, and Faith was certain she flinched again. "What are you saying?"

But he didn't have time to answer. The front door flew open, and Nicole walked in. Faith automatically looked for a gun, but the woman appeared to be unarmed. Still, that didn't make this a welcome visit. She'd had more than enough of Beck's family today. Because of his father and brother's impromptu visit, Aubrey had had to go to a safe house.

"Her brother stole from me," Nicole announced.

That got Faith's attention, and she changed her mind about this visit. It might turn out to be a good thing. "You've seen Darin?"

But Nicole didn't answer her. Instead, she turned her attention to Beck. "That killer was at the ranch." She shuddered. "He was there and could have murdered us all."

"Let's go into my office," Beck suggested.

Faith silently agreed. Though they were the only ones in the reception area, it still wasn't the place to have a private discussion.

"I don't want to go into your office," Nicole insisted, and she wouldn't budge. "I want you to make her tell us where her creepy brother is so you can arrest him before he murders me like he did his mother and sister."

Beck held up his hands. "Faith doesn't know where Darin is. No one does. Now, what happened to make you think Darin wants to kill you, and what exactly did he steal?"

"He took a tranquilizer gun from the medical storage room in the birthing barn."

Faith pulled in her breath. A tranquilizer gun had been used to incapacitate both her mother and sister before they'd been strangled.

"I have proof," Nicole continued. She pulled a disk from her purse and slapped it onto the reception counter. "He's there, right on the security surveillance. He took it two and a half months ago, just days before the murders. He knew where it was because we've kept it in the same place for years, and as you well know, he used to work at the ranch part-time before all that mess at the motel."

Oh, mercy.

If this was true, it didn't sound good. Right up until the time of the murders, her brother had worked on and off as a delivery man for Doc Alderman, the town's only vet. The police had investigated the vet's supplies, but he could account for both of the tranquilizer guns in his inventory. Neither of those guns had prints or DNA from her brother. It was the bit of hope that Faith had clung to that Nolan had perhaps used a tranquilizer gun to set up Darin.

"And you just now noticed this tranquilizer gun was missing?" Faith asked.

Nicole still didn't look at her. She aimed her answer at Beck. "We haven't had to use it in ages. One of the ranch hands went in there to get it this morning to sedate one of the mares, and that's when we realized it was missing. Darin Matthews took it."

"That's on this disk?" Beck picked it up by the edges.

"It's there. It took me a while to find it. The security

system in the storage room is motion-activated, and since the ranch hands hardly go in there, the disk wasn't full. I played it, and I saw Darin."

"You're sure it was him?" Beck asked before Faith could.

"Positive. You can see his face as clear as day."

"And you can see him take the tranquilizer gun?" Beck pressed.

Nicole dodged his gaze. "Not exactly. He moved in front of the camera, but what else would he have been doing in there?"

"Maybe delivering something for Dr. Alderman?" Faith immediately suggested. "Did you check with the vet to find out if he'd sent Darin out there to the ranch?"

"He had," Nicole said through clenched teeth. "Even though I'd told Alderman that I didn't want Darin anywhere near us."

"So maybe Darin was just delivering supplies," Beck concluded.

"Then what happened to the tranquilizer gun?"

"It could have been misplaced. Or someone else could have stolen it."

Anger danced through Nicole's cool blue eyes. "You're standing up for her again."

"I'm standing up for the truth," Beck corrected.

Her perfectly manicured index finger landed against his chest. "You're standing up for the Matthews family. I don't understand why. You know what they've done to us. The cheating, the lies."

"Pete cheated that night, too," Beck countered.

The color drained from Nicole's face, and she dropped back a step. "I expected this from the likes of her. But not from you." And with that, Nicole turned on her heels and hurried out the door.

Faith stood there silently a moment and tried to hold on to her composure. "Thank you," she said to Beck.

He turned and faced her. But he seemed unmoved by her gratitude. "I'll look at this disk," he said, his words short and tight. "And if there's any hint that Darin or anyone else stole that gun, I'll send it to the crime lab."

She nodded. "I expected that. I never expected you to give my brother a free ride. If Darin's guilty, I'll do whatever's necessary to catch him, and I'll support your decision to arrest him."

He searched her eyes, as if trying to decide if she was telling him the truth. Then he motioned for her to follow him to his office.

Faith did, and her heartbeat sped up with each step. The moment he made it into his office, Beck turned around to face her again.

"After watching the way Nolan reacted to you, I need to know." But he didn't ask it right away. He waited a moment, with the tension thick between them. "Is Nolan Aubrey's father?"

There it was. The question she'd been dreading.

Well, one of them anyway.

"Is he Aubrey's father?" Beck demanded when she didn't answer.

Faith shook her head, stepped farther inside and shut the door. "Maybe."

"Maybe? Maybe!" That was all he said for several seconds. Seconds that he spent drilling her with those intense and suddenly angry eyes. "You don't know who fathered your own child?"

"No, I don't."

Faith took a deep breath and braced herself for the inevitable fallout that would follow. "Because I'm not Aubrey's biological mother."

Chapter 10

Beck dropped into the chair behind his desk, squeezed his eyes shut and groaned.

"I know, I should have told you sooner," Faith said. "But I had my reasons for keeping it a secret."

He slowly opened his eyes and pegged her gaze. "I'm listening." Though he was almost positive he wouldn't like what he heard.

Faith sat first. She eased into the chair as if it were fragile and might break. "Sixteen months ago, Sherry showed up at my apartment in Oklahoma. I hadn't seen her in months, but she was pregnant and needed money. I gave her what cash I had, and when she left, I realized she'd stolen my wallet. It had my ID and driver's license in it."

Beck didn't say a word because he'd already guessed how this had played out.

"The following day when Sherry went into labor, she used my name when she admitted herself to the hospital. She even put my name on Aubrey's birth certificate. I didn't know," Faith quickly added. "Not until after she checked out of the hospital two days later. She broke into my apartment and left Aubrey and a letter on my bed."

"Hell," he mumbled. He had guessed the part about Sherry being the birth mom. But not this. "She left a newborn alone?"

Faith nodded and swallowed hard. "Aubrey was okay. Hungry, but okay. Needless to say, I was a little shaken when I realized what Sherry had done."

Beck leaned closer, staring at her from across the desk. "Why didn't you tell anyone?"

"Because of the letter Sherry left. I have it locked away in a safety deposit box in Oklahoma if you want to read it for yourself. But Sherry told me in the letter that Aubrey would be in danger if her birth father found out she existed. 'He'll kill her,' Sherry wrote. 'You have to protect her. You can't tell anyone or she'll die.'" Faith shuddered. "I believed Sherry."

Yeah. Beck bet she had. He would have, too.

"You covered for your sister, again, just like you did ten years ago outside the motel with Pete."

Faith nodded. "I had to protect Aubrey. I loved her from the moment I laid eyes on her."

He understood that, too.

Beck wanted to be angry with Faith. He hated being lied to. He hated that she hadn't trusted him with something this important. But if their situations had been reversed, he might have done the same thing. All he had to do was look at the things he'd done to protect his own family.

"I'm sorry I let you believe she was mine." Faith swiped away a tear that slid down her cheek. "But she is mine, in every way that counts."

He didn't want to deal with Aubrey's paternity just yet. But he had to find out if this was connected to the case.

"Nolan could be the father," Beck said more to himself than to Faith. "But if he knew, he would have already tried to use her to get money."

Faith mumbled an agreement. "Sherry told me she'd kept her pregnancy a secret. That no one knew, except our mother and Darin. She left Austin when she starting showing and stayed in Dallas until the day before she came to see me."

Beck wasn't sure he could take Sherry's account at face value, but something must have happened to make her want to hide the pregnancy and her child. Or maybe the woman simply didn't want to play mother and conned Faith with that sob story. It felt real.

"If Aubrey's father is someone other than Nolan, he hasn't made any contact with me," Faith continued. "And if he'd talked to Sherry, she probably would have let me know. She was so worried about him finding out about Aubrey."

Beck thought that through. If Aubrey's birth father was the person responsible for the attempt to kill Faith, then why had he shot at her? If he wanted something—money, for instance—then why hadn't he gotten in touch with her so he could blackmail her?

"I don't think this is connected to the case," she added, her voice practically a whisper now.

"Maybe not, but we need to know for sure."

She shook her head and looked more than a little alarmed. "How can we do that without endangering Aubrey?"

"Do you have something of hers that would have her DNA on it?"

She stood, and he could see the pulse pounding on her throat. "I have her hairbrush in my purse, but I don't want her DNA tested. I believed Sherry when she said Aubrey could be in danger."

"I'm taking that threat seriously, too. But we have to know who Aubrey's father is. He could have killed Sherry and your mother. We have to rule him out as a suspect. Or else find him and arrest him."

"I know." A moment later she repeated it, and the fear and frustration made her voice ragged. "Sherry often had affairs with married men."

"And one of those men might not want the world to know he has a child." Beck stood, too, and walked closer to her. "So here's what we do. I'll package the hairbrush myself so that no one, including my deputies, will see it. Then I'll seal it and send it to the lab in Austin. I'll ask them to compare the DNA to Nolan's. And to mine."

Her eyes widened. "Yours?"

He obviously needed to explain this. "I'll ask Sgt. Caldwell to give the results only to me. But I want him to leak information that he did some DNA testing and that I'm Aubrey's father."

"What?" Her eyes widened even more.

From the moment the idea had popped into his head, he figured she'd be shocked. Still, this was a solution. Time would tell if the solution was a successful one. "If everyone believes I'm Aubrey's father, that'll stop Nolan or anyone else from being concerned that they've produced an unwanted heir."

With her eyes still wide, she shook her head. "Beck, this could backfire. What happens when your family finds out?"

Oh, they would find out. No way to get around that.

"They won't be happy about it, but it doesn't matter. This will keep Aubrey safe."

He hoped.

But there was another reason he wanted his DNA compared to Aubrey's. Beck was positive he wasn't the little girl's biological father, but he couldn't say the same for his brother. Or even his own father.

If Aubrey was his niece or his half-sister, then the test would prove it.

And if Aubrey was the primary motive for murder, that might mean there was a killer in his family.

From where it lay on the coffee table, Beck's cell phone softly beeped again. An indication that he had voice mail. He didn't get up from the sofa and check it. Didn't need to. He'd already looked at the caller ID and knew the voice mails were from his father and brother.

He did check his watch though. It'd been six hours since he told Sgt. McKinney to get out the word that Beck was Aubrey's father. To make the info flow a little faster, Beck had told his deputy, Corey, the same necessary lie. The Rangers knew the truth. Corey didn't. He hoped Corey had leaked the little bombshell all over town, especially since Beck hadn't said anything about keeping it a secret.

Those two calls wouldn't be the only attention he'd get from his family. If he didn't answer their calls, they'd drop by for a visit—maybe even tonight. This time though, Beck had put the slide lock on. His father wouldn't be able to just walk inside as he'd done that morning. He'd also set the security system so if anyone tried to get in through any of the doors, the alarm would sound. Hopefully no one in his family would be desperate enough to try to crawl through a window.

He glanced at the numbers he'd written down when the bank manager had called him just minutes earlier. It was one of two other calls that brought bad news. Beck wasn't sure what to do about the second, but as for the first, he needed to investigate the bank figures from his father's account. Those numbers added up to trouble. They were yet another piece of a puzzle that was starting to feel very disturbing.

"Mommy misses you so much," he heard Faith say.

She was sitting on one of the chairs in the family room, just a few feet from him, with her phone pressed to her ear. She had her fingers wound in her hair and was doing some frequent chewing on her bottom lip. She was obviously talking to Aubrey, and it was the third call she'd made since the Ranger, Marita, Tracy and Aubrey had arrived at the safe house.

It wouldn't be the last.

This separation was causing her a lot of grief. Grief that Beck felt as well. But this arrangement was necessary. And hopefully only temporary. Once he'd caught the killer, then Faith could bring Aubrey home.

Wherever home was.

He doubted she could go back to her house, not with the attic death calendar and the shooting incident.

Faith got up from the chair and made her way to him. She held out the phone. "I thought you'd want to tell Aubrey 'Good night.'"

He did, but Beck knew all of this was drawing him closer and closer to a child that he should be backing away from. He needed to stay distanced and objective.

But he took the phone anyway. "Hi, Aubrey," he told her.

She answered back with her usual "'i'" and babbled something he didn't understand, but Beck didn't need to understand the baby words to know that Aubrey was confused. She was probably wondering why her mother wasn't there to tuck her into bed.

"Your mommy will be there soon," he added.

The next syllables he understood. She strung some Da-da-da's together. Such simple sounds. Sounds Aubrey didn't even comprehend, but they were powerful.

"Good night," he said and handed the phone back to Faith.

"Good night," she repeated to Aubrey. "I love you."

Faith hung up, stood there and blew out a long breath. "It's hard to be away from her."

Beck settled for a "yeah."

She put her phone on the coffee table next to his and then looked around as if she didn't know what to do with herself. "I cringe when I think of the prenatal care Sherry would have gotten when she was pregnant. She wouldn't have taken care of herself. But thankfully, Aubrey turned out just fine."

"You've done a good job with her. You're a good mother, Faith."

Her eyes came to his. "I'm sorry about lying to you. For what it's worth, I'd planned to tell you today."

He believed her. It riled him initially, but ultimately brought them closer.

Like now.

She stood there, just a few feet away, wearing dark jeans and a sapphire-blue stretch top, something she'd put on after showering when they'd returned from his office. Her hair was loose, falling in slight curls past her shoulder.

She looked like the answer to a few of his hot fantasies.

His body wanted him to act on the fantasies, to haul her onto his lap so he could kiss her hard and long. Of course, because this was his fantasy, the kiss would be just the beginning.

And all that energy would be misplaced because he needed to do everything to make sure there wasn't another attempt on her life.

Forcing his mind off her body, he picked up copies of the three blackmail letters and spread them out over the coffee table so that Faith could see them. "With everything else that's happened today, I haven't had a chance to go over these. They could be important."

She made a sound of agreement, sat down on the floor near his feet and picked up the first one. "I find it interesting that Sherry sent the letters to both your father and brother. By doing so, she implicates both, which means she could have had a recent affair with either of them."

"Or neither."

Faith didn't look offended by that. She stayed quiet a moment, apparently giving that some thought. "True, but then why would she think she could get money from them unless there'd been some kind of inappropriate relationship? Because Nicole hated Sherry so much and blamed her for her emotional problems, an affair with either would have upset her. Both Roy and Pete would have wanted to prevent Nicole from finding out."

She paused, and her gaze snapped to his. Her eyes widened. "The DNA tests," she said. "You wanted to compare Aubrey's DNA to yours so you'd know if Roy or Pete is Aubrey's father."

He nodded.

"Beck, this could be a nasty mess if one of them is."

He nodded again.

"Oh, mercy." She dropped the letter on the table and tunneled her hands through the sides of her hair again. "What happens if it's true, if one of them is a DNA match?"

"Then I'll deal with it." Which was his way of saying that he didn't know what he'd do. Still, he and Faith had to know the truth, and this was one way of getting it. DNA could also exclude his relatives and hone right in on Nolan.

Shaking her head, she leaped up from the floor. "I'm not giving up custody. I've raised Aubrey since birth. I love her—"

"You're not going to lose her," Beck promised, though he had no idea how he'd keep that promise. If necessary, he'd just continue the lie that he was Aubrey's father.

He felt as if he were anyway.

Because he was losing focus again, Beck forced himself to look at the letters. "The third letter is different from the other two," he continued.

It took her a moment to regain her composure, but then she glanced at all three letters. "Yes. Sherry asks for more money in the third one. Maybe because Nolan pressed her for more. Ironic, since his car was probably worth less than a thousand bucks. He would have tried to get everything he could from her, all the while threatening to go to the police to report her for car theft. With her priors, she would have gone to jail."

That made sense, but he wasn't sure that the rest of

it did. "Why would Sherry have typed the letters, especially since she put her name on them, visited my father and told him what she wanted? These letters are physical evidence and prove attempted extortion."

Faith lifted her shoulder. "Who knows why Sherry did what she did. Maybe she thought she could bluff her way out of extortion charges if she was arrested. She could claim she didn't type the letters." Faith paused. "You think someone else did?"

Now it was Beck's turn to shrug. But he also stood so he could deliver this news when they were closer to eye level. "The bank manager called when you were on the phone with Aubrey. It took some doing, but he found that my father had taken money from his various investment accounts. A little here, a little there, but it all added up to ten grand."

She walked closer and stopped right in front of him. "That's the exact amount Sherry was demanding in the first two letters."

"Yes. And she might have gotten it." His father might have paid Sherry off. He'd deal with that later, after he'd put more of this together.

"But if your father gave her the money, then why the third letter?" Faith asked.

"My theory is that someone else might have continued the blackmailing scheme."

"You mean Nolan." She didn't hesitate.

Neither did he. "Or your brother. Or even your mother. All it would have taken is knowledge of Sherry's plan and a computer to type the letters."

She bobbed her head, took another deep breath. "Nolan could have done this, and when Sherry threatened to expose him, he could have killed her."

That's what Beck thought, too. Nolan could have killed Sherry's mother if the money had been left with her. She would have known Nolan had a part in the scheme.

Because he was watching her, he saw Faith go still. "Is Nolan still being held at the sheriff's office?"

Hell. He hated to tell her this. "No. His lawyer showed up, and he was released about a half hour ago."

"I see." The words were calm enough, but the emotion was there in her expression and in her body.

"If I can get just one person at the Moonlight Bar to say they saw Nolan leave early on any of the three nights in question, then I should have enough to ask the DA to take this to a grand jury."

"In the meantime, Nolan is a free man. And he might stay that way. There's enough reasonable doubt, especially with the security disk of Darin in that barn."

Her voice didn't crack. Her eyes didn't water. He didn't touch her, but he did move closer.

"Some homecoming," she mumbled. She tried to smile at him, but it turned into a stare that ran the gamut of emotions. "But at least we're on the same side."

Oh, yeah. And more. They'd moved from being enemies to being comrades. To being…something else that Beck knew he should avoid.

But he didn't.

When Faith stepped closer, he didn't step back. He just watched her as she reached out and touched his arm lightly with the tip of her fingers.

"How badly would this screw things up?" she asked.

"Bad," he assured her.

She nodded. Didn't step back. She didn't take her caressing fingers from his arm.

"I'm not good at this." Her voice dropped to a silky whisper. "But I'll bet you are."

Beck couldn't help it. He smiled.

And reached for her.

Chapter 11

Beck's mouth came to hers, and just like that, Faith melted. The intimate touch, the gentle I'm-in-control-here pressure of his lips. The heat. They all combined to create a kiss that went straight through her.

She couldn't move. Couldn't think. Couldn't breathe. The kiss claimed her, just as Beck did when he bent his arm around her waist and pulled her to him. The sweet assault continued, and Faith could only hang on for the ride.

Or so she thought.

But then he stopped and eased back just a bit. That's when Faith realized her heart was pumping as if she were starved for air. She blamed it on the intense heat Beck had created with his kiss.

"You need a minute to rethink this?" he asked.

Did she?

Beck stood there, waiting. Breathing hard as well. Looking at her.

Faith looked at him, too. At those sizzling blue eyes.

At that strong, ruggedly hot face. And she looked at his body. Oh, his body. That was creating more firestorms inside her.

Because her right hand was already on his chest, she slid it lower and along the way felt his muscles respond. They jerked and jolted beneath her touch. It was amazing that she could do that to him.

Beck didn't touch her. He stood there with his intense eyes focused on her and his body heat sending out that musky male scent that aroused her almost as much as his kiss had done.

Her hand went lower, while their gazes stayed locked. A muscle flickered in his jaw. His heart was pounding. Hers, too. So much so that she wasn't sure if that was her own pulse in her fingertips or if it was Beck's.

When she made it to his stomach, she slipped her fingers inside the small gap between the buttons of his shirt and had the pleasure of touching his bare skin.

You can do this, she told herself. She wanted to do this.

"You still need time to think?" Beck asked her. She was surprised he could speak with his jaw clenched that tight.

"No." She eased her fingers deeper inside his shirt, loosening a button until it came undone. "I don't need any more time."

Before the last syllable left her mouth, he kissed her. It was hard and hungry. If it hadn't fueled the need inside her, it would have been overwhelming. Suddenly, she wanted to be overwhelmed. She wanted everything she knew Beck was capable of giving her.

With their bodies still facing each other, he scooped her up in his arms. Faith wrapped her legs around him, and he immediately started toward his bedroom. They bumped into some furniture along the way. And a wall. Neither of them were willing to break the kiss so they could actually see where they were going.

Beck used his foot to shove open the door. The room was dark, with only the moonlight filtering through the blinds and thin curtain.

Several steps later, Faith felt herself floating downward. Her back landed against his mattress. And Beck landed against her with his sex touching hers through the barrier of their jeans.

She didn't want any barriers. She kicked off her shoes and went after his shirt.

Beck went after hers, stripping it over her head and tossing it onto the floor.

Everything became urgent. Frantic. A battle against time. She cursed her fumbling fingers but then gave a sigh of pleasure when she got his shirt off and put her hands on him. He was all sinew and muscle. All man.

And for the moment, he was hers for the taking.

So Faith took.

She kissed his chest and explored some of those muscles. Not for long though. Beck had other ideas. He unhooked the clasp of her bra, and her breasts spilled out. He fastened his mouth onto her left nipple and sent her flying.

Mercy, was all she could think.

He kept kissing her breasts and lightly nipped her with his teeth; all the while he worked to get her jeans off. She worked to get his off, too, though she had to keep stopping to catch her breath.

Her jeans surrendered and landed somewhere on the floor where Beck tossed them. Faith shoved down his zipper. He shoved down her panties. And for only a moment, she felt the cool air on the inside of her thighs.

The coolness didn't last.

Beck kissed her. The heat from his mouth warmed her all right and had her demanding that he do something about the fire he'd created inside her.

He stood and rid himself of his boots and jeans. She wished the light had been on so she could see him better, but the moonlight did some amazing things to his already amazing body. The man was perfect.

Beck reached in the nightstand drawer and pulled out a foil-wrapped condom. Safe sex. She was glad he'd remembered. She certainly hadn't.

He tugged off his boxers while he opened the condom. She got just a glimpse of him, huge and hard, before he came back to her, moving between her legs.

Faith forced herself not to think. She wanted this to happen. With Beck. Right here, right now.

Their eyes met. The tip of his erection touched her in the most intimate way and sent a spear of pleasure through her. She gasped and gasped again when he pushed deeper.

Wow.

With just that pressure, that movement, that sweet invasion, she was certain this was as much of the tangle of heat that she could take. She felt on the verge of unraveling.

But Beck stopped.

In fact, he froze.

Faith wanted no part of that. She hooked her leg around his lower back and shoved him forward.

There was a flash of pain. But it was quickly overshadowed by a flood of pleasure.

Beck didn't move. He stayed frozen.

She focused, trying to see his face, and the confused expression she saw there probably matched her own. He had questions.

"You're a virgin?" he asked.

Now it was her turn to freeze. "Sort of."

Sort of? Sort of! She wanted to kick herself for that stupid response. And she wanted to kick herself again because the moment was gone. Even though the need was still there, racing through her, she knew this wasn't going to continue until Beck got an explanation.

She caught onto him when he tried to move off her. "I tried to have sex with my boyfriend in college, but it didn't work out. I panicked."

"You're twenty-eight," he reminded her. This time, he did move off her. He landed on his back next to her and groaned. "There would have been other opportunities since college."

"One other, a few years ago. I panicked then, too." Faith hesitated, wondering how much she should say, but since she'd already messed this up, she went for broke. "When I was fourteen, one of Sherry's drunk boyfriends sneaked into my bedroom one night and tried to rape me. He didn't succeed, obviously. Darin came in and hit the guy with an alarm clock. Anyway, it took me a long time to get over that."

Beck cursed under his breath. "You're over it now?" he asked, staring up at the ceiling.

"I'm over it." Beck seemed to have cured her. Amazing that he could do what therapy hadn't.

He turned on his side and faced her. "Why didn't you tell me before I got you onto this bed?"

"I didn't want to explain what'd happened in my past.

I wanted to have sex with you. And besides, I didn't think you'd notice."

"I noticed." It sounded as if he'd worked hard to keep the emotion and maybe even some sarcasm out of his voice. "Did I hurt you?"

"No." Since that sounded like a lie, she tried again. "Just a little, that's all."

This time the cursing didn't stay under his breath. "I'm sorry."

"No need to be. I'm not."

He stared at her, groaned and looked up at the ceiling again. "You just turned my life upside down. Now I've got positive proof that my brother's been lying all these years about what happened in the motel. And everything I'd ever thought about you was wrong."

"You thought I was a slut." She put her hand over his mouth so he wouldn't have to confirm that. "Everyone did. Because everyone believed I was just like my mother and Sherry. Guilt by association. But the truth is, I went in the opposite direction. I didn't want to be anything like either of them."

He stayed quiet a moment, before he reached for her and pulled her to him gently, and just held her.

"I never wanted to be any woman's first lover," he said. "It was sort of a badge of honor for some guys in high school. Not me. I figured it created some kind of permanent bond that I wasn't sure I wanted."

That stung a little. Was he saying he was sorry this had happened? Apparently. Because he wasn't doing anything to continue what they'd started.

"You don't owe me anything, Beck," she assured him.

"Oh, I owe you. An apology for starters for the way I've treated you." He kissed the top of her head. Cursed softly. And looked down at her. "What the hell am I going to do with you now?"

Though he probably didn't want her to answer, she considered pointing out that they were naked on his bed. But a soft thump stopped her from saying anything. The small sound came from the direction of the window. It sounded as if someone had bumped against the glass.

Beck shot off the bed.

"Get down on the floor," he told her.

Her heart banged against her rib cage, and Faith did as he said. Beck ran into the bathroom and seconds later emerged with his boxers on. He gathered up his jeans and started to put them on while he reached for something in his nightstand drawer.

A gun.

That got her moving.

She hurriedly crawled around, collected her clothes and got dressed. Once Beck had on his jeans, shirt and boots, he raced to the window. Pressing himself against the wall, he peered out the edge of the blinds.

"Hell, someone's out there," he let her know.

Her heart banged even harder. "Who is it?"

"Can't tell. He's dressed all in black, and he's crouched down near the rosemary bush in the side yard."

A ringing sound sliced through the silence. It was her cell phone. She'd left it in the family room.

"Stay put," Beck instructed. But a moment later, he cursed again. "The guy looks like he's trying to sneak away."

Oh, mercy. She didn't want him to get away. If it was Nolan, they could use this to arrest the man for trespassing. If he had a weapon, even better, because they could possibly charge him with criminal intent.

Beck started for the bedroom door. "My cell's not in here either. Use the phone by the bed and dial nine-one-one. Ask for backup. But I don't want sirens. I want a quiet approach so we don't scare this guy off."

She dialed the number as he asked. The dispatcher answered right away, and she relayed what Beck had told her. The dispatcher said he would send the night deputy immediately.

"Are you thinking about going out there?" she asked Beck the moment she hung up.

"I need to catch this guy," was his uneasy answer.

The silence lasted several seconds. "I have another gun on the top shelf in the closet," he instructed. "Get it and then stay low while you follow me to the back door. Lock it when I leave and set the security system. I won't be long."

"You don't know that. This guy could shoot you."

"I'm the sheriff," he reminded her. Plus, if he could end this tonight, then Aubrey wouldn't be in danger.

Her little girl could come back home.

"I'm doing this," Beck insisted.

Faith considered arguing with him, but she knew it would do no good. She hurried to the closet and took the .38 from the shelf. They crouched down and hurried to the back door.

"Be careful," she told him. But that was it. All she had time to say.

"Six-eight-eight-nine," he explained, disarming the security system so it wouldn't go off when he made his exit. He shoved a set of keys into his jeans pocket. "Lock the door, reset it and then get back into the bedroom. Stay on the floor. I'll let myself back in when I'm finished."

And just like that, he hurried out.

Faith followed his instructions to a tee, added a prayer that he would be okay, and headed to the bedroom. She hadn't even made it there when the house phone rang. Five rings and the answering machine kicked in.

"Sheriff Beck Tanner," the machine announced. "I'm not here, so leave a message. If this is an emergency, hang up and call nine-one-one."

She waited, her mind more on Beck than the caller. And then she heard the voice.

"Faith?"

It was Darin.

She scrambled across the room and picked up the phone. "Darin, it's me. I'm here."

"I'm here, too. Outside Beck's house. I need to see you. I have something to show you."

Oh, God. Beck was out there expecting to catch a killer. He might shoot Darin by mistake. Of course, there was that possibility that Darin was the killer.

"I'm in the yard," Darin continued. "By some rose-bushes. There's a window nearby."

So he wasn't by the rosemary. He'd moved from the side yard to the back, where Beck had just exited. They'd probably just missed each other. She needed to tell Beck what was going on, but he didn't have his cell phone with him.

"I won't hurt you," Darin promised. And for a moment, she remembered her brother, the one who'd saved her from Sherry's drunken boyfriend. The brother she loved.

With the cordless phone in one hand and the gun gripped in the other, Faith crawled back toward the kitchen. Toward the window with the roses.

"What do you need to show me?" she asked Darin.

"Sherry had some pictures of her with a man. I found them, and I think they're important."

It was likely the photo that Sherry had sent Pete and Roy, the one that proved she'd had the affair that might earn her some blackmail money.

When she reached the kitchen window, Faith lifted her head a little and looked out. She didn't spot her brother. "Darin, listen. Beck's out there, and if he sees you, he might shoot first and ask questions later. So I want you to stay put. Don't run. Don't make any sudden moves."

She saw something then. Was that a shadow in the shrubs or was it Beck?

She couldn't tell.

"Stay down," she told her brother in a whisper. She waited until Darin had gotten to the ground. Then she opened the window several inches, and in a slightly louder voice, she said, "Beck?"

Nothing. Not even from the other end of the phone, and she wondered if Darin had hung up.

Faith lifted the window a little more. The shadow didn't move. "Beck?" she called out.

She waited. Not long. Seconds, maybe. And a swishing sound came right at her. It happened in the blink of an eye.

Something tore through the mesh window screen.

There was a stab in her neck. Sharp and raw. But she didn't even have time to scream.

Faith felt herself falling, losing consciousness, and there was nothing she could do to stop it.

Beck stayed close to the house so he could use it for cover in case something went wrong and so he could make sure no one got inside to go after Faith.

The figure he'd seen in the yard might be a kid playing a stupid game, but with everything else that'd happened in the past two days, he couldn't take the chance. He also didn't want to leave Faith alone much longer, so that meant he had to find this guy and take care of the situation—fast.

He hoped it was Nolan so he could arrest him. Or beat him senseless, whichever came first.

Hurrying but keeping his gun aimed and ready, Beck went to the front of the house and looked around the corner. No one was there so he moved across the porch toward the side yard where he'd first seen the figure.

He silently cursed when he didn't see anyone there.

Had Nolan or Darin gotten away?

From up the street, he saw a cruiser approaching. The siren was off, but the deputy had his headlights on. He turned them off when he was about a half block away, parked the cruiser and got out. It was Deputy Mark Gafford. Beck motioned that he was going to go back around the house.

Beck stepped down from the porch and into the side yard where his bedroom extended to just a few feet from that rosemary bush. He glanced inside the bedroom window but couldn't see Faith. Good. That hopefully meant the killer couldn't see her either.

With the deputy now covering his back, Beck got moving again. Staying in the shadows. Keeping watch. He half expected someone to ambush him at any moment. Because after all, Sherry and her mother had been ambushed. But with each step, he heard nothing, saw nothing.

Until he made it to the backyard.

Someone was on the back porch at the door, dressed

all in black. Could it be the same shadowy figure that'd been in the rosemary?

"Hold it right there!" Beck called out. He ducked partly behind the corner of the house to use it as cover in case the person fired.

But there was no shot.

The person bolted off the porch and began to run.

"Stop!" Beck yelled.

The guy didn't. Beck jumped on the porch in pursuit. From the corner of his eye, he saw Faith. On the kitchen floor.

His heart fell to his knees.

He called out her name, the sound ringing through his head, and he got a glimpse of the darkly clad figure rounding the corner, out of Beck's sight.

Beck didn't chase after him. Instead, he raced to the back door, forgetting that it was locked. God, he had to get to her.

There was blood on her neck.

"Watch out for a gunman," Beck yelled to his deputy, hoping the man would hear him.

He fumbled through his pocket for his keys. It seemed to take an eternity before he got the right one into the lock. Finally, it opened, and despite the fact he'd triggered the security system and it started to blare, he ran to her.

She wasn't moving.

Trying to keep watch to make sure the gunman didn't return, Beck pressed his fingers to the side of her neck that wasn't bleeding.

He felt her pulse. It was faint. But it was there. She was alive.

For now.

He reached up, yanked the wall phone from its cradle and jabbed in nine-one-one.

"Sheriff Tanner," he said, the second the dispatcher answered. "Get an ambulance out to my place now. Faith Matthews has been shot."

He tossed the phone aside and checked her injury to see what he could do to help her. She wasn't bleeding a lot, and he soon realized why.

The injury wasn't from a bullet.

Beck reached down and plucked the tiny dart from her neck. And he felt both relief.

And fear.

Because someone had shot her with a tranquilizer gun.

Just the way her sister and mother had been shot, right before someone had murdered them.

Chapter 12

Faith forced her eyes open. No easy task, because her eyelids felt as heavy as lead. Actually, her entire body felt that way.

She glanced around and saw she was in a bed in a sterile white room. A hospital. That's when she remembered what had happened in Beck's kitchen.

Someone had shot her.

Her hand flew to her neck, to the thin bandage that was there. The skin beneath it was sore, but she wasn't actually in pain.

"Someone used a tranquilizer gun on you," a man said. "You're going to be okay." It was Beck. He was there. It was his voice she'd heard, and next to him stood Corey, his deputy.

"We didn't catch him," Beck added with a heavy, frustrated-sounding sigh.

"But you saved me. I didn't die," she mumbled.

Beck shook his head and walked closer. "You didn't die." His face was etched with worry, and judging from his bloodshot eyes, he hadn't slept in a while. Faith had no idea how long it might have been.

"How long have I been here?" she wanted to know.

Beck eased down on the side of the bed beside her and pushed her hair away from her face. His touch was gentle. "All night. It's nearly ten o'clock. There was enough tranquilizer in that dart to knock out someone twice your size. That's why you had to stay the night here in LaMesa Hospital."

"Ten o'clock?" That was too long. She had to find out who'd done this to her. She also had to check on Aubrey. Faith tried to get up, but Beck put his hand on her shoulder to make her lie back down.

"How are you feeling?" Corey asked.

So that it would speed things along and get her out of that bed, Faith did a quick assessment. Well, as quickly as her brain would allow. It felt as if her thoughts were traveling through mud. "I'm not in pain." She touched her throat and looked at Beck. "I guess you got to me before the killer could try to strangle me?"

"I got to you," Beck assured her, though that had not been easy for him to say. His jaw was tight again.

He was blaming himself for this.

Deciding to do something about that, Faith sat up. Beck tried to stop her again, but this time she succeeded. "How soon can I leave?"

He didn't look as if he wanted to answer that. "The doctor should be here any minute to talk to you."

She hoped he didn't hassle her about getting out of here. She wanted to get in touch with Marita and check on Aubrey. And her brother. She had to talk him into surrendering, or he was going to end up getting himself killed.

"Darin called me last night after you went outside," she explained to Beck. "He was there in your yard, but I don't think he's the one who shot me with the tranquilizer gun. I think someone else was out there."

Beck nodded. "There were two sets of tracks. I'm hoping I can match one of the sets to Nolan."

Good. That was a start and might finally lead to Nolan's arrest.

"I also had your neck photographed so the crime lab can compare your puncture wound to Sherry's and your mother's. The killer didn't leave the actual darts at those scenes so the lab can't make that comparison. But if the puncture wounds match, then we know the same person's responsible for all three attacks. Plus, they might be able to get some DNA from the dart I pulled from your neck."

And she prayed that DNA wouldn't belong to her brother. "Any sign of Darin or Nolan?"

Beck and Corey exchanged an uneasy glance. "No." Corey handed him an envelope that he'd been holding, and in turn Beck gave the envelope to her. "Darin left this by the rosebushes."

"Are these the pictures?" she asked, opening the envelope. "When he called last night, he said he had Sherry's pictures."

"And he obviously did," Corey mumbled. "I found them when I was processing the crime scene." He hitched his thumb toward the door. "I'll get back to the office and see if there's been any news about the case."

Faith waited until Corey was gone before she took out the first photograph. It was blurry and similar to the one in the blackmail letter. In the shot, there was a man lying asleep on a bed, and he was covered from the waist down with a white sheet. Maybe it was Pete, or even Roy, but it could have been Nolan with a wig.

In the second photo, someone had moved the sheet to expose the man's bare leg. Faith saw the spot on his thigh. A birthmark, she decided. She looked up at Beck for an explanation.

"Pete, my father and I all have that same birthmark."

Oh, no. Since she was dead certain that wasn't Beck in Sherry's bed, that left Roy and Pete. "The birthmark could be fake," she pointed out. "Nolan could have learned about the birthmark from Sherry and then painted it on to incriminate them."

Beck gave a crisp nod, an indication he'd already considered that. So why did he look as if that was a theory he didn't want to accept?

Faith tucked the second picture behind the third one. The last one. Again, it was a blurry shot, not of the man in the bed. This one was taken from long range, and it took Faith a moment to realize it wasn't Sherry.

It was a shot of her and Aubrey.

It'd been taken at the park about two months earlier. Right about the time the blackmail letters had been sent to Roy and Pete.

Faith drew in a sharp breath. "You think Sherry planned to use Aubrey to blackmail someone?"

But she didn't need an answer. She knew. This was exactly the kind of reckless thing Sherry would do.

"I have to go check on Aubrey," Faith insisted. She got out of the bed, and Beck looped his arm around her to steady her. If he hadn't, she would have fallen—her legs felt like pudding.

"Aubrey's fine," Beck assured her. "I talked to Sheriff Whitley less than a half hour ago. No one has attempted to get into the safe house. You can't go check on her. It's too risky. Someone might try to follow you."

The disappointment was as strong as her concern for her daughter. But he was right. Faith couldn't take the danger to her child's doorstep. However, that didn't mean she had to stay put.

She was wearing a hospital gown, but Faith spotted her clothes draped over a chair. Wobbling a bit, she reached for the jeans and top.

Beck had her sit on the bed while he put on her jeans. It was a reminder that he'd done the exact opposite the night before when they were on his bed, and despite the hazy head and the punch of adrenaline, she remembered the heat they'd generated.

When she met Beck's gaze, she realized that he remembered it, too.

"Are you *really* okay?" he asked.

"I'm really okay." She was still wearing her bra, and he slipped off her gown and eased her stretchy blue top over her head so that she could put it on. "This wasn't your fault."

"Like hell it wasn't."

Because he looked as if he needed it, Faith put her arms around him. She would have done more. She would have kissed him for reassurance, both hers and his, if the door hadn't flown open.

Pete and Roy.

Apparently, there wasn't much security at the small-town hospital if anyone was allowed to march right into her room. That in itself was alarming enough. But her alarm skyrocketed when she spotted the blood on Roy's shirt. The man also had what appeared to be several fresh stitches on his forehead.

"Well, isn't this cozy?" Pete barked.

Faith stepped away from Beck as quickly as she could. But Beck didn't step away from her. He stood by her side and slipped his arm around her waist.

"What happened?" Beck asked his father.

Roy looked at her. "I had a run-in with your brother about a half hour ago."

Oh, God. "Are you hurt? Is Darin hurt?"

"My father's obviously hurt," Pete interjected before Roy could answer. "Darin is a sociopath and a killer."

"What happened?" Beck repeated, sounding very much like a cop now.

Unlike Pete, there was no anger in Roy's expression or body language. Just fatigue and spent adrenaline, something Faith could understand.

"I went out to the stables to check on a mare, and Darin was there," Roy explained. "He said he wanted to talk to me, but I didn't think that was a good idea. I grabbed my cell phone from my pocket to call you, and Darin tried to stop me." Roy lifted his shoulder. "I don't think he meant to hurt me. He just sort of lunged at me, and we both fell."

"Dad cut his head on a shovel and needed stitches," Pete supplied.

"What about Darin? What happened to him?" Beck wanted to know.

"He ran off, but I think he was hurt." Roy touched his wounded head and winced. "He was limping pretty badly."

As much as Faith hated to hear that, she hoped it would make Darin seek medical attention, and then maybe, finally, she could talk to him.

Roy looked at her. "I heard what happened to you. Could have been worse."

"Much worse," she supplied. "I'm sorry about what went on with my brother. He's scared, and he needs help."

"He needs to go back to the loony bin," Pete jabbed. "And maybe you do, too." But he didn't aim that last insult at her but rather Beck. "What's this I hear about you being the father of her kid?"

So the info had indeed been leaked, though it was ironic that the first question about it had come from Pete, the man who might very well be Aubrey's biological father. Faith didn't want to know what kind of problems that was going to create if he was. Of course, the alternatives were Roy and Nolan. Nolan was a jerk. Possibly even a killer. And Roy seemed too decent not to own up to fathering a child.

But then maybe Sherry hadn't told him.

"You didn't mention a word to us about the baby," Roy continued where Pete had left off. "Or about being with Faith."

"Because I knew you wouldn't approve." Not exactly a lie. They wouldn't have.

Pete's hands clenched into fists. "So you're saying it's true, that you are the kid's father?" But then he relaxed a bit. "Oh, wait. I get it. You slept with her on a down and dirty whim, and then she claimed you got her pregnant. And you actually believed her?"

Roy caught onto Pete's arm. "If Beck thinks the little girl is his, he must have a good reason to believe it."

"I do," Beck supplied. "I also have a good reason to believe that Pete lied ten years ago. You didn't sleep with Faith."

The anger flushed Pete's face. "You're taking her word over mine?"

"No. I'm taking what I know over what you said. I think you lied because you thought Nolan would pound you to dust if he found out you'd been with Sherry."

She expected Pete to return fire, but he didn't. He went still, and it seemed from his expression that he was giving it some thought. Several moments later, he scrubbed his hand over his face.

"I wasn't afraid of Nolan," Pete finally said. "And I don't remember what went on in that motel room."

Pete seemed to be on the brink of an apology, or at least an honest explanation, but Beck's cell phone rang. Pete shook his head again, and she could tell that he'd changed his mind about saying anything else.

"What?" Beck snapped at the caller.

That got everyone's attention. So did Beck's intensity. He cursed and slapped the phone shut.

"That was Nicole," he explained. "She said she just found a dead body in the west barn at the ranch."

Beck caught onto Faith's arm to stop her from bolting from the cruiser when he brought it to a stop in front of the west barn at his family's ranch.

"I have to see if it's Darin," she insisted.

Not that she needed to tell him that. From the moment he'd relayed Nicole's message, Faith had been terrified that the body belonged to her brother.

Beck figured it did, but he didn't say that to her.

Still, he couldn't discount the altercation Darin had had with Roy just an hour or so earlier. His father had even said that Darin was injured. Maybe he'd hit his head, and that had caused his death.

That wouldn't make it any easier for Faith to accept.

This was going to hurt, and Beck wasn't sure she would let him help pick up the pieces.

Nicole was there, standing in front of the dark red barn, waiting. There wasn't a drop of color in her face, despite the cold wind whipping at her.

"I have to go in first," he instructed Faith. He drew his weapon, just in case. "I have to do my job."

He didn't wait for her to acknowledge that. Behind him, Pete and Roy pulled up. And behind them was Corey. All three men barreled from their vehicles.

Beck got out and held out his hands to stop them from going any farther. "Corey, I need you to wait here with Faith. Pete and Dad, you wait with Nicole. As soon as I've checked it out, I'll let you know what's going on."

None of them argued, maybe because none of them were anxious to have a close encounter with a dead body.

"I couldn't see his face," Nicole volunteered. "But it's a man, and he's dead in the back stall. There's blood, a lot of it," she added in a hoarse whisper.

Pete pulled her into his arms, and Beck gave Corey one last glance to make sure he was guarding Faith. He was. So Beck went inside.

The overhead lights were on, so he had no problem seeing. The barn was nearly empty, except for a paint gelding in the first stall. He snorted when Beck moved past him. Beck walked slowly, checking on all sides of him.

With the exception of six stalls and a tack room at the back, there weren't many places a killer could hide.

If there was a killer anywhere around.

But Beck figured Darin would be the only person he'd find inside. That meant he'd have to interview his father about the fight he had with the man, and Beck only hoped that he had told the truth. He didn't want to find out his father had shot an unarmed man.

Beck spotted a pair of boots sticking out from the back stall. Judging from the angle, the guy was on his back. He wasn't moving, and there was a dark shiny pool of blood extending out from his torso. Nicole had been right—there was a lot of it. Too much for the person to have survived.

Keeping his gun ready and aimed, Beck went closer. There was a piece of paper on the open stall door. The top of the page was slightly torn where it'd been pushed against a raised nail head that was now holding it in place. Beck decided he would see what that was all about later, but first he needed to ID the body and determine if this person was truly dead or in need of an ambulance.

More blood was on the front of the man's shirt. And in his lifeless right hand, there was a .38. The barrel of the gun was aimed directly beneath his chin.

Yeah, he was dead.

Blood spatter covered his face, too, and it took Beck a moment to pick through what was left of the guy and figure out who this was.

"Hell," Beck mumbled.

He looked at the paper then. Hand-scrawled with just three sentences.

I killed them. God forgive me. I can't live with what I've done.

He left the note and body in place so the county CSI crew and the Rangers would have a pristine scene to process. That was if Nicole hadn't touched anything. He wanted them to find proof that this was indeed a suicide or if someone had staged it to look that way.

Everyone was waiting for Beck when he came back out, including Sgt. McKinney, the Ranger who was still investigating the tranquilizer gun incident from the night before. But it was Faith that Beck went to.

"It's not Darin," he told her.

Her breath broke, and she shattered. He felt the relief in her when he pulled her into his arms. "It's Nolan Wheeler."

Blinking back tears of relief, she looked up at him. "Nolan?" she repeated.

So did Pete and Nicole. "What was Nolan Wheeler doing here?" Pete asked.

"Apparently killing himself. There's a suicide note."

"I'll have a look," the Ranger insisted, going inside.

Faith shook her head. "Nolan committed suicide?"

Beck couldn't confirm that. "According to the note, he couldn't live with himself because of the murders he committed."

He saw the immediate doubt in Faith's eyes and knew what she was thinking. On the surface, Nolan wasn't the suicide type.

So did the man have some "help"?

"Why would he have done this?" Corey questioned.

Beck was short on answers. "Maybe he thought we were getting close to arresting him."

That was the only thing he could think of to justify suicide. But why choose the Tanners' barn to do the deed? As far as Beck knew, Nolan wasn't familiar with the ranch.

"What were you doing in the barn?" he heard his brother ask Nicole.

Beck pushed aside his questions about Nolan because he was very interested in her answer.

Nicole, however, didn't seem pleased that all eyes were suddenly on her. "I was looking for my riding jacket. I thought I left it in there." Pete didn't jump to confirm her answer, so she sliced her gaze at Beck. "Why would I do anything to Nolan Wheeler? I hardly know him."

"You went to high school with him," Corey pointed out, earning him a nasty glare from both Pete and Nicole.

"I won't have Nicole accused of this or anything else," Pete snapped.

Nicole nodded crisply. "There's only one person here who had a reason to kill Nolan, and that's Faith."

Beck was about to defend her the way Pete had Nicole, but he spotted the Ranger walking back toward them. "I used my camera phone to take a picture of the suicide note and sent it straight to the crime lab. They'll compare it to Nolan's handwriting. We've got some samples on file that we've been comparing to the threats written in the attic."

"And did Nolan write those threats?" Faith wanted to know.

Sgt. McKinney shook his head. "The results are inconclusive, but we might have better luck with this suicide note since whoever wrote it didn't print."

Before the last word left the Ranger's mouth, Beck saw a movement out of the corner of his eye. He turned, automatically drawing his weapon. So did the Ranger and Corey. Pete shoved Nicole behind him.

Darin Matthews was walking straight toward them.

"Darin?" Faith called out.

Beck caught her arm to keep her from running toward

her brother. Darin was limping and looked disheveled, maybe from the altercation he'd had with Roy.

"Don't shoot," Darin said. He lifted his hands in a show of surrender.

"Are you hurt?" Faith asked.

"Just my ankle. I think I sprained it when I was here earlier."

Roy took a step closer to the man. "You mean when I ran you off or when you killed Nolan?"

Darin froze, and his eyes widened. "Nolan's dead?" And he looked to Faith for confirmation.

"He's dead."

"I didn't do it. I came here because I've been sleeping in one of the barns while I've been in town looking for evidence to clear my name. I didn't kill anyone, and I didn't help Nolan do it, either." He took in a weary breath. "But I'm tired now. I need to rest."

"You'll have to get your rest at the sheriff's office," Beck let him know. He walked closer and patted Darin down. He wasn't armed, but in addition to the limp, there was a nasty gash on the back on his head. It was no longer bleeding, but it looked as if it could use some stitches.

The Ranger's cell phone rang, and he stepped aside to take the call.

"Darin will have to be cuffed," Beck let Faith know, and he kept a grip on her until after Corey had done that.

When he let go of her, Faith ran to Darin and hugged him. "I want to go with him."

Beck didn't even try to argue with her. He knew it would do no good. He motioned for Corey to get Darin into the cruiser. He and Faith would follow it, first to the emergency room and then to his office, where he'd eventually have to lock up Darin.

"I'll do whatever you need me to do," Darin insisted. He looked at Faith. "You're not in danger anymore. Nolan can't hurt you."

"And I'll help you," Faith promised. "I have attorney friends who can defend you if you're charged with anything. There's a lot of evidence, and when it's all examined and processed, I think it'll prove you're innocent."

Beck hoped the same thing.

Nicole walked closer to them. "Now that this is over, and the killer's been caught, there's no reason for Faith to stay at your house any longer. We can finally get back to the way things were."

Beck shook his head. "This case isn't settled." And Faith would stay with him until it was.

He didn't want to think beyond that.

"We might be one step closer to getting things settled," the Ranger announced, rejoining them. "That was the crime lab. We'll need to do more analysis, of course, but the handwriting expert says the suicide note appears to be a match to Nolan Wheeler's."

"So he did write that note," Nicole concluded.

Beck considered a different theory. "Perhaps he wrote it under duress?" While a gun was pointed to his head?

The Ranger shrugged. "Maybe, but according to the expert, there are no obvious indications of hesitation. There probably would have been if he'd been forced to write it."

Well, that put a new light on things. Nolan had confessed to the murders in that note. Maybe Darin had been telling the truth about his lack of involvement? Maybe he wasn't a killer, and Nolan had been the one to orchestrate all of this so he could get the money from Sherry's blackmail scheme and her estate.

"We should go." Beck caught Faith's arm and led her toward his cruiser.

With her barely out of the hospital, he didn't like the idea of her having to accompany him to the station, but he didn't want her alone, either. Besides, she would want to be there when Beck questioned Darin. And when the questioning was done, the loose ends would be tied up into a neat little package.

So why did Beck have this uneasy feeling in the pit of his stomach?

Why did he feel that Faith was in even more danger than ever?

Chapter 13

Faith's mind was racing. She was mentally exhausted after spending most of the afternoon with her brother. But she was also hopeful.

Because soon she'd get to see her little girl.

She'd already called Marita, and the nanny had told her they would be on their way back when they got everything packed up. With luck, Aubrey would be home within the next three hours.

Well, not home exactly. But back at Beck's house, where they'd stay another day or two until she could decide something more permanent.

She climbed out of the cruiser, went inside the house and into the kitchen. Because it suddenly seemed to take too much energy to go any farther, she leaned against the wall and tried to absorb everything.

So much had happened in the past twenty hours. Too much to grasp at once.

Nolan was dead and no longer a threat to Aubrey and her. Her brother was at the LaMesa Springs hospital receiving treatment for the head wound he'd gotten from the altercation with Roy. Once the doctor released him, Darin would still have to undergo an intense interrogation. Maybe the evidence against him would even have to go to a grand jury. But Beck had promised her that Darin would be given fair treatment and that he personally was going to recommend that any assessment come from the county mental health officials.

Her brother might finally get the help he needed.

Beck came in behind her, took off his jacket and hung it on the hook on the mudroom door. "How's your neck?" he asked.

It took her a moment to realize what he meant. The tranquilizer dart wound. Even though it hadn't been that long since the injury, she'd forgotten all about it. "It's fine," she assured him.

The corner of his mouth lifted. A weary smile. "You're not feeling any pain because Aubrey will be here soon."

Faith couldn't argue with that, so she returned the smile. She took off her coat and hung it next to his. "Thank you for letting us stay with you."

It seemed as if he changed his mind a dozen times about what to say. "You're welcome."

His response was sincere, she didn't doubt that, but there was something else. Something simmering beneath the surface. "Your family won't like me being here. I'll make plans to leave tomorrow."

No smile this time. He took off his shoulder holster, and with the weapon inside, he placed it on top of the fridge. "No hurry. I don't want you to make any decisions based on my family. Truth is, I'm fed up with them. And I'd like for Aubrey, Marita and you to stay here for as long as you like. Or until at least we have everything sorted out with your brother. It's a big place, lots of room, and we can get to know each other better."

"You've known me for years," she pointed out.

He lowered his head. Touched his lips to hers. "But I want to know you *better*."

The kiss was over before it even started. It was hardly more than a peck. But it slid through her from her lips all the way to her toes.

"That sounds sexual." Or maybe that was wishful thinking on her part.

"It is," he drawled. "But the invitation isn't good for tonight. Tonight, you'll rest, take a hot bath and spend time with Aubrey when she gets here. In a day or two, I'll work on getting you into my bed again."

There it was. More heat. She'd been attracted to men before but never like this. Nothing had ever felt like this. It scared her, but at the same time, she wanted more.

"Don't look at me like that," he warned.

She touched the front of his shirt with her fingertips. "Like what?"

"Like you want to get naked with me."

"Oh." Maybe she looked that way because that's exactly what she wanted. "I'm at a disadvantage here. I've spent my entire adult life pulling back from men. I don't know how to stop you from treating me like glass. I don't know how to make you take me the way you would a woman with lots of experience. I don't know how to seduce you."

He shrugged. "Breathe."

Faith blinked. "Excuse me?"

He leaned in, whispered in her ear, "This is all about you, Faith. Just you. To seduce me, all you have to do is breathe and say yes."

"Yes." She pulled in a loud breath, and with that, his mouth came to hers.

This time, it wasn't a peck, it was a full-fledged kiss. His mouth moved over hers as if he knew exactly what to do to set her on fire.

It worked.

Faith leaned against him—until she could no longer do the thing that had set all of this into motion. She couldn't breathe. And she didn't care. She'd take Beck's kisses over breathing any day.

His left arm went around her waist, and he pulled her to him. The embrace was gentle. Unlike the kiss that had turned French and a little rough.

Faith broke the intimate contact so he could see her face. "No treating me like glass," she reminded him. "And I'd rather not rest tonight if you don't mind."

He stared at her, and she could see the debate that stirred the muscles in his jaw. "All right."

That was the only warning she got before he hoisted her up. Face-to-face. Body against body. And he delivered some of those kisses to the front of her neck and then into the V of her top.

Faith automatically wrapped her arms and legs around him. His sex touched hers and sent a shiver of heat dancing through her. She wanted him naked, now.

She went after his shirt as he carried her toward his bedroom. Buttons popped and flew, pinging on the floor, and her frenzy of need for him only fueled the fire. She got his shirt off and kissed his neck. Then his chest.

He made a throaty sound of approval and, off balance, he rammed his shoulder into the doorjamb. Faith wanted to ask if he was okay, but he obviously was.

Beck kissed her even harder, and instead of taking

her to the bed, he stopped just short of it, and with her pressed between him and the mattress, he slid them to the floor. While he kissed her blind, he unzipped her jeans and peeled them off her. Bra and panties, too, leaving her naked. He quickly covered her left nipple with his mouth.

The sensation shot through her.

His hand went lower, between her legs, and his fingers found her. He slipped his index finger through the slippery moisture of her body and touched her so intimately that Faith could have sworn she saw stars.

"Breathe," he reminded her.

She thought she might be breathing, but couldn't tell. The only thing she knew for sure was that she wanted him to continue with those slippery, clever strokes.

And he did.

He touched and created a delicious friction that brought her just to the edge.

Faith caught her breath and caught onto his hand. "You, inside me," she managed to say, though she didn't know how she'd gotten out the words. Speech suddenly seemed very complex and not entirely necessary.

She shoved down his zipper, which took some doing. He was huge and hard, making it difficult for her to free him from his jeans and boxers.

Even though her need was burning her to ash, she took a moment to fulfill a fantasy she'd had for years. She got him out of those jeans, took Beck in her hand and slid her fingers down the length of him, all the while guiding him right to where she wanted him to go.

He reacted with a male sound deep within his chest. He buried his face in her hair. His breath, hot against his skin. His mouth, tense now, muffled a groan, and he kissed her. His tongue parted the seam of her lips as his hard sex touched the softness of hers.

Her vision blurred. She reached to pull him closer. Deeper into her. But he stopped and cursed.

"Condom," he gutted out.

Still cursing, he reached over, rummaged through his nightstand drawer and produced a condom. He hurried, but it still seemed an eternity. The moment he had it on, Faith pulled him back to her.

Despite the urgency that she could feel in every part of him, Beck entered her slowly. Gently. Inch by inch. While he watched her. That wasn't difficult to do since they were face-to-face with her straddling him. He was watching to see if he was hurting her.

He wasn't.

The only pain she felt was from the hard ache of un-filled need. A need that Beck was more than capable of satisfying.

She could see how much this gentleness was costing him. Beck didn't want to hold back anything, and Faith made sure he didn't. She thrust her hips forward.

Beck cursed again.

"It's better than I thought it'd be," she mumbled. A shock since she'd been positive it would be pretty darn good.

"Yeah," he said.

He stilled a moment to let her adjust to this intimate invasion, but the stillness only lasted a few seconds and a kiss. He moved, sliding into her. Drawing back. Then sliding in even deeper. Each motion took her higher. Closer. Until her focus honed in on the one thing she had to have.

Release.

Beck had taken her to this hot, crazy place. He'd made her feel things she'd only imagined. And he just kept making her feel.

He slid his hand between their bodies, and with him sliding in and out of her, he touched her with his fingers, matching the frenetic stokes of his sex. He kept touching. Kept moving. The need got stronger. Until she was sure she couldn't bear the heat any longer.

Beck seemed to understand that. He kissed her. Touched her. Went deep inside her. A triple assault. And it happened. In a flash. Her orgasm wracked through her, filling her and giving her primal release.

Breathe, Faith reminded herself. *Breathe.*

There were no barriers. No bad blood. Nothing to stop her from realizing the truth.

She was in love with Beckett Tanner.

Well, Faith was breathing all right.

Her chest was pumping as if starved for air, and each pump pushed her sweat-dampened breasts against his chest. There was a look of total amazement on her face.

She was practically glowing.

Beck knew he was somewhat responsible for giving her that look, and when his brain caught up with the now sated part of his body, he might try to figure out what he was going to do about that look. And about what'd just happened.

For now though, he just held her and tried not to make any annoying male grunts when the aftershocks of her climax reminded him that he was still inside her. Not that he needed such a reminder.

"That was worth waiting for," she mumbled.

He kissed her, tried to think of something clever to

say and settled for another kiss. But he would have to address this sooner or later. Faith obviously wasn't a casual sex kind of person. Neither was he. But it suddenly felt as if he had more than a normal responsibility here. A commitment, maybe.

After all, he was her *first*.

He certainly hadn't expected to have that title once he was past the age of twenty. Maybe she'd have some emotional fallout from this.

Maybe even some regrets.

Beck realized she was staring at him. Her breathing had settled. There were no more aftershocks. But she had her head tilted to the side, and she was studying him.

"What?" he prompted.

"I'm just trying to get inside your head." She smiled. It was tentative. Perhaps even a facade. "Don't worry. This doesn't mean we're going steady or anything." Still smiling, she moved off him and stood.

Beck caught onto her hand before she could move too far from him. All in all, it wasn't a bad vantage point. He was still sitting. Looking up at her. She was naked. Beautiful. Glistening with perspiration. And his scent was on her.

He wanted her all over again.

"I need a drink of water," she let him know. She leaned down and kissed him. "Then I think I'll take a bath before Aubrey gets here."

He had some cleaning up to do, too, and rather than sit there and watch her dress, Beck got up, gathered his clothes from the floor and went into the adjoining bathroom.

While he cleaned up and put his jeans back on, he glanced at the tub. Should he run her a bath? Probably not. It would only lead to more sex. Once was enough for her tonight. Plus, despite her "going steady" remark, she had some feelings she needed to work through.

He certainly did.

The house phone rang, and he went back into the bedroom to answer it. "Sheriff Tanner."

"It's Corey. Is Darin Matthews with you?" His words were harried and borderline frantic.

That put a knot in Beck's stomach. "No. He's supposed to be at the hospital with you."

Corey cursed. "Darin was sedated so I went to the vending machine to get a Coke. When I got back, he wasn't in his bed. I guess he wasn't sedated as much as I thought. I've looked all through the building and the parking lot. He's not here."

Darin couldn't have gotten far with that injured leg. Beck hoped. Unless he stole a car.

"Don't put out an APB just yet, but if one of the Rangers is still around, let him know so he can look for him. Faith and I will drive around, too, and see if we can spot him. Darin's probably looking for her anyway."

"One more thing," Corey said before Beck could end the call. "The Ranger lab in Austin put a rush on that DNA test you ordered. They faxed the results over, and the dispatcher brought it to me while I was looking for Darin."

Great. He needed those results, but he had to resolve this problem with Darin first. "The results will keep," Beck let him know.

Cursing under his breath, Beck hung up and reached for his boots. He should probably call Marita and Tracy and delay Aubrey's homecoming, just in case Darin had some kind of psychotic episode.

Beck reached for the phone again, but stopped when he heard the soft sound. A thud. He stilled and listened. But there wasn't another sound. Just the uneasy feeling that all was not right.

"Faith?" he called out.

Nothing.

That knot in his stomach tightened. Hell. Why hadn't she answered?

The answer that came to mind had him grabbing the gun from the nightstand.

Beck started for the kitchen.

Chapter 14

Faith opened the cupboard and reached for a glass. But reaching for it was as far as she got.

The lights went out.

She heard footsteps behind her. Before she could pick through the darkness to see who was behind her, an arm went around her neck, putting her in a choke hold.

A hand clamped over her mouth, and she felt the cold steel of a gun barrel shoved against her right temple.

Oh, God. What was happening?

Nolan was dead. The danger was over. Who was this person, and what was going on?

She didn't wait for the answers. Faith rammed her elbow into her attacker's belly. She might as well have rammed it into a brick wall because other than a soft grunt, the person didn't react.

"What do you want?" she tried to say, but his hand muffled any sound.

Still, there were sounds. Footsteps, both his and hers, as he started to drag her in the direction of the back door.

Beck would likely hear the sounds, even though he might still be on the phone dealing with the call that'd come in. Once that call was finished, he would begin to wonder what was taking her so long to get a drink of water.

Then Beck would come looking for her.

And this person might shoot him.

He jammed the gun even harder against her temple when she started to struggle, and Faith had to try to come to terms with the fact that she might be murdered tonight. She thought of Aubrey, of her precious little girl. And of Beck. He would blame himself for this because he hadn't been there to protect her. But Faith didn't want him there. She wanted to live, but not at the expense of Beck being killed.

The man opened the back door, and cold air rushed inside, cutting what little breath she had. He tried to push her outside, but Faith dug in her heels. If he got her out of the house and away from Beck, he'd just take her to a secondary crime scene where he'd do God knows what to her.

But why?

And that brought her back to the question of whom.

Had Nolan hired someone to do this last deed? A way of reaching out from beyond the grave to settle an old score with her?

Of course, there was another possibility. One she didn't want to consider—maybe somehow her brother had gotten free. Maybe he really was a killer after all and had come to eliminate the last member of their family.

"Faith?" she heard Beck call out.

Her attacker froze for just a moment and then resumed the struggle to get her out the door. She tried to warn Beck, but her assailant's hand prevented that.

"What the hell's going on?" Beck called.

Though it was pitch-dark, she spotted him in the hallway opening just off the kitchen. She also saw him lift his gun and take aim.

The attacker stopped trying to shove her out the door, and he pivoted, placing her in front of him. He even crouched slightly down so that his head was partially behind hers.

She was now a human shield.

"Who are you?" Beck demanded. He squinted, obviously trying to adjust to the darkness. He reached out for the light switch on the wall next to him.

"Don't," her attacker growled. He kept his voice throaty and low, but there were no doubts that this was a man. A strong one. He had her in a death grip, and the barrel of the gun cut into her skin.

Beck didn't turn on the light, but he kept his gun aimed.

"I'm leaving with her," the man said. He was obviously trying to disguise his voice. That meant Beck and she probably knew him.

Inching sideways and with her still in front of him to block Beck's shot, the man started dragging her back to the door.

Faith didn't know whether to fight or not. If she did resist, he might just shoot Beck. However, the same might happen if she cooperated.

Beck inched closer as well, and because she was watching him, she saw his eyes widen. He didn't drop his gun, but he did lower it.

"Pete?" Beck called out.

The man's muscles went stiff, and he stopped. She heard every word of his harshly whispered profanity.

"What the hell do you think you're doing?" Beck demanded. He came even closer.

"Stop," the man said. Not a muffled whisper this time. She clearly heard his voice.

It was indeed Pete, Beck's brother.

"Well?" Beck prompted. "What the hell are you doing?"

"What's necessary." With that, Pete jammed the gun even harder against her. She could smell the liquor on his breath, but he wasn't drunk. He was too steady for that.

"What's necessary?" Beck spat out. "How did you even get in here?"

"You gave Dad the codes to disarm the security system and I used the key you gave me for emergencies. I didn't want you to be part of this," Pete said to Beck. "I wanted to take care of her before you noticed she was missing. She's a loose end."

Beck shook his head, and his expression said it all. He couldn't believe this was happening. "Put down your gun."

"I can't. I have to fix this." Pete groaned and took his hand from her mouth. "I've made a mess of my life."

"You can fix things the legal way," Beck insisted. His voice was calm, and he took another step toward them. "Put down the gun."

"It's too late for that. I killed them, Beck. I killed them all."

Oh, God. It was true. Pete was a killer, and he had her in his grips.

"You mean you killed Sherry and Annie?" Beck clarified.

"Yeah, I did. But it was all Sherry's fault. I swear she tricked me into that affair. When I saw her at the Moonlight Bar, she came onto me, got me drunk and then took pictures of me when I was sleeping. She blackmailed me. And I gave her the money. I gave her exactly what she wanted—ten thousand dollars that I got from Dad's accounts. Look where it got me."

"Start from the beginning. What happened?" Beck asked.

"The beginning? I'm not sure when it all started. But killing Sherry was an accident. I swear. I used the tranquilizer gun from the stables and drugged her so I could reason with her. But the drug wore off too soon, and when she started struggling, I had to strangle her."

"It wasn't premeditated," Beck explained. "You could maybe plea down to manslaughter. That's why you need to put down the gun so we can talk."

"Talking's not going to save me. Sherry's death might not have been premeditated, but the others were."

Until that statement, Beck had managed to maintain some of his cop's persona, but the grim reality of Pete's confession etched his face with not just concern but shock. "What do you mean?"

"After I killed Sherry, I tried to get the money back so Dad and Nicole wouldn't find out, but Annie wouldn't give it to me. She said she wanted it and more. A lot more. She wanted fifty thousand dollars. That's when I had to kill her. I couldn't keep paying her off, and I knew she'd tell Nicole."

It was so hard for Faith to hear all of this. She hadn't been close to Sherry or her mother, but both of them had been killed for money. For greed. And to cover up an affair that Sherry had probably orchestrated just so she could blackmail Pete. If he hadn't been thinking from below the belt, Pete might have figured it out before things got this far.

"I thought after I killed Annie that it'd be over," Pete continued, his voice weary and dry. "But I got another letter demanding more money. I thought it came from Nolan. That's why I put a gun to his head and made him write that suicide note. But he insisted right up to the end that he hadn't sent any blackmail letters."

"You killed him anyway," Beck said. It wasn't a question.

"Nolan Wheeler deserved to die." Pete's voice was suddenly defiant. "He'd been skirting the law for years. I did the world a favor."

"The world might not agree," Beck countered. "I certainly don't. You killed three people, and you're holding a gun on your brother and the assistant district attorney. Where's the justice in that?"

Pete stayed quiet a moment. "It'll be my own form of justice. I can't let either of you live. Especially Faith. This afternoon there was another blackmail letter in the mailbox. She put it there. I know she did. There couldn't be anyone else."

"You don't know that. It could be one of Sherry's friends. Besides, Faith's been with me all day. She couldn't have put the letter in the mailbox."

"I don't believe you," Pete practically shouted. "You're covering for her because you're sleeping with her. You chose her over your own family."

"Maybe I did," Beck conceded. Unlike Pete, he kept his voice level and calm though Faith didn't know how he managed to do that. "But it's my job to protect her." He took another step toward them. "Put the gun down, Pete, and let's talk this out."

"No. No more talking. I'd wanted to do this clean and nearly succeeded last night. I got the tranquilizer in her, but then you came to the rescue. Just like tonight. But the difference is, tonight I'll kill you, too."

"I'm your brother," Beck reminded him. "Think what killing me would do to the family."

"I can't think about that. I have to protect Nicole. She's my first and only concern. I have to make sure she never learns about any of this. The only way for that to happen is for you to die."

Pete re-aimed his gun.

At Beck.

Faith felt the muscles in Pete's arm tense. She saw the realization of what was about to happen on Beck's face. He couldn't shoot at his brother because he might hit her. Pete, however, had no concern about that since he intended to kill them both anyway.

She yelled for Beck to get down. With the sound of her voice echoing through the house, Faith turned, ramming her shoulder into Pete. He hardly budged from the impact, but it was enough to shake his aim.

The bullet that Pete fired slammed into the wall next to the fridge.

Beck lunged at them, and the hard tackle sent all three of them to the floor. Beck's own gun went flying, and it skittered across the floor. And the race was on to see which one would come up with Pete's gun.

Faith managed to untangle herself from the mix. She got to her feet and slapped on the light. Pete and Beck were practically the same size, and they were in a life-and-death struggle.

She waited until she spotted Pete's hand. And the gun. Faith went for it, dropping back to the floor, and she latched on to his wrist. Somehow, she had to keep that gun pointed away from Beck.

Beck drew back his fist and slammed it into Pete's face. The man was either tough as nails or the adrenaline had made him immune to the pain because he hardly reacted. In fact, Pete twisted his body and slammed his forearm into her jaw. The impact nearly knocked the breath from her, but somehow Faith managed to hang on to his wrist. She dug in her nails and clawed at any part of his flesh that she could reach.

Beck threw another punch. And another. The third one was the charm. Pete's head flopped back onto the tile floor. Dazed and bleeding from his mouth and nose, he groaned and mumbled something indistinguishable.

"The gun," Beck said.

Beck wrenched it from his brother's hand. He pulled in a hard breath and reached again, this time to roll Pete on his stomach so he could subdue him.

"Call nine-one-one," Beck told her.

"You're sure?" she asked, though she knew he had no choice. This was attempted murder. But Pete was still his brother. A lesser man would have wanted to try to resolve this without the law and tried to keep it a family secret.

Beck nodded. "I'm sure. Make the call."

She got up to do that, but before Faith even made it to her feet, the back door flew open, hitting her squarely in the back and sending her plummeting into Beck.

"Oh, my God," someone said.

Nicole.

Pete used the distraction of his wife's arrival to ram his elbow into Beck, and grab his gun.

Faith couldn't scramble away from him in time. Pete

latched on to her hair and dragged her in front of him again.

"January fourteenth," Pete said as if in triumph. "Faith dies."

His brother's words were like stabs from a switchblade. It was the threat written in the attic. A threat Beck hadn't announced to anyone other than law enforcement, which meant Pete had been the one to paint that threat on Faith's attic walls.

Oh, man. Things had really gone crazy. And worse, it might turn deadly if he didn't do something now to stop all of this.

Beck's gaze connected with Faith's. She was scared. And shocked. But he could also see determination. She wasn't just going to stand there and let Pete kill them. She was a fighter, but this fight might cause Pete to pull that trigger even faster.

"Pete, what's going on?" Nicole asked.

Nicole looked at Beck, her eyes searching for a logical answer. But he couldn't give her one. There was no logic in any of this. Another of Pete's affairs had gotten him into trouble, and he'd been willing to kill to keep his secret.

"Pete killed Annie and Sherry Matthews. Nolan Wheeler, too," Beck explained to Nicole. "Now, he's going to put his gun down so we can deal with this."

Beck hoped.

"I killed them for you, Nicole," Pete insisted.

She gasped and stepped back. Good. So Nicole wasn't in on this. Maybe, just maybe, she could talk Pete into surrendering.

"Tell Pete to put his gun down," Beck instructed Nicole.

She gave a choppy nod. "Please, Pete. Do as Beck says."

"Faith's blackmailing me. She sent me a letter today. Left it in the mailbox—"

"No. She didn't." Nicole shook her head. "I sent the last two letters."

Beck hadn't thought there could be any more surprises tonight, but he'd obviously been wrong. "You?" he questioned. "Why?"

Tears filled Nicole's eyes. "Sherry called me two months ago and told me about her affair with Pete. She faxed me copies of the pictures of them together."

"Oh, God." Pete groaned. "I'm sorry. So sorry."

"I know." Nicole blinked back the tears, and her voice was eerily calm. "But I was upset, and I wanted to leave you—after I punished you. So, after Sherry and Annie were killed, I sent a third letter. This afternoon, I put the fourth one in the mailbox. I wanted you to suffer. I wanted you to think that your indiscretion would be punished for a long, long time."

Pete cursed. He glanced at Faith and then cursed some more.

"Faith didn't do anything wrong," Beck said. "You need to let her go."

"Yes," Nicole agreed. "Let her go. Let Beck handle this."

"I can't. Don't you see what has to happen here? I've already put the plan in place. I waited at the hospital until I could get Darin alone, and I forced him to leave with me. There are no security cameras in the entire place so it was easy. Then I left him on the side of the road about a mile from here."

"No," Faith mumbled.

Beck silently mumbled the same. With Darin hurt and possibility medicated, he shouldn't be out on his own on a cold winter night. It was a cliché, but he could literally die in a ditch somewhere.

"Darin will try to go home, but he won't have an alibi," Pete continued. "He'll be blamed for Beck's and Faith's murders. Then we can start over, Nicole. I swear, no more affairs."

That just pissed Beck off. His brother was willing to kill Faith and him rather than take responsibility for what he'd done. Somehow, he had to get Faith out of harm's way and subdue Pete.

"Do you hear yourself?" Beck snapped. "I knew you were self-centered and egotistical, but I had no idea you'd stoop to this. Think it through. You plan to kill me and Faith in front of Nicole? What kind of future can you have with that hanging over your heads?"

"Beck's right," Nicole added. "I could never stay with you after what you've done."

"You tricked me with those letters!" Pete shouted.

"Letters?" Nicole threw right back at him. "I didn't murder anyone. Nor would I. Did you honestly think I could live with a killer?"

Pete slowly aimed his attention at Nicole. The change in his brother's expression wasn't subtle. Rage sliced through his eyes, and the muscles corded on his face. "I did this all for you, and this is how you treat me?"

"You didn't do this for Nicole." Beck wanted to get Pete's attention off Nicole and Faith and back onto him. Because it looked as if his brother was about to start shooting at any minute. "You did this to cover up what you'd done. Well, the covering up has to stop."

"Who says?" He pushed Faith onto her knees and put the gun to the back of her head.

She looked up. Her eyes met Beck's. "I love you," she said, silently mouthing the words.

Oh, man. Oh. Man. That hit him, hard, but he knew he couldn't think about it. Later—and there would be a later—he'd deal with her confession.

A sound shot through the room.

Beck was certain he lost ten years of his life. It took him a moment to realize that Pete hadn't fired. The phone was ringing.

"Don't answer that," Pete ordered. "You," he said to Nicole. "Get down on the floor next to her."

Nicole frantically shook her head. "You're going to shoot me?"

"Yeah." This was no longer the voice of his brother. It was the voice of a cold, calculated killer. "I love you, Nicole. I always will. But I won't give up my life for you. I'm not going to jail for you."

The answering machine kicked in on the fifth ring. "Faith, it's Marita. Pick up."

"No," Faith whispered. She repeated it as Marita's cheerful voice poured through the room.

"I guess you're celebrating, but I wanted you to know we'll be there in about ten minutes. Aubrey's sacked out, but I'll wake her when we arrive so you can get some hugs and kisses."

Hell. Ten minutes. He couldn't have Marita, Tracy and especially Aubrey walking into this.

"I gave Marita an emergency key," Beck let Faith know. And that meant if they didn't answer the door, which they wouldn't be able to do at this point, then Marita might let herself in.

"You couldn't hurt a child," Beck told Pete, trying one last time to reason with him.

Pete met him eye-to-eye. "I'm fighting for my life. I can and will hurt anyone who gets in my way."

Beck believed him. This wouldn't end with a successful surrender. It would end only when he managed to stop Pete. He might even have to kill his own brother. But he would if it came down to that.

He wouldn't allow Pete to hurt anyone else.

"Go ahead," Beck instructed Nicole. "Get on the floor."

The tears were spilling down her cheeks now, and her eyes were wide with terror.

"Trust me," Beck added. "Get on the floor."

Nicole gave a shaky nod. Using her right hand to steady herself, she started to lower herself to her knees.

Beck waited.

Watching Pete.

His brother glanced at Nicole. Just as Beck had figured he would do. It was just a glance. But in that glance, Pete took his attention off Beck and Faith.

That was the break Beck had been waiting for.

He dove at Pete.

Though Beck was moving as fast as he could, everything seemed to slow to a crawl. He saw the split-second realization in Pete's eyes. And then Pete reacted. He didn't turn the gun on Beck.

But on Faith.

Pete lowered the barrel of the semiautomatic right toward the back of Faith's head.

And he fired.

Chapter 15

Faith moved as quickly as she could, but she figured it wasn't nearly fast enough. She braced herself.

Death would come before she even knew if Beck had heard her. "I love you," she'd said. It might be the last time she ever had a chance to say that to anyone.

She was feeling and hearing way too much for Pete's bullet to have killed her. Instead, she realized that it'd smacked into the tile floor less than two feet from her.

Pete's bullet had missed her.

The sound of the fired shot was deafening, and it roared through her head, stabbing into her eardrums. It was excruciating, but since she could feel it, she knew she was very much alive.

So was Beck, thank God.

With his momentum at full speed, Beck crashed into Pete, and into her. Pete's gun dislodged from his hand and landed somewhere behind them.

"No!" Nicole yelled. She scrambled to the side to get away from the collision.

However, because Faith was directly in front of Pete, she wasn't so lucky. She was caught in the impact, again. Caught in the middle of the struggle. But this time, the stakes were even higher.

Aubrey was on her way there.

"Run!" Beck told her.

From the corner of her eye, she saw Nicole do just that. She threw open the back door and rushed out into the night. Maybe the woman would call the deputy. But as distraught as Nicole was, Faith couldn't rely on her for help. She and Beck had to stop Pete.

"Now!" Beck snarled to her. "Get out of here."

Faith wiggled her way out of the fight and somehow managed to get to her feet. But before she could run, Pete latched on to her ankle and tried to pull her back down. She fought, kicking at him, but he was pumped on adrenaline now and was fighting like a crazy man with triple his normal strength.

Then things got worse. The doorbell rang.

"We're here," Marita called out.

Marita's announcement nearly caused Faith to panic, but she forced herself to concentrate on the task. She gave Pete another hard kick, and that broke the vising grip he had on her. She felt him reach for her, and he groped at the floor.

Faith ran. But not out the back as Nicole had done.

Frantically, she looked around for Beck's gun. She didn't see it, and it took her a moment to figure out why.

Pete had it.

Oh, God.

Pete had the gun.

"Come in!" Pete shouted to Marita, dodging a fist that Beck had tried to send his way. "Beck needs help."

"No," Faith countered. "Stay back." And she hoped they'd heard her and would do as she said.

She looked around the floor for another weapon and remembered Beck's service pistol. Faith grabbed it from the top of the fridge where he'd put it right after they'd returned from seeing Darin.

"Stop!" she yelled.

Pete didn't. Neither did Beck. Pete managed to land a hard punch on Beck's jaw, and the momentum sent him backward. The two men weren't separated for long because Beck dove at him.

The doorbell rang again, and it was followed by a knock. "What's going on in there?" Tracy asked.

Faith hurried to him and held out his service revolver. Beck snatched it from her hand and got up off the floor.

Pete did the same.

And the two brothers met gun-to-gun.

"Don't," Beck warned, his voice a threatening growl.

The corner of Pete's mouth lifted. A twisted, sick smile. "You think a bullet can go through your front door?" He didn't wait for Beck to answer. "Because I do. God knows what a bullet would hit…"

Pete didn't have to aim in that direction. Faith realized his gun was already pointed there. Just to Beck's right. And that put it in line with the door.

Oh, God. That nearly brought Faith to her knees. Her baby was in danger.

"Try to warn them and I'll shoot through the door," Pete warned. "I have nothing to lose."

Faith didn't cower. "And you have nothing to gain from hurting my child."

"True. But it'll be nice to see you suffer."

Every inch of Beck was primed for the fight, and his

face was dotted with sweat from the struggle. "Faith did nothing to you."

"Yes, she did. She came back. She made me think she'd written that blackmail letter. She made me believe I had to stop her. The woman's just bad luck, Beck. She always has been."

Faith saw Beck's finger tense on the trigger, and he had his attention fastened to his brother's own trigger finger. One move, and Beck would shoot him. Faith didn't doubt that. But what she did fear was that even if Beck shot him that Pete would still manage to shoot.

Aubrey could still be in danger.

She heard the scrape of metal, a key being inserted into a lock, and she glanced at the front door.

Just as it opened.

"No!" Faith shouted. And she automatically turned in the direction of the door. She had to block any shot that Pete might take.

She only made it one step before the bullet rang out.

Beck didn't even wait to see where Pete's bullet had hit.

Or who.

He couldn't think about that. Right now, he had to stop Pete from firing again. Each shot could be lethal.

Still, Beck couldn't stop the rage that roared through him. Pete had put Aubrey and Faith in danger. To save his own butt, his brother had been willing to hurt a child.

Beck grabbed Pete's right arm. He wanted to shoot his brother. To end this here and now. But Beck couldn't risk another shot being fired.

Not with Aubrey and Faith so close.

Faith yelled something, but the blood crashing in

Beck's ears made it impossible to hear. Besides, Beck only wanted to concentrate on the fight.

Beck dropped his gun so he could use both hands to try to gain control of Pete. His brother was fighting him, trying to re-aim his gun in the direction of the door. Beck wasn't able to get his finger off the trigger.

Pete fired again. The shot landed somewhere in the ceiling, and white powdery plaster began to rain down on them. Good. As long as that shot wasn't near the others.

Beck heard the sound then. A cry.

Aubrey.

Every muscle in his body turned to iron. *God, was the child hurt?* Or maybe it was Faith who'd taken the bullet. Maybe both were injured. Hell. He could lose them and all because of his selfish SOB of a brother.

"You can't save them," Pete growled.

It was exactly what Beck needed to hear. Not that he needed a reminder of what was at stake, but his brother's threat was the jolt that gave Beck that extra boost of adrenaline. Nothing was going to stop him from saving Aubrey and Faith.

Nothing.

From the corner of his eye, Beck saw Faith running toward the front door. There was no color in her face, and she appeared to be trembling. But she was headed in Aubrey's direction. Hopefully, she'd take the child and run. He wanted them as far away from there as possible.

With both his hands clamped onto Pete's right arm and wrist, Beck used his body and strength to maneuver Pete backward. Toward the wall. Pete didn't go willingly. He cursed, kicked and spat at Beck, all the while using his left fist to pound any part of Beck that he could reach.

Beck slammed him against the wall. The impact was

so hard that it rattled the nearby kitchen cabinets. Still, Pete didn't stop struggling. Beck didn't stop, either. He bashed Pete's right hand against the granite countertop. The first time he didn't dislodge the gun.

But the second time he did. Pete's gun fell onto the granite.

Even though he was unarmed, Pete was still dangerous. So Beck didn't waste even a second of time. He caught onto his brother's shoulder and whirled him around, jamming his face and chest against the wall between the cabinets and the mudroom door. There wasn't much room to maneuver, but Beck wanted to get Pete onto the floor, facedown, so he could better subdue him.

Pete didn't cooperate with that, either, but Beck had the upper hand. With his forearm against the nape of Pete's neck, he put pressure on the backs of his brother's knees until he could get him belly down onto the tile floor.

By the time it was done, both Pete and he were fighting for air. Both of them were covered in sweat and blood from their cuts and scrapes.

But it was finally close to being over.

"Faith, are you all right?" Beck called out.

Since he'd expended most of his breath in the fight, he had to repeat it before it had any sound. And then he waited.

Praying.

He didn't hear her say anything. No reassurance that she was okay. But he could hear footsteps. Frantic ones. Something was going on in the living room. Before he could call out to Faith again, there was another sound.

The back door opened.

It was Nicole.

"Let Pete go," she said. Her voice was trembling as much as her hand.

And she had a gun in her hand.

Beck cursed. He didn't need another battle when he hadn't even finished the first one.

"Nicole," Pete said through his gusting breath. "I knew you'd come back for me."

"I didn't do this for you. What you did was stupid, Pete, but I can't let you go to jail. Despite what you've done, you're still my husband. Part of me still loves you." She turned her teary eyes to Beck and pointed the gun right at him. "I'm a good shot," she reminded him. "Now let him go."

"Go where? Pete's a killer. What if he turns his anger on you?"

"He won't. I'm the reason he killed."

"He could hurt someone else," Beck reminded her. "You'd be responsible for that."

"What do I care if Faith Matthews and her bastard child are hurt?" Her attention went back to Pete. "I'll get you out of this, and then we'll be even. I want you to leave and never come back."

That wouldn't be good enough. Beck knew Pete wouldn't stay away. As long as his brother was alive and free, Faith and Aubrey would be in danger.

"I can't let him go," Beck insisted.

"Then I'll have to shoot you," Nicole insisted right back.

And she would.

Beck could see it in her eyes.

She'd already crossed over and left reason behind. She was going to save Pete whether he deserved it or not.

Nicole adjusted her aim so that it was right at Beck's

shoulder. She wasn't going for the kill, but it didn't matter. The shot could still be deadly, and even if it only incapacitated him, it would leave the others vulnerable.

Cursing under his breath, Beck readied himself to take evasive action. He'd roll to the right, dropping to Pete's side. It might cause Nicole to think twice about shooting. But then it would give Pete the opportunity to break free.

"Nicole!" someone yelled.

Faith.

Hell. She'd come back.

Nicole automatically looked in the direction of Faith's voice. Beck couldn't see her. She was behind him.

But he saw the movement of something flying through the air.

Nicole tried to adjust her aim. But it was too late. A coffee mug slammed right into Nicole's hand. Maybe it was the impact or the surprise of the attack, but Nicole dropped the gun.

Pete went after it.

So did Beck.

Both of them scrambled across the floor toward it.

Above them, Nicole moved as well. Faith, too. Beck could hear Faith's footsteps, and he knew she was going after Nicole.

And Faith might get hurt in the process.

Beck caught onto Pete and slammed him against the floor. Nicole reached down, to help Pete or get the gun. But reaching was as far as she got. Faith grabbed Nicole and with a fierce jerk, she yanked her back. It was the break that Beck needed. His hand clamped around the gun, and this time, he came up ready to fire.

"Move back," Beck told Faith.

Nicole reached for her to try to use her as a shield, but Faith darted across the room just out of Nicole's reach.

"Don't move," Beck warned Pete when he tried to get up. His brother turned his head, and their gazes connected.

Beck made sure there were no doubts or hesitation in his eyes. Because there certainly wasn't any of that in his heart.

"I will kill you," Beck promised.

Pete laid his head on the floor and put his hands on the back of his head. Finally surrendering.

Chapter 16

Faith frantically checked Aubrey again.

She hadn't seen any blood, or even a scratch, but she had to be sure that Pete's shots hadn't harmed her child.

"No, no, no," Aubrey fussed, batting Faith's hands away. The little girl rubbed her eyes and yawned. She was obviously sleepy and didn't want any more of this impromptu exam.

Deputy Winston rushed in the door. He had his weapon drawn, and he hurried past them and into the kitchen. A moment later, the Ranger, Sgt. McKinney, followed. Then Deputy Gafford.

Finally!

Even though it'd been only minutes since her nine-one-one call, Beck now had the backup he needed. And once she had the all clear that it was safe to check on him, she would. Well, she would after Marita had taken Aubrey into the bedroom away from Nicole and Pete.

She prayed Beck was all right.

In the distance she heard the sirens from an ambulance. And she heard footsteps. Faith looked up from her now fussy daughter and spotted Beck.

Oh, God. He was bleeding. There was a gash on his forehead. His left cheek. And both hands were bloodied.

"The ambulance will be here any minute," Faith told him.

He looked at her. Then at Aubrey. He seemed to make it to them in one giant step, and he pulled them both into his arms. Faith's breath shattered, and she was afraid she wouldn't be able to hold back the tears of relief.

"Is she hurt?" Beck asked. His voice was frantic. "Are you hurt?"

Faith pulled back so she could meet his gaze. "We're not hurt. You are. I called the ambulance for you."

His breath swooshed out. "You're not hurt." He repeated it several times and drew them back into his embrace.

Aubrey rubbed her eyes again and babbled something. It sounded cranky, and Faith figured she was about to cry, but her daughter maneuvered her way into Beck's arms and dropped her head on his shoulder.

"I'll see if I can be of assistance in the kitchen," Tracy volunteered, trying to give them some privacy.

"Want me to take Aubrey?" Marita asked.

"No," Faith and Beck said in unison.

"All right then. I'll just go outside and let the EMTs know what's going on." Marita took a step and then stopped. Her forehead was bunched up. "What exactly is going on?"

He and Faith exchanged glances. He didn't let go of her. But then she had no plans to let go of him either.

"My brother is about to be arrested for three murders," Beck explained. "Nicole will be taken into custody as well since she tried to assist him with his escape. And we need to look for Darin. He's out there somewhere and needs medical attention."

"Oh. I see." Marita turned pale. She waggled her fingers toward the sound of the sirens. "What should I tell the EMT guys? They'll be here any minute."

"Have then come in and check out Faith," Beck insisted.

Other than some bruises and maybe a scrape or two, Faith knew she was fine. She couldn't say the same for Beck. He'd need stitches for that gash.

"And I want them to check out Beck," Faith added as Marita went out the door.

"I'm okay," he insisted, kissing Aubrey's cheek. He kissed Faith's, too. "At least now I am. For a minute there, I thought I'd lost you."

"Me, too," she managed to say. Her emotion was too raw to talk about.

There was movement from the kitchen, and a moment later, Pete appeared. Handcuffed. Corey had a hold on him. The other deputy had Nicole cuffed and was walking her to the front door.

Pete stopped, and Beck automatically turned so that Aubrey wouldn't be near the man. "There's nothing we have to say to each other," Beck insisted.

But Pete didn't speak right away. He stood there, volleying glances among Beck, Aubrey and Faith. "You fell hard for her, didn't you?" He didn't wait for Beck to confirm it. "That's how I feel about Nicole."

"You were ready to kill her," Faith pointed out.

"I wouldn't have. *Couldn't* have," he corrected. "Love really messes you up." His attention landed on Aubrey again. "I know she's Sherry's kid. Sherry showed me her picture. One she'd taken in a park, and she tried to convince me that I was the one who got her pregnant."

That gave Faith another jolt of adrenaline. "Did you?"

Pete shook his head. "Not a chance."

Faith desperately wanted to believe him. "And since you've been so truthful in the past, I should just take you at your word?"

"He's telling the truth," Corey volunteered. "This time, anyway. I saw the DNA results from the Ranger lab. He's not the father. Neither are you, Beck. It's Nolan Wheeler."

Nolan. In hindsight, it didn't surprise her. Not really. Sherry had spent most of her life breaking up and then getting back together with Nolan.

"He might have fathered her," Beck mumbled. "But Nolan was never her father."

Faith couldn't have agreed more. If the man hadn't been dead, his DNA connection to Aubrey would have caused her stomach to go into a tailspin. Because Nolan would have spent the rest of his life trying to figure out ways to use Aubrey to get what he wanted.

"Get my brother out of here," Beck instructed the deputy.

Pete didn't protest. He looked straight ahead as he was escorted out. Nicole was next. She didn't even try to say anything. Tears were streaming down her cheeks, and she made a series of hoarse sobs.

However, Deputy Gafford did stop. "On the way over, I got a call from the hospital. Darin Matthews is back there. He's not hurt, and he wanted me to check on Faith, to make sure she was all right."

Faith was so glad that Beck was holding on to her. Her brother was safe. Pete hadn't hurt him. And better yet, he was receiving the medical treatment he needed. She would check on him as soon as things had settled down.

Whenever that might be.

It might take her years to forget how close she'd come to losing Beck and Aubrey.

"The other Texas Ranger is with Darin now," the deputy continued. "Will there be any charges filed against him?"

"No," Beck quickly answered. "But I want him to have a thorough psychiatric evaluation."

The deputy nodded and escorted Nicole out.

Faith looked around and realized they were alone. The house was quiet. Her heart rate was slowly returning to normal.

"Are you really okay?" Beck asked.

But the silence didn't last. Before she could answer, there was the sound of hurried footsteps, and she automatically braced herself for the worst.

Roy came rushing through the front door.

He looked at Beck. At Aubrey. Then at her. He'd no doubt passed his other son and daughter-in-law and knew they were under arrest. But his concern seemed to be aimed at Beck.

"Son, you're bleeding," Roy greeted him.

"Just a scratch," Beck assured him.

"He needs stitches," Faith insisted.

Roy agreed with a nod, and he put his hands on his hips. He looked around, as if he didn't know what to say or do. "I just spoke to Corey and the nanny, Marita. They told me what happened in here."

"Yeah," was all Beck said.

"'i,'" Aubrey babbled to Roy.

There were tears in Roy's eyes, but he forced a smile

when he returned the "hi." He hesitated. "I'm sorry. So sorry for what Pete did. I knew about the blackmail and the payoff, but I swear I didn't know he'd killed those people. And I didn't know he would come after the three of you. I'm sorry," he repeated, aiming this one at Faith.

She gave his arm a gentle squeeze. "Thank you."

Roy turned those tearful eyes to Beck. "What can I do? Give me something to do. I can't go home and sit there."

"You can go to my office and call Pete and Nicole a lawyer. They're going to need one."

"Of course. I'll do that. And if you need anything, just let me know."

"I will."

"Make sure he sees the medics," Roy whispered to Faith. He gave her arm a gentle squeeze as well and went back out the door just as the medics were coming in

Beck held up his hand to stop them. "Could you give me a few minutes?" he asked.

That halted the two men in their tracks, and they looked at her for verification. "Just a few minutes," she bargained. But only a few. She wanted that gash checked.

Aubrey fussed and babbled, "Bye-bye," but Faith didn't think she wanted to go with Roy or the medics. She smeared her fist over her eyes again and whimpered.

"It's okay," Beck said to Aubrey, and he lightly circled his fingers over her back.

"Da, Da, Da, Da," Aubrey answered. Not in a happy tone, either. But it was a tone Faith recognized. Her baby was on the verge of a tired tantrum.

Beck must have sensed that because he caught onto Faith's arm and led them to the sofa. Once he'd sat down, he moved Aubrey so that her tummy was against his chest. She dropped her head onto his shoulder and stuck her thumb in her mouth. Within seconds, her eyelids were already lowering.

Faith smiled. "Tantrum averted," she whispered. Good. She didn't have any energy left to deal with anything. "I might have to call you the next time she gets fussy."

Beck angled his eyes in her direction and stared at her. She'd thought the light comment would have given him some relief. It was certainly better than the alternative of her falling apart.

"You said you loved me," Beck reminded her.

That kicked up her heart again. She'd planned on having this discussion later. After some of the chaos had settled. "Yes, I did say that." Because she wanted to dodge eye contact with him, she checked Aubrey. Sound asleep.

"You meant it?"

But before he let her answer, he leaned in and kissed her. He winced because his lip was busted. Hers, too, she realized when his mouth touched hers. She didn't care. That kiss was worth a little pain, and it was the ultimate truth serum. She was going to lay her heart out there and let him know exactly how she felt about him.

She hoped he wouldn't laugh.

Or run the other direction.

"I meant it," she answered. "I love you." Beck and Aubrey were two things in her life that she was certain of. "I'm crazy in love with you."

His face relaxed a bit. The corner of his mouth even lifted in a near smile. "Good. Because I'm crazy in love with you, too."

A sharp sound of surprise leaped from her mouth. "Really?" She heard her voice. Heard the shock. "You're sure it's not just the lust talking?"

"The lust is there," he admitted. He reached out and pushed her hair away from her face. "But so is the love. You did me the honor of letting me be your first lover. Now I'm asking if you'll let me be your last."

Mercy. That was not a light tone. Nor a light look in his eyes. Still, Faith approached that comment with caution. "Are you asking me to go steady?" she joked.

"No. I'm asking you to marry me."

Oh. *Wow.*

Her heart went crazy. So did her stomach. Her breathing. Her entire body.

Was this really happening? She wanted it to happen. Desperately wanted it, she realized. But she hadn't expected it.

As if to convince her, he kissed her again. And again. Until he was the only thing she could think of. Beck had that kind of effect on her. He could make even the aftermath of chaos seem incredible. Heat and love just rippled through her.

"I don't want you to call me when Aubrey's fussy because I want to be there, close by, to hear her myself. I want to be her father, and I want to be your husband."

"You're already her father," Faith said. And it was true. "Aubrey chose you herself." She had to blink back happy tears. "She made a good choice."

"I'm glad you think so. Now, to the rest. I want to be your last lover. Your only lover. What do you think about that?"

Faith didn't have to think. She knew. There was only one answer. "Yes."

* * * * *

YOU HAVE
JUST READ A
HARLEQUIN®
INTRIGUE®
BOOK

If you were **captivated** by the **gripping, page-turning romantic suspense,** be sure to look for all six Harlequin® Intrigue® books every month.

HALOHIINC1012R

The Edge Emergency Department, Chicago
Monday, June 4, 5:30 p.m.

Dr. Devon Pierce listened as administrators from more than a dozen hospitals in metropolitan areas across the nation bemoaned the increasing difficulty of maintaining emergency departments. Once the opening discussion concluded, Devon was the featured speaker.

He rarely agreed to speak to committees and groups, even in a teleconference, which was the case today. His participation required only that he sit in his office and speak to the monitor on his desk. He much preferred to remain focused on his work at the Edge. There were times, however, when his participation in the world of research and development was required in order to push his lagging colleagues toward the most advanced medical technologies. Emergency treatment centers like the Edge were the future of emergency medicine. There was no better state-of-the-art facility.

Devon had set his career as a practicing physician aside and spent six years developing the concept for the center's prototype before opening it in his hometown of Chicago. The success of the past year provided significant evidence that his beliefs about the future of emergency rooms were correct. This would be his legacy to the work he loved.

The subject of cost reared its inevitable and unpleasant head in the ongoing discussion, as it always did. How could a person measure the worth of saving a human life? He said as much to those listening eagerly for a comment from him. All involved were aware, perhaps to varying degrees, just how much his dedication to his work had cost him. He'd long ago stopped keeping account. His work required what it required. There were no other factors or concerns to weigh.

Half an hour later, Devon had scarcely uttered his closing remarks when the door to his office opened. Patricia Ezell, his secretary, silently moved to his desk. She passed him a note, probably not containing the sort of news he wanted if her worried expression was any indicator, and it generally was.

You're needed in the OR stat.

"I'm afraid I won't be able to take any questions. Duty calls." Devon severed his connection to the conference and stood. "What's going on?" he asked as he closed a single button on his suit jacket.

Patricia shook her head. "Dr. Reagan rushed a patient into surgery in OR 1. He says he needs you there."

Ice hardened in Devon's veins. "Reagan is well aware that I don't—"

"He has the surgery under control, Dr. Pierce. It's…" Patricia took a deep breath. "The patient was unconscious when the paramedics brought her in. Her driver's license identifies her as Cara Pierce."

A spear of pain arrowed through Devon, making him hesitate. He closed his laptop. "Few of us have a name so unique that it's not shared with others." There were likely numerous Cara Pierces in the country. Chicago was a large city. Of course there would be other people with the same name as his late wife. This should be no surprise to the highly trained and, frankly, brilliant members of his staff.

"One of the registration specialists browsed the contacts list in her cell phone and called the number listed as her husband."

Devon hesitated once more, this time at the door. His secretary's reluctance to provide whatever other details she had at her disposal was growing increasingly tedious. "Is her husband en route?"

Patricia cleared her throat. "Based on the number in her contacts list, her husband is already here. The number is yours." She held out his cell phone. "I took the call."

Devon stared at the thin, sleek device in her hand. He'd left his cell with Patricia for the duration of the teleconference. He hated the distracting vibration of an incoming call when he was trying to run a meeting. Normally he would have turned it off and that would have been it, but he was expecting an important work call—one that he would pause his teleconference to take if necessary. So he'd assigned Patricia cell phone duty with instructions to interrupt him only if that call came in, or if there was a life-or-death situation.

He reached for it now.

"Thank you, Patricia. Ask the paramedic who brought her in to drop by my office when he has a break."

The walk from his office in the admin wing to the surgery unit took all of two minutes. One of the finely tuned features of the Edge design was ensuring that each wing of the emergency department was never more than two to three minutes away from anything else. A great deal of planning had gone into the round design of the building with the care initiation front and center and the less urgent care units spanning into different wings around the circle. Straight through the very center, the rear portion of the design contained the more urgent services, imaging and surgery. Every square foot of the facility was designed for optimum efficiency. Each member of staff was carefully chosen and represented the very best in their field.

As he neared the surgery suite, he considered what his secretary had told him about the patient. The mere idea was absurd. There'd been a mistake. A mix-up of some sort.

Cara.

His wife was dead. He'd buried her six years and five months ago.

SIN AND BONE by Debra Webb
is available June 2018!

www.Harlequin.com

HIEXP0518

Need an adrenaline rush from nail-biting tales
(and irresistible males)?

Check out **Harlequin® Intrigue®**
and **Harlequin® Romantic Suspense** books!

New books available every month!

CONNECT WITH US AT:

Harlequin.com/Community

**ROMANCE WHEN
YOU NEED IT**

SGENRE2017

Reward the book lover in you!

Earn points from all your Harlequin book purchases from wherever you shop.

Turn your points into *FREE BOOKS* of your choice
OR
EXCLUSIVE GIFTS from your favorite authors or series.

Join for FREE today at
www.HarlequinMyRewards.com.

Harlequin My Rewards is a free program (no fees) without any commitments or obligations.

MYR17